SECRETS OF THE ERILAZ

M.J. STRUVEN

Secrets of the Erilaz

By M.J. Struven

Dedicated to my wife, who said she'll finally read this once it's published.

"Erilaz is a Proto-Norse word that appears in Elder Futhark inscriptions and is often interpreted to mean "magician" or "rune master"."

Part 1: The Sinner

Chapter 1

A final burst of fireworks lit up the sky with flowers of blue and red, and a black sheet of darkness cascaded down towards the hills in the distance. Naryan's face dimmed and was overtaken by shadows as the echoes of the fireworks diminished, and the sound of clapping and cheers rose up to him from the courtyard below.

He half sat, half crouched on the steep shingled roof of a tower, the door to his solar ajar on the balcony to his right, and the flicker of firelight emanating from within. He hiccuped and drained the remainder of the wine from his goblet, turning to make his way along the roof back to the interior.

A shingle loosened itself as he crawled, and his foot slipped towards the edge of the roof. His heart raced as he grasped at the brick-tiled shingles, managing to catch himself with his fingertips and regain his footing. The goblet, at that moment the least of his worries, slipped out of his hand and bounced once on the roof with a metallic clank, before disappearing into the darkness below. He sniggered, thinking of the commotion that it would cause amongst the guests when it landed beside them, and only worried for the briefest moment that some court member's head would be bashed in. It was a very tall tower.

Not that there's much brain to damage anyway, he thought to himself with a chuckle as he flipped his leg over the balcony wall and landed on the terrace. He entered inside from the cool night air, feeling the warmth from the small fire lit in his hearth, and seeing the flicker of shadows that it sent throughout his room. He hopped over to his postered bed and fell backward onto it, his blankets enveloping him as the room swam and he closed his eyes.

His eyes were heavy and he had no plan to reopen them that night when his slumber was interrupted by tapping on his door.

"Naryan, you in there?" Sherry's voice was unmistakable, even through the closed wooden door. He swallowed and managed to get control of his languid tongue long enough to call out,

"Ya, come in."

The door swung open and Sherry walked in, chatting as she closed the door behind her.

"I can't stand this thing. I hate dressing up. It's just not me."

Her attire was a laced-up velvet green corset, and a dress of the same color that fell to her feet and billowed at her legs as she walked.

"You should just take it off and come lay in bed." Naryan said without sitting up. He grinned to himself.

"Ha-Ha, very funny. I told you we're not doing that anymore. Oh god, are you naked? Naryan, put your clothes on!"

"You don't even want to have yours on, why should I put mine on?"

"It's not that I don't want to have *any* clothes on–I just don't want *these* clothes on."

Naryan sat up and beckoned to her with a single finger and the most sultry look he could muster. He was promptly hit in the face with a pair of trousers while Sherry retorted,

"I told you, we're not sleeping together anymore. It just complicates things. Now put on your clothes and come back downstairs. It's the first of May–your father's birthday!"

"What's so complicated? No feelings, no dowries, and it's fun to keep a secret from everyone."

Sherry didn't smile.

"Fine, I'm going to the great hall–come if you want, or not. I don't care."

Sherry blinked, and Naryan was already up from the bed and standing next to her. The shadows cast onto him from the fire kept just enough of his groin to her imagination. Not that she needed to imagine anything anymore.

He reached down and grabbed her hand, raising it to his lips and giving it the softest kiss. His eyes did not break from hers. He reached the back of two fingers out to caress her cheek, before pulling her close to him by the back of her neck. Her eyes closed as she felt the caress of his lips, and the sickly-sweet aroma of wine.

They lingered there together for a second before their lip-lock tightened and he pushed his groin against her, grabbing and lifting the back of her leg as he did so. Their kisses were long and each of their hands ran over the other's body, grasping desperately onto whatever they could. The two of them now were pressed against the wall, and their kisses subsided for a moment as they pulled away and, nose-to-nose, looked into each other's wild eyes. He now turned away from her, still holding her hand to lead her toward the bed.

She took a single step to follow him before wrenching her hand away from his. He turned to look back at her and could see the glaze of her eyes in the firelight. She flashed a curt smile before wheeling away, pulling the door closed behind her with a clatter. Outside the door she paused; her lip trembled and she puffed out a sharp exhale of breath before gathering her dress up and heading down the stairs.

Naryan chewed on his cheek for a moment before gathering up his own clothes from the floor, struggling to don them, and following her to the party.

The servants that Naryan passed in the hallways nodded and greeted him as he walked, each of them bustling and carrying some sort of prepared food or drink to wherever they were headed. He ignored most of them, only stopping a tray-bearing servant carrying goblets of wine. The servant smiled wryly,

"You look like you could use two, your highness."

Naryan ignored the quip, as he was clearly already drunk. Still, he grunted in affirmation and grabbed another, double-fisting the goblets as he meandered towards the great hall where the feast was commencing. The night was still very young.

The great hall had a row of pillars set out from each wall, to support a high ceiling. The ceiling itself was adorned with painted art displaying heroic deeds, and trimmed by engraved marble. More than a hundred sconces lined the walls and pillars, and braziers hung from long chains that attached themselves to the ceiling to give a bright and cheery glow to the entire room. Courtiers, servants, and commoners, all milled around the room, engaged in laughing, song, food, and conversation.

He saw the table at the head of the great hall where his father sat, and started to make his way towards his own seat there, when a curt voice caught his attention.

"Ah Naryan, so glad you could join us."

A woman walked towards him, the crowd seeming to part as she moved. She was cold, tall, and beautiful in her own rights, and his step-mother Rhondia's stern face told him that her mood was tense.

"Look at you," she said, her hands moving across his jacket to pat down his collar and straighten his sleeves. "You'd at least think you'd give your hair a comb before showing yourself in public. And your mouth too. It could use a good scrubbing. I could see your lips stained purple as soon as you came through the door."

He grinned to show that his teeth were purple too, before taking a sip from one of his goblets.

"Are you so drunk you've forgotten if you're right or left handed? You really should just drink one at a time. Let's make sure there's enough to go around."

"I'm ambidextrous, actually." he said, "but sure–I'll finish one." He downed an entire goblet in one go and offered her the empty vessel, his cheeks ballooned with wine.

"You might as well have just stayed in your tower if you are going to make a scene about everything."

She turned away, immediately finding a servant to charge, leaving Naryan standing with a mouthful of wine and one empty goblet.

"Yes, of course my queen…" he heard the servant's voice trail off before being lost in the chatter of the hall. He swallowed, leaving the goblet on the nearest table, and glanced over to see Sherry's profile and brown braided hair from across the room. He knew she was pretending to be engrossed in a conversation, but was clearly ignoring him.

He shrugged and began the search for food, though his attention was instead caught by a corset pulled tight over a bust nearly popping out the top. Her face was fair and her locks were a flashing blonde–a stark contrast to Sherry's. Perhaps he'd bedded her before, he couldn't quite remember for that night had been a blur, but she'd certainly do for now. She was an old knight's daughter, or something to that effect, and though her name eluded him he swooped in nonetheless with a,

"M'lady" and a kiss on each cheek, perhaps lingering on the second cheek a little longer than necessary.

"Your highness," she replied in turn, "it has been quite some time! I believe the last time our paths crossed was nearly three months ago."

"Three months? It feels like years, for far too long a time to pass without admiring your beauty." he smiled.

Her eyes glanced down at the ground for a moment as she held back a smile, before looking up again at him and giving a soft laugh.

"Come, take my arm," he said, offering it to her, and she grasped it. He pulled her close to his body as he escorted her through the hall, aiming towards Sherry's direction. He took a sip of wine from his remaining goblet and swallowed.

"Tell me," he said, glancing down at her breasts, "how have these three months been then?"

"There is not much of consequence to tell," she shrugged,

"You do know there is always a place for you here, should you ever desire to visit the capital. There are always exciting things happening. And if you couldn't find anything of interest, I have some nice tapestries to admire in my tower."

"I would very much like that."

"Excellent! Send me a letter and it shall be done. In the meantime, I have some matters to attend to."

He glanced over towards Sherry again, and from the way that she was turned, he could tell she was certainly keeping her peripheral vision on him.

He grinned, grasping the lady's chin gently between his thumb and forefinger, again placing a kiss on each cheek before sending her on her way. Her figure was certainly nice to admire as she departed as well, and he shook his head with a chuckle as he watched her leave.

The 'matters to attend to' were in fact a table laden with pastries and meats that he'd spotted, and so he headed towards it with a grin of a different kind. He arrived and grasped up a plate, taking sips of wine and periodically setting his goblet down as he moved, while gathering delicacies on a pair of plates he balanced on the other hand.

"Need help with that?" he heard Sherry's voice behind him. He studied a roasted drumstick from a large bird, taking a bite and savoring it, but not turning to acknowledge her.

"I thought you were mad at me." he managed to get out, between swallows.

"Oh, I am. I just wanted to let you know that you're going to look like a buffoon when you get up to your seat and see there's already a plate waiting for you."

Naryan swallowed another bite, then turned to look at her.

"Oh, you made me a plate?"

"No, you oaf. You have servants for that. They made everyone at the table a plate."

"Oh yea." Naryan tossed the drumstick on his towering plates, grabbed his goblet of wine and started towards his seat at the front table.

As he approached, he saw that his father spoke to a baron, and Naryan grimaced that he would have to endure an evening of political guff. The king made eye contact with him and gave a smile as he approached. He waved off the baron with his hand, who gave a quick bow and dispersed, seeing his short time had lapsed.

"Ah, Naryan It's so good–" spoke his father as Naryan walked closer, but his sentence was paused mid-breath, and a rush of wind was let from his mouth, as if his lungs had expelled all their contents in a single cough. His mouth agape, twitched, and his chest heaved, nothing more than a squeak of air escaping the back of his throat. The king's eyes bulged wide as he looked toward Naryan, and Naryan, puzzled, looked behind him to see what his father was looking at. He saw that there was nothing behind him, and he turned back to his father just in time to see the man's lids close over his rolled eyes, before twisting where he stood and collapsing to the floor.

Naryan yelled, dropping his plate and goblet to the floor, and sprinted to his father. The wine spattered on the ground and the drumstick rolled until it came to rest at a chair's foot. All eyes in the room turned on the pair. He knelt, holding his father's head in his hands and felt a weakening pulse on his neck. The king's chest still convulsed, mouth wide attempting to draw in air, and Naryan put his ear to his father's mouth to listen. He felt the gentle brush of wind against his ear, but it did not come from within the king's mouth, rather blowing over it as a breeze blows over the tip of a candle.

"Move boy." The stern voice broke Naryan from his focus, and he felt himself hauled back by his collar, and thrown away to the floor. Galen, a tall wiry man dressed in long brown robes knelt then beside the king, listening with his ear against the king's lips.

"Silence!" he shouted, and the room's murmurs quieted. "He's not breathing. I must check his air passage."

Galen opened wider the king's mouth with one hand and tilted his head back to peer deep into the king's throat.

"I see nothing." he said, before scooping his finger towards the back of the king's mouth.

"I feel nothing," he also remarked. "Who saw what happened?"

Naryan babbled,

"He stood to greet me and then gasped for air before falling over."

Galen grimaced.

"Breathe into him!" shouted Naryan,

Galen paused, but said nothing as he watched the king's visage darken to deeper shades of blue.

"Do it!"

Galen shook his head.

"Fine," continued Naryan pushing towards his father again, "I will."

"Do not put your mouth on him boy, for if he was poisoned you will also perish."

"I don't care!" screamed Naryan. His throat clenched as he reached his hands out to grasp at his father's fallen form. He slipped, trying to pull himself up to crawl, but Sherry pulled at him from behind.

"Let me go you bitch!"

Shocked, she released him, and he scurried again on his hands and knees towards the king. He was then caught on each arm by the king's guard, and restrained, and he watched through blurred vision as his father expired on the ground next to where he lay.

Chapter 2

"He is little more than a grown child, and unfit for kingly duties."

"Unfit or not, he is the next in line, and the coronation must be held. With hundreds of years of tradition, there's no reason it should stop now."

Naryan stood in the hallway outside the cracked door to the council chamber, eavesdropping on the discussion of his fate. Rhondia was speaking with Murdock, the Duke of Rowan, who held the highest seat in the court of Satoria next to the now-deceased king. It was unfortunate, Naryan thought, that his step-mother was not the one defending him behind his back.

"I do not argue against his coronation," continued Rhondia, "but it's clear that we must seat wise advisors next to him so he doesn't make rash decisions. Satoria's alliances already lie in a delicate balance."

The sound of Murdock pouring himself a glass of wine drifted through the door.

"Any king is only as good as his advisors," Murdock agreed, "and you and I can both admit that Naryan must have close watch kept over him. We cannot afford a war with Chromer to the north, whilst we defend our trade routes in the south. Our only true allies lie in Concordia, and they would not come to our aid in light of open war. You are right–his brash tongue must be watched at all times, and we must consider seating additional ambassadors to send tribute to our neighbors."

"You would have us give away the Satoria's treasury as tribute? I would just as soon levy an army with those funds so at least hope to make some return on the investment."

"War," replied Murdock, "is not an avenue that anyone wishes to travel."

"No," said Rhondia, "but the threat of war itself is often enough to gain respect and riches from those who fear it."

Murdock smiled.

"What I appreciate about you, Rhondia, is your political keenness. Many ladies in the court hold their position only for prestige and the gifts of tributaries. Your advice may actually enact change."

Rhondia smiled and replied,

"I should hope so."

Murdock sipped his wine and continued,

"But back to the tale of our young prince–excuse me–King. His decisions must surely be sifted, and he must be kept under close watch for attempts on his life."

"Can we then be certain that my late husband's passing was of someone's hand?" asked Rhondia.

"Hm, no, we cannot, though the circumstance is surely concerning, and should at least give us reason to keep a closer eye on your comings and goings as well. Our late king's cadaver has been thoroughly investigated for signs of foul play. If it was murder then it was not poison for our chemists know of all poisons and their reactionary agents, and found nothing on his lips nor clothes."

Rhondia nodded.

"Good, I'm glad to hear it. Though, I should think it was not a murder at all, and merely a stroke of ill luck on his health. Galen said that when he came to his aid, the king was not breathing. Perhaps the man had forgotten how in his old age."

Naryan's nose twitched, and he pushed open the door to reveal himself.

"It distresses me to hear that you slander my dead father."

Both Rhondia and Murdock shared a startled glance before regaining composure.

"Ah Naryan," said Rhondia, "up early this afternoon I see." She made a show of glance out the window to see how high in the sky the sun sat. Murdock cut her off before they could start a tiff,

"How do you fair in light of your father's passing, what was it now–two days gone?" he asked.

"Worse off than many others, I presume. I came to seek consolation for my distress and find my step-mother deep in the throes of political gossip instead of wearing black and weeping her newly deceased husband. And before you ask how much I've heard, I've heard it all. No, I don't *want* the throne thrust upon me, but it is a responsibility that I will accept, *mother*."

"Curb your sarcasm you little sot," Rhondia snapped, "my heart is surely pained at your father's passing, but Satoria must still be looked after lest we be found vulnerable. There will be time to grieve, but first there are matters to attend to. Go drown your sorrows in another pitcher of wine while the adults discuss the fate of the kingdom."

"*My* kingdom." snarled Naryan. "And that is no way to address your king."

"You haven't been crowned yet, child."

"No, but I was acceded the moment my father expelled his last breath. You would do well to remember that."

Rhondia's eyes narrowed for a second, but she set her jaw and nodded.

"Yes, your highness."

A knock at the door interrupted the rising tension. A servant was there, followed by a dark-cloaked man with his hood up, leaving his face encased in shadows.

"Your boarded guest, Einar, my lady." The servant bowed and left, and the robed man entered the room. Naryan's eyebrows raised as the man entered, and he looked at Rhondia, a snicker lingering in the back of his throat.

"A priest, Rhondia? I have never known you as one to practice religion."

Rhondia gave him a stern look.,

"My sorrows have driven me to look for answers that I do not have. Let us show a little respect to our guest. He is an itinerant, and I've requested he perform your father's funeral ceremony.

The man raised back his hood to show that his head was shaven, and his ears were gauged with studs of chipped obsidian. He was gaunt, almost emaciated, but still youthful, and his gaze bit back at Naryan. He nodded his head once in acknowledgment, but he said nothing.

"I never found my father one to find hope in sermons spouted by fablers. He found joy in the teachings of science and the concrete lessons therein learned. We should respect his wishes in death as though he were living, and not desecrate his tomb with blessings of fabricated deities. He would wish us to celebrate his life with a feast, and speeches in memoriam."

"Time changes people in their age. Fate has brought Einar to our doorstep; he is a blessing in an hour of woe." said Rhondia.

"I will not have my father's funeral turned into a theater for proselytization. I do not know this man, nor have I heard of his religion, though I can say with certainty that all the religions that have been placed before me have done nothing but spew falsehoods."

Einar studied them for a moment before speaking in a smooth, but adamant tone.

"I do not come with falsehoods, nor to evangelize to the unwilling. Those who wish to believe, will believe, and those who do not wish to believe..." his voice trailed off, as if the ending was inconsequential.

Naryan surveyed his Rhondia and Einar before rolling his eyes and shaking his head with a snort.

"I'm not in the mood for petty squabbles. My word is final, but I do think it's time for some of that wine you mentioned. I'll see you at the funeral."

A column of nobles and courtiers waded amongst each other to take their seats. They were dressed in their finest attire and wore their most solemn faces amidst whispers that echoed off the stone walls. The funeral was held in the great hall and the casket itself lay closed, not far from the very spot where the king had perished. It was a little morbid, Naryan thought, to be holding the funeral in the same place. Yet, there could hardly be found a

15

cathedral or church in the entire city, and the few that did exist in Satoria were not fit for the funeral of a king in size, nor adornment.

He watched from the large doorway, not yet entering the Hall. The room, as large as it was, looked suffocating, and he inhaled a deep breath through his nostrils before turning away. The sad toll of a bell rang from a tower, signifying the commencement of the ceremony, so he tilted back his head and poured in the remaining wine, only then realizing he had nowhere to put the empty vessel. He looked around for a moment before finally tossing it into a marble planter next to the entrance.

He sauntered up the aisle towards the front of the room where Rhondia already stood, veiled in black and bowing over the casket. He felt all eyes on him as he approached it, and the weight of the situation pressed on him. His stomach tightened, as did his throat, but he clasped his jaw to hide the tremble of his lip, and bowed his head to hide his glossy eyes.

He knelt at the casket, his stomach heaving as he released a sob, and let his forehead fall against the gold-engraved wood with a knock that echoed through the hall. He finally let himself weep, the tears from his eyes mingling with his nasal discharge to drip off the end of his nose, his sobs the only sound in the room.

Rhondia placed her hand on his shoulder, and he looked up at her, startled.

"What, do I smell of wine?" he choked out. "Am I disheveled? Am I a disgrace? Leave me to grieve."

Rhondia's eyes also glistened as they looked at each other, and she shook her head.

"Your sorrow is apparent," she said, "and for that I do not fault you. Just know that your kingdom now looks to you and your behavior in your father's passing."

At this reminder he let loose a wail, and turned so that his back was now to the casket with his head leaning back onto it.

Einar now stood there in front of him, silently watching, his hands folded in his robes and a grim look set on his face.

Naryan looked up with red eyes, finally able to hold back his sobs, and now only occasionally pausing to catch his breath with a wavering inhale. His lip turned up to a sneer as he looked upon Einar, and he rose, pointing at the man.

"What is he doing here?."

Rhondia set her lips and shot him a sharp glance, but said nothing.

"What's your name again? Hiney? Depart now. Guards!"

Einar's eyes were set upon Naryan, and he did not move, even in light of the king's order. Guards from either side of the aisle came at Naryan's beckon, hands on hilts as they approached.

"You are not welcome here." spat Naryan, still aggressing towards Einar. "You disgrace the memory of my father."

The guards were now near to the front of the room, each coming to one side of Einar. As they drew nearer he broke eye contact with Naryan and moved his hands around him with a twirl. They were curled in a peculiar manner, and his fingers moved as though they painted in the air. The faintest glow of golden glimmer could be seen trailing from his fingertips, as a symbol took shape in the air in front of him.

A rush of wind filled the great hall, extinguishing the flames of all of the hanging braziers and wall sconces in an instant. Smoke from each of the extinguished flames rose from where the lamps now smoldered, but coalesced into a swirl with Einar at the center.

Naryan covered his face with his arm, coughing into it as the guards waved their hands to clear the smoke from around them.

Garments from the audience now lay strewn about on the ground, and a beam of sunlight coming through a stained-glass window illuminated the empty spot where Einar had once stood.

Chapter 3

"This is ridiculous. I've never seen such a movement in my entire life. He's only been here a few days and the whole city is trying to convert."

Sherry sat across from Naryan, expecting a response. They were seated in a well-lit room with a crackling fire and Naryan, per usual, was drunk. *At least he's wearing clothes this time,* Sherry thought, taking a gentle sip of her own wine.

Naryan brooded for a moment, his brow furrowed.

"It's bullshit. All of it." he said, mesmerized by the fire. "I don't believe it." He took a deep sip.

"I don't know how that *wasn't* real. How do you fake that?" asked Sherry.

"I bet he had a host of people all open the doors at the same time, which created a draft to blow out the torches." Naryan said, glancing up. Sherry sat up straight.

"Let's try it!"

"Nah, I'm feeling lazy today."

"You're *literally* the king. You can do whatever you want. You also have people to do it for you."

"I don't think it was that," said Naryan, shaking his head. "It was something else. This doesn't make any sense."

Sherry shrugged and said,

"I mean, maybe magic is real."

"Oh, don't you go getting crazy on me now too. Half the kingdom is in an uproar, and the other half doesn't even believe it happened. I was there and I'm nearly on the half that doesn't believe it happened."

"It's kind of hard to deny it. There were three hundred witnesses."

Naryan grimaced and paused before speaking again,

"And then he just disappears. Gone. For nearly three days. Now he's back like nothing happened."

"I mean, I wouldn't say he's acting like nothing happened. I see him walking around the streets acting the part, speaking to his new followers. You should just banish him. You're the king."

"Oh, I've considered it, but he is in Rhondia's favor. She's probably his main proselyte at this point. She's enough of a hassle as it is, without riling her up about banishing her new-found priest."

"I hear my name being spoken, and I certainly hope that it was not ill." Rhondia appeared in the room behind them. "Naryan, what are you doing here? You're supposed to be at court."

Naryan didn't take his gaze off her, but did take a long pull of his wine.

"Court? You know the place where a king sits and lays out decrees and judgements, and manages diplomacy of the kingdom?" she crinkled her nose and a scoff escaped the back of her throat. "You're hopeless. You have subjects and courtiers awaiting you–the least you can do is show face."

Naryan swirled his wine.

"I think I'll cancel court today."

A sigh of exasperation escaped Rhondia's mouth.

"You can't just *cancel* court. "

Naryan tilted his head back and raised his voice, shouting,

"Court is canceled!" he looked back at her. "See, I just did."

Sherry snorted into her wine and looked away towards the window, trying not to spit out what was in her mouth. A little dribble did escape the corner of her lip, and she wiped it away with her sleeve, eyes darting to see if anyone had noticed, before regaining her composure.

Rhondia glared at him, enunciating her words,

"Your father would be ashamed of you."

She wheeled on her heel and strode out of the room, leaving Naryan to bite his lip and stare into the fire.

"Well," he said, "I suppose I should go to court."

"Make way for the king!"

The herald's announcement rang through the courtroom where there were already quite a few people awaiting his arrival, each of them much more well-dressed than he. They all stood and bowed as he walked through the door, and someone handed him a long parchment of what he could only assume was the agenda. Sherry, who walked in behind him, took a seat towards the rear of the room. He glanced down at the parchment with a grimace and carried it with him to the throne.

He sat down, looking next to him to see a crown and scepter lay on an ivory-inlaid dark wood table adjacent to the throne. His eyes flashed and he saw scenes of his father wearing it, his smiling bearded face filling out the entirety of the crown, and waving the scepter as he gave edicts. He absentmindedly reached his hand out to caress the gold plate of the crown, and felt the room stiffen with all eyes on him.

He picked it up, holding it in front of him and turning it between his hands as he admired his reflection in it. He turned it, so that its base faced him and nodded his head forward for a second, as if he were to don it.

"My lord." a voice next to him whispered. It paused as Naryan turned his head to look at the advisor to his right. He was a round-faced man, clean-shaven, and looking uncomfortable in court clothes that did not well-fit his plump frame. Naryan's mouth pulled into a tight line as he looked him over.

"Might I suggest," the advisor continued, "that you refrain from donning the crown until your coronation has passed. It is a long-lived custom that even your father upheld."

Naryan stared at the man, frozen in a tableau and still holding the crown. He blinked once, still keeping eye contact with the advisor, and moved the crown up higher towards his head. The advisor's eyes were wide, and he swallowed as he watched Narayan's hand's move up until even his hair was rustled by its edge.

At the last moment Naryan pulled the crown away from his head, placing the crown back onto the table, and letting out a barking laugh. The advisor let out a breath of relief, and nervous laughter emanated from other members of the court. Sherry, still sitting in the back, rubbed her forehead with her hand and rolled her eyes.

Naryan caught his breath after a moment, turning to the advisor.

"You, what's your name? I like you."

"My name is Domery, my lord."

"Domery. Domery, ok, I think I can remember that but you might need to remind me once in a while."

Domery nodded.

"Yes my lord."

"So, what do we do here? I see this list, who's first?"

"If I may?" Domery reached out his hand for the parchment, which Naryan gladly surrendered. Domery ran his fingers along the top of the page, reading under his breath until he called out,

"The court recognizes Constable Cormack to come forth with a grievance, on behalf of those who keep safe the city."

A man stepped up before the throne, and bowed his head. He was large and round, and a goatee with a poorly-kept mustache adorned his lip.

"My lord, I am the Constable of the capital–I'm sure you remember me from your youth?"

"Hm, yes," nodded Naryan, "Do not worry–I have already forgiven you for the times you hauled me to my father after halting whatever fun I was having."

The man smiled curtly and nodded his head once, not realizing that he'd needed forgiveness, and unsure if he should now be worried that he was remembered after all. He continued nonetheless,

"I come before you today, my lord, in light of civil unrest that has spread through the capital, and even the countryside.

"Civil unrest, you say?"

21

"Yes, my lord."

"And what, pray tell, is causing this civil unrest? Are they too heavily taxed?

"My lord," whispered Domery, "I would not bring up the subject of taxes at this time, for it is *always* a sore point amongst your subjects."

Naryan waved his hand at Domery, who closed his mouth and retreated back behind him. The constable continued,

"No, my lord–the people are uneasy and divided, for some of them seek to gain wisdom from Einar. Many others do not believe what he says, and it causes riots in the streets."

Naryan's nose twitched at the mention of Einar.

"What then do you believe Sir Cormack?"

"Ah, I'm not a knight, my lord."

Naryan rolled his eyes.

"Whatever. What do you think of this man, goodman Cormack?"

Cormack glanced from side to side to see the reactions of the courtiers, before shuffling his feet and looking back at Naryan.

"My lord, I am a simple man. I believe that which I have been taught, and the precepts described to me under your father's rule have been those of logic. The math and sciences that I have been educated in, do not allow for such mysticism. I have never witnessed anything that I would describe as miraculous, nor seen the dead walking as ghosts, nor do I pray to any god. In short, I do not believe in the magical nor mystical for I have seen no evidence of either."

Nararyan smiled and nodded, but he was cut short by a voice that rang out in the court.

"You weren't there goodman Cormack–what do you know? I saw it with my own eyes!"

Cormack's head turned to see who spoke. The courtiers parted to allow the speaker to step forward–a tall, handsome man around Naryan's age with brown hair that collected itself around his shoulders. Shawn was his name; he was well-dressed in a white tunic, trimmed in gold with ivory buttons running down the front. He stepped forward, ignoring the protocol of the court's recognition, and stood next to Cormack, clasping his hands behind his back.

"You were also there, Naryan. You were closer than anyone. You cannot deny what you saw."

"I have not yet made up my mind as to what I saw." said Naryan.

"I do not know the *cause* of what we saw," continued Shawn, "but my skin was not fooled by the wind that brushed over it. My eyes were not fooled to see all the fires in the hall extinguished in an instant, nor my nose by the smoke that lingered where Einar stood.

"Truth is the root of the matter here." he continued, "All our lives we have been raised as Cormack has described–to place our trust in the validity of reason and science. You and I both. If there is a world full of magic that surrounds us, and my eyes have been closed to it all this time–I would be sorely disappointed. Would you not?

"I am frustrated with the possibility that I have been lied to my whole life about what our world is! And if I should find that I was purposefully deceived, then my frustration would instead be anger."

Naryan looked past the men in front of him to see Sherry, sitting on the edge of her seat, breath held as she watched her brother speak. Silence finally hung in the air, until Naryan broke it,

"What would you have me do? I have two people of opposing views in front of me now, and I cannot yet be the judge of which of them is right."

Shawn interjected,

"Send forth an inquisition to question Einar's validity. If he truly is an oracle of a god or possesses some magic, then it must be made public. We do not deserve to live a life so deceived."

Naryan nodded once and looked at the other.

"And goodman Cormack, what would you have me do?"

"Peace in the streets," said Cormack, "is all that I desire my lord. People loot storefronts, saying that the end is nigh, and those with opposing views on Einar assault one another, each calling the other heretics."

Naryan snorted.

"I can hardly believe that the kingdom has degraded into religious zealots arguing in the streets. Perhaps I should have Hiney banished, or executed."

Cormack folded his hands behind his back and nodded in agreement, but Shawn protested,

"You are dull to waste such opportunity. Profound knowledge may lie with this man. If you kill him, it will be lost, and if you turn him away he will evangelize another city to our detriment. No, there is no choice but to see if he speaks the truth."

Naryan set his jaw for a moment, looking at the two men before him.

"Fine then," he said, "Bring Hiney before me and I will pass judgment upon him."

Both Cormack and Shawn nodded their head once in a bow,

"Your highness," spoke Cormack, "I will bring him before you…"

His sentence was cut short by the hall door bursting open. In the doorway stood three men; they were uniformly garbed in robes of dark red that flowed behind them, and black cords twisted around their waists. One stood in the front of the other two, leading them forwards in the hall with furrowed brows.

The king's guards on either side of the door moved towards them, hands on the hilts of their swords, but the man in front held out a parchment, sealed in red wax and snapped at them.

"Stay your posts and do not hinder us, for I come bearing a message from Chromer, the greatest power in the north."

The four guards wavered for a moment, glancing at each other before escorting the men towards where Naryan sat on the throne.

Cormack and Shawn, turning at the commotion, saw the escorted trio coming down the aisle towards them, and moved out of their way as they came to stand in front of the king. The guards now stood on either side of Naryan, wary of the visitors.

"Halt your court, for we come bearing tidings," spat the man. As he came to stand in front of Naryan, "Who sits here on the king's throne? I must speak with him."

"I am the king." replied Naryan, and watched them for a response. The man let a scoff through his nose as he shook his head.

"I have never seen you before. So, a new king now sits on the throne, and already overreaches his bounds. You should know your place, young one."

Naryan enunciated as he replied,

"I sit here now as my father has perished. I would watch your tongue while you speak to the king."

The man stared at Naryan, eyes unwavering as he replied,

"Your father was wise, for he knew his place. Now you must learn yours."

Naryan bared his teeth at the man, standing up from his throne and grasping a sword from one of his guard's hands. He stepped twice to the man, sword pointed out towards the man's throat. The man scoffed and shook his head,

"Such brashness." His eyes still did not break away from Naryan's, even with the blade nearly tickling him. He raised his hand to show the sealed parchment that he held, and smiled.

"Kill me if you dare, but it does not matter, for war is already declared on you." He tore open the sealed parchment and threw it at the Naryan's feet. Naryan looked down at the black words scrawled on the parchment, and the broken seal of Chromer. Whispers emanated from the courtiers in the chamber, and Naryan lowered the sword, stooping to collect the parchment.

He unfurled it and read, unaware of the gaze of the entire room on him. He looked up again at the man who watched him with a sneer on his lip.

"Why? What has been done to deserve this?" Naryan asked as his brow tightened.

"You are accused of assassination, and all clues point back to Satoria. Your people will pay for this fell deed."

"Assassination?"

"Don't play coy with me. My king was murdered, smothered in his sleep so that he even turned blue from the asphyxiation. But you should already know that, for the torn colors of your house guard were discovered, wrapped in thorns of a tree near his window."

"Two kings now dead?" said Naryan, "I sense something awry. Let us discuss this for a moment."

"Don't try to fool me with this sudden ruse of your father's death. I doubt even that he is dead; perhaps he is ill and you are playing foolhardy games on the throne. Perhaps even he has planned this trickery and now rules from behind closed doors." He tilted his head back and yelled, "Come out good king, and face the wrath that will be brought upon your people!"

Naryan's lips twisted up and he clenched his jaw as he heaved the sword in his hand towards the emissary from the low position where he'd held it. Naryan yelled, even as the man brought his arm up to defend himself. The blade glanced off his forearm, sliding up along the man's sleeve until it came to his bare hand, severing the bottom half of it from his wrist. Gasps filled the room and the guards on either side of Naryan rushed forwards, shoving the man's companions to the ground and standing over them, swords drawn to their necks.

The emissary bent over, clutching his arm close to his body. The blood ran down his elbow in uneven pulses to leave echoes of heavy dripping in the courtroom, and painting uneven spatters of red onto the floor. The man dropped to his knees, the scorn in his face dissolving as he looked up at Naryan. His vision darkened around the edges before simply looking at him and shaking his head,

"You fool." were the last words he spoke, as he collapsed next to the portion of his severed hand. The crimson on the ground was no longer in neat drips, but now streaked across the floor by the man's red robe, and the red of the robe perfectly matched the blood that now soaked into it. Naryan dropped the sword to the floor with a metallic clatter that echoed through the chamber, and shook his hand as he turned to walk away.

Chapter 4

"The emissary certainly did not hesitate to speak the truth with his final breath."

Naryan looked up at Rhondia who stood with her arms crossed, staring down at him. A servant dabbed at Naryan's forehead with a cool cloth while he lounged on a chair with his legs resting on a velvet footstool in front of him.

"I can't believe you would do such a thing. Do you know what kind of position this leaves us in?"

Naryan scowled,

"I told you court should have been canceled."

"When will you learn that quip and wit are not the appropriate responses to every comment? You are a king now. You must act like one. Not slaughtering emissaries in your court would be a good step in the right direction."

Naryan gazed off at a wall and said,

"Yes, it did make quite a mess of the floor..." he looked back up at Rhondia,

"They had already declared war on us anyway. How worse can they retaliate? He was simply the first casualty."

"Don't pretend like this was some well-thought out plan of first strike. You let your temper get the best of you and you threw out what little bit of civility might have been salvaged from this pending war."

Rhondia had more to say, but was cut short as Murdock strode through the open door, another man in tow, who was in turn followed by Domery. The new man was tall and lean, clean cut and in military uniform, not in the fancy attire of the court.

"My lord, if I may interject." Domery said, gesturing towards the man, "This is Sir Sylvian–commander of Satoria's armies–in case you have not yet been acquainted."

Sylvian gave a courteous nod, not breaking eye contact with Naryan, his hands clasped behind his back. Naryan looked at him, then at Murdock, then at Rhondia, then back to Murdock as if waiting for something.

Domery poked his head out from behind the other two and spoke,

"Erm, my lord–you may want to discuss the state of our outer land's defenses and the preparation of our armies."

Naryan stared at all of them, unblinking, before finally rolling his eyes to the ceiling with an exhale, and gesturing in a circular motion with his hand.

"Go on then–advise me."

Sylvian stepped forwards,

"Thank you for the audience my lord. I will first say that our standing army is in good strength and well-equipped. Locally and in the surrounding hamlets we maintain a standing army of two thousand at all times, with another two thousand trained in reserve. I estimate available conscription from the surrounding population at another four thousand. If we were to conscript from the cities in the west we could double that–though it would certainly create dissent in your subjects. Bear in mind, also, that they would need to be trained and equipped if they are expected to do battle, let alone the journey here.

"At this moment, however, there is no army massed, for they are spread at their posts across our borders, and garrisoned within their various home cities and hamlets."

Naryan looked Sylvian in the eyes, nodding as if he understood, before speaking,

"Tell me then of our foes. What does Chromer have at their disposal?"

"It's hard to say, my lord. I doubt they would mass their entire force to assault us all at once. They will most likely strike at our bordering cities to draw our forces to defend, and play a game of mobility."

"That's not what I asked. How large an army are we dealing with?"

Sylvian stiffened,

29

"Yes my lord. Our best estimates would say they could amass an army of more than twenty thousand."

Naryan sat up.

"Twenty thousand? They have more standing now as we could muster altogether?"

"Well yes, my lord. They do aim to maintain a stricter hold on their territories, and certainly collect more tribute and conscripts from them."

"Why do we not aim to keep a force large enough to contend with our most outspoken foe? I would think this wise–would you not?" posed Naryan.

"Upkeep of an army is expensive, my lord. Also, things have not been necessarily tense with them until certain…recent events unfolded."

Naryan grimaced.

"I suppose not."

Sylvian gave a curt nod.

"What's done is done my lord."

Naryan chewed on his cheek for a moment before replying.

"So then, what can we expect from them as far as aggressing towards us? They delivered a decree of war, so I can only assume they are a step ahead of us. Where will they strike first?"

"It is likely that they will weaken the defenses of our outermost territories, rather than amass an assault to our heart. The more damage done to the countryside and the more our forces are spread thin, the more difficult it will be to meet them in open war when the time comes."

"Send out scouts then, so we know where they will first strike. If we are to be at war, then let it be a war we shall win."

"It has already been done my lord."

"Well," Naryan raised his eyebrows, "it sounds like you've got everything handled then. As you were." He rested his head back against the head of the chair and rested his eyes, beckoning the servant with the damp cloth to return.

Sylvian, still standing tall, clasped his hands behind his back and cleared his throat.

"My lord, if I may."

Naryan opened his eyes again and raised his head, looking towards the ceiling before motioning with his hand to continue.

"Any outright war with Chromer is not a war that we can win; there isn't a subject in the kingdom that doesn't know this. Plans for troop movements, supply trains, and the stockpile of armaments have already been set in place, but If negotiations are already a failed tactic, then we *must* boost the morale of the army. Every man must fight like ten."

"Ah yes, a feast! A great proposition."

Sylvian's mustache bristled as he struggled to keep his lips pursed.

Domery spoke up, peeking out again from behind the other 2 men,

"My king, perhaps what Sir Sylvian is saying, is that a good place to start would be to visit the outer hamlets. The people there certainly do not yet know of this pending war and would welcome a visit from their king who will guide them to safety. Then, we can also discuss the defensibility of each hamlet, and strategize a plan of action."

Naryan thought for a moment,

"What other options do we have?"

Domery huffed and withdrew back behind the other two men. Sylvian replied,

"It is also customary, my lord, that the king accompanies the army as it travels, and that you show face on the battlefield. They are, after all, putting their lives on the line for you."

Naryan furrowed his brow.

"Is that safe?"

Sylvian cocked his head.

"It is battle, my lord. None of it is safe."

"I'm not an imbecile–I know that battle is not safe. Is traveling safe?"

"Apologies my lord..."

Rhondia interjected,

"Just save us all the time of this feigned strategy and admit to us that you will lock yourself in your keep with a large store of wine until all the countryside has been ravaged."

Naryan tore the cool rag off his forehead and stood, staring at Rhondia.

"You take me for a coward, but I am not. I have an idea–and this is what I shall do. I will go to the outer hamlets and visit them. I shall survey the lay of the land and we shall discuss the defensibility of each of them, and whether or not they should be strategically sacrificed and the people relocated."

Domery could be heard sputtering behind the other two men and his now crimson face peeked around from the side of Murdock, who elbowed him and said,

"That is a fine idea you have, my lord. Come now, walk with me and we shall discuss provisioning your caravan."

Chapter 5

"Are you ready, my lord?"

Naryan stood with Sylvian, surveying the caravan. It was set to be a single day and night's carriage ride to the hamlet of Sallow Hill. Sallow Hill was to the north east, and the first in a line of three that were parallel to the north-south running Chromer border. Steeds had already been sent ahead to the watering posts that lined travel routes, to provide fresh legs along the journey so that they could continue without needing to stop.

The caravan itself consisted of three carriages that would bear the two of them and other strategists to the outer hamlets, two platoons of foot soldiers, a company of cavalry, and two wagons of provisions. His own carriage was evenly in the middle of the caravan, and the two horses at its front eyed servants carrying large barrels of wine to load onto the rear of the carriage.

"Nearly," he replied to Sylvian, and turned to see Rhondia approaching. She came and stood next to him for a moment, looking between him and the caravan before saying,

"One would not have to jump to conclusions to guess which gaudy carriage is yours. Let's hope that assassins are not yet out for you."

"Hm yes, I will miss you too Rhondia, and also wish you safety."

"Perhaps flaunting your riches on the cusp of war is not a wise move. Nor is the drunkenness you're clearly preparing for." She looked him up and down, "And your attire insinuates you a fop."

"The war has not started yet, and I only wish to be afforded a few luxuries before I dig into the trenches of a long defensive campaign.

"I'm sure I'll see you back here in a week."

"You think Chromer will surrender that quickly? Well, thank you for your vote of confidence; I wasn't exactly sure you believed in me."

33

Rhondia exhaled,

"If you want this to be a short war, you'll consider enlisting the aid of Einar."

Naryan stopped eyeballing the barrels of wine and straightened his lip from the sneer that showed at the mention of Einar.

"I've got enough problems as it is without the dissent he's causing throughout the city. I've got half a mind to have him executed or banished. It will mostly depend on the mood that I'm in when I give the order."

"Your stubbornness will cost many lives."

"Do you *actually* believe this, Rhondia?"

"How can I not? I have seen this magic, as have you."

"Rhondia," Naryan started, before pausing to study her for a moment. "For all of the squibbles and snide remarks that we trade, I know you to be keen. Part of me wishes to listen to some hidden wisdom you seek to share, and the other part wishes to forsake all advice you give, just to spite you. Still, even another part of me thinks that you've been made a fool, and I myself refuse to fall victim to his ruse. I will not have him involved in this, even in the most desperate moment. Now, I depart."

Rhondia pushed an exhale through her nose as they turned their separate ways, and Naryan headed toward the caravan.

He came to it and surveyed a thick muck that lay between him and the carriage's entrance. A growl of disgust lingered in the back of his throat before he began tip-toeing through the mud to reach the doorway. The heels of his boots left deep imprints in the mud, and a plop of suction was released with each step that he took. He finally came to the doorway and flung it open as he stared down at his now certainly-ruined boots. A presence within the carriage caused him to raise his eyes, and he saw Sherry's form sitting comfortably in the interior, already enjoying a goblet of wine.

"I've been watching you through the blinds for some time now. I find it quite the entertainment to watch a macaroni who now thinks himself a war commander, schlepp through muck."

He put his hands on his hips and looked up at her sternly, before raising his hand to her, palm down.

"Well, the least you can do is help me up."

Sherry paused and watched him for a moment, before finally taking a pull of her goblet and smiling at him with her mouth still touching the rim of the goblet while her eyes peered over its top. She reached out her hand,

"Of course m'lady."

Naryan sat on a fur-covered bench and began pulling off his muck-covered boots, struggling to get his heel from each of them, and finally piling them under his bench. Nearly out of breath, he looked at her,

"Well, now that that's done—what are you doing here? And where's the wine?"

"Oh, the wine barrels are in the back. Did you not see them as you came over?"

Naryan feigned a glare as he looked at her. He reached for his boot and stuck his foot halfway in before pulling it off and looking at her,

"Will you get me some wine?"

Sherry looked over at her own boots that were already near the door, then at her stocking-covered feet as she wiggled her toes. She looked back at him and innocently smiled while shaking her head.

"Fine then," he threw his boot on the ground. "I order you to get me some wine."

Sherry scoffed, her mouth half-open in disbelief.

"Are you really pulling the 'king' card on me? You wouldn't dare."

"Oh, watch me. I wonder what everyone will say when they find out that a would-be assassin snuck into my carriage to end the war early. They will sing praises that I was able to fend them off long enough for my guards to arrive. Guard! Guard!"

Sherry, now wide-eyed, swallowed a mouthful of wine and stood to don her boots near the door.

"I'm sorry my lord."

Naryan smirked as footsteps outside signaled the approaching guard, and the door to the carriage was pulled open.

"Yes, my lord?"

"Bring me some wine. In fact, make it a casket."

The guard, as annoyed as he was, kept a stern face.

"Certainly, my lord."

While Naryan waited for the guard's return, he stared at Sherry with a smile playing on his lips. Her jaw was set as she held the goblet close to her face while she brooded at the carriage wall, not acknowledging him. All too pleased with himself, he chuckled as the guard returned with the casket and closed the carriage door behind him.

As soon as the door was shut Sherry got up and slapped him on the arm.

"I can't believe you!" She slapped him again.

"Ow, hey, stop that! Guard! Guard!"

Sherry retreated instantly to her side of the carriage again, but the guard's footsteps returned and the door was wrenched open. He peered his head inside as Naryan collected himself and looked at the guard,

"Thank you for the wine."

The guard nodded and again retreated as the door shut.

Sherry snapped at him,

"You know you're an ass, right?"

Naryan smirked at her,

"I've been told it's my best feature."

And so as they traveled, the night passed, and with each bump of the carriage, it seemed that the casket drained itself a little further until even the light sloshing from within disappeared. Naryan held the casket in one arm and his goblet in the other, and had been very free in his doling out of wine between the two of them. Their lips and teeth were stained purple, and hiccups often interrupted their sentences as they conversed into the long hours of the night.

"So I know that it's been hours," Naryan slurred, "but you never did tell me what exactly you're doing here in my carriage. You do know that we're on a very dangerous mission to the outskirts of my kingdom. Very dangerous."

"I'm not really sure now that I'm here." Sherry swirled the little bit of wine that was left in her goblet and drained it. "I suppose I was just bored. Sometimes I need a little adventure. The manor can be stuffy."

"Oh, and do I provide you the excitement that you so crave?"

Sherry put down her goblet and rose, lifting the now-empty casket from the crook of Naryan's arm and settling into it herself.

"Excitement? Let's not get ahead of yourself–you're not that exciting. I'm not sure, perhaps I just missed you."

Her eyes gazed up at him in the light of the single lantern that flickered inside the carriage.

He glanced down at her and then studied his own nearly-empty goblet.

"You know, we'll be there soon. I can't decide if I should get some rest or some more wine. I do sleep well when I drink wine though; perhaps tonight will be the best of both worlds. Will you get me some more wine?"

"I'll oblige you this time."

She pushed herself up and stooped to collect the casket, holding it to her ear and shaking it. There was barely a slosh from the interior.

"I'm sorry m'lord. We seem to be out of wine."

Naryan grimaced as she continued,

"Since we're out of this wine, why don't you have some Sherry?"

He looked up at her as she dropped the casket to the floor and flipped her hair over her shoulder, straddling him in a quick motion. With her right hand she grasped the back of his head and with her left she held the front of his neck, bringing their mouths together and locking lips in tight embrace. They held there for a long moment until finally they pulled apart, gasping for breath. The severance lasted only a second before they came back together even more desperate than before. He dropped the goblet to the ground with a clank, and a small dribble of wine leaked to the floor, even as she felt his hands grab her hips and slide her further up his lap.

She lofted herself so that his head was leaned back as she kissed him from above, and rhythmically moved her hips across his until she could feel him rising through his trousers. Their lips played with each other, and her hands ran through his hair, grasping it while the ebb and flow of their lips synced with waves of her hips.

Sherry felt his hands fumble for a moment at the hem of her shirt until they found their way beneath it and onto the small of her back. They caressed her as they moved, coming to her front and gliding up to her chest until his fingers brushed the tips of her breasts. She shivered and bit his lower lip between her teeth with a sharp inhale while pulling tight on his locks woven between her fingers. A soft moan lingered in the back of his throat, even as their tongues found each other again and danced between the open curtains of their lips.

Naryan grasped her haunch, holding tight as he rolled her onto her back and laid her down across the bench. He steadied himself with his right leg on the floor of the carriage, and his other knee rubbing between her thighs as he leaned down to give attention to the soft skin of her neck. He moved up it, his breath giving her a shiver as he reached her ear, and she reached her hand down to his loin to feel him erect through his pants.

His body clenched for a moment at the first touch, then continued with newfound enthusiasm as she massaged him while their lips found each other again. His right hand grasped tightly to her hair as their lips rhythmically moved, and she felt his left hand pulling at the bottom of the dress that she wore. It entered from the bottom of the dress and moved up her leg until he found the skin of her midriff and the band of her undergarments at her waist.

He pushed into it, going further down to her lower lips; her whole body quivered as she felt it and she found new invigoration as she rubbed his member. His fingers went lower to her crevice, feeling its wetness, and he gathered some on his fingers before sliding back to her labia and caressing it gently.

She forgot the motion of her hands as she focused on the pleasure that he brought her, and she grasped onto his shirt with balled fists as she moaned.

"Have me." The words escaped her lips between gasps, and he stripped his trousers down in a smooth motion. She fumbled to pull her own undergarments down as he did, and wrapped her legs around his waist to pull him close to her. She reached down and grasped his member, guiding it to her crevice and teasing him with its exterior. She felt her moisture on his tip, and glided her hand across his shaft to spread it down further. She felt the pulse of his heart in her hand, and pulled him in closer until he had just barely entered her. They hung there for a moment before she was able to relax; he pushed into her and she enveloped him, even as they both let out heavy exhales. In between gasps the utterance,

"Oh, I love you." escaped her lips. His eyes were closed as he steadied himself on the carriage wall, and one of his cheeks pulled into a smug grin. They gyrated together and she felt the tension building within her as his tip rubbed on the same spot within her over, and over.

"I love you." She said again, smiling and looking up at his profile in the dim light.

He opened his eyes for a moment to glance down at her with his own smile, bending to give her a kiss, even as their bodies squirmed together in unison. She pulled away from the kiss and brought his ear down to her lips as she whispered,

"Tell me you love me."

He lifted his torso up so that he was above her, and looked down at her; her large pupils stared up at him, eyebrows raised and lips curled into a soft smile.

Naryan put his finger on her lips.

"Sssh."

He closed his eyes and arched his neck back, living in the moment of ecstasy. Sherry's eyebrows narrowed the slightest, even as her lower lip trembled.

"Naryan," she said, "Please?" as she reached her hand up to place it on his face. He grasped her hand and kissed it, but did not look down at her. "Please." She said again, her voice cracking into a beg, but he did not acknowledge her. "Please."

His breaths became more shallow and frequent as he felt the desperation building with him. Sherry unwrapped her legs from around him and tried to push him away with her hands.

"Stop. Naryan." she snapped. "Look at me."

He did look down at her, but his eyes were narrowed to ferocity instead of the tenderness she craved. He pushed harder into her so that she slid further across the bench with each thrust until she felt her head pressing against the wall of the carriage.

She pushed against the wall with one hand for leverage, and against his chest with her other, but he grasped her arm and pinned it against the seat of the carriage's bench.

"Naryan, *stop!*" she yelled, and slapped him across the face. He bared his teeth at her and grasped that hand too, bending it at an unnatural angle as he raped her. His brow furrowed with intensity as he rammed into her over, and over until her neck was now forced into an uncomfortable angle against the wall.

"Stop!" she cried again, weaker this time. "Stop. Please. Please." and her words trailed off even as she resigned her form to him. Her throat tightened and her lower lip curled even as the tears forming around her eyes blurred the interior of the carriage, and his indifferent face.

Naryan's grip on her arms loosened, even as his eyes became less wild, and he let out a guttural exhale as he came.

"I'm done." he rasped, "I'm done." He collapsed backward over the trousers on his ankles to sit against the bench opposite her as he caught his breath.

Sherry lay there for a moment, still exposed to the air, as she clenched her teeth and her eyes furrowed in fury. She sat up, pushing her garments down to cover herself again, and rose to strike him. Seeing his drained face, however, her own face contorted to grief, and she instead burst out through the carriage door and ran into the dark night.

Naryan sat up, watching her disappear through the door and called out,

"Sherry, wait! Where are you going?"

He stooped and grasped his undergarments, pulling them up as he jumped out of the carriage and stumbled to the ground. He managed to push himself to a stand as he now pulled up his trousers, and chased Sherry into the darkness of the woods. He heard the shouts of the soldiers in the caravan behind him as he followed her crashes through the underbrush deeper into the forest.

Chapter 6

Thin branches lashed across Naryan's face as he ran, and he felt the coolness of the night air on the blood that seeped to the surface of his skin. He ran by a dim moonlight, only guided by the sound of crushing leaves as Sherry escaped him. His head swam from the wine he'd consumed, and he struggled to keep his balance by steadying himself on thick tree trunks as he moved.

He realized that he'd forgotten his boots in the carriage when he smashed his foot into a protruding rock, and hopped along on one foot for a moment before falling to the ground and rolling. Twigs stabbed into his back and rocks clubbed at his body before he finally sat up. He nursed his injured foot, seeing then that his socks were shredded and his feet bleeding, only unnoticed prior due to his focus on the chase. He listened for a moment, hearing the sounds of Sherry's crashes disappearing further into the forest before yelling out for her. The sounds completely dissipated into the night, and a growl of disgust lingered in his throat as grabbed a stick and threw it into the darkness.

He pushed himself up off the ground and with his sleeve he wiped away the sweat that now beaded on his brow. He felt the cool forest air now cooling his smeared forehead and caught his breath before, gingerly stepping on his now noticeably painful feet one at a time as he tip-toed through the forest. He yelled out again and listened for a response from either Sherry or his guards, but heard nothing.

"Useless guards," he said aloud to himself. "can't even catch two barefoot people in the woods."

Having wholly lost his bearings, he headed back in what he thought was the direction he'd come. He had no clue how much ground he'd covered as he'd chased after Sherry, but after more than an hour's walk, he was sure that he'd been going in the wrong direction. The night air now chilled him, and he tucked his arms tighter against his torso with a shiver, and rested his chin on his chest as he pushed onwards.

A while longer he walked until a flicker of light in the distance caught his eyes through the trees. Reinvigorated, he pushed on quicker now, seeing the lights multiply as he muttered under his breath how unhappy he was to be with his guards once he was a bit warmer.

"Aw shit. Sherry." he said audibly, then brushed it off. She'd be fine; he'd send out a search party for her in the morning, if she wasn't back already. She was probably faster than he, and had a far better sense of direction anyway. As he approached nearer to the lights he found that they weren't the lanterns of the caravan that he'd expected, but standing torches lining the perimeter of a camp of red tents at the end of the forest. Slower he approached, now crouching and forgetting all sense of cold.

There were more than a few tents, perhaps fifty, spread across the open countryside. At a quick estimation of their size he figured there were two hundred men, and the flags raised above the tents bore the insignia of Chromer. The crackle of a nearby fire caught his attention, voices carried to him as he now carefully chose his steps to get within earshot. His heart pounded and he dared barely breathe as he picked his way along the tree line and finally came within sight of the men.

The flickering fire cast shadows on their grim faces as they spoke,

"I cannot say that they even know we come." said one. "This is not a well-guarded keep, but merely a town of hovels. They will not expend resources to defend it, for it is neither a strategic location, nor easily defensible. Cheer yourselves. We will soon be on our way."

Another of them grunted and threw a stick into the fire, staring deeply into it.

"I am plenty cheerful." said another, in a less-than-cheerful tone. "I just wonder why we need to camp another night when we could set a flame to it now and be done. The longer we're here the higher chance of a scout stumbling upon us."

The one who spoke first looked at him.

"We will not be scouted. They were only delivered the declaration of war but a few days passed. Even if they knew we were coming, they would expect us to come from the northeast, not to have waded the river. They will not contest Sallow Hill anyway–they will give it up, and it will be the first of many to fall."

Naryan recalled the large map of the Satoria that had sat in his father's study, and swiveled his head to see the silhouette of mountains off to the distance in the east against the night sky. They were hardly tall mountains, but certainly enough to create impassable terrain for an army, and the range marked the easternmost border of his lands. He turned away, slowly picking his steps again until he was certain he was out of earshot of the men, set the mountains to his left, and ran as fast as he dared.

If he'd known where he was when he'd jumped out of the carriage, he would have found Sallow Hill just a few minutes walk away. It was unfortunate that he'd been set off his course for a long walk, or rather, Naryan thought, perhaps it was fortunate that been set off course and stumbled across the Chromerian adversaries.

He found the dirt road leading to Sallow Hill with a short walk through the forest, realizing that this short walk meant that the enemy was much nearer than comfortable, and would certainly be ready to attack in the morning.

Sallow Hill wasn't much of a hill, a large mound at best, and was named for the rather ugly dark-yellow flowers that bloomed on it in the spring and quickly died in the heat of the summer. It sat in the middle of a large forest clearing that now contained small farmsteads and some livestock, but not much else. The main part of the town itself was surrounded by a small wooden palisade that skirted the bottom of the large mound, and housed no more than a few hundred inhabitants, most of them farmers or peasants who would probably leave at a moment's notice if they had anything better going for them.

Naryan ran along the road now, glad that his numbed feet couldn't feel the bloody scrapes and bruises he was sure to find in the morning. He saw the bob of lanterns leaving from the town's gate and ran to them, shouting.

"Sylvian. Sir Sylvian! Where is Sir Silvian?"

Lanterns bee-lined for him from all sides, the soldiers gathering around him in a commotion.

"My lord, this way. We're glad to have found you." said one.

"Sylvian. Where is he?" spat Naryan between breaths.

"My lord, he's in the Hall of Sallow Hill organizing a search for…you."

Naryan pushed past the soldiers without thanking them, sprinting again towards the hamlet. The soldiers fell in, confused, and followed behind him.

Naryan came to the door, ignoring guards that bowed as they saw him coming, and pushed through it, still shouting for Sylvian.

Sylvian turned and stood, bowing at the sign of Naryan, but with an eyebrow raised.

"Your Majesty. Where have you been?"

"Nevermind that. And never mind how…" Naryan caught his breath for a moment. "Chromer. They're here. A rabble of two hundred men, merely a morning's walk to the north."

Sylvian studied Naryan's scratched face, tattered clothes, and purple lips for a moment.

"You're sure, your majesty?" he asked.

"Do I look in a tale-telling mood?"

"No, my lord." Sylvian nodded once and turned to a soldier. "You there, take another and scout them out. Be silent and bring word promptly." The soldier nodded and turned on his heel, jogging out of the door.

Naryan spoke again, frenzied.

"Vacate the people. Ring the bell. Call for reinforcements. It must be cavalry if they are to arrive by morning."

"My lord," Sylvian paused, "do you think it wise to act so hastily? War is often a game of patience and slow moves."

"They are very near. There is no time for slow moves. Wake the people!"

"If Chromer is as near as you say, we should not ring the bell lest they be alerted that we're aware of them."

"Fine." said Naryan, "then send for the cavalry."

Sylian's cheek twitched.

"Your majesty. Perhaps we should discuss the strategic value of our Hamlets and other landmarks, and decide which we should devote resources to defending."

"I overheard them speaking. They think we won't defend anything. They called us cowards and aim to take all of our lands." he pointed his finger at Sylvian. "You'll do as I say. Now call for reinforcements."

Sylvian turned to a guard,

"Send a light rider to Satoria and gather fifty horsemen. Tell them to come from the north of Sallow Hill to flank Chromer when they come."

"Fifty only? More. I want none of them to survive."

Sylvian's mustache bristled.

"A hundred then."

The soldier nodded and trotted away before Naryan could shout at him, but Naryan's anger was still turned to Sylvian.

"Did you not hear me? They think we are nothing–cowards. They think they will take what we have without a fight. Why do you call for scant forces? We should crush them!"

"Your majesty. We do not have limitless resources to call upon at a whim. We must not only manage this fight, but the state of the city, the state of other provinces, and future fights to be had in this looming war."

Naryan scowled, but nodded and said,

"Fine, as you see fit. Now, wake the subjects. They must flee while we defend the hamlet."

"You there." spoke Sylvian, "Take a few men and start alerting the people door-to-door. They must gather a few belongings and depart immediately. Send riders south to the other hamlets too and tell them to prepare to evacuate as well."

"Good." Said Naryan. "The people will be safe. Let us now discuss the defense of Sallow Hill."

"Defense, my lord?" puzzled Sylvian.

"Yes, Sallow Hill will certainly fall in this state. These are but wooden buildings and a thin stockade to surround them."

Sylvian tilted his head slightly,

"You do not intend to fully defend Sallow Hill, do you? My lord."

"Of course."

Naryan did not break his gaze from Sylvian, who then realized he was serious.

Sylvian's eyes looked heavenward for a moment as he took a breath through his nose and replied,

"War is not some glorious game. These men will die. Look around, we did not come with a war party but merely a few men to guard you. We have barely a hundred foot soldiers and cavalry combined. We cannot defend Sallow Hill. And even if we did have a force here to defend it with, what is the cost of lives to defend this small hamlet? What of value is there to defend?"

"Where is the line? Should we let them take but a little land? A little town here, or there? Our pride and lands are at stake."

"Ah, your pride. Is your pride worth the lives of everyone here? You too shall die if we stay, and," Sylvian's voice hushed, "if you leave the men will certainly relinquish their posts. They will not fight to die if you will not."

"I do not intend to fight and die–is this not why we are calling for reinforcements? We only must hold the line until they arrive, at which time the cavalry will certainly smite them to ruin."

"So, you intend us to hold up against an army in a town of sticks and straw? We certainly cannot meet them in the fields with half their number. My lord, let us reconsider. We should evacuate the citizenship and leave the town to flame"

"Sallow Hill *will* stand. We must fortify it, with what little time we have. I say a trench at the perimeter with wooden stakes pointing out, to impale Chromer as they run at us."

"My lord, we have not come prepared for this. We have no picks, or spades, and must fell trees to shape stakes. Even if this is your command, we also have no time."

"Then I want the palisade fortified, and guarded. Sallow Hill will stand."

Though it was still the dark of early morning, Sallow Hill now bustled with the evacuation of civilians, woken from their slumber by torch-bearing soldiers banging on their doors. Gaunt-faced men towed their wide-eyed wives and crying children behind them, carrying ragged sacks of what little belongings they had. They left in a long line, escorted by but a few soldiers on foot, whom others whispered were the lucky ones.

Naryan stood in what could be considered a small tower against the north wall, though it was little more than a raised platform with corner posts holding a pointed thatch roof over it. He stewed as he overlooked Sallow Hill's short wooden palisade wall to see the moonlight bathing wisps of fog that hovered over fields of wildflowers, and the dark forest behind.

Flickering torches on posts illuminated the ground below him, and along the fence he could hear the heavy breathing of his soldiers as they toiled away at reinforcing the palisade.

In front of the fence, soldiers set freshly shaped stakes of two cubits to protrude from the ground at an upward angle to keep the enemy away from the wall. It was maybe enough to slow down any massive charge against the wall and make a few steps falter, but it would not stop them.

Having brought no tools of their own, they commissioned them from the local populace, who unceremoniously dumped axes, shovels, spades, picks, and hoes in a pile at the south entrance before their evacuation. Nobody complained, and nobody looked back.

Never mind the pending battle, Naryan's foul mood was enhanced by the fact that Sylvian was nowhere to be found. He was sure Sylvian was hiding away so that he didn't have to heed any more of Naryan's commands, for he'd put up quite an argument in the face of the stubborn decision to defend Sallow Hill. Naryan ignored the hushed conversations of the soldiers who were clearly concerned at his decision, set his jaw, and laid out his expectations.

His decision was made out of concern for his subjects, he thought, as he ran his hand up one of the corner posts and looked towards the forest. Where were they to go if their homes were destroyed? Their livelihoods were here, their belongings were here, and their families were here. And he couldn't have homeless refugees roaming the capital—that wouldn't do. Plus, losing an economy like this, small as it was, would certainly affect the tax income. Chromer's reach would only grow more aggressive if they gave up the outer hamlets without a fight. No, this was the right thing to do; perhaps some of his men would die, but when the cavalry arrived in the morning—all would be set right. Chromer would wonder why their men had disappeared, and why the least defensible Hamlet in Satoria stood unscathed.

His thoughts were interrupted by a throat clearing just below his perch, and he looked over the edge to see that Sylvian had returned, and he was now garbed in light armor; a shining breastplate with leather sleeves ending in gloved hands, thick chaps with tall boots, a sword at his side, and a ridged barbute helmet on his head. A peasant stood next to him, perhaps forty years of age, a sack tossed over his back, and wearing garb fit for the fields. He looked wide-eyed up at Naryan, as Sylvian introduced him.

"My lord, I bring before you one of your subjects, who wishes an audience before you."

Naryan nodded and smiled.

"Of course, bring him nearer." he motioned. "I'm glad to finally see some gratitude. I knew the people of Sallow Hill were of good spirit. I'll have you know, once this ordeal is behind us, I fully intend to repair any damages to the town, and budget for some better infrastructure. I tasted your well water and it wasn't too pleasant. Also," he motioned with his hand, "this whole place could use a little sprucing up–with the roofs and all."

The man bowed his head as he approached and glanced at Sylvian before speaking,

"Well you see, my Lord, that's the thing." he stuttered. "There are actually a few men in your guard whose roots are here in Sallow Hill. My son is one of them, among others, and we have seen and greeted them this evening."

Naryan Smiled.

"I'm glad to see that Sallow Hill has produced such fine soldiers. I will be sure to give them commendations once the town is made safe."

The man swallowed.

"We're certainly grateful for your concern, the people of the town do not even see reason to shed blood for its defense."

Naryan's eyes narrowed.

"I'm not sure I follow."

The man looked at Sylvian again and started to speak, but closed his mouth as Sylvian nodded at him and interjected.

"What he's trying to say, my lord, is that the people of Sallow Hill would not even defend it with their blood."

The man nodded and spoke again.

"Fields can be resown elsewhere, buildings, rebuilt. I would rather see Sallow Hill fall than bury my son, and the children of my neighbors."

Naryan scowled.

"Unless you're going to pick up a sword, old man, I suggest you depart here with your family. I see the last of the evacuees leaving now." Naryan nodded towards the south entrance and the man hastily bowed and turned to leave without another word. Sylvian grimaced and also turned to leave, but Naryan called out to him.

"Sylvian, a word."

Sylvian stood at attention, looking up at Naryan's post with his arms folded behind his back and his lips drawn tight.

"My lord?"

"If I catch you causing dissent amongst my subjects again, I will relieve you from your post, and your head from your body. Do I make myself clear?"

"Your Majesty, I simply wish to bring to your attention the desires of your subjects. They are a simple people, and do not wish to get caught up in the wars of kings. We should not squander the scarce resource of life, to defend unstrategic lands."

"Sir Sylvian. Your head. Am I clear?"

Sylvian nodded once.

"My lord."

He started to turn, but saw that Naryan's gaze was drawn across the fields to movement coming from the forest, even as rays of a red dawn began to glow from the treetops to the east. Naryan looked down to Sylvian and said,

"They're here."

Sylvian climbed a short ladder to the platform to stand next to Naryan, and saw dark movements along the treeline as the Chromerian raiders began to emerge a few hundred yards away. They formed thick ranks, and Sylvian glanced over at Naryan.

"A rabble of two hundred, you said? In my estimation it is more like five hundred, well-equipped and well-organized."

Naryan looked at Sylvian with a scowl and replied,

"You think that I've made a rash decision, but it is a calculated one. I do expect that the cavalry you called will be here in time, or else it seems our lives are forfeit."

Naryan looked at his soldiers. They were all garbed in the same attire as Sylvian from their heads to their feet, except with thick leather vests instead of breastplates. Instead of swords, each carried a long spear in their hands, and a round shield was bound to their backs. Their faces were grim, and the sound of muttering voices and retching men filled the otherwise still town. Naryan saw Sylvian's curt court demeanor change as he barked tense orders to the men from their perch,

"Form a line. Face the wall. Spears in front. Lift them high. You will hold this ground with your lives! It is your king's command. He stands with us today and bids us to defend our lands! You will not give in until your final breath!"

Sylvian turned to Naryan with a wry smile,

"Would you like a spear and shield, my lord?"

Naryan's stomach turned and he ground his teeth as he looked out at the lines of Chromerian soldiers. He shook his head at Sylvian's question without looking him in the eye. Sylvian barked a laugh under his breath,

"So be it." and he turned again to face the battlefield.

The Chromerian lines marched forward as one unit until they were a hundred paces away, and a lone figure on horseback approached the defenders of Sallow Hill with a steady cadence. The rider came close, until he was only a short stone's throw away, and spoke,

"I will be frank–I did not expect to come upon Sallow Hill and find defenders here." he laughed under his breath, "Let alone so few. Nonetheless, since you are here I will offer to treat with you. Depart this hill and leave it undefended, and we will spare you for another day in battle. These are my full terms."

Sylvian responded in kind,

"Your terms are rejected. Take your army elsewhere, for you attack a sovereign kingdom, unprovoked."

"Sir Sylvian," the man responded, "it is unfortunate that we do battle today. I am not an emissary, so I will not argue for or against the righteous cause of a war. Nonetheless, you and I both know that the commands we are given, we must heed. You are bid to defend, and I am bid to aggress; we will both attend to our duties."

"Then why do you pretend to offer a treat, Sir Goden?"

Sir Goden reached into his red cloak and withdrew a blue and white cloak, holding it high. As it fell and unfurled, the insignia of Sotoria could be seen embroidered onto it.

"Perhaps this will change your mind, for this man was waylaid in the night as he departed here, I can only assume he was to return with reinforcements."

Murmurs rippled through the Sotorian line, and the spears wavered as the defenders fidgeted. Sylvian glanced at Naryan who could not bear to keep eye contact.

"I am sorry for his soul," replied Sir Sylvian. "But did you catch the pigeon as well?"

A chuckle escaped Sir Goden's throat and he shook his head.

"Sir Sylvian, We will see. We will see."

He threw the cloak to the ground and wheeled the horse so that it turned, and he rode back towards the lines of his army. Naryan watched him depart, and looked at Sylvian who muttered under his breath,

"And so our fate is sealed."

Chapter 7

As part of the preparation, the defenders of Sallow Hill had removed some of the standing beams every few feet so that they could peer through the wall. Through these ports they watched the Chromerians march closer and closer until their ranks were near to the palisade. Here they stood, banging weapons on shields and yelling at those behind the wall.

Though tall for a palisade, it now felt short and brittle, a mere paper-thin defense against the raiders. The few men that guarded Sallow Hill had spread themselves across its perimeter, and they now readied themselves for the crash of foes against the wall.

The first rank of Chromerians roused together with a yell and moved forward as one wave, slowly at first, until they had reached full speed. A hundred men ran to the palisade, jumping up as they reached it and hoisting themselves up and over the weather-dulled pointed posts. A few made it to the top and were then greeted by spears from the defenders, pointing up at them as they vaulted the walls. The stabs from the spears waylaid the first wave, and many Chromerians fell from the wall to the ground, dead inside the of Sallow hill.

Those who were unable to vault the wall, the lucky ones some might say, found themselves pressed up against the wall and harassed by spears jabbing through the removed slats in the palisade. Realizing these were not weaknesses in the wall they retreated away from it.

Naryan looked over at Sylvian.

"See. See! The defense is working! Already have weakened their numbers."

Sylvian shook his head.

"I count twenty dead, no more, and their numbers have not dwindled by much. That was merely a tease to the defenses. I would not hold such high expectations."

Having now regrouped, a row of archers appeared amidst the Chromerian ranks.

"Wary of archers!" Cried out Sylvian to his men, and the defenders unstrapped the shields from their backs, holding them above their heads.

"Where are our archers?" questioned Naryan,

"How many times must I remind you, your majesty, that we did not come prepared to fight a battle, merely to escort you across the countryside! We are at their mercy."

In front of the archers, a row of men walked forward bearing torches, and the archers dipped their arrows to the flame before bending their bows. A volley of arrows rose from the Chromerians as one cloud, falling down upon Sallow Hill. None of the defenders were pierced by the arrows, for there was room for the few of them to shelter against the near side of the palisade wall, but arrows scattered across thatch-roofed buildings and caught them to flame.

Each of the arrows that landed on the roof started only as a small spout of fire, but in only a few moments the flames were caught by the morning breeze and spread across the buildings. Crackles from the thatch roofs soon turned to a deep roar of flame that grew as Sallow Hill burned.

The ranks of Chromer moved forwards again, this time the entire force instead of just a few, and they sprinted full speed into the wall with shields raised. Some bounded off the wall before they then were pushed again from behind by their allies, coming up to it and pressing against it with the might of a thousand legs.

Spears that poked through the defensive ports were ripped from the defenders' grasps by many hands, or hewn by swords and axes until the shafts splintered. Sections of the palisade began to tilt under the pressure of the pushing men, and the palisade posts uprooted, toppling inwards onto the defenders. Caught beneath the falling wall, the Satorian defenders were crushed under the weight, and trampled further as the Chromerians rushed into the interior of Sallow Hill.

A mere fifty Satorian soldiers now circled in the center of Sallow Hill in one final stand as they looked over to Sylvian and Naryan for the call to retreat. Chromerians spilled in through the now many openings in the fragile palisade and the Satorians found that they were caught between a rushing wall of men and walls of flaming buildings behind them.

Naryan jumped down from the post, as did Sylvian, and they ran towards the south Entrance of Sallow Hill.

"Fall back!" Shouted Sylvian to the men. "Fall back, for we are routed!" Naryan was already far ahead of him, sprinting without looking back.

The soldiers needed no second order, some of them hoisting their spears as the charging Chromerians, and others dropping their weapons where they stood to turn and run. They had a small head start on the Chromerians, and the fearful adrenaline coursing through their veins sent them sprinting away faster than the Chromerians could chase them. The assaulting army did not give further pursuit, instead turning their attention and their torches to the remaining buildings, and their cheers of a Chromerian victory carried on the wind.

The day was further dawning as the retreating Satorians ran south without even a glance back, when they saw ahead of them a dark horse approaching at full gallop. The men scattered, fearful that it was a Chromerian pinscher to cut off their retreat, but there was only a single horse with a lone figure, and their head was fully cloaked. The rider did not acknowledge them, but galloped past them towards Sallow Hill, and Naryan saw a glimpse of Einar's face beneath his hood as the wind whipped at its corners.

Naryan slowed and turned, seeing that they were no longer chased, and the others slowed as well to watch as Einar approached the south wall of Sallow Hill. Pillars of smoke billowed up from the buildings within, and orange flames could be seen licking up at the base of the pillars. At the entrance was a band of Chromerian soldiers, and they grouped at Einar's approach. He lept off of his horse a ways away from them and moved his hands through the air.

As they moved, light hovered in their path until a symbol was drawn in the air where his fingers had traced.

The Chromerians watched, unsure of the hooded man, until he had traced a few symbols in just a moment, and they hovered, bathing him in soft golden light. Small stones then ripped themselves up from the earth around Einar, countless flying at as though they were loosed missiles. Their bodies thudded with the pummeling of stones even as they still fell, and Einar was already tracing new lines with his hands. The symbol dispersed in a flick of light, but a moment later it was as if each ember on Sallow Hill had split into a hundred, and each lick of flame had blossomed and grew, until the whole the hamlet was consumed in a raging mountain of flame.

Chromerians scattered from the conflagrated area, dropping their weapons as they went, for the metals of their swords were now red-hot, and the poles of their spears burning charcoal. They too burned, for the heat of the air itself boiled their skin and caught their attire aflame. Everything within the bounds of Sallow Hill burned; Chromerians fell as they ran, some pulling themselves along the ground to keep their heads from the smoke, even as the glassy slag along which they inched burned into their faces.

Einar's silhouetted form then raised his arms again, drawing another symbol, and he clapped his hands together on it. A shockwave emanated from him, knocking over Naryan, Sylvian, and the other men, even though they were not nearby to him. The walls and buildings of Sallow Hill were then blown away as but a puff of dust in the wind, and the fires were extinguished instantly so that where there had been a raging inferno moments before there was nothing but flattened earth covered in soot. Nothing now stood where the town of Sallow Hill had been; not a beam was still raised, nor were there any forms remaining of those who had been battling only moments before. It was still, and silent.

Neither Naryan, Sylvian, nor the remaining Satorian survivors moved from their places as they watched Einar remount his frightened steed, calming it with pats on its neck as he padded towards them. He approached them at a slow trot, and they could see blood running from the horses' ears and nose as it came nearer. Many of the soldiers too, at the sight of this, felt their ears, finding blood on their fingers and realizing that they too were bleeding from the shockwave that had emanated from Einar.

Naryan stared at Einar as he rode nearer, and Naryan's eyes narrowed, as caressed his chin and folded his arms.

"I suppose you're expecting some thanks."

The horse stood still and Einar looked down at him.

"Thank your mother. She insisted that I ride, the moment the pigeon came."

"We had reinforcements coming. You weren't needed"

Einar nodded his head behind Naryan, who turned to see a cloud of dust on a hill in the distance, signaling that the reinforcements were still a ways off.

"A little slower than a lone rider, I'd say." said Einar, "I suppose it's good that I arrived early, for it looks like you weren't able to hold the hamlet."

Naryan grimaced for a second,

"No, we could not hold it, but you can see," he looked at Sylvian, "that I did make the right call. Whether by the hand of Einar or the hand of the calvary, Sallow Hill was the perfect bait to bring this army to its knees."

"Your Majesty," protested Sylvian, "They were but a small force of men who were not well equipped to siege a defended town, nor expecting to fight anything other than peasants. It was a raiding party, no more, not a grand army of Chromer. And *we* would not have prevailed over anything without…" his voice trailed off and he eyed Einar.

"Yes, about that," continued Naryan, "You will speak of this to no one." he turned and looked at the surviving soldiers. "None of you."

The soldiers stood, fidgeting while some looked around at each other, and others stared at the ground.

Einar looked down at Naryan from his mount, a smirk playing on his lips.

"And I, your majesty?"

Naryan squinted at him.

"What's your game, Einar?"

"Game? I have no game. I merely have come to help Satoria in its hour of need. And I have no love for Chromer. They've turned a violent eye to my kind in the past."

"Your kind? What are you then?"

"I am a man, no different, from you." he gestured around at the soldiers, "Or you, or you, or any of you."

Naryan scowled.

"After witnessing this feat here today, you are not welcome in Satoria. Your magic has left an ill taste in my mouth and a pit in my stomach. It is unnatural."

The soldiers tensed, looking between the king and the Erilaz, before Einar replied.

"No, perhaps I am not welcome in Satoria, but elsewhere I am hunted to be killed, so I welcome a little discomfort in comparison." he nodded his head at Naryan, "Your majesty" and turned his horse to ride off in the direction of the approaching reinforcements.

The survivors gathered together around Naryan and began to trudge the road towards the approaching cavalry, who were still a ways off judging by the approaching cloud of dust. Silence hung over them, every man in concerned thoughts as to what they had witnessed, and hesitant to discuss it in front of Naryan. Sylvian broke the silence.

"So then, my lord, if we are to not discuss here today how will we explain what happened? A hundred men defended against five hundred? A town burned to the ground without so much as a lump of charcoal remaining? No bodies of the fallen to return to their families, and no trace of the defeated Chromerians?"

"You are all mighty warriors to be commended. That is all. You fought valiantly to defeat them, though the town was caught aflame and we could do nothing." said Naryan. "Tonight we will have a feast in your honor. And not a word of this, from any of you. I want to hear tales of how each of you killed ten men, and we will drink to it."

Chapter 8

The war with Chromer had not progressed since Sallow Hill, which was a good thing for Naryan, since Satoria's hands were full with its own citizenry. Three weeks had passed since the battle, and it was clear that none of the soldiers had held their tongues about what they'd witnessed. Naryan sat at the council table, alone, stewing in his thoughts and deciding his next course of action whilst the city raged against itself.

News of Einar's latest miracle had spread like wildfire and refueled the zealots in the city proclaiming that they had been lied to their whole lives, and that Einar was a god here to save them. Even more fervent were the non-believers who denied any claims, since they themselves had not witnessed any of it. A mere fifty eye-witnesses were not enough to sway them, for the soldiers themselves were, '*Certainly* bought and paid for by the crown.' No, to the non-believers, a conspiracy was afoot and they were to discover it.

Naryan's thoughts were interrupted as the doors swung open, and Murdock, Sylvian, and Rhondia strode in, clearly in the midst of conversation.

"Well something *must* be done," said Rhondia. "We cannot let things lay as they are with Chromer, for greater tension is building–I can feel it. "

"I agree." added Murdock, "Chromer will grind us to the ground without a miracle."

"Ah, but there's the thing–we have a miracle worker among us…" her voice trailed off as she spotted Naryan sitting at the head of the council table. Her demeanor stiffened and her lip curled as she turned her attention to him, "Oh your majesty, we didn't expect you here."

"I was just looking for some peace and quiet. I could use a break from all of this talk of battle and miracles."

"A break?" Rhondia snapped. "You'd think a king would have duties to attend to, what with a war having just started, but you've been nowhere to be found."

"I go here and there."

"Yes, but *there*, more often than *here* in the council chamber. Which is why we didn't expect you *here*."

"Well now that I'm here," he said, "Go on." and motioned with his hand. "I want to learn more about this miracle worker that you've heard of."

"Oh," she said, her voice dripping, "do you mean the one that you witnessed decimate an entire army of Chromerians with but a few motions of his hand? That one? The one that Sir Sylvian here said you are trying to suppress knowledge of to the people? The one and the same?"

Sir Sylvian stiffened at his name being mentioned, but Naryan didn't seem to notice while he stared down Rhondia,

"I'm sick of hearing his name, and I've yet to decide what to do with him."

"What to do with him? He is a powerful tool to be used–that's what! The end of our war with Chromer will not be of the desired outcome unless he intervenes. Murdock knows it, Sylvian knows it, I know it, every peasant from the milkmaid down to the vagrant in the street knows it. Do you know it? I'm sure you do, for you are lazy, not stupid. What course of action do you then propose if not enlisting Einar?"

Naryan winced at the final enunciation of Einar's name and stood.

"Am I not the only one here whose spine tingles when he is nearby? Am I not the only one curious as to where he has come from, and why he has come to us now? In my youth I of course fantasized that fables of magic were true and that I could have access to this power. Now that I see it in front of me not as a fable but as truth I am disgusted by it, for it reeks of evil intent."

Murdock spoke up,

"Is not the weapon of magic the same as any other weapon? Bent to the will of the wielder? I do not see this magic as evil, merely a tool to be used as needed. Nor, do I see Einar as evil; eccentric, perhaps, but not evil."

"What then do you know of the magic? Something that you're not telling me? You seem well-versed in its morality." asked Naryan.

Murdock shook his head,

"I know no more of it than you, I simply speak what I have seen."

Naryan pointed his finger at the three of them,

"Something is afoot, I know it. Two kings dead, a war declared, a fabled magician appears. Do you not see a game being played here? By whom, I cannot say, but I am uneasy."

He turned away from the chair and stalked back and forth for a moment, while they watched him. He turned on his heel to look at them.

"It's decided. He should be slain."

Murdock looked heavenward for patience. Rhondia glared at him. Sylvian shifted ever so slightly. Naryan continued,

"He causes dissent in subjects in an already tumultuous time. This, and the fact that after now seeing his power, it is easy to discern that it is too much for one man to control. Who is to say that he would not come and slay us all and usurp the throne." Naryan's eyes glazed over as he stared off into the distance. "I am fearful of his spells, for I saw how he manipulated the fire and melted the Chromerian army. There was nothing left there on the ground, not even the bones of the dead. No one should wield that kind of power."

Sylvian and Murdock looked at each other, neither wanting to break the silence. Rhondia did not hold back,

"Naryan, my lord. Do you not see the value of this opportunity? Chromer will soon be on our doorstep and we do not have the armies to waylay them. Einar will be of great use. Not only could he single-handedly defeat the invading armies of Chromer, but he could undo their walls and their keeps, purge their castles and conquer their royalty. We would be rid of their looming shadow forever! Then, we could go further to the north, where not even our traders have gone, and create roads of gold to bring back wealth. Then we can secure our footholds in the west where the territories mumble about us. Then he can melt the snows of the far north to reveal the fruitful lands beneath and we can rid our lands of famine. The potential that he holds, Naryan, is too great to let go to waste. I beg you to see this."

"I will not have it. Einar will be slain, for I cannot stand the sight of him." finalized Naryan. There was silence while the four surveyed each other, but Rhondia broke it,

"Perhaps this is your wish, but plans are already in motion, for I have instructed Einar to summon more of his order to come here."

Naryan's head cocked,

"More?"

"Yes, sorcerers powerful and valiant to help us battle the Chromerians. Chromer will stand no chance, for Chromer hates magicians with a passion, and those who stand against our enemies are our allies."

"From whence did they manifest? I've never heard of them before and suddenly you can conjure up an army of them? The subjects can barely handle one without the kingdom tearing itself apart!"

"Perhaps it is time," interjected Murdock, "to tell the people the truth."

"The truth?" questioned Naryan. "What is the truth? I do not know the truth."

"The truth," Murdock continued, "is clearly that there are those in this world who wield a power greater than the common man. I did not believe it until now, nor did Sylvian until his eyes witnessed it, just as you did not until you witnessed it. We were ignorant before, but now the truth is plain as day, and it must be told to the people."

"What good would telling the people do?" questioned Naryan.

"Perhaps," answered Sylvian, "It would calm their angst; right now they are sided against each other for they do not believe what the other believes. If the truth were put in front of them as plain as day, only a fool would not believe."

"Truth or not be told to the public," said Naryan, "the mages should not come. I have already said that Einar should be slain, for his powers are unsightly and should not be held by a man. In fact, now that ten more are coming they should all be done away with.

"Who is to say that they will not kill us all in their sleep with their magic? Surely if Einar can defeat an army of five hundred by himself in an instant, many of them would decimate tens of thousands with ease. There is nowhere safe in the world with these men alive. We should all live under their shadow if they take hold of the kingdom. Surely they will kill the nobility and turn the monarchy into a theocracy."

"It is too late," Rhondia said. "They are coming, and will be here by nightfall."

Naryan looked at her, uneasy as she spoke, and tilted his nose up as his eyes squinted and his jaw clenched. He swallowed, looking at the three of them waiting expectantly for his answer.

"I'm not sure who you think I am, Rhondia. Perhaps a dimwit, or lazy, or haughty, or dandy, or even full of avarice and cowardice. I am none of these, and while perhaps I am still learning what I am, I know that I am not violent. My stomach turns at the thought of battle, and my innards clench when I see the sick on the street. Verily I am proud, and will defend what is ours by right, but only out of compassion for our subjects. I am a compassionate man, even for our foes, and I do not care for conquering lands. I do not care to grow the kingdom's coffers, nor to enslave people to do my bidding.

"I would rather enjoy a hot afternoon with a cool drink in the shade, or feasts in the night where I can sleep after with a belly full of wine, or laugh with my friends at a crass joke told at an ill time. I am no warrior or conqueror, and I will not turn my kingdom into a machine of war."

"You hypocrite." spat Rhondia, "for you slayed a man in your own courtroom out of spite and now you order the killing of mages. I do not know your angle, but you must heed our council and make use of Einar, while the time is right. All of us demand it."

"You will *demand* nothing of your king–I will make the demands. And how *dare* you call me a hypocrite!" Naryan now was in her face, pointing his finger at her and he stared into her eyes. "I am not violent, but I am no pushover either–I already said I will defend our kingdom. No man is perfect, least of all me, but I am a good man."

A sneer played on Rhondia's lips before she spat,

"Good? I'm sure Sherry would disagree with that sentiment, you pitiful despoiler."

Naryan drew his lips, lost images of the night in the carriage flashing in his mind. He closed his eyes for a moment, his inebriated moment of defiling coming to the forefront. The memories had been nearly written over by his discovery of the Chromerian force in the woods, the battle of Sallow Hill, the citizen's buzz of Einar, and the defensive strategy of Chromer on their doorstep. His throat clenched, Sherry's anguished face outlined against the seat of the carriage as he thrust himself on her. His stomach turned and he looked at the floor as Rhondia spoke in the silence,

"Yes, I know of your foul deeds, for she returned here, haggard and famished from her dangerous return journey, telling tales that no mother would hear. The poor girl is lucky I found her and brought her in, lending her a solar and keeping her safe from your gaze this past week. I would not set her in front of her defiler.

"It would be better if you philandered with someone who is not the daughter of a noble, for the annoyance you've caused is insufferable. At least go find some bar wench who won't complain."

Naryan quieted his voice as he spoke,

"Where is she?"

"She is no longer of your concern, so that you may no longer be a concern to her. This is the final word of your mother, which is of more value than that of a mere subject.

Naryan Screamed,

"Bring her to me!"

"No!"

Naryan reached out and slapped Rhondia across the face, turning her head with the blow and leaving a reddened mark.

"How dare you deny your king!"

Rage grew in her eyes and she spat out,

"How dare you strike your mother."

Naryan snarled back,

"You are no mother of mine."

"So be it then, I gladly rescind all claims of mothership from you–and I am happy to be rid of them."

"You will be rid of your head if you don't abate your snide remarks."

Naryan pushed out of the room's great wooden doors, and stormed down the hall. A silence settled in as the two men stood beside Rhondia while she caught her breath. She glared in the direction of Naryan's exit, and a few moments later her collected voice to speak again,

"He is proving himself more of a child every day, and unfit to rule a kingdom. He is weak, too amiable, and will not do what needs to be done for Satoria, especially those acts of hard decision. It seems time he went the way of his father."

In the night, ten mages on horseback galloped towards a small gate at the side of the curtain wall to the castle's outer bailey. There, a hooded figure opened it and ushered them in.

Chapter 9

"You called for me?"

Einar now stood in front of Naryan, only the two of them in the room as the door thudded shut behind the guard who had escorted Einar. The room was bare-walled and bare-floored, save for two tall-backed chairs facing each other and a small fire in a hearth that cackled from fresh wood and a recent stoking. A single window cast to the floor the red glow of dusk falling outside. Naryan sat in one of the chairs and motioned for Einar to sit in the other.

"Yes, please sit." Naryan watched Einar for a while before opening his mouth to speak, but cutting it short with a barked laugh. He pursed his lips and recollected himself before continuing, "You know, I was thinking of calling you here to have you executed." He watched Einar for a reaction, but Einar did little more than blink and tilt his head slightly to the side. Naryan continued,

"We both know that wouldn't have gone well though, so I decided to spare my men's lives and save you the trouble of waving your arms around."

"You're so kind." Einar replied.

"Instead," said Naryan, "I've decided to personally thank you for your intervention at Sallow Hill."

"Oh? I was under the impression that you didn't like me."

Naryan rose from his seat and paced.

"Recent conversations have made me rethink my position. I've decided that you're too valuable an asset to not be on good terms with, and that this division in the kingdom must come to an end. What do you say about becoming," Naryan paused and waved his hand in the air, "The High Archmage of Satoria?"

"An asset?" Einar raised an eyebrow, then shrugged. "Well, I've never cared for fancy titles."

"Fine, you can have whatever title you'd like, so long as you heed my commands."

"And if I don't?"

Naryan stopped pacing and bit his cheek. He paused another moment and exhaled, almost resigned.

"Then I shall have you executed."

"I thought we already discussed how that would play out for you and your men."

Naryan scowled. Einar continued,

"You said that you called me here to thank me, but it seems more of a proposition–and I've still not heard a thanks."

Naryan rolled his eyes in exasperation,

"Thank you. There, I've said it. Are you always this confrontational?"

A smile played on Einar's lips, but he said nothing.

"I want to learn." bumbled out Naryan. This caught Einar's attention, and he replied.

"Be my guest. Nobody is stopping you."

"I want you to *teach* me."

"And what do I get in return? Will you promise not to slay me when you are my equal?"

"I'm not sure what idle threats you want to hear..." said Naryan.

"How about no threats?" suggested Einar.

"Fine, bribery then." clapped Naryan, "Riches–all that you can imagine. Women–all that you can have. Wine–all that you can drink. You will live like a king. You will live like *I* do."

"Ah, but you see–" said Einar, "therein lies the problem, for you cannot live like you do and live like I do. Our lives are in opposition to one another, and in order to have one, you must forsake the other."

"What do you want then? Name it, and it is yours."

"Peace." Said Einar. "I want to live in peace."

"Peace." Scoffed Naryan. "You say peace even after you decimate an army of men with a few waves of your arms. Never have I seen such raw power before. How can you cry "peace" as a living weapon?"

"A peaceful life does not mean that one is not strong. A peaceful man is not a good man, unless he has the capability of violence, for if he has no capability then he is not peaceful, merely weak. In slaying a few, I hoped to save the lives of many. Chromer is familiar with magic, and they hate it, but they fear it more. I hoped to end this war before it started."

"What then, is a peaceful life to you?" posed Naryan.

"I wish to live here in Satoria, unbothered, as I have in the past. I wish to bring prosperity back to these lands."

"The past?"

"Yes, I did, well over a hundred years ago, for I am certainly older than I look, and Satoria looked differently as well. But, that is a story for another time."

"Why do you speak in philosophies and riddles? A simple yes or no will suffice. Will you teach me?" Asked Naryan again.

Einar rose and looked at Naryan, who was still standing, his arms folded across his chest. He studied Naryan for a moment before replying,

"Your spirit is too weak." he inhaled through his nose, "I can feel it in its infancy. No, you must teach yourself." With that he gave the nod of a bow and exited the doorway, leaving Naryan grinding his teeth.

The castle was quiet in the now dark hours of the morning, but still Naryan was awake, weary and red-eyed as empty flasks littered the ground around him. He stared into the hearth from his tall-backed seat, as seared memories of the conflagration at Sallow Hill glowed back at him from the flames. In his eyes, the darkened grains of the wood amidst the glowing embers took the shapes of the burning men, their forms disintegrating as the flames licked at them.

"Teach myself?" he scoffed aloud.

Naryan's head swam, and he reached out his hand toward the flame. His vision blurred and he cocked his head as if to clear the wine's influence from his sight, as he attempted to center himself.

"Focus, perhaps." He twitched his fingers and turned his hand as if to grasp the fire within his palm from where he stood; nothing happened.

"Rage then!" He gritted his teeth and flexed his hand into a fist until it shook, but there was still no change in the small fire. He pushed himself to stand, catching himself as he stumbled and reached out with both hands, palms out, even letting out a yell, but the flames still licked lazily towards the chimney as they always had.

A yell of disgust escaped his throat and he shoved one of the chairs over with a thud, kicking an empty wine vessel out of his way as he shuffled his feet towards the door. He left the scrape of the spinning bottle in the room behind him as he set out into the hallway, heading towards his tower to retire. The sound of his padding through the otherwise empty halls was the only thing echoing in his ears, and he steadied himself on a wall.

He looked out a window nearest to him, where he could see his tower far away and silhouetted against the night sky. He squeezed tight his eyes before peering at it again. Flames rose out from the slitted windows and his balcony, and smoke blotted out the stars above. Though the tower itself was stone and could not be caught aflame, the interior was rich with furs and linens and wood furniture, and it was clear that they were burning.

Naryan let out a yell of alarm and rushed down the hallway towards the wing of his tower. A glow further down the hallway, and the echoes of shouts, told him that the problem was more widespread than just his chambers. He slowed at the sound of pounding footsteps in the corridor, and Sylvian burst around the corner, sword drawn, nearly colliding with him. Wild eyes adorned his usually stoic face,

"My lord! You're safe! Come!"

Naryan paused and pointed.

71

"But, the fire! It's in my room. We must gather the fire brigade."

"There's no time. They're after you. We must run."

Sylvian grabbed Naryan by the arm and turned him, pulling him as he led him.

"My clothes, Sylvian. My tapestries!"

Sylvian shook his head,

"There's no time. To the throne room."

As they ran, Sylvian continuously blew bursts into a shrill whistle, and doors opened all up and down the hallways at the alarm. Still, they ran faster until the din was behind them and they came again to dark and quiet hallways, finding themselves then at the entrance to the throne room. The thick double doors were shut, so Sylvian pushed them open and ushered Naryan inside. The room was dark, save a single hanging brazier at the center that was never extinguished. Sylvian slid in behind Naryan, trying to catch his breath as he spoke, and pushed him towards the throne.

"Behind the throne. The secret way–you must exile."

"Exile? Sylvian, what is this?"

"A coup." a calm third voice spoke out in the courtroom. The two of them started, seeing then a shadowed figure slouching on the throne just ahead of them in the darkness.

"Show yourself!" shouted Sylvian, brandishing his sword and stepping forwards.

The figure raised his hand, fingertips glowing as he drew a symbol in the air, and flames from the brazier arced out to light torches that lined the rest of the courtroom. The room glowed alive and Naryan and Sylvian saw the hooded man on the throne had another hooded figure standing guard at his side.

"Einar." spat Naryan. "How dare you usurp me. I even thanked you!"

"Einar?," chuckled the figure. "I am no stale old man like Einar." He rose and threw back his hood to show that his head was shaven like Einar's, but he was indeed a different man.

"No doubt he scuttled off when he heard of my coming; I will deal with him if I must, but we turn now to the task at hand." He turned to the still-hooded figure on his left. "Curtis, let us put your mettle to the test. He should be of no issue."

Curtis lifted his hood to show that he was little more than an adolescent. His head was also shaven, but his young cheeks showed no stubble, nor were there any wrinkles on his skin. He set his jaw and inhaled, raising a shaky hand in the air as his fingers began to glow.

Sylvian then, recognizing danger in the movements, crossed the distance in a few smooth steps and plunged his sword into Curtis' chest without even a twinge in his cheek. Curtis' eyes bulged and his hands dropped to feel the sword as he looked down and saw blood dribbling across his robes. Naryan was frozen as Sylvian let out a curt yell,

"Run!"

In the next movement Sylvian withdrew the sword from the sheath of Curtis' falling body, and turned to the man in the center. The man's hand was already raised and drawing in the air, even as Sylvian brought the sword down towards his bare head. The sword, however, stopped as if gripped in the air by an invisible hand. It quivered for a moment and then was twisted from his grip and discarded to the ground behind him. The throne room rang as the sword clattered along the floor, and Sylvian looked down at his now mangled hand that had attempted to grasp the sword as it was wrenched from him.

He let out a cry of pain and clutched his injured hand with the other, before lowering his shoulder to ram into his foe. He was stopped in his movement after a step, and was then twirled towards the ceiling so that he hung upside-down by a single leg in the air. The man's face was calm as he moved his hands again, and fire from the hanging brazier rushed in a tight funnel toward Sylvian's head. Sylvian screamed as the fire whirled and whirled unnaturally around his head until the skin had seared from his face and the pink of his muscle beneath began to char.

The man said nothing to Sylvian, who could do nothing except release whimpers of pain from his barely open lips. The man moved over to the pale-faced Curtis who now lay on his back with his hands pressing into the wound in his chest, inhaling quick, shallow breaths. The man watched him for a moment before again raising his hand to draw in the air.

Sylvian's chest convulsed and the garments over his whole body began to sop with blood. Naryan could see that Sylvian's exposed hands had begun to expel beads of crimson across every bit of their surface, as though a sponge was being wrung, and the blood congealed in the air as it flowed in a river towards Curtis' chest. The man's fingers twitched further, and Curtis' chest mended itself closed as he inhaled a deep gasp.

Naryan's stomach turned, but he felt himself running on shaky legs towards the double doors through which they'd come. As he came to it he felt a rush of wind brush past him and the doors ahead pushed themselves shut. He hit the doors with a thud and pulled desperately on the rings of the handles, even as the doors quivered and held themselves secure. He pounded with both hands, screaming, and felt the hairs on his neck raise as the two mages moved in closer behind him.

"Now Curtis, remember—write clearly and cleanly and feel it in your gut."

Naryan turned to see that a pale but now-healthy Curtis was standing before him, hand outstretched and drawing in the air again with glowing fingers. Naryan grit his teeth and took a step towards the two of them, attempting to aggress, but felt the breath expelled from his chest in a burst of wind. He attempted to inhale, but no air would even enter his throat. He ripped at his chest garments with both hands, even as he fell to his knees at the feet of the two mages, and watched them as the edges of his vision blurred to black.

Then, even as his surroundings became nothing more than echoes and a dream, the double doors behind him burst open and he felt himself hoisted to the ceiling in a rush of wind. Even though the wind flipped him up with a powerful burst, he was gently laid onto the ceiling as if it were a soft bed, and he felt air rush into his lungs again with a gasp. He watched from his upturned position as a single man slid into the room riding on a wave of the wind, knocking the gust into his two foes.

Curtis was taken by surprise and thrown across the floor where his head rapped on the ground and he was laid unconscious. The other, however, caught his footing, and streams of white wind passed around him leaving him untouched. He crooked his hands as if to beckon the flame from the hanging brazier, and it rushed from behind him heading towards Naryan's savior.

Einar's hands carved through the air, glowing fully as he wrote the runes, and expelled the fire away in a burst as it rushed upon him. He dropped to a knee, now writing in the dust of the floor, and the square floor stones of the throne room tore themselves up from their settings. Rows of them popped, all at once, and a mound of earth grew up from the ground to fill the room between himself and the other. He looked up and locked eyes with Naryan, who felt himself dropping in a flip from the ceiling. He was caught right side upward by the wind and felt it rushing through his garments as it set him onto the ground.

"Run." said Einar, and Naryan affirmed with a single nod before following him in a sprint through the castle's corridors.

Chapter 10

They ran through the darkness of the castle, and though they could barely hear the echoes of distant yells, they still felt as though foes were at their heels. Neither of them looked behind for pursuers as they went, continuing until they passed through the main barbican and came to the side gate in the castle walls. It was left unguarded in the commotion, and so they exited into the night.

For as thin as he looked, and as old as he claimed he was, Einar easily led the race to safety. Naryan lagged behind with a hand holding his cramped side, no doubt from the wine that sloshed around in his stomach with every step, his long-standing habit of consumption lending no aid to his fitness either. Einar went to the southeast and seemed to have an idea of where he was going, so Naryan followed him, gasping and out of breath, and falling further behind with every step.

Even as the sun began to rise, they ran along the roads, putting more and more distance between themselves and the castle. Farmlands spread out from the capital, and sparse trees littered the countryside where they ran. Off in the distance behind hills and across rivers and plains, the Satorian Forest lay, and that was where Einar headed.

Still, it was a long way off, and Naryan could not carry on any longer.

"Einar." he gasped out as he hobbled behind. "Einar!"

Einar turned and waited in the middle of the road for Naryan to come, arms crossed, and not the slightest bit out of breath. Naryan stopped a few feet from Einar, and hunched over, hands on his knees as he gulped in air. Between gasps, he managed to get out,

"How much longer?"

"How much longer until what?" replied Einar.

"Until wherever we're going."

"Are you following me?" posed Einar.

Naryan looked up while catching his breath, before finally standing up,

"Are you not leading me somewhere?"

"I am headed somewhere, but I have never said I am leading you anywhere.

"Back at the castle you said to follow you."

"No," said Einar, "I said to run. I gave no direction after that. Here we are, hours of trekking later, and I assumed that you knew where you were headed, and our paths merely led in the same direction. So, if this is not the case–*why* are you following me?"

Naryan rolled his eyes.

"I...don't know. I don't have anywhere else to go."

"Well, that's a pity."

Einar turned to walk again.

"Where are you going? Can I come with you?" asked Naryan.

Einar looked towards the forest for a moment.

"I am going to the depths of the forest. You are free to go to the forest if you wish–after all, it is a very large place."

"How long will it take to get there?"

"So many questions. At this pace, we'll be there by dusk. If you hurry, you could arrive faster."

"Faster? We could not go faster unless we had horses." Sputtered Naryan. "Why the forest?"

"Safety, for my old home is there, though it has now been abandoned since I left it, and I did not think I would be returning so soon, if ever."

"Hmm, yes," replied Naryan, "How inconvenient that you must return to your home. I apparently no longer have a home, since I have been thrust into exile."

Einar shrugged.

"Each man has their own struggles to overcome, I suppose." Einar turned back towards the road. "I now continue."

"Continue? I've just got here to rest! You're fresh because you've rested this whole time watching my approach." Einar turned back to Naryan,

"I was never tired. I only stopped when you called."

Naryan glared.

"Can't you just port us there with some conjured magic?"

"No," Einar chuckled, "it does not work like that, though I do suppose I could fly–that could be faster than walking."

"You can fly?"

"When the need arises, though it's more of a floating glide, really. I'm not sure how you'd keep up though, since you don't know how."

"Show me."

Einar cocked an eyebrow.

"I don't take kindly to snapped orders."

Naryan rolled his eyes,

"Please, it would be so nice and would really make my day if you could, show me, just this once–please?"

Einar ignored the biting sarcasm and cheerily replied,

"Ah, some manners finally."

He crooked his fingers and their tips glowed as he whirled his hands in the air, and a rush of wind caught around his feet and whipped through his robes. Dust kicked off the ground and into Naryan's eyes, but he still managed to see through squinted lids that small pebbles around Einar's feet were blown away, even as his heels lifted a few inches from the ground. The wind continued to rush around them both as Einar crossed his arms and looked down at Naryan. A moment later, the wind slowed and died, as Einar's feet were gently laid back to the ground.

"Impressive." said Naryan after a pause. He turned his head slightly, "Now could you cast this spell of flight on me?"

Einar nodded.

"Yes, I could."

Einar watched Naryan, who stared expectantly back at him. A long pause.

"Well, will you?" asked Naryan. "Oh" he said, "Please."

Einar smirked,

"As you wish."

Even as Einar's hands began to move the wind had already started to kick up around Naryan's feet, whirling the dirt and wind around his garments. He felt the pressure from his heels decrease, even as the wind lifted him up from the ground. The wind pressured all around him, and he felt the wind rushing past every underpart of his body that was parallel to the ground. His heart jolted at the first feeling of his feet no longer supporting him, but it was as though the air had wrapped him in its arms and laid him into a pool of water that whirled around him and kept him afloat. It was loud as the wind filled his ears, but he looked down at Einar and grinned.

"Ready to go?" he yelled.

Einar shook his head, even as the wind began to let Naryan down, and he stumbled, catching himself.

"I cannot summon two breaths of wind, with the precision needed to fly us independently," said Einar.

"Carry me with you then," said Naryan. "Please."

"I will not carry you in my arms like a child, nor let you ride me as a steed."

Einar turned and looked the way that they'd come and squinted, before continuing,

"But we are followed. Come now, or go your own way, but we should not stay here." He turned his back to Naryan and walked down the path. Naryan glared at him for a moment before waving his arms furiously through the air, and then peered curiously at his crooked fingers to see if they glowed.

"No," smirked Einar without turning around, "Not like that."

Naryan ran after Einar, finally catching up to him, and still trying to wave his arms.

"Will you teach me?"

"Do you not remember when I told you no?"

"Yes, but our circumstances have changed."

"Perhaps *your* circumstances have changed; now you have even less means to threaten and bribe me with."

Naryan kicked a pebble as they walked, and his lip curled in disgust. A shadow crossed Einar's face as he turned behind them to again survey their trail.

"They come quickly. They will be upon us soon. We should hide." Naryan turned and saw an approaching cloud of dust kicked by horses coming up the road after them. There were no trees to hide in, nor boulders to hide behind, so they bounded off the road and into the fields of golden grain that spread out to their right and left as far as they could see. Out into it they waded, leaving trails of trampled stalks behind them until they crouched a stone's throw from the road. Einar twirled his glowing finger and a wind whisked through the trampled grain, lifting it back up again to hide their trails. Then, they waited.

It was not a long wait, for only a couple minutes passed until they felt the drumming of hooves in their chests and the frothing mouths of the animals in their ears. Two cloaked and shaven riders approached on the road, standing in their stirrups and riding the horses hard. Past the hidden two they flew, the rhythm of the hooves beating on the ground nearly as loud as their hearts beating in their ears.

A whistle then, from one of the riders halted the two horses and their hooves skidded on the hard dirt of the path as the cloud of dust in their trail caught up and puffed into them. The horses turned, hooves still prancing as the riders urged them back up the road near unto where Naryan and Einar had slipped into the field. One rider looked at the other,

"They're here." he said, and nodded his head towards the fields. "Einar," he cried "Come out!"

The two riders dismounted, the crunch of their feet on the path audible from where the other two were hidden.

"We have no quarrel with you, Einar." shouted the other. "Just give up the king and you can be on your way."

Naryan swallowed and looked at Einar whose intense gaze tracked the two men through the swaying grain.

"How did they find us?" whispered Naryan. A sharp glance from Einar bade him hold his tongue.

"There's nowhere to hide. Even if your form hides, we see you plain as day."

The man pointed directly to where the two of them hid, and grinned as his eyes pierced to their hiding place.

"They see us, the same as we see them." said Einar.

"How?" asked Naryan.

Einar shook his head,

"No time."

The man lost his patience, and wrote a rune, releasing a burst of wind that blew down the grain all around them. They were then exposed in the middle of the field, their cover now pressed to the ground. The two riders glanced at each other and then laughed at the sight of their quarry hunched together in the open field.

"Come, Einar." The first said, "bring him here and you can be on your way. We have no quarrel with you, even though Solis is a bit sore." The second chuckled.

Naryan and Einar straightened to a stand and surveyed the two mages who casually watched them from the road. Naryan swallowed and looked at Einar, whose eyes narrowed at the other two.

"No," he said, "I don't think that will be necessary. Look at him," he gestured to Naryan, "he is pathetic. He poses no threat; there is no need to take him back."

The mages looked at each other and laughed, before turning back to Naryan and Einar. Naryan bit his tongue.

"Pathetic or not," the first mage said, "we shall be bringing him back–alive or not. The queen has demanded it."

At this, Naryan burst out.

"Queen? She is no queen–she is a usurper who has commanded regicide. She is no more than my late father's wife. She holds no power in the Satoria. I am the king and you shall do as I say."

The two mages' faces tightened; they did not laugh.

"Come now," the second said, "I do not care for titles and I tire of this conversation. Einar, hand him over and there will be no trouble."

Einar turned squarely to Naryan and reached his hand out to place it on Naryan's shoulder.

"Naryan," he said loudly, "my friend." He gave a sigh and glanced at the other two mages. "I do not think I can win a contest against the two of them." he shook his head and looked at the ground. Naryan's throat tightened as he tried to swallow.

"Run," Einar muttered in a whisper, "and do not turn."

Naryan looked back at Einar's face, which was still staring intently at the ground. He in turn glanced down and saw that the tip of Einar's foot was aglow as he scratched a symbol into the dirt. He finished the arc of the symbol and turned back toward the two mages on the road saying,

"But I think I'll give it a go."

The earth split between his legs with a crack, arcing like lightning on the ground toward his two foes. Naryan turned and ran deeper into the fields even as a cavern opened its mouth beneath the two mages and their horses. The whinnies of the horses carried through the air as the earth swallowed them up and boulders and loose dirt tumbled on top of them. The mages were quick with their own sparkling fingers and the wind held them up above the pit, their garments flapping in the swirling air around them.

Einar, however, did not merely watch, for his hands were already writing. A gust of wind emanated from him and pushed towards the suspended mages, sending one of them spinning wildly towards the ground where he landed on his back with a thud.

The other pushed forward his own wall of wind so that he was not touched, and landed on the ground beside the sinkhole with a puff of dirt at his feet.

Einar caught movement out of the corner of his eye and saw the mage that he had toppled to the ground was writing in the dirt with his finger. Einar twirled his hands to lift the mage into the air with a gust of wind. The mage's hands desperately reached out towards the earth and his limbs flailed as he was lifted, and after only a few short feet he was slammed back into the earth head-first with a crunch. His broken spine left him twisted on the ground, and crimson leaked from a gaping crack in his skull.

Still, it was too late, for he had scribed his rune. As Naryan ran through the fields, he felt the soil loosen beneath his feet and he tumbled to the ground into a sifting pile of dirt and pebbles. The soil moved and sifted itself as a wave across the surface of the field, carrying a helpless Naryan in its midst back toward the battling mages.

The remaining mage flashed a glance at his deceased ally and snarled at Einar. Einar looked over to see that Naryan was again near unto them, his limbs spreading out of the pile of dirt in which he lay, struggling to free the dirt from his face so he could breathe.

In that instant the mage reached into his cloak and pulled out a small vial, which he smashed onto the ground at the foot of the stalks of grain that filled the field. A spark flickered and a flame burst out of the vial, and the mage was already writing his runes so that the flames spread from their small source, pushed outward by a rolling ripple of wind. The fire fed on the golden stalks for a moment and grew into a whirling inferno all around. The fire then collapsed towards Einar from all sides, leaving black and red glowing stalks of charcoal in its wake. But Einar was not helpless, for he had already conjured his own wind, and the flames swirled in a vortex around him, leaving him unscathed.

Naryan had managed to scrape the dirt from his face, and wriggled himself free from the grasping hands of the dirt, rocks, and roots. He stood, gasping for air, and with every breath felt a sharp pain in his abdomen. He grimaced and reached down to see that blood was smeared on his filthy hand, and found his side was riven.

A sharp rock protruded from the dirt, and its edge was covered in blood and tufts of linen from his shirt.

He put his hand to his side again with a wince, and looked up to witness the swirl of flames close to engulfing Einar, the eye of the flaming vortex thinning with every pass of its circumference. The mage on the road held his jaw, still conjuring runes, while Einar stood stoic in the center with his arms crossed and eyes set on his foe, before he noticed Naryan had risen. He gave a barely perceptible nod towards the ground, and Naryan looked down to see a rock at his feet.

Naryan stooped and grasped it, then brought back the projectile and hurled it. It clapped into the side of the mage's head and shook him for a moment, and while it did not lay him unconscious, a break in his concentration gave Einar the respite he needed.

The swirling flames rose above Einar's head into a pillar that then arced to touch down as a cyclone onto the mage on the road. The flames ate him, tearing round him in circles so that his clothes were consumed and the skin melted from his frame. His screams were barely perceptible amid the sound of rushing wind, and silence then settled onto the scene as the mage crumpled to the ground to a charred ending.

Einar looked over at Naryan who gave a satisfied nod, before losing his equilibrium and collapsing towards the ground. A bed of air written by Einar caught him as he fell, and carried him behind Einar as he set off again towards the forest.

Chapter 11

"Good to see you finally stirring."

Naryan's eyes fluttered open, but he squeezed them tight again in an attempt to keep out the blinding sunlight that poured onto his face. He pulled his arm over his head so as to shut out the cheerful chirps of the birds outside, and immediately felt the pain in his side. He grit his teeth as a growl lingered in the back of his throat, and he pushed himself up on one arm to survey his new surroundings.

It was a single room, humble, to say the least. A fire in a small fireplace of stones cobbled together crackled on one side of the room, and a table and single chair from which Einar surveyed Naryan was only a few steps away. A chest and the bed that Naryan now lay on were the only other commodities in the room, and Naryan noticed that even the thatch roof was in poor shape.

"You couldn't fix yourself up a more lavish abode with some of your whirly-finger magic?"

"Modest, yes, but it's a nicer home than you have at the moment."

Naryan rolled his eyes and replied under his breath in a sing-songy voice.

"It's a nicer home than you have at the moment."

He directed his attention back to Einar,

"I was at least expecting some gingerbread walls adorned with sweets, to lure children."

Einar stood and began rummaging in the chest as he spoke,

"Children? Not to my taste. Too tough, and not enough meat on them. I'd prefer courtiers with soft hands and thick midsections. Perhaps I should lure them with wine. Here, you'll want to put a clean shirt on; that one is ruined."

Einar rose and tossed a coarse brown shirt to Naryan, who winced as he struggled to catch it. He unwrapped his own shirt, seeing blood drip to the ground from the sopping cloth.

"I will prepare a poultice," said Einar, and continued to rummage in the chest while Naryan grit his teeth,

"Why don't you just heal me up with some blood magic or something."

Einar stiffened and turned.

"What do you know of blood magic?"

"I mean, I don't *know* anything myself, but those two mages from the courtroom–the elder one basically brought the younger back to life with it. Curtis–I think that's what his name was."

"Solis cast blood magic?"

"Sure, if that's what his name was. Sylvian skewered Curtis with his sword and the elder mage healed him. Oh, Sylvian…" Naryan paused and bit his lower lip. "He…is deceased…in the most horrific way. How he screamed." Naryan furrowed his brow and swallowed at the thought of Sylvian. He took in a deep breath through his nose and continued,

"So is this blood magic evil?"

Einar shook his head.

"Evil? No. No magic is evil, though it is perhaps distasteful. Magic is merely a tool, put to use by its wielder. Would you say a hammer is evil? A hammer can be used to construct a house, or cave in a head–the wielder decides its use. I'm simply wary of Solis. "

"If it's not evil then why don't you mend me up?"

"It's not a matter of evil or not evil–it's a matter of the cost. With what blood would I mend you?" Einar barked a laugh, "Not my own. Not in a thousand years."

"Even after I saved you yesterday? Well, I see how you repay your debts."

"Debts? If anything you're still indebted to me. First Sallow Hill, and then the courtroom." Einar shook his head, "No, the king here certainly paid no mind in his arithmetic."

"What about this blood?" asked Naryan, gesturing to the blood now pooling on the floor. "It's my own blood–can you not use that?"

Einar shook his head.

"No, that blood has lingered in the air and is now too foul for healing. I should not poison your veins with it. For you, the poultice it is."

He slapped the poultice hard onto Naryan's side, who let out a gut wince and stumbled back to sit on the bed.

"Poultice and rest, my friend. Poultice and rest."

Naryan woke again to the sound of chirping birds and realized it was another new morning. He pushed himself up off the bed and hobbled to the door, teasing it open to find that the house sat in a clearing of the forest; blue skies and a few clouds were above, and soft green grass carpeted the floor of the clearing. Einar sat with his back to the door and greeted Naryan as he exited.

"Welcome–I'm glad to see you're still alive…for now at least. You've slept for two days."

Naryan trudged over to where Einar sat, and lowered himself onto a small boulder.

"Two days? That's nothing. I once slept off a drunken stupor for three. I will say though, waking without a throbbing head is something I could become accustomed to–I haven't done it in a while and it's quite nice."

He trailed off as he saw that the chirping that had awoken him was coming from a few small birds that hopped around on the ground in front of Einar. They fluttered their wings often and chirped their songs, but did not fly away.

"A bird-whisperer too, Einar? How many of these pets do you have"

Einar laughed.

"No, not quite pets. I've caught them, and they're our dinner."

"Caught? How?"

Even as he asked, a bird flew overhead of the others and immediately fell to the ground amidst the others, flapping its wings profusely, but to no avail.

"Easy," replied Einar as he motioned with his hand, "I have a pillar of air here in the center of the clearing, from which I've pulled out half of the volume."

"I see nothing." said Naryan.

"Do you usually see air?" posed Einar, before continuing, "The birds cannot fly where there is less air to lift them, so they simply fall. Here, they do not know why they cannot fly, soon forgetting they ever could, and now walk aimlessly in circles, ready to be plucked."

Naryan nodded.

"I see. How much magic do you use in your daily life? I have only seen you thus far in combat. Are magic spells useful otherwise?"

Einar studied him for a moment and nodded.

"Yes, it is as useful as your imagination can make it. Satorian was once filled with those gifted with this imagination, and so it grew to greatness."

"You mentioned mages in Satoria once before, but I have never heard of this. Where did you come by this tale?"

"It is no mere tale," replied Einar, "it is the truth of history. But, it is a history that has been hidden from you–for what reason I cannot guess."

"Tell me then, if you'd oblige." Naryan said, nodding his head towards the ground where the birds fluttered, "I think we'll need to wait for a few more than that for dinner."

Einar gazed off into the distance as he recounted,

"More than a hundred years ago Satoria was a land like no other; its people had rid themselves of their vices and were chaste. There was no forced prohibition of these vices, but abstinence was a celebrated trait, and with this temperance each mind was in harmony with its own body. Clean bodies led to clear minds, and clear minds led to unhampered communion with their spirits, and so they were powerful mages. Things were as they were meant to be upon the creation of this plane, for this wisdom was brought to Satoria by Erilaz from the cold north.

"And there was peace, for even Chromer dared not tease Satoria. Chromer had not held onto arcane knowledge themselves, and dared not meet Satoria in open war, even though peace was a core tenet of their philosophies. If one cannot cause harm they are not peaceful, merely weak, but Satorians kept whet their talents and were feared.

"Satoria was wealthy, for each citizen could do the work of ten. Fields sowed themselves in an evening, ores were smelted in an instant, and tall towers were erected in days. There was peace, for those who had surplus gave freely to those who were unable.

"But the surplus of one generation verily leads to the corruption of the next. The values of the elders slowly waned in favor of the reckless and rebellious youth. They wondered at senses dulled with ground leaves and distilled drinks, spreading their habits as chic, until the practices had crept into the annals of culture, and the once-youths now held public offices. Even those of advanced ages soon partook, seeing that the vices were not of an immediate detriment as they had been told in the past. Still, the power of slow and unnoticed decay whittled away at them, until they awoke one day to find that their bodies were blind to their spirits, and could not be rekindled.

Einar scowled. "And so, the wisdom of a thousand years was lost in but a generation."

Naryan grimaced,

"Were you an elder or a youth at this time?"

"I was but a youth, and I cannot say that I did not have a hand in the matter, for I myself partook in those voguish habits."

"It must not have been that bad," said Naryan, "for you have more power than any I have ever seen."

Einar let out a gruff chuckle,

"I am nothing of my former self, nor was I even particularly talented in my generation. I have practiced and practiced to rid myself of the detriment of but a few years of vices, but I still feel merely a flicker of my spirit, where before there was a raging flame."

"I still find it strange," said Naryan, "that merely a few generations have passed since this time you speak of, and nothing in our history books speak of it. Surely there would be elders alive today whose parents had lived this."

"Ah yes, a question I myself have pondered many times." said Einar, "I have arrived at the conclusion that was a plan well-contrived and purposeful, set in place to upend Satoria and dull the population. By whom? I cannot say, though it is easy to point a finger at Chromer, who now sits comfortably in power.

"First they corrupt the youth, then infiltrate the culture, then they put clout in the wisdom of science instead of the arcane, and then they hide history so that no one even knows an inkling of the truth. It is hidden in layers undiscoverable, for hiding the truth is easier than fighting the truth.

"They must have rooted their agents deep in Satorian stewardship to keep the populace complacent and unaware of their own history; yes, someone you know could be a powerful mage and instrument of Chromer. They would now be of advanced age, and inconspicuous to avoid detection."

Naryan thought for a moment and then shook his head.

"No one comes to mind."

"A new question arises though." said Einar, "What will this person do now that mages are brought openly to Satoria? Surely if Chromer was behind this all along it is not in their best interest to be openly fighting a war with mages. Perhaps their hundred-year plan has been foiled by a stroke of luck."

"Stroke of ill luck, I dare say," grimaced Naryan, "for here I am in the wilds with a stranger and nothing to call my own. Where though were these mages hidden? Have they been exiled as you have been, all this time?"

Einar shrugged,

"Some, perhaps, and perhaps others have been hiding in plain sight amidst the populace. I do not know, for there is no council held among us. Some of them, such as Solis, I am aware of, though our terms are clearly shaky."

"Shaky?" asked Naryan. "Rhondia said you summoned them to Satoria."

Einar shook his head,

"I did no such thing, for I am little more than a hermit and have not kept contact with any other Erilaz. As for the coming of these men, perhaps a new movement of self-awareness is arising. Part of me is glad for it, but the other part of me is wary, for without guidance the lust for dominance will corrupt the powerful, and I cannot say that these Erliaz are as meek as those in the Satoria of old."

"Rhondia." spat Naryan. "That bitch must have called those mages to have me murdered. Treason and attempt at regicide, that's what it is. I knew we weren't as familial as we could be, but I never knew she had it in her to try to off me. I'm not sure how she knew of the mages; I thought you were involved, but now you've said that's not the case."

"Yes, strange indeed." said Einar.

"You must teach me to defend myself." announced Naryan. "They will certainly come for me again."

"Oh, will they?" said Einar, rising. "Well, you should be off then. I don't want them coming here to bother me. I feel as though we'd burn down the forest in a scuffle."

"You mock my circumstance." Spat Naryan. "Do not forget how I saved your life. You should teach me so I can better defend myself, and you, as the need arises."

Einar raised an eyebrow and stood.

"Defend yourself, hm? Fine, let us begin. Plant your feet like so."

Naryan watched Einar, copying his stance.

"Now," continued Einar, "raise your hands like this," as he balled his fists in front of his face.

Naryan copied again, jaw set as his eyes tracked Einar.

"Now," said Einar, "you'll want to always keep your hands in front of your face so as to block the incoming blows. Quick steps now, side-to-side, forward, and back, duck your head, and throw blows with a twist of your torso and the spring of your legs, not just the strength of your arm."

Naryan rolled his eyes and dropped his hands down to watch Einar shadow box nothing in particular in the middle of the clearing.

"Are you done?" asked Naryan.

"Oh, we're done?" Einar stopped and straightened out his robe, coming back to Naryan and sitting on the ground again in front of the birds.

"I know how to box. Teach me to defend against my foes!"

Einar shook his head.

"Did I not give good instruction? Who will you be fighting, save for drunks in a tavern? You're no longer a king and therefore the quality of your foes will have greatly decreased."

Naryan let out his frustration in a gurgle that turned to a yell, and he stepped forward and kicked toward the birds on the ground. He connected with a couple of them, and a puff of feathers floated around as the others scurried away. His foot, however, misjudged the lack of airflow in the column and cut through it with no resistance. His foot swung upward and he slipped to the ground where he pounded it with a balled fist in frustration.

"You see," said Einar, peering down at him, "this is why I am hesitant to teach you. You are but an angry child and you must learn to control your physical form before you can control your spirit."

"Don't spew moral judgment at me from some pulpit, Einar." said Naryan. "It is not your place to decide what is right and what is wrong for me."

Einar shook his head.

"Though you are not what I would call a 'model of upstanding character' I do not believe you to be evil. There is much evil in this world, but the nightly indulgence of alcohol alone in one's chambers is not the highest evil. Fool-hearty, but not evil. No, this is not about the moral high ground. It is about learning to put aside your impulses, for if you wish to learn the ways of magic, discipline is paramount."

Naryan glared at Einar, his voice rising further and further as he spoke,

"How can I have discipline when my father is dead, my *mother* has betrayed me, my kingdom has been ripped away from me, mages come to kill me, I have pushed away the only one who has ever loved me, and I am now nothing but a vagrant in the forest? Tell me. Tell me!"

"Now," replied Einar, "Is the best time for discipline, for you must reinvent yourself and unlearn a lifetime of habits if you are to truly master your spirit."

"Teach me then. I have nothing but time." Said Naryan.

Einar smirked,

"That is truly all you have, for even the clothes on your back are borrowed." He paused for a second and looked at Naryan. "Perhaps now is the time, though I'm not sure how you'll fare with a lifetime of indulgence seeping through your veins."

Naryan stood and said,

"Einar, I have nothing. I am now nothing. Make me into something new."

Einar laughed.

"I will not make you into anything–you must do all the making yourself."

Their eyes locked but Naryan said nothing–he just stood there with balled fists and breathing heavily. Einar smiled and broke the silence.

"Fine then–I will teach you."

Naryan cocked his head and narrowed his eyes.

"Why a sudden change of mind? What's the catch?"

"You have merely pricked the pity in my heart–like a helpless stray cat. And you're right–we probably have enemies coming to kill us both. I suppose you could help a little. How are your literacy and calligraphy skills?"

Naryan shrugged,

"I mean, I write the common tongue just fine. What's that got to do with anything?"

"Let me first clarify what we are, for this bit of knowledge will better shape your understanding."

Naryan nodded, but did not blink, watching Einar with rapt attention. Einar continued,

"We are physical beings, yes, surrounded by a physical world, but there is more to us than that, for we are also spirits, dwelling in a different plane. Your physical form is blind to the spiritual, but your spirit craves to be one again with your body. Your spirit is decrepit and weak; I can barely feel you, as but a candle lit in a foggy night. You crawl to and fro as a blind man, feeling your way through a cave of horrors. You have been tricked, taught you are nothing but a body to eat food, and drink wine, and shit and piss, and mate, and that life is to repeat this cycle until the end of your days. You have been told that what you see with your eyes is the only truth–but there is more!

"I questioned your literacy, for you must learn to speak to your spirit, and the language of the spiritual is a written one, inherent to their being. When I draw the runes, I am directing my spirit's actions, and our spirits are powerful. The matter of this world is but energy in its raw form, and spirit is the purest form of energy. Just as matter begs to be refined, so does your spirit beg to bend to your mind's will, and when you can speak to your own spirit, then you will have mastered the world around you."

Naryan scowled and shook his head,

"This lesson goes above my head. Teach me the rune of a spell and let's see if I can cast it."

"No," snapped Einar, "You misunderstand what I've told you. Here and there we are called magicians, mages, or sorcerers, but those are all misnomers for we are warlocks. We do not learn spells, we do not create magic, there is no magic in the world around us–we call on a power from a higher plane to enact our will upon the world; we call on our own spirit. When you learn to write the runes, the language of your spirit, it will do your bidding. Or more appropriately, you will do your *own* bidding when it is finally understood. You have the power to shape your own world, Naryan, but the means have been hidden from you.

"Still, the motions themselves mean nothing. Even with the perfect calligraphy, your spirit would not be able, for it is weak, and you have never spoken with it. It is as a baby, learning to speak for the first time, and you must rebuild the bond that you have dulled with your vices. When you have refined this communion, it will speak to you as well."

"I will hear voices in my head?"

"Well, no" corrected Einar, it is more of a sense to things you cannot see on this plane. Come, sit like this. You must first learn to shut out everything around you. Shut out the birds, the rustle of the wind in the grass and trees, and more importantly, you must silence your own mind."

Einar sat cross-legged on a soft bed of grass and closed his eyes as he inhaled deep through his nose. Narayan struggled to the ground and raised an eyebrow as he watched Einar. Einar did not open his eyes, so Naryan closed his own eyes and sat in silence. A mere few moments later he opened one eye to again observe Einar. The Erilaz was still silent, the rising and falling of his chest the only sign of his life, and his eyelids drooping peacefully.

Naryan shut his own eyes again and tried to inhale through his nose, but did not feel the satisfaction of a breath until he yawned and felt the airflow into the bottom of his lungs. He swallowed and scratched at a bit of grass that poked at his ankle before folding his arms.

This isn't so hard. After Einar teaches me his spells I'll be able to head back to Satoria and take back the throne. I'll ruin anyone that tries to stop me. Rhondia—I can't believe she'd do this to me

His fists tightened at the thought of Rhondia.

I'm going to kill that bitch. She's treated me like shit ever since my mother died. Oh, my mother—she was so sweet. What drove my father to choose Rhondia in her stead? They're nothing alike. I

95

have no bad memories of my mother. I feel if she had raised me I might have turned out differently. Perhaps I could be a better person if my mother was still around. Not that I don't like myself. Sure, I'm rough around the edges but overall I'm proud of who I am. I care for people, as much as I can; surely that's a good measurement by any standards. When was the last time I hurt someone? Ok, throwing that rock hurt that mage, but that was really self-defense. They were going to kill me and probably Einar. It was the right thing to do.

Let me think–before that? I definitely don't hurt any of the servants. They all like me. They're happy to bring me wine whenever I ask. If I was rotten to them I'm sure they wouldn't oblige.

Sallow Hill? Sure, some people died, but I didn't do any killing. That was all the soldiers–that's on their conscience, not mine. Honestly, Einar has more blood on his hands than I've ever had. Oh yes–Einar. What's he doing?

Naryan opened one eye to lend a quick glance to Einar, who had not stirred. Naryan shut his eyes again.

I wonder what he's thinking about. This seems like kind of a boring life–just sitting here, thinking. I don't think I could do this forever. I've got to get up and move around sometimes. I love the energy of being around people. There's such a buzz of excitement when I'm in the great hall with a goblet of wine in each hand. I wonder when the last time he had a drink was? I could really use some wine right now. Ouch, my side still hurts.

He fidgeted and felt a sharp stab in his side. He took a breath in through his nose and opened his eyes to see Einar was watching him, his lips pursed into a smile.

"You are not peaceful within. You must learn to just…be."

Naryan exhaled through his mouth and brought in a deep breath through his nose, closing his eyes.

I bet he's watching me again.

He opened his eyes and saw Einar was indeed still staring at him.

"Just, be."

Naryan nodded and closed his eyes again. He felt the brush of the wind over his hair, the warmth of the sun on his skin, and heard the tweets of the birds in the clearing around him. He straightened his posture and took in another breath, and for the next few minutes he only felt his chest rise, then fall with each exhale. A shiver ran down his spine even though he was not cold, and static lingered behind his closed lids. The staccato of the birds melded together into a single piercing buzz that soon overtook his mind before it faded to nothing, and finally white overtook his vision.

He felt all around him so intensely that he became formless and felt nothing. He was now nothing, and everything; a single blade of grass in a field, a single star in the night sky. Then, he heard the whisper of his name from deep within the cavern of his mind that echoed louder and louder until it reached a full crescendo.

It all rushed away in a moment and his eyes sprang open to find that dusk was now settling over the clearing, and Einar was not seated where he was before. Naryan pushed himself up from the ground, feeling the ache in his knees that had not moved in hours. Einar's voice spoke from behind him,

"So, how does it feel to finally meet yourself?"

Chapter 12

The two of them sat at the table in the hovel; Einar picked through a bowl of porridge and a dismembered bird, but Naryan had pushed his own meal away and was looking deep into the flames of the fire.

"It knew me. He knew me."

"*He* is no different than you. You are simply discovering yourself. It is merely as if you are exercising an atrophied muscle; you must rebuild your mind's connection to relearn your strength."

Naryan replied,

"Feeling him there was like…pulling back the covers for a breath of fresh air after hiding beneath them. It was like throwing open the shutters to let sunlight into the stifling darkness of a room. I can breathe again. I can see again."

Einar barked a laugh.

"This is just the beginning. You are still suffocated and blind."

"Again." said Naryan, "I want to hear him again."

"*He* is always with you, for he is you. To reach him, you must simply meditate as you learned today. In time, as you practice, your tether will strengthen, and the effort needed to commune will be less."

"How can I speak with him?" Asked Naryan.

"There is only writing."

"I heard him speak to me. He said my name."

Einar shook his head.

"You must have imagined it. There is no speaking, and no hearing, only runes to commune with them, and a sense of guidance. There is no tongue that they speak, but you will feel the urges of their guidance as your bond strengthens."

"The runes then." said Naryan, "teach them to me."

"What then would you learn?"

"Fire. I've seen you weave fire; teach me that."

"Firstly, I do not control fire, I merely manipulate the wind on which it rides. Secondly, I would as soon have an infant grasp a greatsword. It is too unruly for you to wield, "Einar smirked, "though, your death would certainly relieve me of the responsibility of further training. No, let us start with something more simple: a summon."

His finger glowed as he whisked it through the air, and the crate near Einar's bed dragged itself along the floor with a long scrape until it rested in front of him."

Naryan raised his eyebrows and nodded,

"Show me again." he said.

Einar motioned again, and the crate pushed itself back to its resting place.

"Was that not a different rune?" Naryan asked.

"Ah yes, very perceptive." replied Einar. "Each rune is not a static spell that always has an effect, but more a sinogram that conveys direction in context of the circumstance. Remember, you are communicating with your spirit, and your spirit is not stupid. It sees all that is going on and understands—it simply requires direction.

"The slightest difference of a line in the sign can convey a completely different meaning, but allows for greater precision. Each sign is, in a way, a written sentence of instruction in regard to a subject, object, and verb. Of course, you can direct with adverbs as well."

As Einar spoke he motioned with his hand, and Naryan's chair jerked up towards the ceiling, halting as his head neared the rafters. Naryan's knuckles whitened as they gripped onto the edges of his seat, even as Einar's next motion lazily let Naryan down towards the floor.

"Swiftly, slowly, gently, violently." Einar chanted under his breath as the chest scooted in random directions across the floor while his fingers drew in the air, leaving glowing lines in their wake. Naryan's chair settled down on the floor again as the chest finally came to rest in front of Einar, and he dug in it for a moment, coming out with parchment and a quill. He spread the parchment out in front of them on the table, drawing first two lines perpendicular and intersecting in the middle.

"Divide each rune into a trichotomy." he said, labeling each segment and motioning to them. "In this section here you put the subject, here the verb, and here the object. There are no letters in this language, only hieroglyphs, and each hieroglyph can be expounded upon by modifications to them. Thus I can clarify to '*swiftly-place*, the *blue-cloak* to *here*' by only the slightest modifications to the motion '*slowly-place*, the *blue-cloak* to *there*.'" behind them a blue cloak maneuvered itself back and forth across the single room as he wrote on the parchment. "Now you see why I questioned your calligraphy skills."

Naryan nodded and bit his cheek before responding,

"Right. So that means I've just got to learn a new language and how to write it, and I'll be off to re-take my throne in a jiffy." he slumped into his chair and ran a hand through his hair with an exhale.

Einar leaned both his hands on the table to get closer to the pouting Naryan.

"This will be no easy task. Better to give up now and return to your wine, than to exert the energy and spend the time, only to give up later. At least you would live out your days in ignorant bliss rather than know what you've lost."

"But it's already too late." said Naryan, "I've seen and I know, and I cannot stuff the cat back into the sack." He gazed at the symbol sketched on the parchment for a moment before continuing, "Ok, I will try."

He took in a deep breath and stared at the symbol as he focused on gliding his finger through the air to trace its form. He completed it and looked over at the chest to see that it did not even quiver, and that his fingers did not glow like Einar's. He took in a breath and traced again, as Einar stared watched his movements, and again there was no response from the chest. Naryan set his jaw and drew again, and again, each time increasing the precision and speed until his hand was a flurry. He finally banged down on the table in frustration and threw himself down into the chair, burying his face in his hands and gripping his hair.

"Oh look, it moved!" Einar exclaimed, and pointed to the chest as it moved itself across the floor by an inch and quivered. Naryan sat up straight and looked at it in disbelief, before glancing down at Einar's glowing foot to see that he had drawn a rune into the dirt of the floor.

"You bastard." said Naryan. Einar grinned.

"I'm only trying to cheer you up. Keep at it and you'll get it eventually. Your spirit must strengthen itself before it can truly interact with the world–and that chest is quite heavy."

Naryan sighed,

"Something simpler. What else can you teach me?"

Einar thought for a moment before responding,

"I could teach you to call a breeze–perhaps that would be best. It is nice to stay cool on a warm day."

Naryan waved his hand,

"Yes, sure, let's start with that."

Einar nodded and rose, saying,

"Ok, come outside. I don't want you inadvertently conjuring a tornado in my house." Naryan rolled his eyes and followed Einar into the clearing where the first rays of dusk were beginning to turn the sky into reds and oranges above the treetops.

"Stand here," Einar said, pointing, "and watch this sign carefully. It is a simple sign, but do not forget that the slightest distinction can greatly change the meaning. It means *slowly-wind-to here."* As he drew the rune in the air with his finger a breeze rustled through the leaves of the trees and brushed across his cloak. He continued moving his finger as he spoke,

"And now to continue it, 'slowly-whirlwind-here', 'slowly-wind-to there." and Naryan saw leaves picked up by the breeze whirl once around Einar before the air brushed along his own skin and dissipated.

"Are you ready?"

Naryan shrugged and exhaled, eyes focused intently on the empty space in the air in front of him and drew the simple rune into the air. Nothing happened. He hung his head for a moment but then raised it again, took in a breath, and crafted the symbol. His finger did not glow, but the hairs on the back of his neck raised as a breath of wind caressed him. He spun around to look at Einar, half-expecting him to be laughing after having drawn his own rune to trick Naryan, but Einar's arms were folded, and he gave a nod of approval.

"See, there you have it." he said. "You're well on your way. But we must have a rest now."

"Rest? I've only just learned!" Naryan whirled his hand again to draw the rune, but there was no effect. Again he tried, but still nothing.

"You have never exercised this muscle before–it must be strengthened." said Einar. "For now, come and rest."

Naryan resigned to him and followed Einar back into the hovel.

"Runes," said Naryan as they entered the door, "teach me more."

"Perhaps there are a few more that I could show you," said Einar, "but I was never a very good teacher, and the nuance of the more complex signs should be seen as they are written. No, my grimoire would be best suited for teaching."

"Show me then," said Naryan. "I'm ready."

"Ready or not, and I would err on the side of 'not'," replied Einar, "it is not here."

"Then let us fetch it. Where is it?"

"Well, I, as most people, keep my belongings where I live, and I have most recently lived in Satoria, in your castle."

Naryan nodded,

"I see. Well we'll just need to go get it then, won't we."

"We? I have no need for it–I know all its contents."

"Well I don't, and I can't just get it myself–they'll just kill me. I'll need you for protection."

Einar thought for a moment,

"So let me understand; we are surely safe here, for it is unknown that we are here in the forest, but you would like to put us where it is the least safe, so that we may be *more* safe than we already are, while here in the forest? You are certainly perplexing."

"You don't *care,*" snapped Naryan, "because you have had nothing taken from you!"

"Wrong." interjected Einar, "They do have my grimoire. And a chest with some robes, but I suppose that *is* about all."

Naryan scowled as Einar continued,

"Now let us think–perhaps the cause of your angst is that you *care* too much."

"Perhaps you do not care because you have so little." spat Naryan.

Einar smiled.

"What you mean as an insult is surely wisdom. Let us dissect it."

Naryan crossed his arms,

"I'm in no mood for a lecture."

Einar's eyes flickered for a moment in anger,

"If I am to instruct you in the manner of these runes, you will listen to what I have to say, in *all* regards."

Naryan's chin raised a little and his eyes narrowed but he bit his tongue and nodded. Einar continued,

"You are bound to the whim of your fleshly form and it controls you. If you lust for wine, or riches, or women, or possessions, your mind will dwell on attaining these things, and your ego will be tied down by them. But, if you cast them out, your spirit will be independent and strong and you will learn to find identity in their lack. In all things learn moderation, and if you lack the temperance, then abstinence is the way. This is why, to gain these abilities you have never had, you must live in a way you have never lived before.

"Do you desire this knowledge?" now posed Einar. Naryan gave a single nod, arms still crossed. This time, Einar raised his voice,

"Do you desire this knowledge? A simple nod will not suffice–you must yearn for it within your being. You must lust for it above all else, for in order to gain it, you must forsake all else you value. But this is not a violent lust, it is a controlled burning perseverance, for when you covet many things they will slip from your grasp, but when you are in control of yourself, and bend your spirit to your will, all other things will be within your attainment." Einar's voice fell again to a calmer cadence as he continued,

"You must give up the things you want, to gain absolute control of yourself, so that all those things will surrender themselves unto you. So, what is it that you most desire?"

"To reclaim the throne." said Naryan, without hesitation.

"Then you must give it up, so you can focus on learning your spirit. Once you have mastered your spirit, the throne will come unto you."

Naryan sung back to Einar in his own tone, waving his arms around

"You must give up this to gain that, and forsake your desire to gain your desire." he laughed, "this is all nonsense. Just show me the runes and I will learn them."

Einar gripped his fists together and clenched his jaw, nostrils flaring. He brought in a deep breath then exhaled, and after a brief pause, he laughed. His now relaxed hand stroked his chin and a twinkle returned to his eyes as he put his hand on Naryan's tensed shoulder.

"You know," said Einar, "you certainly do know how to strike a nerve in me; thank you for the reminder of my imperfections. I don't remember the last time I was angry." he thought for a moment before continuing, "Before, I hoped that you would forsake this path. I foresaw my passing you in a gutter someday, purple lips adorning a smile as you looked up at me, trying to remember where you knew me from. I thought your stubbornness would be detrimental to your advancement, but now I think it will be your greatest strength so long as you learn to apply yourself. I've made up my mind–I will teach you, in spite of this mirror you hold to me."

Naryan watched as Einar moved over to the chest and dug through it for a moment, coming up with a small sackcloth pouch. He untied it, reaching his fingers delicately into it, coming up with a few shriveled stems and caps of thin, brown mushrooms. Einar smiled and held them out in his palm to Naryan.

"Let us accelerate this, and really open your mind."

They did not taste good, Naryan thought as he gagged on the chewy mass. His throat refused to swallow and his stomach churned as he gagged again and finally choked it down with watery eyes. Einar stood, watching.

"I was going to give you some berries to mask the taste, but have it your way."

Naryan feigned a smile as he held in a retch, and gulped water from a cup that was set on the table.

"Oh," said Einar, "that's been there for months." He heartily pounded Naryan on the back while Naryan managed to give him an obscene gesture from his doubled-over position. He coughed a bit more before finally standing up and wiped the saline from his eyes. He took in a deep, wavering breath and looked at Einar,

"Ok, then how long?"

Einar shrugged.

"Who can tell? An hour? Two? Best be patient and think not on it. Go, and meditate outside, alone. I will rest."

Einar ushered Naryan outside and shut the door a little too hard on him, as he stepped into the now cool night air. Naryan scratched his head and looked around the clearing, walking to the center and sitting where he could look up at the night sky. The moon was full and its glow lit the clearing so that he could even see flowers and blades of grass around him. Crickets chirped, and the sounds of the forest enveloped him from all angles.

He crossed his legs and closed his eyes, and focused on his breathing. Thoughts did not ceaselessly flow across his mind this time, but they came one-by-one, a trickle of them that he was able to deflect. He was aware of each thought, and instead of the consciousness flowing as it willed, he was able to purposefully silence it, until his mind was a blank canvass and the cadence of his breath was deep and steady.

As he reached this state, his mind's canvas stretched, clear and pure as if this was the source of all white light, and it rushed towards him, placing him on it. He was there, in the plane, alone, no, not alone, for he felt another presence, a mere shimmer of light a long way off. He was drawn towards it, an eternity of walking until he was exhausted from the journey, and he'd forgotten who he was. He then looked behind him and saw a different formless shape, a dark and ghastly blotch on the white plane, trailing him from far behind.

A whisper of his name drew him nearer unto the bright shimmer ahead of him, but as he came closer, it retreated, and he felt shame emanating from it, shame that it was but a shimmer instead of brilliant radiance. The form of a wavering hand took shape and reached out to him from the shimmer, drawing a rune as it moved, and looking upon it Naryan knew it as a greeting. He returned the greeting in kind and stepped closer again, but the shimmer retreated further away, hesitant in its feebleness.

Naryan then felt behind him a dark presence, and turned again to see that the blotch now loomed next to them. He stood between the blotch and the shimmer, his id and his ego, as they each surveyed the others. He knew that the despondency of the shimmer was due to its neglect, and that the blotch easily subdued it, for it was gorged by his carnal desires.

The white plane began to dissolve, giving way little by little to the forest clearing where Naryan sat. The shimmer and the blotch materialized with it, facing each other as apparitions, until the blotch turned its attention to Naryan. It overshadowed him, tendrils seeping out to wrap themselves around his head, and he felt thirst, and lust, and gluttony, engulfing his mind.

The shimmer did not stand idly by though, for it moved forward in his defense and thrust itself between Naryan and the blotch. But, it was frail, and the blotch began to envelope it as it came closer to Naryan, until only the slightest glint of the shimmer escaped its pitch-blackness.

Naryan then felt no sadness, only apathy, at the shimmer's defeat. Thus, he was set to acquiesce to the cravings of his thirst, and libido, when Einar's words echoed through his mind,

"But, if you cast them out, your spirit will be independent and strong."

He rose, invigorated by the anger he felt at the waste of his life and now faced the blotch. Reaching both hands out, he drew a rune, a summon that had no subject, only direction: *swiftly-to here.*

The huge blotch was rent in two with a burst of light that emanated from its gut, and there, in its place was the shimmer. It rushed to Naryan's side, and they watched while the blotch's two parts collected themselves together again with a screech. It then charged towards them, its tendrils conveying itself across the ground, and maw agape to consume them.

Naryan then wrote again, remembering in detail the rune that he'd seen Einar conjure, but with his own change: *swiftly-whirlwind-here.* The shimmer took heed, and Naryan saw that it grasped and crinkled the air itself in its hands as if it were a sheet, and blinked in circumference around him so that it was here, and then there, and then everywhere all at once. The wind whipped around him even as the blotch drew nigh, and the wind began to dissolve it so that it became a thousand separate grains, and was whisked away to the plane in defeat. He breathed heavily as he surveyed the now peaceful clearing, and saw that the shimmer now stood in front of him, a little taller, and a little brighter than before. It too then began to dissolve from the clearing, and he reached his hand out towards it as he heard it call his name.

Chapter 13

The morning was still early when Naryan rose from the bed, finding that Einar was no longer in the chair where he'd been slouched and sleeping. The cool air of the morning drafted in through the open window and the bed of coals was covered in ash, only a wink of red showing from beneath the snowy white.

He threw back the single blanket from the bed, stretching towards the ceiling for only a moment before nearly bounding towards the door to find Einar, and tell him what he'd seen the night before. Out into the forest clearing he went, calling for Einar as he opened the door, but stopped mid-call. Einar was seated, cross-legged in the center of the clearing with a dozen written runes surrounding him, hovering in the air and glowing, undispersed.

"Einar," Naryan started, but he was cut short by a curt,

"Silence." from Einar.

Naryan seated himself near the hovel, watching as Einar wrote another rune and examined them each in turn before finally pushing his hands out to cast them. He then rose, brushing a few leaves from his robes and turned to Naryan, greeting him,

"Good Morning."

"What was that?" asked Naryan. "I've never seen you cast so many runes before."

"A series of directives, step-by-step, to be completed all at once."

"And what were those commands?"

"We must know what is going on outside of our little fortress," he nodded to the hovel, "I have sent my spirit on an errand to bring news of our adversaries and their certain hunt for us. Some circumstances require different actions, so it must all be pre-written, lest he return here over and over again for instruction. Though he is quick to traverse this plane the distances are long, and it may take some time."

Naryan's stomach grumbled.

"What's for breakfast?"

108

"Breakfast?" said Einar,"There's no time for breakfast! Too much food dulls the mind. So much to learn in so little time. Come this way." and he bustled off into the forest with Naryan in tow.

Despite Naryan's pestering questions of what they were doing and where they were going, Einar gave little answer, and the coolness of the dawn turned into the heat of the morning as they picked their way along an unused trail. After a while, Naryan's ears picked up the sounds of a small stream, and they went until they came to it, and Einar stooped to drink.

"Ah, we're here, finally." said Einar and he stood and wiped the back of his mouth with his robe sleeve.

"All that way just for some water?" asked Naryan. "You'd think you'd have chosen a spot closer to water for your home; this is quite inconvenient."

"Inconvenient to walk an hour for water, yes," replied Einar, "but usually I can conjure what I need from the leaves in the trees and the dew that has settled onto the earth. However, my spirit is occupied for the time being, and yours is useless. I also figured you could use a little exercise, judging by how poorly you kept up with me the other day. Now, gather some of that clay."

Naryan bit his cheek, looked at Einar, and then looked at the clay.

"Ah," said Einar, "please."

Naryan chuckled and stooped to collect a handful of clay and held it out to Einar.

"Now roll it into a ball, and flatten it. Keep it thin, but not *too* thin."

While directing Naryan, Einar walked a few steps, searching the ground with his eyes until he came to a branch. His fingers walked along the branch until he found a twig, which he snapped off, stripped the bark from, and then whittled the tip with his teeth.

"With my spirit away, I will take the opportunity to write these runes for you, for if he was here, he may think I was directing their casting. Make a few more while I work. We must be quick though! My cousin once wrote runes in a book, thinking his spirit was to be away for longer, but upon his return caused a tornado in my uncle's home. He was whipped harshly, to say the least."

Naryan flattened two more lumps of clay, handing them to Einar one-by-one, and wiped his hands on his clothes. Einar scratched symbols into the clay tablets with the stick, and they disappeared into his cloak as he finished writing each of them.

"Come now," he said, rising, "let us return."

Naryan nodded, and they set down the path they had come. Naryan asked,

"What did you write on the tablets?"

"They are for you," Einar said, "for I must endow you with some agency if you are to be an asset and not a liability. Though, they must be fired in an oven to reach full maturity."

"Why must they be fired?"

"When they are crafted," said Einar, "they must be imbued with intent, and they must be broken in order to bring that intent to fruition. When fired, they will crack easily when smashed to the ground, and your spirit will know your intent."

"What will these runes enact?"

Einar pulled them one-by-one from the innards of his robe, explaining the drawn runes as they walked,

"This is *swiftly-earth-rise*. Know that the earth will rise where you cast it down, for if you are writing the rune in the air you would need to clarify *where* it should rise.

"This is *swiftly-whirlwind-here*, which you already know of.

"This is *swiftly-whirlwind-there*. I'm going to assume you can figure what they will do."

"That's it?" asked Naryan. "Why didn't you make me more?"

"Well you only made me six tablets so I've made you two of each." said Einar. Naryan paused to look over his shoulder at the direction of the stream, and hesitated. He then jogged to catch up with Einar, who had not stopped.

"Why did you make these three kinds then?"

"You must understand," said Einar, "that most runes are written with specific indication of that circumstance. These are a few generic directions that do not need much in the way of specifics."

"Well," said Naryan, "Best I learn how to cast my own then."

"Best indeed." said Einar, and they trudged in silence the rest of the way to the hovel.

When they arrived, Einar bid Naryan to stoke and rebuild the fire, and then lined a brick inside the small hearth with the tablets to fire them. He surveyed the fire for a moment, perking up and inhaling with closed eyes.

"He has returned," he said, beckoning Naryan outdoors. Let us see what news he brings."

Einar sat cross-legged in the middle of the clearing and closed his eyes whilst Naryan watched from the side. His eyes moved rapidly behind his eyelids all the while, and the cadence of his breath varied from slow and controlled to quick and sporadic. Finally, after a short while, he opened his eyes and rose, moving past Naryan without a word and went back into the house. Naryan followed, asking,

"Ill news?"

Einar nodded,

"Ill news."

Naryan grimaced,

"Well then, let's hear it."

"Eight Erilaz remain, since two have fallen by our hands. These eight, however, do not garrison in the city standing idly by, for they have gone out into the lands searching for us."

"They shouldn't find us here though," said Naryan, "for we are deep in the woods and left no trail behind."

Einar shook his head,

"If it were even just a skilled tracker following us I would agree, yet these Erilaz are no fools, and certainly send out their spirits in search of us, as I have done of them. The essence of my spirits is as a beacon to theirs, and they certainly will find us without issue. I must depart from here, for hiding is not an option."

"Where will we go?"

"Did you not hear me? I said *I must* depart. You will not come with me, nor should you stay here either. Speed is my only ally now, and they will not find you if you leave here, for your spirit is still dull."

Einar started gathering a few things from the chest and slipped them into a bag that he threw over his shoulder.

"How do you know what he tells you?" Asked Naryan.

"I read the runes he writes," said Einar.

"You're leaving so quickly–I'm afraid I will never learn."

"This is no skill to be honed–it is innate within you. Control your vices, and it should be no trouble at all in little time."

Einar paused at the door, motioning to tablets at the hearth,

"And do not forget those, for they may be your only defense until you learn the runes."

"What should I do?"

Einar shook his head as he looked Naryan up and down.

"Do what you will, and do what you must. You no longer know who you can trust, and only you can find your path."

He sighed and looked around the hovel, one last time.

"I would teach you more, but there is no time. You must learn on your own. Find my grimoire at the castle, for it may help you learn. Meditate often and read the runes written in your mind. And do not follow me." He whooshed out the door, leaving it to swing on its hinges in his wake.

Naryan listened to the crunch of his footsteps disappear into the distance until only the sound of birds remained. He moved to the hearth, gathering a scrap of cloth along the way, and collecting the now-hardened clay tablets, setting them on a mantle stone to cool. He then turned to survey the rest of the single room, and spoke aloud to himself,

"Didn't leave much for me now, did you Einar?"

He went to the chest, pausing for a moment before he threw it open. He expected to find at the very least a magical stick. But it was, in fact, empty. Naryan exhaled, chuckled, and kicked it, and the lid slammed back down. He turned to survey the sparse room to see what else he could salvage, but there was nothing save a dark brown and hooded robe. He donned it, tightening it with a cord that hung at its waist.

He felt that the tablets no longer burned to the touch so he placed the rag on the floor, setting the first tablet down, then layering the cloth between it, and the next, and the next, so as to ensure they did not crack. He twisted the end to a knot and tied it to the cord at his waist, heading out the door and down the trail. With every step, he felt it bump across his leg, and the faint scrapes of the tablets as they rubbed against one another.

Chapter 14

The road back to Satoria was to be long, and much slower than when there were Erilaz on his trail. He strolled along the shaded trails in the forest that soon turned into paths in the sunny fields, and widened themselves into cobblestoned roads as he approached nearer to the capital. When he'd first left the hovel, he hadn't seen anyone else in days, but as he came closer to the capital, the roads became more and more populated with merchants and travelers. Noone recognized him as he went, though he did not mind it, for he burned the signs of the runes over and over again in his vision with every step.

Having no food or drink with him when he'd departed in the late morning, he stopped here and there when he saw fruit trees on the side of the road, and drank from a stream that shared the same direction as the road for a while. With every mile that passed, the weight of the tablets on his belt was a reminder of his goal.

Dusk finally began to settle over the roads, and Naryan saw the lights of a small settlement in the distance. He came to it, finding it little more than a tavern, a shop in a nearby structure, and a few lights of homes adorning the hills in the distance. Two horses were tethered to a post outside and he eyed them, considering forgoing a meal and sleep, and cutting his time in half with a ride through the night. Instead, his stomach rumbled, so he trudged to the tavern, lifted his hood to his head, and pushed the door open to find the glow within.

It was a single room with a bar in the back, no keep to be seen. Short tables lined the edges of the room, and in the center were lines of long tables with lanterns on them, but nobody sitting at them. One table at the edge of the room had three plain-clothes men at it, and another with two Satorian guards. All in the room turned to look at him as he surveyed the scene.

"Well close the door will yeh," said one of the men from the table of three. "You'll let the horse flies in." Naryan grabbed the handle and pulled the door shut behind him before walking towards the bar, still looking around.

"Pour yerself something that you'd like and just leave the coin on the bar." said the man.

"Well," said Naryan, "I don't have any coin–I was hoping to trade some labor for a meal and a room for the night."

The man grimaced.

"I've done all the chores, and we don't take kind to vagrants here. You best be heading off."

"An inn that doesn't take kindly to vagrants?" Naryan posed, "You must not get much business then."

The man shook his head,

"No, you misunderstand. We just don't like vagrants without coin. Now get, before I put my taxes to work." he nodded his head at the guards on the other side of the room.

Naryan scowled and turned back to the door, making sure to leave it open as he exited, and eying the horses again. He moved towards them, seeing that they bore the saddles of the Satorian crown, and that they certainly belonged to the guards inside.

They're really mine anyway, he thought as he looked behind him towards the ajar door. He checked, and no eyes peeked at him through the windows so he walked to the horses, and began untying the rope that tethered one to the hitching post.

Behind him the clunk of footsteps on the wooden floor approached the door,

"The bastard left it open." he heard the voice say from within. "I knew he was no good." The man's head poked out the door, and he caught Naryan with the tether between his hands. His eyes narrowed and he called out to the other men within,

"The horses!!"

The clamber of the guards from within was apparent, and the sound of chairs falling and tables being pushed out of the way came from within the door. Naryan struggled with the knot for a moment before finally getting it free from the hitching post, just as the man at the doorway was knocked aside, and the two guards came rushing out.

Naryan started to mount the horse, but it wheeled, spooked by the commotion, and his boot slipped out of the stirrup. He stepped back down to the ground as the guards closed the distance, brandishing spears they had grabbed from their stands at the door. Naryan swore and took off on foot around the corner of the building, seeing the inn-keeper's face surveying him from the window at the back of the inn. He sprinted faster around the next corner of the building, then coming into full contact with one of the guards who had run to cut him off.

The two bounced off each other, staggering to catch their footing, but Naryan had lighter attire so he recovered quicker and pushed the guard over again as he rose. He heard the other guard and turned his head to see him charging around the corner of the building behind him. He took off again, but as he stepped the fallen guard held the shaft of his spear out to tangle his legs and trip him. As Naryan fell he twisted his body so as to not crush the tablets, and landed on his side, where he was quickly reminded of his wound. By the time he recovered his bearings the other guard was standing above him, and he felt the rap of the guard's spear against the side of his head.

Not unconscious, but quite disoriented, he felt himself grabbed by each arm from behind, and dragged around to the front of the building. His eyes were half-shut, but his ears picked up the sound of his feet scraping along the dirt path until he was dumped in front of the tavern, and he heard the pants of the guards catching their breaths. He sat up, holding his head with one hand, while the clunk of boots down the stairs signified that the civilian inhabitants had come outside to view the commotion.

"We oughta kill you," said the first guard as he pulled back Naryan's hood. "Thievery of the crown's steed?" he paused, studying the dazed Naryan for a moment, before looking at the other guard.

"Isn't this this prince?"

Naryan raised his head up, a black eye already swelling from where the spear's shaft had contacted the side of his face.

"No, it can't be." said the second. "He's got no flagon in his hand." The two laughed. The second motioned to the barkeep, "Bring a lantern, I need a good look at him."

Naryan retorted,

"*King*, actually. And you'll be forgiven if you just help me up."

The two guards didn't move. The first said to the second,

"I mean, it does look like him, but what's our luck?"

"Good, apparently." said Naryan, "You've found me. I've only just managed to escape a maniac magician who has held me captive. What word comes from the capital? When I last left the castle was aflame and mages ran amuck."

"Mages?" said the first guard, "What nonsense is this? Perhaps he *has* been drinking."

The barkeep returned, lantern in hand, and gave it to the first guard who held it above Naryan and peered at him.

"Do you know nothing?" Naryan tried to rise, but the butt of the second guard's spear pushed against his chest to prevent him.

"There's a bounty on his head," said the second, "I saw word of it not two days ago."

"You can't put a bounty on the king." laughed Naryan.

"King no longer," replied the first, "for any 'king' that murders his commanders and sells out his own kingdom to Chromer for coin deserves not the throne. The queen now rules, and we will be better for it." he turned to the other guard, "Do you remember if the bounty was dead, or alive?"

Naryan interjected,

"What of the mages? There were ten of them that came to overthrow the throne, and they set the castle aflame. Have you heard nothing?"

The second guard shook his head,

"Look at him, he's certainly gone mad. That preacher left, and since then talk of magic has reduced again to folktale. You're too late on your trends."

Naryan sputtered,

"If I was lying, could I do this?"

He reached his hand out to draw a rune, finishing it with a flick of his finger–but nothing happened. He focused and tried again, and again, before the guards both broke out in laughter.

"Perhaps a bounty was too harsh for this one. He probably wouldn't survive much longer out in the woods without someone to wipe the spittle from his face and change his soiled clothes. I'd say the pillory for him, more so he doesn't hurt himself than others."

Resigned, Naryan asked,

"What's the bounty?" as he reached for the pouch on his belt.

The guards watched him reach for it and laughed.

"More than you can carry in that." he nodded with his head towards the pouch. "The promise was of an estate and servants, a hundred years wages, and the title of lord. I think we'd take that over whatever you can carry in that pouch. I'd like to get fat and lazy in my old age."

"No no," Naryan said as he fumbled with the cloth, "Let us count my coin." He finally untwisted it and grasped his fingers around the first tablet.

The guards laughed again,

"What is this, some counterfeit made by a madman in the woods? I've seen children with better craftsmanship than this. Here, let us have a look at it."

Naryan made as if to hand it to the guard, but then threw it to the ground where it shattered with the clank of breaking pottery.

The wind whirled around him, lifting the guards into the twisting air and ripping the spears from their grasps. The lantern in the guard's hand smashed to the ground and the swift air dragged the oil-fueled flames along the ground until they spread into the whirlwind, catching the guard's cloaks aflame and burning them as they screamed. The wind only spun for a few seconds before it began to die, the flames evaporating first and the guards falling to the ground. Naryan reached out and caught a spear in his hand with a clunk as it passed him, and looked to see the innkeeper and two counterparts running off into the night.

Light from the tavern's open door spread onto the scene; the first guard quivered on the ground, moaning, his face blackened, and the second lay face-down, unmoving. The living guard's eyes opened as he rasped for breath, and widened as he saw that Naryan was unscathed and watching him. Naryan stepped towards the guard, and his stomach twisted, seeing what he'd done. The guard's eyes widened and his breaths grew quick and shallow.

"What is the greater mercy?" Naryan asked. "To let you live, feeble and scarred, or to end your misery?"

The guard swallowed and pushed out with weakened breaths,

"End me." he rasped. "To live, like this, is no mercy." and he tilted his head back as much as his weakened neck would let him.

The word "Fuck" escaped Naryan's turned lips as he drew the edge of the spear's leaf end-to-end across the man's neck with a quivering hand. His own throat tightened as he saw the pinkness of the muscle beneath the blackened skin of the throat. Then, the lines of red came dripping forward, pulsing with the beat of his heart. They spilled down further onto the charred uniform as the man's head fell to the side, but his eyes locked onto Naryan. Naryan stood there, gritting his teeth, watching as life drained from the man's eyes while he expelled his last breath.

"Fuck. Why? Why did you do that?" Naryan whispered aloud to the man's limp face.

Naryan turned away, not wanting to gaze upon the deeds done by his hand, going now to the other guard lying motionless on the ground. The other guard had indeed perished, though it was a bloodless death for his neck was broken after having landed on his head. Naryan hung his head, looking at his subjects, for even though they were his enemies in that moment he'd had no hatred towards them. He only acted in the moment out of necessity, and now their lives hung on his conscience.

Naryan took the sword from the guard's belt and stripped the man, cutting off pieces of the uniform that were burned. He then donned what clothing remained, garbing himself in the helmet and armor, and dragged the bodies to the side of the tavern.

The tethered horses watched him out of the corner of their eyes, and when he was done he came to one, untied it, and rode off into the night towards the capital.

Chapter 15

The ride to the capital took a few more hours, and Naryan knew he only had just as many more hours of dark remaining. He overlooked the city from a hill on its outskirts before riding down into the city that surrounded the castle, seeming to be nothing more than a lone guard on his patrol. He passed through the city streets unharassed, with nothing more than glances from the few citizens out at this hour. As he approached, he formulated a plan in his head.

One of the perks of often burning the midnight oil in a drunken stupor was that he could survey the guard's patrols from his tower, and knew them by heart. The side door to the castle courtyard was certainly the answer here, and he found an alley in the city where he tied the horse, and continued on foot the remainder of the way. Out of the city he went, into the dark wood outside the castle's wall, and picked his way along the inside of the treeline until he came to the small gate. It was locked, and unguarded, for it was not well-known, and fortunately, he knew where a key was hidden. He felt around the wall near the small gate for the loosened stone, finally wriggling it as his fingers touched it. He pried along the edges of the moss, pulling it loose and finding the brass key there. He put the key into the hole, turned it, and with little more than the squeak of a hinge he let himself through the gate.

This portion of the outer bailey was a rather large, flat area that drew a semi-circle around the inner ward, with a well-kept lawn and a few evenly placed decorative trees. It was not much more than a well-kept garden, and there was not much cover for him to traverse without being seen. He looked across the castle, up at his tower silhouetted against the night sky, and got a sense of longing to be back in his bed. He then saw in his mind's eye the memory of flames licking out of the windows and shook away the feeling, focusing instead on the task at hand.

He avoided the path that ran directly from the gate and lawn towards the inner ward's barbican, instead hugging the wall and traversing along its circumference while keeping in the shadows. He realized that the guards were fewer than usual, probably pulled from their posts to attend to the looming war with Chromer, and thanked his luck. The keep was not under lockdown for the city was not besieged, so getting in would not be too difficult.

He watched the rounds of the guards from the shadow of the wall, keeping low and near shrubbery where he could. He looped around the full perimeter of the wall, coming to the point where the curtain wall and the inner ward's wall met it, a thick corner that rose high. On the opposite side of the wall from him, to the rear of the fortress, was a forest. It was considered unpassable by any large company of men, for it was thick and near to the wall–a natural barrier and defense of the city's rear.

He looked up where the walls met, and knew that unless he were to risk exposure, this was to be his path. Fortunately, it was a path well-known to him, for in his youth he often scaled the wall to sneak back into the keep when he had stayed out lurking through the city streets later than he should have. He knew where the cracks in the stone were for footholds, and the chipped mortar for finger holds, and though his fingers and boots were surely larger than when he'd last scaled it, he was confident he could even find the path in the dark.

He stepped up to the wall, lifting his knee to place his boot on the first protruding stone, and began the ascent. It was a thirty-foot climb, and harder wearing the confining armor of a guard than when he'd worn the light garb of a young prince. Halfway up, he managed to wedge himself partly in the corner of where the two walls met and rest, before continuing his ascent. This corner where the two walls met was the base of a tower that rose up from the inner ward's wall, and once he was level with the top of the wall, he had to scale perpendicular to his climb to reach an area that was not the solid wall of a tower.

A fall would most likely not kill him, but it would certainly not be pretty, and he let loose the breath he was holding as he finally grasped onto the corner of a merlon and pulled himself through the crenel. He landed on the wall's walkway with a slight clink of metal and looked around to see if anyone had seen him. It didn't appear as much, so he crouched and moved towards the door of the tower to his left and pushed it open, entering into the stairwell that would take him to the lower floor of the inner ward.

The emissary's quarters, where Einar had been staying, was on the far side of the castle from where he had snuck through, and he now had to make his way across the entirety of the castle without being discovered. The good news was, however, that having already infiltrated the inner ward and being dressed as a guard, he could go nearly wherever he pleased–so long as he didn't run into a commanding officer who had any sense of wits about him regarding the patrol patterns.

As he went he passed a few servants, but there were few out at this hour, and the ones that were out had duties to attend to such as oiling the lamps and sweeping the floors. His helmet cast shadows on his face to hide it from prying eyes, and he and the servants gave each other courteous nods as they passed one another, but nothing more.

Through the hallways he walked, sure of his direction, and while he was tired, he operated on the fuel of excitement. Though he was trying to keep the steady, almost lazy cadence of a guard on patrol, he hurried his pace when he looked through the windows and saw the sky begin to lighten with sunrise. He didn't think it prudent to be waltzing around the castle in broad daylight, as the temperament of the guards whose armor he now wore gave him a lack of faith in who his allies actually were.

As he rounded a corner near the council chamber, he saw three figures standing in front of it, for torches were always kept lit here, and they cast long shadows on the floor of the hallway. He hesitated for a second, but continued forwards for he had already passed the edge of the corner, and it would be suspicious for him to turn away now. He heard their voices as he came closer.

"It was nice of you to come see me off." echoed Shawn's voice in the hallway. Shawn stood with his back to Naryan, his long brown hair pulled neatly into a tail, rather than the flowing style he usually kept. His garb was no longer that of a courtier, but he wore the plain and padded undergarments that complimented plate mail. Next to him, also with his back to Naryan, stood Shawn's squire, and across from the two of them stood Sherry. She was not of her usual cheerful demeanor, but wore a solemn face, and plain garments.

Naryan's footsteps echoed in the hall behind them, and both Shawn and the squire turned to give him no more than a glance, before returning their attention to Sherry. Sherry stepped forward to Shawn, standing on her toes to reach up and envelope him in a hug even as Naryan passed them, and their eyes met through the apertures of his helm. Naryan set his jaw and his eyes gave her a stern look, and she gasped, stiffening at the realization of his presence, but continued the embrace until Naryan had passed by them.

As Naryan continued down the hall away from them, he heard Sherry speak,

"Be safe brother."

"I'll be fine–really. I'm there more for show than to do battle. I'll be mostly strategizing in the commander's tent sipping a goblet of wine."

He rounded the next corner, picking up his pace, and moved further down the next hallway until their voices disappeared, often looking back to see if he was followed. The emissary quarters were now closeby, and he came to their entrance. There were 8 rooms, four on either side of a long hallway lit by flickering torches placed on the wall between each door. The quarters were not lavish, but were private and reserved for long-distance travelers who came for an audience with the crown, whether it be diplomacy, trade, or tribute. This was where Rhondia had provided Einar with accommodations when she'd taken a liking to him.

Naryan stood in the hallway, unsure exactly in which room to start his search. He thought back for a moment, trying to remember if there were any other emissaries that had come for an audience while Einar was staying there, and couldn't think of any.

Knowing Einar, if given the choice, he would have picked the quietest room, furthest from any commotion, so Naryan went to the back left room and grasped the handle. He pushed on the door, feeling no resistance of a lock, and peered inside to ensure that it was unoccupied. It was, and he slipped into the room, closing the door behind him.

Oftentimes regularly visiting emissaries would make requests for their rooms–flowers, tapestries, and the like, but this room was sparsely furnished, just as Naryan would have expected from Einar. A pair of shoes was abandoned by the door, as was a single satchel sitting on a wooden side table near to the bed, but nothing more. He went to the satchel, pulling the drawstring to open it, and rummaging through its contents. His hands passed over a thick leather-bound book, and he removed it from the satchel, running his fingers over its title-less and black-ridged spine.

He took in a breath and opened it; when opened it sat comfortably in the palm of his hand, and each page was well-folded so that it stayed open to the chosen page and did not flip of its own accord. The inner pages were of a thinly-sliced beige tanned hide, and the symbols written therein were calligraphed with clean black-ink lines.

He flipped through a few of the pages, seeing written runes with descriptors in the common tongue, keeping the same structure of sentence that Einar had taught him. There were a hundred staves, at least, judging by the thickness of the book, and Naryan smiled as he tucked the grimoire back into the satchel and further stuffed that into the chain mail of his armor. He moved again to the door and went through it, moving down the emissary quarters' hallway, and coming to the 'T' where it intersected with the main hallway. As he approached he heard the patter of footsteps coming towards him, so he stiffened as if he was standing guard over the hallway, when he saw Sherry approaching.

She saw him in the hallway and came towards him, looking over her shoulder as she went, and pushed him deeper into the hallway with her hand on his chest, hissing,

"What are you doing here? You're going to get yourself killed!"

"I'm glad to see you." he said, grasping her in an embrace. She stiffened, allowing it, but then pushed him away to look him over.

"This isn't a game." she continued, in a whisper, "They're looking all over for you. There's a bounty on your head."

Naryan nodded,

"Yes, I know," he nodded, motioning towards the guard outfit, "I relieved this of the last man who told me there was a bounty."

"Playing dress-up isn't going to help." she said. "You've got to get out of here."

"And go to where?"

"I don't know, but not here."

Naryan watched her. Her brow was furrowed and her jaw was clenched, but her eyes glistened in the torch light.

"I'm not sure if you've noticed," he said, "but this is my home."

"I'm not sure if you've noticed," she said, "but you're not exactly welcome anymore. Word spread around that you killed Sir Sylvian and then ran off, and now everyone thinks that you're mad. Rhondia is sitting on the throne, and she's tightened up the edicts around here."

"I didn't kill Sylvian." said Naryan.

Sherry's eyes narrowed as she studied him for a moment, then said,

"I believe you. But nobody else will."

Naryan moved to pound the wall with his fist, but then thought better of it. He paced a few steps up the hallway and back, then looked at her again,

"What of the mages?"

"Mages?" Sherry replied.

"Yes, the mages. There were ten of them–well, now eight. Einar and I killed two of them."

126

"I don't know anything about mages–though I have seen Rhondia with some new unknown courtiers recently. I just thought I didn't keep close enough tabs on court politics, so I didn't worry much about it. But what's this about you and Einar?"

Naryan shook his head,

"There's no time. I do agree–leaving is in my best interest though. Are you coming with me?"

Sherry stepped away from him,

"Coming with you? Why?"

"I don't know, but it's clearly not safe here. There's an ill ambiance in Satoria."

She shook her head.

"No. No, I don't think that's a good idea." she looked over her shoulder again. "I really should get going."

"Fine," said Naryan, "Let's go. Walk with me."

Sherry grimaced for a second, but nodded, and they headed off down the hallway. They walked in silence with nothing but the sound of their feet echoing in the hallway, until they approached a large doorway that led to the inner ward's courtyard.

Coming to it, Naryan broke the silence.

"I'm assuming you rode here–is Nightmare at the stable?"

She nodded as he opened the door and saw that the day had already dawned. Outside, the courtyard in the inner ward was still scarcely populated, save for a few guards standing near the barbican to the outer bailey, and one right at the door where they stood. Naryan, seeing the guard spoke to Sherry,

"Happy to chaperone you to your manor, M'lady." he held out his arm as if to show her the way and she gave him a tactful scowl before heading out the door and down the steps towards the stables. The guard at the door nodded to them as they passed, but said nothing.

They crossed the courtyard unhindered and approached the inner barbican that stood between them and the outer bailey. The outer bailey housed facilitating structures of the castle such as the barracks, a smith, the storehouse, and more importantly–the stables.

Only two guards stood at the inner barbican, and they passed them by without incident, walking then the distance to the stables. Entering it they found Nightmare hitched alongside a few other horses, all of them already saddled and bridled for the guards to use throughout the day. Sherry came to Nightmare, untied her, and led her to the entrance of the stables while Naryan chose a horse for himself. They mounted together and trotted towards the outer barbican.

A set of four guards manned the outer barbican and gatehouse, and Naryan breathed a sigh of relief as they neared it and saw the road leading out of the castle and towards the city. But as they came nearer to the gate, he stiffened, for he saw ten foot soldiers bearing spears with bows fastened to their backs, and a man in black robes coming around to the front of the gate. They were already entering into the gate as Naryan and Sherry approached, so they waited off to the side of the pathway as the troop came through.

The man in the black robes stopped to speak with the guard at the gate, as he passed by, and Naryan overheard their conversation,

"Are we the first to return? What news of Solis or the others?"

"None, sir." replied the guard. "You are the first to return–and I've received no word of their coming."

The robed man nodded and continued to follow after the ten soldiers, barely noticing Naryan and Sherry as they took pause on their horses. Naryan did not look at him, but stared ahead towards the gate, and as soon as the man passed he goaded his horse towards the main gate, Sherry in tow.

Behind him, the man in the robes stiffened, pausing mid-step as if he'd heard a noise, and wheeled round. Naryan felt naked and exposed, a feeling reminiscent of the field where he and Einar had futilely hid from the mages on the road. He knew he was discovered, for the mage's spirit could glimpse his own.

"You there," said the man. "Stop."

Naryan looked at Sherry and kicked his horse, which took off at a gallop down the road. He heard Nightmare's hoofbeats behind him, and shouts from the guards as they turned and gave chase. Shy of ten seconds the horses sprinted, and Naryan thought they were free, but the Erilaz had written a rune. Naryan's horse faltered as the ground beneath it writhed, catching its hooves as it ran, and tripping it. One of the horse's right legs snapped as it misstepped, and the bone protruded through its leg as it came skidding to its knees, throwing Naryan off to the side.

Sherry wheeled Nightmare, missing the loosened soil, and pulled her reins to come beside the fallen Naryan. There was a whir in the air, and then a thud, and then another, as arrows planted themselves in the ground around him, and he pushed himself up to a stand off of the thrashing horse. He looked back at the gatehouse and saw that the company of ten soldiers had paused to form a line, and held their bows bent. As one he saw them volley, and a moment later heard the shout to loose.

The arrows arced towards them, and as he saw them silhouetted against the backdrop of the castle he knew that some of them would hit their marks. His mind raced, and he reached his hand into his mail to feel the pouch with the tablets. His fingers tugged at the pouch, but it was too deep and still tied, and he knew he could not pull a tablet from it in time.

Time slowed as he saw Sherry's face, brow furrowed as her eyes darted between him and the volley. He released the pouch, instead exhaling and putting his palm out in front of him to draw the rune: *swiftly-air-away*. Light glowed from his fingers as he did, and Sherry's hair swept round her head in the wind that emanated from him. The arrows were nigh unto their marks, but the burst pushed them off their course so that they bounced and clacked onto the road around Sherry and Naryan. Sherry's mouth was agape, but she was interrupted as Naryan pulled himself up onto the rear of Nightmare, and Nightmare bore them away down the road at a full gallop.

Chapter 16

They headed immediately north away from the city, taking a smaller path away from the main road so as to not run into any curious eyes. Nightmare galloped full speed for a few minutes until she'd lost her vigor, the weight of two riders being more than she was accustomed to. Still, they pushed her on at a trot until they'd checked behind them enough times to be sure they weren't followed. Nightmare panted and foamed at the mouth, and eventually they dismounted, leading her to a stream near the road to take an uneasy rest.

It was still morning, and the cool air helped calm them as they sat in silence on a patch of thick green grass while Nightmare watered.

Naran finally spoke,

"Thank you–you know you didn't have to do this."

Sherry nodded, twisting a stalk of green grass between her fingers, but continued to stare at Nightmare.

"You'd probably be dead. It's the least I can do. Though," she paused, "what was that, that you did? I saw you cast…a spell?"

Naryan nodded,

"I've spent time with Einar since I left, and he's taught me some things."

Sherry finally looked at him,

"So it's real then–all that he was doing? Magic is real?"

Naryan nodded. Sherry shook her head,

"I wouldn't have believed it if you told me, but I saw you. How?"

This time Naryan shook his head,

"There's too much to tell, and I'm not even confident that I know what I'm doing enough to explain it. All I know is that there's a part of me that I didn't know existed, my spirit, and we're forming a bond. Everyone has a spirit and can learn this–that's what Einar said at least."

"Since when are you acquainted with Einar?" Sherry asked, "Last I heard you were thinking of having him executed."

"Well," Naryan laughed, "Things change I suppose."

"I suppose they do," she said. She scratched the dirt with a stick, avoiding his gaze.

"I've changed." continued Naryan. He now stared off into the distance, giving a little laugh. "You wouldn't guess it, that such a short amount of time could enact such a change, but it has, and I have. My conscience, Sherry. I feel it.

He took a deep breath, confessing in vulnerability,

"I killed a man for this," he said, motioning to the guard outfit. "two men, actually."

Sherry's posture straightened and she took interest in Nightmare's rump.

"I do feel–justified, for they held me for bounty and I'd certainly be in Rhondia's hands and well on the way to the gallows or a dungeon. But still, even in justice do I feel pity, for they were only men, looking out for their own well-being, and not harming me out of malice.

"And they were helpless." Naryan continued. He clenched his jaw and his eyes glistened as he looked at Sherry. "In speaking to my spirit, I have never felt so unified, so natural, so whole, yet thus far I've only used this for unnatural violence. Even Einar, in all his wisdom, can use it for violent force; how then will I be able to control it, since I am not as wise as he? This is a stewardship that I now have entrusted to me: peace, where I have the potential for great destruction. I now look on the people I've killed with regret–the two guards, even the emissary in my court. In every case I chose to decimate the powerless. What kind of king does that?"

Sherry shrugged, still not looking at him.

"I've come to the realization that I cannot do this by myself. I need you, Sherry. You ground me. I trust you, and you advise me of better choices I can make."

Sherry turned her head to him–fierce.

"What else do you regret, Naryan?"

Naryan thought for a moment before replying,

"My wrath, my drunkenness, my sloth. I realize now that all of these are but symptoms of my own insecurities, and they have done nothing but push people away. If I'm to be a king, I must learn to be merciful and empathetic."

Sherry rose, brushing bits of grass from her skirt,

"But you're not a king–not any longer at least."

Naryan grimaced.

"What about you Sherry, what do you regret?"

She moved to Nightmare, checking her saddle, tightening the billet strap, and inspecting a stirrup.

"Plenty of things." she finally said.

"Tell me."

She turned to him,

"Not that you deserve to know, but…trusting–in hope. And love. And forgiveness of regret." She paused, and shook her head. "It's time for me to go. My father will be concerned, since I was only supposed to see Shawn off." she paused again, "Where will you go?"

"I don't know." sighed Naryan, "But Sherry–don't go. Please. Stay with me. We'll find somewhere to lay low for a while. You're all I have."

Sherry chewed on her cheek and shook her head,

"No."

"Why?" asked Naryan,

She mounted Nightmare and didn't let her voice waver,

"I don't trust you."

Naryan sat with his helmet at his side and watched Nightmare bear Sherry off in the direction of her estate. He let himself fall back onto the patch of green grass where he sat, and ran his hands through his hair with a sigh of exasperation. He stared up at the sky, not noticing that only a few clouds floated across a clear blue canvas as he continuously grasped at grass and aimlessly discarded it.

After he'd picked the ground around him bare, he pulled out the grimoire and looked it over. He opened it, reading through the pages and seeing inscriptions in the common tongue, placed alongside the runes. Each had a description, but there were also staves of runes combined that allowed for more complex biddings of the spirit. Here he studied them for a while, learning the chapters and pages and organization of the grimoire until he grew restless.

He then rose, gathered the helmet, and headed back to the road. Off in the distance a windmill stood on a hill, surrounded by fields of grain, and he set his course for there, no other destination in mind. As he walked along the trail, it again became a cobbled road, and dwellings sprouted up around him. The homes themselves were far apart, often with a homestead and livestock surrounding them, but they condensed themselves closer and closer together until they formed a town with a square and a well in the middle of it.

He stopped at the well, pulling up the bucket and holding it to his face for a long draught. A townsman, resting on a weathered stool in the shade of an inn's tilting overhang called out to him,

"You don't suppose you need a mug for that do you? Don't need you getting your filthy spittle in our only bucket. You should know, our buckets don't grow on trees like they do in the capital."

Naryan swallowed some of the water in his mouth, and spit the rest out in the direction of the man. The man sneered,

"All you from the capital are the same–no respect. I'm surprised you even would soil your feet by coming to our dirty little hamlet. Lost your horse, have you? Looks like the king is filling his army with dolts these days."

"There's no longer a king–haven't you heard? The Queen rules now." said Naryan.

"No king you say? Well, You wouldn't be happening to bring a decree that the queen will no longer levying taxes on Grainridge, would you? If not, then it makes no matter to me who rules in the capital. They're all the same–lining their own coffers with what little we have, and taking our young men to war." he spit on the ground. "Take that as your next tribute."

Naryan set the bucket down on the rim of the well.

"I'm not here to collect tribute, nor young men for a war that I myself want no part of."

The man chuckled,

"Ah, a deserter then?"

Naryan shrugged,

"Something like that. I wouldn't suppose you know of an inn to stay a while, do you?"

The man nodded his head towards the building behind him,

"Best inn in Grainridge, so long as you've got the coin to pay."

Naryan feigned patting a coin pouch under his chain vest. The man smiled and said,

"The best room in the house for our honored envoy?"

"A modest one will do."

The man grunted,

"Times must be tough if even the corrupt guards are cutting back their spending. Come this way."

The man brought Naryan inside the inn, leading him through a front tavern and to a hallway lined with a few shut doors and a rear exit from the structure. The man opened the first room, motioning for Naryan to enter.

"I'll be collecting payment every third day," he said. "But the first three are payable up front." he nodded towards Naryan's fake inner coin pouch.

"Certainly," said Naryan, "Let me just strip my armor and I'll bring it out to you."

The man grunted and left as Naryan surveyed the room. It was nothing more than a filthy-looking blanket atop of what appeared to be straw-stuffed sacks, resting on a wooden box on the floor. Certainly a step down from his own room in the keep, but he hadn't slept there in over a week by now, and this was not dissimilar from Einar's hovel anyway. Even after seeing the state of the room,

Naryan wasn't so sure that these weren't the expensive accommodations, and that he was going to be expected to pay handsomely for them. There was at least a bed after all.

He didn't remove his armor, and instead snuck out the back door of the inn, hoping to explore a bit more of the hamlet before night fell.

To the rear of the inn was an unkempt garden, nothing growing in it but weeds and surrounded by a leaning garden fence made from sticks. The buildings on either side of the inn continued on to form the town square on the other side of the buildings, and he snuck through a narrow alleyway towards it. The innkeeper was no longer sitting on the stool in the front, which was good since Naryan didn't feel like answering any questions about why he hadn't paid his rent, nor taking any more jabs about being from the capital. It was good, he thought, that nobody knew his identity out here–for more reasons than one.

There were a couple of people milling around the town square, one leading a goat, another carrying a screaming child, and an old woman sitting next to a cart laden with what Naryan could only assume was produce from surrounding fields. His stomach rumbled as he saw it, and the old woman eyed him as he approached.

"You don't be comin' to tax me now, you hear. I can barely get by as it is."

Naryan grimaced.

"Oh, of course not. I'm not sure what kind of guards you're used to, but I pay for my goods."

She peered at him through squinted eyes.

"Well then, what will you be havin' today?"

He examined the produce, his fingers moving across heads of lettuce, carrots, and eggs, before coming to rest on an apple. He picked it up, and moved his other hand to the inside of his vest as if to search for his coin. He felt around for a moment, then said,

"It seems that I've left my purse in my room at the inn. I'll need to go get it.

The lady stood up and snatched the apple from his hand. His stomach growled again.

"I'll be taking that then–it'll be waiting here for you."

Naryan held his face stoic as he nodded, and turned as if to head to the inn. Instead of going inside, however, he hid in the alleyway that he'd come through, and peered his head around the corner so that he could see the lady and cart from across the town square. The square was less populated than before, so Naryan reached his hand into his chain mail and brought out the grimoire.

He flipped through it for a few moments, finding the symbols he was looking for on different pages until he had constructed in his mind the rune that he needed. He reached his hand out and drew in the air, his fingers aglow as he peered around the corner again.

An apple wriggled off the table and rolled along the ground, crossing the entire square and rolling into the alleyway. The woman didn't even notice. Naryan laughed and picked it up. Not *exactly* what he was trying to do, but the result was good enough. He rubbed the apple with his sleeve until it was shiny, then bit off the bit bruised by where it had landed on the ground. The sweet and sour of the apple dripped into his mouth as he bit into it with a crunch, and his mouth watered further. An apple had never tasted so good. He finished off the rest in a few bites, holding large unchewed chunks in his cheeks while he flipped again through the grimoire, searching.

He set his sights on an egg this time, knowing that knew there was less room for error. He wrote a rune again, his cheek still puffed on one side with the apple as he focused. This time the egg flew off the cart, straight across the square, and into his outstretched hand. Grinning, he cracked it on the wall and held it above his tilted head, letting the white and the yolk run into his mouth. This was the first time he'd eaten in what seemed like days, and his stomach ached as his mouth finally tasted food. He threw the shell on the ground, and wrote the rune again, hastily this time in his excitement. The egg rolled off the cart and onto the ground where it cracked and oozed over the cobblestones. The lady at the cart noticed something was amiss and looked around for a moment, before continuing to stare off at nothing in particular. Still hungry, but not wanting to arouse suspicion Naryan slinked off back through the alleyway in the direction that he'd come, entering through the back door of the inn and into his room, and shut the door before falling onto the bed. He was still hungry, and sleep did not come easily.

Naryan was awoken by a pounding on the door.

"Open up in there." The innkeeper's voice was muffled through the poorly-sealed door. "You don't go getting to sleep without paying!"

"Go away." shouted Naryan, "I'll pay you in the morning."

"Damn guards," the innkeeper's voice trailed off as he limped away, "always taking liberties cause they get to carry around a spear."

Naryan flipped over to his back and tried to adjust the very lumpy sack of hay that was supposed to be his mattress. It was smelling more and more of mildew as the night progressed, and sharp pieces of hay poking through the rough sack made him question if it was really the 'best inn in Grainridge'. It probably was the only inn, Naryan realized, so maybe the man wasn't a liar afterall.

He grumbled to himself and closed his eyes, his stomach grumbled again.

Less than two weeks ago I was a king. A king with an army, and a full belly.

He pulled the thin blanket tighter across his shoulder, and turned from one side to the other.

And a nice bed. Einar was right–I had to lose it all and become nothing. But do I really care for those things? I'll have to think on it for a while. They were luxuries, sure, and convenient, but I don't truly miss them. Life is simpler on the road, so long as I could get a little food. Perhaps I could find a small job and stay out of the streets. Perhaps even get my own cottage. Maybe have a few goats and chickens and a nice garden to grow my own food. I could start my own plantation and hire on my own workers.

Naryan shook his head and chuckled,

But I've had more than that. No, that won't make me happy. I've had endless wealth and been miserable. Only a moment ago I just wanted a meal, and in the span of a few seconds I've jumped to an entire plantation. Nothing will make me happy, and so to be happy I must have nothing. There is no step up without avarice taking hold. There is having nothing, or always needing more—no inbetween.

I truly have lost it all. Even Sherry.

His throat tightened at the thought of seeing Nightmare bear her away earlier in the day.

How could she abandon me? What did I do to deserve this? I'm at my lowest, and she leaves me. What kind of terrible friend does that? I could be dead, and she wouldn't care. We used to be friends. She said she can't trust me anymore? Well I can't trust her anymore either, clearly. In my moments of deepest despair, I've never abandoned her. I even recall chasing her through the woods that night when she got upset and left the carriage. Why does she get upset so easily? It's as if the world is against me and I have nothing left. My father is dead, my step-mother calls for my death, Sherry has abandoned me, and my kingdom is in shambles.

It was then that he brushed a tear from his cheek and his jaw set, and his brow changed from soft to a glare, and self-pity turned to vengeance. Anger played through his mind into the darkest hours of the morning, and he still lay awake, red-eyed and sleepless even as the sun began to peek through the shutters of the room.

He was then shaken by a pounding on the door, and he heard the innkeeper's voice demanding his rent, and thoughts of wrath rushed through his head.

Chapter 17

Naryan rose and donned his helmet, grabbed his spear, and tied the tablet pouch to his belt before slamming open the door and staring down the innkeeper.

"Where's your keep fee?" the man spat, "I demand it immediately–you're a thief as far as I'm concerned."

"Thief? You don't know what I am."

He grabbed the old man by the collar and pushed him into the wall where he crumpled. Naryan stepped over the moaning man with barely a glance, and headed to the kitchen. He ransacked through cupboards, finding little more than small sacks of oats for porridge, but that would do. He ripped one open, grasping a handful and stuffing his mouth with the dry grain. He chewed it for a second, but his parched mouth did not accept it well so he found a small barrel of beer and held it above his head, letting the golden liquid pour into his open mouth.

He gorged himself on beer and oats until his stomach bulged against his chain vest, and he wiped his mouth with the back of his hand as he moved towards the front of the inn to leave. He found the old man had crawled out the front of the door and was partially in the square, moaning. Naryan saw that the square was not as empty as he'd have thought it would be for so early in the morning, but it seemed that the town was full of early risers looking to sell their wares before the heat of the day.

The old woman from the produce cart was bent over the old innkeeper, attending to him, and a few men were running over from corners of the square to see the commotion.

"Him." the old man pointed a wavering finger at Naryan as he came through the doorway. "He fell on me. I only asked for my tenant's fee."

The three men arrived, others approaching behind them, and each gave Naryan a wary look for he was still in the guard's attire.

"What's the meaning of this?" spat one of the men. "Attacking the elderly in their own homes? You are not deserved of your post."

"He's a deserter." croaked the old man. "Told me himself yesterday. What kind of man runs from his troubles and then preys on the weak? No man if you ask me."

Naryan glared at him, but said nothing and moved to step over him to leave.

One of the men blocked his path, palm outstretched to stop him.

"I don't know where you think you're off to. It looks like there's a little justice needed here."

"Do not lay your hands on me." growled Naryan, "I'll be on my way and we'll forget this happened."

"There's no forgetting," said the man, reaching out to grasp Naryan's arm.

Naryan wrenched it from him, laying a blow to the man's face with the other hand, and ducking away from the others. The old lady screamed and fell across the innkeeper as anger overtook the posse and they rushed towards him.

He swung the spear around, and the men stepped back, wary of its sting as Naryan held it out with two hands. The men rounded him and Naryan saw that his escape routes would soon be cut off so he took the offensive. He feigned a jab towards one man, who stepped to the side, but then Naryan fully thrust, catching the man and piercing into his side.

It went in deep, for the man was unarmored and wearing only a thin tunic. The man gasped and held his side as Naryan tried to wrench the spear away, but it was stuck deep inside him and did not pull out immediately. Naryan saw that the other men rushed him so he turned to sprint away, but he was laden by the armor and the men caught up to him in a few strides. One wrapped his leg and the other shoulder-charged him, so they tackled him to the hard cobblestones of the town square and further beset him.

A crowd was now drawn from the commotion, and Naryan found himself pinned under a large man who sat on him, while he was beaten from all sides by the others. Gasping for breath, he felt the large man dismount him, while many others grasped onto his legs, dragging him across the square. As he was taken, he saw the body of the man he had stabbed lying in a pool of blood and surrounded by townspeople. Naryan was then raised up and set down onto a wooden chair, and a rope was wrapped around his chest.

One of the men that had subdued Naryan spoke to the gathering crowd,

"This man is a criminal of thievery, assault, and murder in hot blood, all by the eyes of many witnesses–and a deserter. Where is the constable?"

"He is on the road," said another, "headed to the capital."

"Well, we're in need of a verdict."

While men around him were distracted by the discourse, Naryan's bound hands felt at his belt for the pouch of tablets as his heart beat faster. He wriggled his fingers to the interior of the pouch but his throat tightened as he felt crumbs of cracked clay, for the tablets had been crushed as he fell on them in the ruckus. He felt around more, holding his breath, and managed to pull out a single, uncrushed tablet. He glanced down at it to see it was *swiftly-earth-rise,* and he palmed it, biding his time for the right moment, as the man continued.

"Bring the shackles then, until the constable returns."

But the gathering crowd had turned into a mob, and cries of "the gallows" could be heard among the yells. Naryan stiffened at the word, and looked around the square for a gallows, but did not see one.

The man thought for a moment and looked at the mob before nodding, and the crowd grew more wild at his affirmation.

The rope around Naryan's chest was slipped off, and he was hoisted up by his underarms and dragged forward. His helmet was cast away with a clank as it bounced on the ground and his hands were bound in front of him. He looked up to see that a single beam protruded from one of the tallest buildings in the square, and out of the corner of his eye he saw the length of rope being passed from one man to the next through the crowd. He was restrained on either side, and he saw two men hoist another man up to tie the rope around the protruding beam.

The man yelled out to the crowd,

"For his crimes against the public, in the eyes of multiple witnesses, this man is sentenced to death!" he turned aside to Naryan and asked, "Uh, what *is* your name?"

"King Naryan."

The man laughed in return and threw his arm around Naryan's shoulder as he yelled,

"King Naryan is sentenced to death! We're executing the king today–even better!" The crowd jeered. The man looked again at Naryan,

"At least you've got a sense of humor about your death. More of us could use a little jest in life. Unfortunately, there's often not much to laugh at in the face of hunger, war, and the crown's taxes."

Naryan opened his mouth to protest, but the rope was strung around his neck as he was lifted into the air by the men, and a stool was set under him. He felt its edges with his feet, and fought to keep his balance, perched on the thin seat.

"As you'll notice, 'your grace'–our gallows here aren't exactly regulation. Not tall enough for a long drop, only a short one. You might want to," the man motioned to his neck, "not fight it. Just let it happen when you fall. If you tense too much, you might find yourself with nothing but a strained neck and a long death of suffocation. You won't be coming down until you're dead–however long that takes."

Naryan did not look down at the man, but set his jaw and glared straight ahead.

"No sense of humor now, eh?" The man set his boot onto the stool, "Any final words."

Naryan nodded and opened his mouth to speak, but the man interjected,

"Pity." and kicked the stool out from under him.

It was indeed a short drop. Feeling the stool topple beneath him, Naryan purposefully clenched his neck with all his might as the rope's end brought him to a jolt. His neck did not snap, but his vision reddened around the edges from the sharp pain that shot through his nape and down his spine. He felt the noose tighten its grip around him as he swayed to and fro, hanging from the beam as a pendulum.

The man looked up at in reproach, and shook his head with a grimace,

"Shoulda listened."

Naryan tried to inhale but his airflow was inhibited by the rope's clutch, and he felt the rough twine rubbing back and forth against the soft skin of his neck. The mob cheered as Naryan fought to keep consciousness, and wriggled his tied hands. His hands, however, would not come loose. With every extreme of his swing, he rotated a little further until he finally faced the building from which the hanging-beam protruded. His eyes went to the structure's foundation, and with both hands, he cast the tablet to the ground at its cornerstone.

The earth churned beneath the foundation, and a hill of rocks and dirt began to push itself up at the structure's corner. The sound of splintering wood cracked through the air, and the shattering of windows sounded from all around the building. It creaked as its corner was lifted, and its integrity broke as its structural beams were disarrayed.

The beam that Naryan hung from snapped off of the tipping building, and Naryan fell to the ground, landing on his side. The beam bounced off the ground near his head with a hollow thunk, before clattering to a rest. His hands shot to the noose around his neck, loosening it, and he gasped in deep breaths of air.

The noise of the crowd turned to yells of confusion, those nearest to the building backing away as it tumbled. He pushed himself up to his knees and saw that the closest men were a stone's throw away, and hesitant to come near to the building since it still quivered at the new arrangement of its foundation. Naryan wriggled his hands between the ropes, finally freeing them this time.

He stood, looking to flee to the safety of the road, but instead saw the face of the old innkeeper, jeering at him from the crowd. The old man stood healthy without support, and he pointed at Naryan with a cackle. Naryan's head grew hot at the innkeeper's ruse, and he clenched his jaw when their eyes met.

The innkeeper yelled, and a few of the crowd stepped towards Naryan, but he did not run, instead reaching his hand into his mail, feeling for the grimoire, and grasping it. He withdrew it, holding it out in front of him, open, as the front of the crowd approached him, and he traced the written runes with glowing fingers as he read.

Behind him, he heard the mound of earth that had displaced the building sifting, and small stones squirmed themselves loose from it. One by one they whirred by Naryan, hurling themselves into the approaching men. Thuds of the impacts filled the courtyard and the men fell, causing those behind to trip. The mob shifted into a rabble; confusion hung in the air and the commotion turned to yells as they scattered.

Naryan traced his finger in the grimoire again, this time stepping forward towards the center of the evacuating square. The wooden beam which had held him only a minute ago lifted off the ground and spun towards the fleeing men. It contacted the first few, batting them through the air, and Naryan saw their broken bodies flung across the square. He bade the beam to return, and it floated next to him while his eyes scanned for the old man. He bared his teeth as he saw him retreating into the inn, and ran towards it, the beam suspended next to him as he went.

The square was now silent and emptied, save for the bodies of the dead laying scattered across it. Naryan came to stand in front of the door of the inn and touched it. It shifted on its hinges with a squeak, before he thought better and stood aside, writing the beam to crash into the side of the structure. It shot forward straight, like an arrow, cutting down the door and planting itself into an interior wall. Naryan wrote again and it spun, toppling supporting beams and splintering walls. The inn was already decrepit, and stood no chance as its thin walls were torn apart by the whirling beam.

It only took a few moments of flying wood and cracking shingles before the roof caved in as the supports beneath it were destroyed; the entire structure was demolished into nothing more than a pile of debris. He peered through the settling dust until he saw the old man's mangled arm protruding from beneath the refuse. He wrote another rune and the beam turned on its end; he wrote again, and again, and again, the beam now pummeling the same spot incessantly as he screamed until his throat was sore. The beam itself cracked, and he stopped writing, falling to the ground in a fit of coughing as he held his raw neck with both hands.

The courtyard was now quiet, save for his sobbing, and he held his face in his hands as he cried. He threw the grimoire to the ground with a slap, and lay back, his head now resting on the hard cobblestones as his bleary eyes looked up at an otherwise pristine day. While he lay, he felt a moistness on his hair, and put his hand to it. He held his hand in front of his face to examine it, then rose to his knees and saw that a stream of crimson and a stream of purple ran from different sources within the wreckage. His throat tightened at the realization that the crimson was certainly the blood of the broken old man, but then his mind turned to the purple, and he smelled the wine in the air.

He gathered the grimoire from the ground and tucked it into his chainmail before shifting some broken boards and thatch until he found the cracked casket leaking the wine. He pushed the rubble aside until he was able to grasp the casket, and pulled it from the ruins. He turned it around for a moment, finding where it leaked and put his mouth to the crack, sucking wine from its innards until he gasped for breath. He turned the casket over again, finding the cork in its hole, and grasped it with his teeth. He pulled until it was freed, and lifted the casket over his head to drain the wine into his mouth.

It burned his throat but he did not stop, and he chugged mouthfuls of it, even as it spilled over the edges of his chin and onto his clothes. He threw away the empty container and went again to the debris, digging for another casket, for he was sure to find more in the ruins of the tavern. For a while he dug, climbing over ruined walls, beams, and disheveled thatch, until he was able to see another even larger casket deep within the rubble. Still, it was covered with heavy beams, interlocked with one another that he strained to push and pull, with no avail. He pushed out a breath of aggravation before clambering down from atop the pile, and standing in front of the ruins.

He brought forth the grimoire again, writing runes one by one, and the debris sifted, moving beams here and there until finally the casket was free. It lifted itself from the pile, and set itself down onto the ground next to him with a clank. By now a buzz had started to set in his head, and he smiled at the wine in the casket on the ground in front of him. He squatted to lift it, finding that it was too heavy to lift, so he cast a rune to suspend the casket in the air, and another so that the cork pulled itself out. He stood there with his hands on his hips and a look of satisfaction before tilting the casket down to pour into his mouth and drink deep.

Naryan now sat in a daze under the overhang of one of the untouched buildings of the square. He was aware enough to see that the sun had run its course in the sky and that night was now approaching. There had been no sign of the townspeople throughout the day, and he was sure that Grainridge was now abandoned in light of his rampage.

His chainmail was cast aside to the ground in a rumpled pile, and he now wore nothing but a tunic with sleeves rolled up, and plain, coarse pants. The grimoire was tucked into the back of his pants, hidden by his shirt, and his boots were sitting off to the side, tops stained purple by the retching of his indulgence.

The first pile of vomit he'd produced that day had puddled near the front of the inn, thick with the oats he'd gorged himself on that morning. Though it was now dry, crows picked at it, and others arrived to investigate the corpses that lay unmoved from where he'd slain them. His beard was matted with thick spittle, and his clothes smelt of wine and bile, and piss leaked down his leg in his stupor.

His shallow breathing and open eyes were the only sign that he lived, though when he saw that more crows gathered round the corpses, he stirred. He pushed himself up to sit, wavering as he steadied himself on the supporting post of the overhang. He exerted himself to a stand, his limbs languid and head hazy, as he put one foot in front of the other, stumbling towards the nearest corpse.

He waved his arms at the birds, slurring with hoarse voice,

"I'll save you. Gettaway birds. He doesn't deserve that."

Partway to the man he stumbled and fell, and though a few of the birds fluttered, they still stayed–feasting.

"I'll show you." he managed to push out, holding his hand out. He widened his eyes as he focused on the blur in front of him and wrote the rune, *swiftly-whirlwind-there*. Nothing happened. Again he wrote, more deliberate this time, but there was no glow of his fingers, no twisting of wind–not even a breeze drifted across the open square. The pecking and squelching of the birds continued amidst ruffling feathers.

Naryan tried again to stand, but could not, so he dug his fingers into the grout of the cobblestones and dragged himself along, coming closer and closer to the corpse and birds. As he came nigh the birds squawked at him, eventually retreating and flapping away to the other fowl-laden corpses, leaving him to come to the first man. The man's sockets were already gaping, the easy flesh of the eyes already consumed by the fowl, and even the skin on his face and hands were mostly stripped. Bone poked through the man's cheek and in places on his knuckles, and even his clothes had begun to shred from pitiless beaks.

Seeing the man's face, Naryan wretched again, expelling little more than a dripping string of bile that stuck to his beard. He tried to push himself away, but he was too weak, and lay on the ground next to the man as a wave of weariness surged through his body. He closed his eyes and breathed through his nose as his surroundings dulled into blackness and sleep overtook him again.

He did not know how long had passed before was stirred by a sharp pain in his hand, and he shook it, bringing it closer to his body. He rolled, drifted into sleep again, where he dreamt of needles piercing his skin, over and over, on his hands and his arms, and his face. The pain of the needles soon turned to that of bodkins, and he opened his eyes to find that he was covered in crows who pecked at his face and exposed hands. He yelled and shook them off, feeling that blood seeped from nicks in his brow, cheekbones, and eyelids.

He shook his head and saw that the birds still feasted on the other corpses, and pity fell into his stomach like a stone. He still could not stand so he pulled himself again along the cobblestones, coming to the next fallen man. The birds did not even move as he came, instead mocking him with black eyes as they feasted, until finally he pulled himself up by the man's shirt and waved his arms away to scatter them. This man's face too was eaten and gaunt, even worse than the first, for the birds had been at it for a longer time.

He heard caws from behind him and saw that the birds had retreated from this corpse and moved to the one that he had just left. He turned to move back to it, but knew it was a battle of attrition that he would not win. Instead, he collapsed onto the corpse of the man, grasping onto his shirt, his face pushed up against the man's blood-soaked chest as he wailed.

What kind of warrior murders the helpless? What kind of king fells his own subjects? What kind of man drowns his sorrows with wine? No true warrior. No true king. No true man.

He was none of those things—he was just a brash, murderous, drunk. And so he steeped in his sorrows, his tears mingling with the blood seeping from the man's corpse, so that his hair became matted with the fluids. His sobs and gasps for breath, intermingled with exhausted wails were the only sounds in the courtyard for a time, until the clop of horses' hooves on the cobblestones echoed in the square behind him.

He did not even notice them.

The two Erilaz, hooded and cloaked, observed him for a moment, and the crows took their leave from the square en masse with a flutter of wings and echoes of squawks. The two saw the scene of dead men sprawled across the square and the toppled buildings behind, and their noses were offended at the smell of sweet wine mixed with puke and death. The first wrinkled his nose,

"He was here–that's for sure." the first man nodded towards the devastation, "the runner wasn't lying. This was certainly done by his hand."

The second nodded,

"I wonder where he's gone off to, and what got into him. It's very unlike him."

"Ya, well Einar has been a bit touched in the head recently." the man nodded towards Naryan," I wonder if the sot knows where he went."

The two of them sat aloof on their horses, watching with curled lips.

"Well you ask him." said the first.

"Only such a sot would dare stay here in this carnage. He was probably too drunk to even know what happened." the other grunted,

"He is so pitiful that I cannot even feel his spirit," said the first. They both nodded.

"Well, the courier said the hamlet was attacked as the sun rose. Who knows how many leagues away Einar is by now." he nodded to the other and they coaxed their wary horses to the road. "Let us search, and let him grieve for his townsmen."

Naryan woke to the morning sun on his face, though he was still stiff from the cool air. He'd slept next to the corpse all night, and now that he was sobering, he reeled from it. His head throbbed and he moved to the well in the middle of the courtyard and found the bucket near it. He let it down and hoisted it back up, bringing it to his lips to drink the cold water before he finally looked at his reflection in it.

His eyes were bagged and cheeks were gaunt, and his normally well-kept beard was matted and crusty. His breath was rank and his throat was torn on the inside from the bile and yelling of the previous day, and raw on the outside, still bearing the red ring of the gallows. He looked down to see that the padded under-armor clothes he wore were torn and his normally-trimmed nails were filthy and long. He growled at his reflection, finally dumping the cold water over his head and shivering as it ran down his back.

He surveyed the buildings that he'd demolished yesterday, giving only glances to the now cold corpses in the square. He swallowed, his stomach turning at their smell as he passed them by, entering into an untouched building. It was a home, simple and nearly bare, so he stripped his ruined clothing and left it as a souvenir in the hearth. As he stripped, he found the grimoire in his waistband where he'd left it, and turned it over in his hands to inspect it.

When he'd found it, it was unblemished and mystical, but now its cover was bent, and blood and wine had seeped into the binding, staining it. They were reminders of his banes.

He rummaged around until he found clean clothes that fit him well-enough, a bag, and some stale loaves that he stuffed therein. He gave the grimoire one last glance and tossed it into the bag with a sigh, before slinging the bag over his shoulder and heading for the road.

Part 2: The Escapist

Chapter 18

Einar did not even glance back at the hovel, but headed off along the overgrown trail. Naryan would be fine–a little roughing it in the woods wouldn't kill him. Probably. He'd taken a liking to him, even though all his talk of having Einar's head had been wearisome at first. Naryan's behavior was to be expected though–he was little more than an insecure young man with the responsibility of the crown heaped on him. Perhaps being a little less entitled could be a good start, but Einar would deal with him when they crossed paths again. *If* they ever crossed paths again.

Thoughts of Naryan dwindled off as the cadence of Einar's foot and breaths carried him through the woods. He had to get away, for Naryan's sake at least. Reckless as he was, he didn't deserve a death that the other Erilaz would certainly bring.

But to where? Across the sea? He'd be out of their proverbial hair at that point, and certainly not worth tracking down. It was a shame that he'd gotten caught up in this mess. A quick venture into society was all he'd intended, a slow prod here and there before deciding if it was worth it to return. Now after getting caught up in the decimation of a small army and the killing of the two Erilaz, exile was certainly his only option. His victory over the two Erilaz was luck really–he could not contest the strength of the others, for now they would not underestimate him. They'd certainly been honing their skills for conflict in their absence, while Einar had busied himself in other ways.

He'd spent at least the last century in solitude in the forest, and he'd actually enjoyed it. He'd grown fond of the simple things in life; a fresh breeze conjured on a hot day, the glow of a small fire in his hearth during winter, the chirp of birds and the crunch of leaves as he wandered in the forest. He had made his life simple and did not need the complications of riches, or power, feasting, wine, or women. He was happy. And he'd grown to know himself and his spirit in this time. It's amazing what can be accomplished with reprieve from the distractions of society.

Perhaps he would just start a farm and take up drinking again–that would dull him enough to ensure he was never found. He could manage to find some joy in it. Tending to crops and livestock did sound like a lot of work without magic though; he wasn't sure how farmers managed. No wonder they were always so miserable.

The memory of an old friend flashed into his mind–another Erilaz, named Valor. Last he'd heard of Valor the crazy bastard had actually been living in Chromer. He was a good one, Valor. He was the kind of man who would conjure up a laugh boisterous enough to wake up everyone in the house in the middle of the night and then find a way to quell their anger and get them to join in the fun. Often he'd pull a practical joke and clap you on the back afterwards, but then offer to help you with the afternoon's work.

He was different from Einar, for he'd always been at home around the buzz of people, and being the center of attention. It had been a long time since Einar had seen him. Somehow he had managed to hide right under the noses of the most infamous magic haters in the world for most of his adult life, and Einar always wondered how he'd done it. It was a question for another day.

Einar shook his head and thought again on the road ahead of him. Satoria owed much of its wealth to its central location between the surrounding kingdoms. Merchants traveling here and there paid tariffs on their goods in return for protection and well-paved roads. Though Satoria was not densely populated throughout all the lands, the roads were often traveled, and guarded. It was not ideal for someone wishing to remain hidden.

Leaving Satoria was always an option in the long term, but for now, he just had to lay low while the other Erilaz searched for him. He formulated a list of requirements: no local population, not well-traveled, not in the forest near Naryan. His list of options grew thin.

Sallow Hill entered his mind, and he brushed it off at first, but then thought on it again. It had never been high on the list of desirable places to live in Satoria; not close enough to the capital for commerce, and near enough to the edge of the territory to be vulnerable–clearly. It had been just over a month since the raid there, and there was literally nothing left for the people to go back to; they would probably settle elsewhere. Rumors of strange magic would certainly steer any stragglers away from the area as well. He decided then that he'd make for the woods surrounding Sallow Hill, and lay low there until things cooled down.

Einar stuck mostly to the side roads to avoid other travelers, and when he did come across others, a sulky glance from beneath his hood avoided conversation or prying eyes. Every so often he'd stop on the side of the road, writing runes to send out his spirit to search for what may lay ahead. A few quick runes did the trick for these short excursions, and if the other Erilaz were searching for him–it was not here.

The path he took carried him out of the forest and back into the open fields, but instead of heading west to the capital, he headed to the north. The road ran along the forest's edge, never straying too far from it, and never putting him too far out in the open. It provided the reassurance that he could slip into it in just a few moments if he felt he was to be found.

Night was falling, and though he could see the lights of an inn and some houses far off in the distance, he could not risk questions and discovery so he decided to rest within the cover of the forest. It was not an incredibly dense forest, so he made his way in a few stone throws until he found a suitable spot for camp. He cast a rune, beckoning small stones up from the ground. The ground around him shook and the rocks made their way to the surface, twitching to pull themselves free. He gathered them, making them into a ring, and cast another rune so that twigs from the ground around him spun and flung themselves in a pile at his feet. He gathered those too, sparking a small fire from flint that he carried, and coaxing a light breeze to feed the kindled sticks.

As the fire cracked he crossed his legs and sat near it, reaching into his cloak and withdrawing his canteen. He swished it around for a moment, feeling that it was nearly empty, and tilted his head back to drain what little was left. He set it to the side, keeping the lid off, and dug again in his cloak, coming up with a brass dirk wrapped with a leather handle.

While on his travels, he always carried this dirk with him, though it was not meant for combat, for its point was dulled. He wrote a rune so that the dagger suspended itself above the canteen, with its point down. Again he wrote, this rune to chill the blade and another to brush a gust of wind across it. The air left its moisture behind as it brushed across the blade, condensing it on the cooled metal dirk so that water dripped down the blade into his canteen. He moved to sit against a tree a short ways off, and watched the slow drips of water filling the canteen in the firelight. He slept lightly with his head resting against the tree.

The morning came and he rose at first light, jumping up and stretching his cold back before heading back towards the road. As he left he wrote a rune without turning, and dirt kicked itself over the coals of the fire, and the stones flew off, dispersing themselves amongst the trees with a rustle of leaves.

The rest of the walk to Sallow Hill was, thankfully, uneventful. He avoided the other hamlets in line with the journey, opting instead to pick his way around them through the woods, which added some time. Still, he wasn't in a rush, and still made it before the eve of the next day.

Sallow Hill, he thought, should probably be renamed. It was now nothing more than a sooty mound thanks to him. Nothing grew on it, for it was still charred from the battle, and as the crunch of his boots carried him up to the top of the small plateau where the village had once sat. He knew that the fine soot was a mixture of wood and powdered bone and dried flesh. He drew absent-mindedly in the soot with his foot before shaking his head and heading to the far side of the clearing where the forest would provide him some shelter.

He was right–nobody had come back. If they had, they had probably seen that there was nothing left to rebuild and turned to whence they came. The silence in the meadow reminded him that not even birds chirped, and that all life had probably fled this crematory.

He spent his first night at Sallow Hill much like he'd spent the previous night–with a small fire and a wary eye. As morning dawned this day, however, he immediately got to work; if he was going to be spending any time here it might as well be comfortable.

He looked up and saw the blue sky peeking through the greenery; it was only a few feet across. That would not do. It had to be larger for a dwelling–plus he liked sunlight coming in from above the trees at midday. He surveyed the trees and ground around him for a moment, thinking, before writing a rune. The ground where he looked sunk in, creating a hole, deep and wide, and he wrote again a few times until there were five large holes in a row.

He wrote again, this time the ground beneath an oak tree sifted, and the entirety of the tree lifted off the ground. It shook itself in the air, its roots convulsing as dirt rained down on where it had once sat. The sound of crashing branches above him did not draw his attention, nor did the flutter of leaves that cascaded down around him. The tree moved towards one of the holes that he had prepared, its taproot slithering deep into the dirt as the other roots in the system writhed into their new home. Still Einar's hands moved, continuously writing as he worked, and another oak lifted, and another, also planting themselves into the holes that he'd dug, until all the holes were filled, and a neat row of evenly-spaced trees now lined one side of his new clearing

He looked up and smiled, nodding at the larger window to his new clearing that he'd made as the blue sky expanded over his head. Birch trees still littered the clearing, and instead of replanting those as he wrote, they ripped themselves up out of the ground. As they rose the cracking of snapping trunks filled the forest, and they evenly split, creating lengths of logs that lay themselves into cords in the midst of the clearing. The smaller branches with leaves that ran up their trunks also tore themselves off, separating into separate piles, all the while Einar still wrote.

The earth in the clearing was all upturned from the displacement of the trees, and Einar wrote again, this time the stones dislodging themselves from the earth and falling into separate piles in accordance to their size. When this too was done, Einar wrote again, and the larger stones with flat sides embedded themselves in rows in the center of the clearing, forming a simple foundation for what would be his new home. Smaller stones intertwined amidst the larger ones, and the gravel in between those, and they condensed tightly so that they did not even budge as Einar stepped foot onto it for the first time.

He stood in the middle of the foundation and called the birch logs to him with the runes, each of them embedding themselves upright into the ground at the perimeter of the foundation until a wall around its entirety had formed, save where the door would be. He drove in shorter ones in the wall opposite the doorway to leave a window for light, and surveyed the walls that stood just taller than he did. He reached his hand out to feel the driven wall, and pushed against it with his hand to find that it was sturdy.

He nodded in approval and stepped out into the clearing, writing again. A tree opposite him violently shook, its leaves raining down towards the ground, but he wrote again. A breeze now captured them in a swirl so that they all lay together on the ground in a green pile. Einar wrote again, and the leaves picked themselves up into a ball, coming then towards him while packing tighter and tighter. The ball of leaves was in front of him, rotating and condensing until green juice dripped from it, puddling on the ground. The dirt became mud, and Einar wrote until the mixture of water and mud had mixed into a clay. Stones then collected themselves, coming together to build a hearth and chimney in the room, even as the clay molded itself in between the stones, to seal and keep its structure.

Once the chimney rose above the walls, the remainder of the clay spread itself into the empty grooves of the walls, while more branches laid the beams of the roof, and sticks and leaves that had been stripped from the trunks layered themselves on top of the roof beams as a thatch.

It was now nearly complete, save for a door and a bed, and Einar surveyed his craftsmanship. It had taken him less than the whole of an hour. He shook his head, recalling the feats of Satoria in his youth. Now, they were all but peasants, beholden to hammers, shovels, and the stamina of their arms.

It had now been two weeks since Einar had arrived at Sallow Hill, and as far as he was concerned, it wasn't so bad. The peace and quiet, that is. He hadn't seen nor heard another human since he arrived and he was much enjoying the difference from the bustle of the capital. The landscape itself was nothing to glorify though. Beyond the edge of the forest, Sallow Hill was still dark and barren, and the grasslands around it were now browning from the heat of the summer. Still, the trees provided good shade, and his clearing was more and more like home.

He had arranged a few more trees in rows around the perimeter of his clearing and tilled a garden that was now lined with small stones. He had spent some time walking through the surrounding woods, finding wild berries and carrots and onions, and brought the seeds back for cultivation. They had not yet started to grow, and wouldn't for a while, but he kept the ground moist with water pressed from the leaves of the trees and kept the tree's discarded leaves out of his clearing. Much of his days were spent in meditation and retrospection, which he now sat in.

He looked back on the past couple of months and thought on how he'd arrived to the point where he was now, exiled at Sallow Hill instead of his old forest. Pity, was his problem it seemed. He could be alone in his old home if it weren't for pity of Satoria, and in turn, pity of Naryan.

He hadn't often traveled from his old forest home, for he enjoyed the solitude and had everything he needed. Every so often, however, he'd venture to one of the nearby Hamlets and gather any news, or indulge himself in a portion of butchered meat. He came by the occasional rabbit in the forest, but something about the damn bovines just tasted too good to pass up.

His most recent trips to the hamlets had pricked his heart. The filth. The poverty. The malnutrition. The despair. The people were destitute. Einar himself was none of these things. He was not rich, for he did not have money since he did not provide any services, but he was not in want for anything, for he was self-sufficient in every regard. He did not need much so he did not have much, but he did have what he needed. The people did not.

The pity in his stomach had grown, and he began helping the people in the hamlets without their knowledge. His visits became more frequent, and as he came the droughts left, the buildings were no longer in disrepair, and the crops harvested themselves–but the people were unaware of his magic.

He'd often thought of himself as a victim in exile, but seeing the good that he was able to enact in these people's lives, he was pricked in his heart that he should be a champion. He would see magic return again to Satoria, even if he was burned at the stake. He would be its evangelist and stand in the streets of the capital, teaching whoever would learn, so that he could see the day when Satoria would thrive again. If he was killed, then so be it. The people deserved it.

But his plan had failed. His goal had been education and freedom of the populous, but instead, he'd managed to turn himself into a weapon of war–a puppet. He shook his head, trying to clear his thoughts and fall back into a trance of meditation, but his actions continued to eat at him.

Perhaps whoever pushed magic from Satoria had a good motive; perhaps magic had no place in the world, for it could be used for great harm. No, he thought, it was not his place to decide that.

In that moment, he was alerted, for he had written a rune for his spirit to keep watch of the area while he meditated. He jumped up, running to the edge of the clearing and peering towards Sallow Hill. He then saw an Erilaz, robed and alert, walking through the woods towards him.

The Erilaz came straight towards him, not hiding the intent of his path, and called out as he came nearer,

"Einar, come forth!"

He stood, legs spread in stance and eyes wide as he peered for Einar through the trees.

"I know you're there. I come to treat!"

He still hid behind the tree, unanswering, before he felt the Erilaz' spirit watching him, and knew there was no hiding.

"How did you find me?" he called out.

"The same way you'd find someone you were looking for," said the other. "You can't exactly hide."

Einar shrugged,

"And who is it? Arden?"

"Aye." he said, "It's me."

"Well," paused Einar, "What do you want?"

"To talk." Arden took a step again towards the clearing.

"We can talk from here–thank you. Are you alone?"

Arden nodded,

"Aye."

Einar drew a quick rune and saw none other than Arden standing in front of him.

"Ok then, well–go on. You wanted to talk."

"Why did you do it? It's the only reason we're looking for you."

"Do what?" posed Einar.

"You know–kill them."

Ah yes–the Erilaz in the field. Einar grimaced.

"They attacked me. It was self-defense."

"They attacked you? That makes no sense. Why would you destroy half the town? You're a sensible man, Einar. This isn't like you."

"Destroy a town? I don't know what you're talking about."

"Grainridge. What got into you?"

The snap of a twig caught Einar's attention and his head swiveled just in time to see a straight and thick branch missiling towards him, parallel to the ground as if it were hurled. He dove out of the way and it shattered against the tree where he'd been sheltered.

"You fuckin' liar!" shouted Einar from the ground, and he heard Arden let loose his own swears as he started sprinting towards the clearing. Einar saw movement from the direction where the branch had come, and saw another robed figure start running towards him. How the Erilaz had hidden from him, Einar had no clue, but there was no time for pondering.

Einar rose to a crouch, seeing that the other Erilaz in the woods was still coming towards him. The Erilaz stepped over a log, but Einar wrote and the log jumped up, catching the man between the legs and sprawling him to the ground.

Einar ducked behind the house and wrote again, this time directing his attention towards Arden, and the earth beneath him sifted, tripping him. Arden' sprint was broken and fell to his stomach with a grunt, even as the ground beneath him continued to sift, pulling him into it. He clawed at sticks and plants on the ground as he was consumed by the earth, but it did not fully submerge him. The soil stopped churning and Arden wriggled to shake the loose soil from his clothing and pull himself out of the hole, while Einar's attention was caught back to the other Erilaz.

The other was still a way out from the clearing, but he glared at Einar from beneath his hood and wrote his runes as he walked. The trees blocking his path towards the clearing ripped themselves up from the earth, flung aside by the magic, and bounded off the sides of other trees with hollow knocks as he cleared a way forward. One by one they were hurled aside,

160

splintering other trees as they went, and toppling others, all the while the wind rushed ahead of him and cleared the ground of dirt and leaves so that he had a clean path.

The trees between him and Einar now gone, he had unblocked vision of the clearing, and directed the timber one by one toward Einar. In kind, Einar wrote his own runes, grasping the trees near him up from their roots and deflecting those hurled by the other. They met in the air and shattered one another, raining down leaves and twigs until the forest was dismantled. Huge disheveled heaps now sat between the two Erilaz, the white splinters of the trees' interior sapwood poking out from the dark brown of their bark.

Einar grit his teeth and shook his head, now turning to his home and seeing that the walls were constructed of a hundred perfectly formed missiles. He wrote and the roof collapsed as the beams dislodged themselves from the dirt one by one and were loosed towards the aggressor. The man saw them coming, writing to pull a tree up from the ground as a barrier. Some were blocked by the thick trunk, but the beams were thin and some passed unhindered through the branches of the tree to impale and break the body of the Erilaz. The tree fell with a crash to the ground, and silence settled over the clearing.

Einar looked to where Arden had been and saw that he was no longer in the hole, but had managed to pull himself up and was disappearing off towards Sallow Hill. Einar surveyed the carnage of the clearing, and grimaced. So much for having a modest home.

It was clear they were not going to leave him in peace. Exile would do no good if they could find him wherever he went. His spirit shone as a beacon. But the Erilaz whom he had just slain had somehow done it; he'd hidden. Einar had searched for him and, even only a hundred yards away, his spirit was invisible. There was indeed a way.

His mind went again to Valor–the Erilaz who dwelt in Chromer. Einar had to find him and learn his method if he was to ever live in peace.

So, he exhaled a breath and resigned himself from his dream of rekindling magic in Satoria, and set off on the long road to Chromer.

Chapter 19

Einar headed north from Sallow Hill, walking along paths in fields and forests as he headed towards the river that marked the border between the two kingdoms. The White River flowed to the west after a bend, marking Satoria's northern border before it reached the sea far in the west, many miles away. Before the bend it flowed north, down from the mountain range that split Satoria's east-northeast from Chromer's south-southwest, fed by snowmelt from harsh winters.

The Shallows was a settlement at the White River crossing that was much larger than a hamlet– an actual city. Boats coming down the river lay moored in a small bay that had been dug into the side of the river on the east of the city, and then flooded. The city's industry consisted lightly of fishing, but mostly of collecting logs that were floated down from the mountains. These industries and therefore tax revenue, paired with the fact that it was better funded by the capital as a garrisoned city on the border rather than a residential village, made it a place worth living.

There wasn't much in the way of forests around The Shallows, and what trees had been there previously had been logged by the populace to build their homesteads. Unlike most of the other hamlets, some of the buildings were built of stone, evidence again of the kingdom's hand and interest in holding the river crossing.

There was probably some official name somewhere in the tax records, but it was commonly called, rather unimaginatively, "The Shallows". The majority of the White River was thirty yards across, cutting deep into the land where it rushed down from the mountains. Here, however, it spread over nearly three hundred yards, slowing to a lazy drip, and thinning its depth in the process. During the summer months when it was not swelled from rainfall, it was only three feet deep, and easily traversable by foot where the silt had been deposited over thousands of years.

It was a mere day's walk from Sallow Hill to The Shallows, and Einar opted to stay the night away from the city, in order to avoid suspicion. Who knows who had been sent to keep an eye out for him, and he didn't really feel like killing a bunch of people just because something had gone awry and he'd wanted a little comfort for the night. He was a few miles from the outskirts, standing on a hill where could see the torches of the town reflecting on the languid water of the bay when he saw the soldiers. There were just four of them on the road, but they had seen him too, and running would be of no use.

They came to him, not aggressive, but wary, hands casually resting on their hilts as he nodded to them in acknowledgment.

"Greetings," said the first. "A little dark to be traveling on the road at this hour. State your business."

"I am headed to The Shallows now, but was visiting my second cousin in the Hamlet over yonder," he motioned to the southwest, "I'm not from around here though–the name eludes me." This was technically true since he didn't remember the hamlet's name, and he couldn't go on saying that he'd just been at Sallow Hill.

The other guards glanced at the first, but he just looked at Einar while he spoke, nodding.

"Well then, strange business they had going on over there–wasn't it? How long were you there for? By chance you didn't see what actually happened–did you?"

"I was only there for an evening goodman–and I didn't notice anything out of the ordinary."

"You didn't notice buildings upheaved from their foundations and torn asunder from the inside? People say a wizard came and laid ruin to the town. Sounds like a load of shit to me, but if you didn't notice anything I suppose it didn't happen at all."

Einar shook his head,

"I didn't see anything."

"I suppose you didn't." said the guard.

Einar gasped and placed his hand on his chest,

164

"You're not supposing I'm a wizard, are you?"

"No, I don't suppose you're a wizard–just a liar. The town's been emptied for more than a week and the people are afraid to go back. Strange you wouldn't have mentioned an empty and ruined town."

"Perhaps I got the name wrong and have traveled further than that–it is rather late, and I've been walking some time."

"Perhaps you came from Sallow Hill? Notice anything out of the ordinary there?"

The other guards laughed, but Einar shook his head.

"No, that's not where I was. Never even been there before."

"Aye," continued the soldier, "Well now we've got ourselves a conundrum–a liar, caught on the road at night, who doesn't quite know where he is, and we're out patrolling for Chromerian scouts. Perhaps we've bagged ourselves one."

The scrape of swords unsheathing surrounded him, and Einar raised his hands, palms out to show they were empty.

"No, no, you misunderstand–I'm simply lost. I come from far in the south in Concordia. I don't know my way. I was told that I should see The Shallows before I went home, as the view of the river with the mountains behind it is something to never forget."

"A tourist, perhaps–but a liar nonetheless. Either way you'll be coming along. Further questions need answering."

Einar protested further, but did not struggle as they bound him, and the group of them then trudged the remaining miles to The Shallows in mostly silence. He wasn't keen on killing the soldiers, and he did need to go through the town at some point to cross the river anyway, so he went along with it.

The hill where they'd collected him was the highest hill in the series of a few that stepped down towards the plains where The Shallows lay. Up to the top of each hill the road carried them, then down into a gulley cut by a shallow stream at the bottom of each. Reaching the final hill gave them their final vantage point of the lowlands before their full descent, and one of the guards yelled, pointing out towards the river.

Rows of torches that had not been there at their last vantage now before blinked to life on the far side of the river from The Shallows. They fed one another, the ranks growing as the flames were passed along until they numbered two thousand in ten ranks spread along the length of the crossing. Bells tolled from The Shallows, and the town's own torches began to come to life.

"Shit." noted the first soldier, nudging Einar down the hill. "Faster. Looks like your friends are here."

"Friends?" protested Einar, but the men did not answer, rushing along as they approached the outer reaches of the town. For another twenty minutes they passed by homesteads where candle lights began to appear within at the sound of the bells, running until they came to the moat and rear gate of the town which was now flooded with fleeing refugees.

"You two," said the first, catching his breath, "With me. You," he motioned to the last, "lock him up somewhere." and they rushed off towards the river where the remainder of the garrison was readying themselves.

His hands still bound, Einar was ushered to a room filled with crates and barrels, and a flimsy door with slats he could see through was shut on him. He watched the guard lock the door and then disappear, and waited a moment, listening to the shouts that hung in the streets and the bells that still clanged.

The Shallows was of strategic location and therefore well-fortified, and in the shape of a five-pointed star. Its thick wall, topped by crenellations, had its foundations sunk deep into the silt of the riverbed, so that the waters of the White River lapped at its base. The wall was thirty feet tall at the tip of its merlons, but the strength of its defense was that siege towers and rams could not be rolled through the river silt to siege it, and any force crossing the river would be vulnerable as they waded.

Two points of the star jutted outwards towards the river, and nestled in the vertex of these arms was a large portcullis that controlled the passage of those who crossed the White River. At this point in the river, it became too shallow for boats other than canoes to traverse, so a wide moat had been carved around the inland side of The Shallows, built with locks so that boats and their commerce could continue around The city and on towards the sea.

In light of the war with Chromer there was now certainly a larger garrison than the usual hundred that stayed here, and the fort bustled in anticipation. The soldiers meant to hold the river had been quintupled to five hundred, and as orders were shouted to them they lined the walls, their bows at the ready. Provided the Satorian defenders had enough arrows, the two thousand Chromerians would not be enough to storm The Shallows.

The Chromerians knew this, and from far across the river, the shapes of figures assembling siege engines could be seen in the flickering torchlight. They had clearly been at it for hours already in the dark, for the machines were nearly assembled. The soldiers on the wall fidgeted, waiting, the enemy well out of reach of their bows.

Einar waited a while, not wanting to be immediately spotted escaping. Still, he bit at the tethers around his wrists, and discarded the leather straps to the ground. He probably didn't even need magic to break out of the flimsy door, but a quick rune burst it open nonetheless and he stuck his head out to survey the streets.

They were empty, save for a few refugee stragglers leaving the city, so now all he needed was to find how he could get out of the town and cross the river–which could be difficult due to the current circumstance. Yells from the wall grabbed his attention, and through the buildings around him, he looked to the sky to see flaming projectiles hurled from the trebuchets arcing towards the outer wall of the Shallows. A delay, followed by splashes from the far side of the wall signified they had fallen short–but the first shots were just calibrations and there were plenty more to come.

Einar climbed the stairs of a structure near to the wall, and surveyed the progress of the siege. Torches carried by the Chromerians, and stuck in the ground on the far side of the river, as well as the factory line of projectiles being lit, showed that five trebuchets had been assembled over the past hours. The sounds of gears and pulleys squealed, followed by the whir of flames whipping through the air as the projectiles descended upon the city. Only a few fell short of the wall this time, and only a few entered the city, for their goal was not the destruction of the city itself but to break the gate set in the wall at the river. Still, the few that had crashed into buildings in the interior of the shallows spread flame around, and parts of the city burned within.

The engineers now having honed in on the gate with more accuracy, the trebuchets loosed one after another in a line, pummeling the gate, leaving the area in pervasive flames and cracks in the walls.

Einar then saw a man, a robed Erilaz, climb up on the wall near to the portcullis, and the Satorian soldiers spread out from around him as they saw the magic from his runes. Even as the next volley was leashed from the engines across the water, he wrote, and a burst of wind pushed the projectiles back so that they fell short and splashed into the river.

Thinking that the gate was soon to give way, Chromerian ranks had begun to enter into the water to wade across the White River. Now that they were partway across the river and nearer unto The Shallows, the back ranks loosed arrows up at the defenders on the crenellations, while the front rank held shields to defend themselves as they marched. The Satorian defenders did not hold back, loosing their own missiles at the wading Chromerians, all the while onagers fixed on the walls hurled stones that splashed in the water around them.

Another missile was projected from each of the trebuchets in a staggered volley, and the Erilaz on the wall directed them to fall amongst the Chromerian troops as they waded, leaving patches of missing torches amongst their ranks. The Chromerians did not stop their advance, even in the face of the burning oil that now floated atop the water and lit the river in the night.

The Erilaz wrote again. A rush of wind began twisting over the far side of the river, growing larger with every turn of its coil until the stars were blotted out by the dark vortex. The garments of the men on the wall whipped, even though they were not near the vortex, and the once languid river churned. The vortex's funnel descended from the sky, touching down on the river's surface, spraying water out as mist at its base. Water was drawn up from the White River, changing its constitution to a spout, and it accelerated along the length of the Chromerians for a single pass. The riverbed was then barren of water, and men were drawn up along with the water and silt, whirling high into the air along its path. Lightning from the friction in the air spread itself across the sky, illuminating the scene, and thunder cracked all around.

As the vortex reached the end of its pass, it disintegrated into nothing more than a peaceful mist that rained down. The men whom it had drawn up were suspended for a moment as they reached the peaks of their ascent, and they too then rained down along with their spears and shields, and their banners flapped in the wind as they fell. The crescendos of their screams carried across the width of the river and ended with the staccato of their bodies impacting the ground.

The Satorian defense, at first tentative at the Erilaz and his runes, saw the result and shouted a rally, while the Chromerians moved back away from the White River's edge, surveying their fallen. Water from the river rushed in to fill in where it had been drawn away by the wind, and waves lapped violently up at its banks.

The tension in The Shallows lightened amidst their cheers, but it was premature, for in the chaos a Chromerian flat-bottomed boat had glided along the length of the wall in the shadows, and came near to the portcullis. It nudged into the wall beneath where the Erilaz stood, unnoticed, while a figure on it struck a flame and abandoned the craft. The crackling of the fuse only lasted a few moments before the powder ignited.

The explosion cracked into the wall and the fireball billowed, climbing up along the side of the wall towards the sky and blasting away the merlons above it. The vessel itself had turned into shrapnel and peppered the defenders on the wall so that none near it survived. Even the Erilaz lay face down and unmoving, blood seeping from his pierced garments.

The wall was not razed, but its integrity was compromised, for now, a huge crack lay between the rest of the wall and where the gate was inset. Cheers carried from the Chromerians on the far side of the river, and the creaks of the remaining trebuchets started again. Their projectiles impacted again and again at the gate and the crack in the wall so that it was reduced into nothing but a crumbling pile of stone, and the soft interior of the town was exposed.

While the waterspout from the now-deceased Erilaz had waried the Chromerians, their numbers were still not dramatically decreased, for only some hundred had perished. The remainder were invigorated at the sight of the fallen Erilaz and the crumbling wall, and they waded in force into the river.

Einar watched from his perch, while the remaining Satorian defenders loosed their arrows, and fell in number as the Chromerian reply volleys rained down on the walls. Einar came down the stairs and walked through the streets, heading to the mangled portcullis where the city met the river, and through it he watched the Chromerians crossing the river and heading towards him.

He looked down at his fingers, and they glowed for a moment as he started to write a rune, but shook his head. This was no longer his fight. Instead, he hid himself in the shadows of an alley near the gate and watched as the city was stormed by a flood of Chromerian soldiers, and the sound of yelling and broken glass carried into the night.

Chapter 20

The city was now being sacked, but before the Chromerians came into its interior, Einar had left through the east gate which led him to the bay and moored boats. He slid into the water and kept in the shadows of the wall until he was at a place where the river's depth was such that he could stand on the riverbed with only his head showing.

He walked and swam underwater, his feet anchoring him so that he was not swept off course by the current, coming up for breaths of air as often as he needed them. Nearing the other bank he had to swim a little ways up the current to stay away from the Chromerian force remaining on that side of the river, before finally dragging himself up on the bank and resting. It was still night, and it was cold, so he wrote a rune to draw the water from his robes, and they were wrung dry as he continued walking.

He didn't feel safe camping so near to the Chromerian army, so he continued on sleepless for a couple of hours, until daylight started to creep over the mountain.

After the river crossing, the road continued northeast, pushing upwards at an incline towards the interior of the Chromerian territory. He continued on through the day, finally resting again at night before continuing on his journey. The days continued, and he spent them walking the road with his spirit wary so he could duck off it at a moment's notice, and nights spent huddled around a small fire tucked into the woods which he kept near to as he walked. Every day was more of the same and mostly uneventful.

At first, the land was stony and mountainous, giving the impression that the land was rugged and barren. It was, when viewed from Satoria, but after the land inclined, crisscrossing through mountains, it finally dropped into a plateau containing forests and tilled fields and finally, the capital. It had been a 10-day journey in total from Sallow Hill to the Capital, and the nearer to it that he came, the more of a knot he felt in his stomach.

The people of Satoria did not know of magic, and to them, Einar's powers were an anomaly. The Chromerians however, knew of its reality. While they did not know of the spirit, they had long been taught of magic's detriment, and it was feared and hated with whispers. Einar knew they even had a method of finding those of awakened spirit, though he had never seen it for himself.

It was said that there was a perfect orb, set in the midst of Chromer, small enough that it could be held in one's hands. Its weight, however, was immense, incredible for its size, and it took a special harness and two oxen to drag it from where it was found a hundred miles away. How it came to be, none can say, for it was not crafted by the Chromerians, nor those that dwelt in the lands before them. Still, it glowed white when a free spirit came into the city, and it was always kept under watch. Wisps of essence dragged towards it from the direction of a spirit, for spirits were always kept under its watchful eye. Einar had never looked upon it himself, but had heard rumors in his youth of how to escape its gaze.

While approaching the capital, he stopped in one of the Chromerian outlying towns and came to the square, finding the local tavern. It was busy when he arrived, and he strode in, finding a corner table and ordering a drink for the first time in nearly a century. The barkeep poured him a tankard, throwing it on the counter so that the black liquid sloshed over the top and darkened along the surface of the table. That was good malt liquor that was now wasted on the counter. Einar raised his finger to write a rune, but shook his head with a smirk, and just let it be.

He instead ran his finger along the rim of the tankard a couple of times, then dipped his finger in and inhaled with his eyes closed. He did miss it sometimes, especially on hot days, but his life hadn't been unusually stressful, until recently, and it was rare that he thought on it.

He raised the tankard and pursed his lips, drawing a light sip and feeling the tingle of carbonation on his tongue. He swallowed, smiled, and raised the mug to his lips again. He was doing this for his own safety, of course. Getting drunk was a matter of life and death.

The cart ride from the outer hamlet to the Chromerian capital was bumpier than Einar thought comfortable, but for the amount he paid he didn't have a right to complain. It was clear, however, that he could not hold his liquor–in this case, he couldn't even hold his beer. The bumpiness certainly didn't help. He vomited twice on the five-mile ride, retching over the side of the cart, and seeing the driver's twisted lip out of the corner of his eye.

"Rough night, eh?" were the only words the cart-driver said the whole ride, but Einar didn't even respond, just held his head in his hands, closed his eyes, and tried to stop the world from spinning. He often drank from his canteen to cool his bile-burned throat, and it was nice to feel a dribble of water going down, rather than a torrent coming up.

The cart came to a stop outside the city gates and Einar hopped down, landing in a pile of horse manure, before continuing on his way without even shaking the shit off his boot.

"Now you take care of yourself, you hear?" he heard the driver yell after him, and the most he could muster was a hand wave without looking back.

He was still drunk, and would be for a couple more hours in his estimation–that's when the hangover would set in, and he remembered they were his least favorite part of the drinking. Other than the puking, since he wasn't used to the alcohol anymore, he didn't mind the inebriation. It felt good, and he was happy–except for the weakness, that is. And the blindness. Having senses and strengths torn was not enjoyable, but at least he wouldn't be discovered.

Ah yes, Valor–the reason he'd come all this way. Now it was time to find the man who didn't want to be found. He'd been to Valor's house once, many years ago, before Chromer purged itself of magic and the borders were more open. There was no way of knowing if he lived in the same house, or if he was even still alive. Perhaps the Chromerians had gotten to him after all.

Einar shook his head and pressed on; trying to find your way to a place you'd been only once before, while drunk, was not easy. A few wrong turns had him lost, but he stayed on populated streets and out of the alleys, and nobody seemed to think him out of place.

The streets themselves were in a semi-organized grid, but still not as organized as the Satorian capital, whose grid and foundations were laid down perfectly by men and their magic. Here, even a simple error was exacerbated over time, and he found he could guide himself toward the center of the city by studying the precision of the streets to due north/south and due east/west. The nearer to the center they got–the more precisely they were laid.

Thus, he found himself naturally at the center of the capital and drawn to the silver ball. It was placed on a pedestal in the center of the square, guards facing towards it, not away from it, and keeping watch at all times.

He focused on his steps as he approached, and with quite some effort he managed to not stumble. He hoped he didn't look too conspicuous. He watched the guards as he walked, but they paid him no notice, nor any of the others milling around the square. He came until he was near a small fence that surrounded it; not a fence to defend it, but merely to keep tourists' fingerprints from ruining its perfect sheen.

Near it and soldered to the fence was a brass placard, an inscription hammered into its surface.

On the night this treasure was found
In Chariot–shining silver, round
It fell in fire from darkened sky
It smote the hill and there did lie
It starves and seeks with reaching mist
And while it eats I live in list

To stand nearby causes divide
I have no spirit left inside

Einar blinked tight his eyes to straighten out the words, and feigned running his hands over the inscription while he steadied himself and hiccuped. It was curious, certainly, and perhaps some sort of riddle pertaining to the orb and the finding thereof.

He wasn't keen on riddles or poetry. If someone was going to take the time to write all that out he'd rather them just tell him what they meant to tell him. Poets–always taking the fun out of everything. He gagged a little, not so much at the thought of poets and riddles, but just trying to keep down the remnants of ale.

He turned away from it, giving one of the guards a gesture of farewell that was ignored. Einar shrugged and aligned himself with a road heading to the east where he supposed Valor's house was. It was as good a direction as any, and so he stumbled off, leaving the square behind and wondering if he looked as drunk as he still felt.

He went along the street for a mile, his boots catching on the unkept cobblestone road every so often and eliciting a swear each time his toes swelled larger. A couple times he nearly stopped to write a rune to set the stones along the street better, but caught himself. He'd certainly be killed for it, could he even cast the rune in the condition he was in.

What a waste of time, he thought, hiccuping, and managing to actually avoid a protruding cobblestone with this step. *Try to help people, and this is what you get.* Now he was in a land full of people who would kill him if they had the chance, and vulnerable as ever in his drunken state. *I could use another ale though.*

He stopped, looking at a building to his left, and bit his lip. That could be it. He closed his eyes, envisioning what it looked like in the past, but he swayed and they opened again so he could steady himself. Yes, definitely–that was it. When he'd last been here, the city's borders had not extended this far. It was, in the past, a small

175

home, lonely, on the outskirts of town. Now, it was well within its bounds, crowded and dwarfed by structures surrounding it. What used to be a tall tree near the road was now a hollowed stump, probably cut down because its roots had raised some of the cobblestones leading up the steps to the walkway.

The old bastard had been here so long that he was now outliving trees. Einar laughed and shook his head, moving up the short walkway towards the house, and stepping up a few steps. He raised his hand to knock on the frame, pausing for a moment. What if he *didn't* live here anymore? What if they called the guards? What if there was another one of those orbs inside? He'd be caught. Executed.

His wandering mind was cut short by a voice behind him,

"Well? You going in?"

Einar turned to see a gruff man looking at him, arms crossed. It certainly wasn't Valor.

"What, were you gonna knock?" the man scoffed.

Einar stared at him for a moment, hiccuping once before gesturing with a slur and a slight bow,

"Afffter you."

The man shook his head and pushed past Einar, opening the door and entering into the darkened interior. The sound of voices, clinks of pewter mugs, and the smell of beer emanated from within. He followed the man, the springed door clapping him on the back of his heel as he went, and found himself in an ordinary-looking pub that one might have even found in Satoria.

He ordered a beer to tie him over here–much lighter than the drink he'd indulged in earlier, and pulled a chair to a corner table away from the chatter of the other patrons.

Well, Valor certainly didn't live here anymore, and now he was going to be a pain in the ass to find. Perhaps he wasn't meant to find Valor. Perhaps he was meant to live the rest of his life as a sot in Chromer. He raised the mug to his lips and took a draught. He swallowed and smiled. Perhaps that wouldn't be such a bad thing. He could get used to this again–minus the puking. He'd build up his tolerance again in time. He'd go out of the city for a few days, conjure up some of the local currency, buy a house–perhaps the one right next door to here, and retire again. The woods were overrated anyway. There was no beer.

Einar's pensive musings were interrupted by a hand gripping his shoulder while his nose was buried deep into his mug. Startled, he turned to view the interruption, still taking a draught of his drink as he did so. A voice rumbled,

"We don't like your kind here."

Satorian? Mage? Itinerant? His lethargic mind ran down the list of what he could be that was so offensive to the man, and the only reply he could push out was,

"Huh?"

He felt himself escorted to a stand and grasped in an embrace by a man spouting a large brown beard with twinkling eyes hiding behind–Valor's eyes. He laughed, pushing Einar back to his chair where he finally finished the pull on his drink, cheeks now puffed, and watched Valor throw himself into the seat at the table across from him.

"My my, how much has changed! I thought you'd resigned yourself to the chaste hermit's life somewhere down south. Never thought I'd see you walking through my doors. Choking down a beer nonetheless!"

Einar wiped a dribble from around his mouth with a hiccup,

"I wasn't even sure it was your door anymore."

"Eh, I've been here longer than the city itself–though nobody knows it. As far as they're concerned I'm my own grandson! The name's Able, if you get what I mean! This building has been in the family for three generations, and I don't intend on selling any time soon. We've perfected the family recipe." He winked.

"That," said Einar, raising his mug, "I can attest to. Don't you want to keep it down though? What if they hear you?" he motioned with his eyes towards patrons scattered around the pub.

Valor laughed a deep laugh and looked down at his finger as it glowed and wriggled,

"Einar, have you lost your touch? Easy as a little air pocket around us to mask the sound. Plus," he laughed again, "they're not the brightest bunch anyway."

Einar nodded, looking at his nearly-drained mug.

"Ah, another for you?" Valor asked, twirling his glowing hand under the table. A mug resting on the bar crept into the air and flew towards them, hugging a wall most of the way before clanking onto their table with a slosh. A man standing at the bar turned to see what had happened in his periphery, brow furrowed. Valor laughed, nudging Einar with his foot under the table,

"Look, that one almost saw! Good thing he's too drunk to know what's going on."

Einar shook his head,

"You're a brash one."

Valor nodded in agreement, taking a sip from his own mug,

"Perhaps I've gotten sloppy, but I've not been caught in a century, so I must be doing something right."

"What's your secret? And what about the orb?"

"My secret?" Valor grunted. "That's a long story. The orb is also a long story, but slightly shorter so let us start there–for the two are intertwined.

"The orb…" he scratched his head, "Ok, I don't honestly know. Nobody does. Well, I know what it looks like, and the circumstances under which it was found, but how it does what it does…" his eyes went wild for a moment, "…it steals away your ability to do magic." he said, as if telling Einar a secret.

Einar watched for a moment before slamming his mug on the table, laughing.

"Ok, you almost had me for a minute there! I went and stood next to it earlier today!"

"Yea, well if you were this drunk–it wouldn't have affected you. It only affects the healthy."

"Guess I got lucky. What happens when I sober up?"

"It will find you."

"Go on."

Valor continued, somber,

"I've seen it before; when it feels a healthy spirit nearby it emits a glow, though the further away the weaker. A tendril of white emits from it, like a mist, reaching towards the spirit so as to grasp it and draw it in. If the spirit is far it cannot grasp it, but if it is near it will take hold of it. As a spirit draws near, the orb burns white in color until the spirit is consumed.

"Again, the Chromerians know as little about it as I do, for they did not forge it–but they use it to this capability. If you are near unto it, or it finds you..." Valor shook his head and took a swig of his drink. "So, you'd better drink up!" he laughed, "The drinks are on me all day today, but tomorrow you had better start paying, old friend."

Einar did drink, but then asked,

"How then do you hide here in its shadow?"

"The same way I hide from you, or from anyone else seeking me. Simple really–task your spirit with an errand, pointless maybe, far away that will take it a while. While it is gone, it cannot be found where you are, so you are hidden."

"But you did magic," said Einar, "Just now–with the mug."

"Aye, well that's the secret of it I suppose. Give it quick errands only to be sent out again. Now it's in somewhat of a far orbit around you–still near unto you so it returns often."

"Genius really," said Einar. Valor shrugged.

"I'm sure anyone could figure it out."

"They did," said Einar, recounting the story of the forest near Sallow Hill.

"Well," said Valor with a grimace, "perhaps I told Victen when came to visit me. Pity to hear he's dead now."

"That was Victen I slayed?" it was Einar's turn to grimace. "What a shame. I never disliked him."

"Well, many have been deceived and recruited by Solis. It is unfortunate."

"Deceived by Solis?" said Einar. "What do you know of Solis and his recent moves? I'd assume you don't get much news here in Chromer."

"Victen's visit was somewhat recent." responded Valor. "He knew where I was from before–found me just as you did. Solis has been gathering Erilaz together for a while now–trying to get into some mischief certainly, with his ambitions for power."

"He was in Satoria when I left," said Einar. "Who knows how or why he came to be there, but he came in violence and I fought with him."

Valor raised his eyebrow and toasted his drink.

"You fought Solis? I'm surprised you're alive. You were never much of a fighter."

Einar nodded his head in agreement.

"Well, it wasn't much of a fight. More of a distraction while we escaped."

"We?"

"Oh yes, I was saving the new young king from death by Solis' hand. Naryan is his name."

"New king? An actual coup led by Solis? I didn't think he'd actually get anything done. Perhaps I'd have joined him if I'd have known he'd succeed." he slapped his hand down on the table with a laugh before staring off into nowhere in particular. "My my–much happens when you're hidden in a bar, helping other people drown their sorrows. I have a feeling in my gut of foul play afoot."

"Oh yes, there is foul play," said Einar, "but to what scope or end I cannot tell."

"A puzzle!" clapped Valor, "I love puzzles!"

"Well, that makes one of us."

"Let us then consider what we each know and work our way backward! Since you've been a bit more in the know in regards to recent events outside of Chromer, you start first."

Einar thought for a moment and then let out a burp before he spoke,

"Well, I am here now since I am an outcast from Satoria. Before that, well–I've spent many solitary years exiled in a forest in the southeast of Satoria. Before that, well–you know the story of the fall of Satoria, since you were in the heart of it, and left a little before I did."

Valor nodded,

"So you don't know much at all. Right–guess I'll be doing all the talking." he said, taking another sip. "In fact, it seems like you don't even know much of the fall of Satoria."

"What is there to know? We fell victim to our own habits and our greatness crumbled."

Valor nodded,

"Aye, but you speak as if it were a stroke of ill fortune, when it was in fact intended by Chromer. Since I've now been in Chromer a while, I have picked up on conversations here and there–missing pieces of the puzzle that I may not have been privy to, had I not been steeped in local lore."

Einar stiffened.

"Intended? Do tell."

"Patience," scolded Valor, scooting back his chair. "We've got all day! Plus, can't have you sobering up or you'll find my tongue-wagging boring.

He rose, greeting some people throughout the room as he walked and came back with a large pitcher, with which he refilled their mugs. He took a draught, wiping the foam from his beard with the back of his arm, and letting out a belch.

"Aaah, now, where were we? Oh yes, let us return to the orb, for I believe it was this artifact that set in motion the events that led us to where we are today. It was found in a stroke of luck, under no ill intent or design, and brought to be set in the midst of Chromer–merely a gift pleasant to look upon, from an explorer to their king.

"In those days, if you'll recall, magic was alive in Chromer too, though perhaps they were more stoic than we in Satoria, for only the learned were Erilaz, and their secrets were kept safe from the Chromerian masses. They were trained, and sworn to secrecy so that the populace could be controlled, but they were strong, and warriors, and studied their craft wholly for conflict.

"The orb was set in the midst of the city, and as years passed they noticed their spirits weakened, though at that time they did not know the orb was the cause of their frailty. They struggled and trained, and studied, but to no avail, for the orb consumed their souls at its will and they were helpless. They could not let anyone know of their new weakness, so they feigned enlightenment, saying they had given up magic in hopes of equality and that it was too dangerous for any to wield. Thus, magic departed from Chromer, though the people have not forgotten magic, associating it only with violence, and having a hatred for it that continues to this day.

"The problem then lay, however, in the politics of it, for now they were surely disadvantaged to us, their Satorian neighbors. Now, you and I know that we ourselves are not necessarily violent men, yet who is to say the king in that day, had he known what I just divulged to you, would not have thrust himself upon Chromer to crumble it? No–we cannot say, for unchecked power corrupts, and all can fall victim to its seduction. The Chromerians knew this, so they devised a plan, cunning and malicious, to see Satoria's magic also dissipated.

"All I have told you thus far is common knowledge here in Chromer, chronicled in public tomes and even discussed in casual conversation. Many a loose tongue of the common sot here in this very room has given me insights that could have changed the course of history had it been known a century ago. But, none of this was ever whispered in Satoria, for it was kept secret from us.

"Now, Chromer knew they could no longer contend with Satoria in battle, so they decided they would undermine them with schemes. Do you recall those years, perhaps across a decade in our youth, when crazed Erilaz sometimes took to the city streets, causing mayhem and death? They were said to be insane, citizens who too often communed with their spirits and lost control–but those were lies, for they were seduced and commissioned by the

Chromerian crown to terrorize their own communities, and once they were slain, their families would live in wealth.

"With people now dwelling in fear, the Satorian crown realized the danger of magic, thinking their own citizenry had acted out in violence, and knew that action had to be taken. They themselves peddled to us those things which dull; you know, for you and I both partook and even now partake.

"But here comes the crux of the mystery–information less easily ascertained, even here in Chromer, for it is often alluded to but never spoken. It is said that there was an infiltrator to the Satorian court, and these attacks were brought by the agent as evidence to persuade Satoria of the dangers of magic, and therefore to dilute the Erilaz. You and I and a few others clung to our souls while watching the power of Satoria crumble in but a few generations. We were outnumbered and fearful of being seen as strange and violent in our own land, so we exiled ourselves to the wild. A few of us here, and a few of us there, we lived, but we are now dissipated and lost, and the knowledge of spirit will die with us.

Einar listened, but he stared at the wall while his eyes glazed as he thought back on those days.

"So, now you know what I do, and perhaps we can live and die together as drunks."

Einar smiled, though his eyes were still moist.

"My friend, I would do this, but I must confess–I am here now because I am resigned to it, but it is not what I desired. I am a solitary man, true, still I am compassionate, and it aches my heart to see the struggles of mankind. They toil, and sweat, and starve, and die, when they have the innate capabilities to rid themselves of their fleshly adversities.

"Nearly two months ago I left my humble forest home, thinking I could live among the people of Satoria again, and teach them what they could do. I saw myself a messenger of hope to the destitute–but I have failed. Now I am exiled again, leaving Satoria a worse place than when I came to it.

Valor nodded,

"Well, we've all failed in our own ways, have we not? Why do you think I live here? Now tell me, since I have no news from outside Chromer, other than whispers of war–what was the crux of your failure?"

"As I mentioned before, it was Solis and some others. They were summoned, somehow by Rhondia–the now-queen of Satoria, though how she knew of them or found them I cannot say for the last I heard they were spread throughout the land."

"A queen rules now when there is a living king? I would ask to delve further into the matter, but politics bore me–so do not digress."

Einar nodded,

"All is intertwined in politics these days. If you are not privy to it then you will be disadvantaged. There is much to tell I suppose, though I am more concerned with answering questions of the future than retelling events of the recent past. The meat of the question is–how did she know who they were, and how were they beckoned? She must have been helped."

"She must have," nodded Valor, "but these are answers that I do not have for I have been preoccupied with fermented cereals and ledgers for the last century. It is all I know now."

Valor rose,

"I have things I must attend to, but know, my friend, that you are welcome here. If you want to make yourself useful around the pub I can offer you a modest wage. Just lay low, keep drunk, and we can live out the rest of our days in peace."

Einar nodded,

"I suppose it is best as such." and he then sent his softened spirit to the wilds to do nothing but twirl leaves in a gust.

Chapter 21

Nearly a month and a half had now passed Einar by while in Chromer, making it the 21st of August. He dwelt in little more than a cleared pantry in Valor's pub, and though it was not even modest, he was used to less. His bed was little more than a pile of sacks stuffed in sacks in the corner, and the smell of cereals wafted from it whenever he fell to it to rest. Still, it was glorious, and every night he slipped into a restless sleep with the room spinning round him and the remnant of a smile curling his lip.

His days were spent slinging pints and scrubbing floors, and while he was normally a solitary man, he'd grown accustomed to the regulars who sauntered through the door, often with a point towards him and a boisterous yell of greeting. They now knew him by name and welcomed him as a *refugee from Satoria, where life was a pile of shit.*

And oh, the laughter. Each day was a ruckus, overused jokes echoing across the room eliciting the same riotous guffaws from men laughing at little more than talk of their own dicks. He could barely tell you their names, but they still gripped each other in greeting, and grasped their arms around each other as they drank. They told tall tales, sang crass songs, and carped over their mistresses into the hours of the morning when they stumbled home, and Einar retired to his pantry. Was he happy? Probably not. Still, his dulled mind didn't know the difference, so long as his belly was sloshing.

The heat of the summer baked the small room, causing the smell of beer, and sweat, and vomit to permeate it. He made it his mission though to keep it clean, and keep it clean he did—even without the aid of magic. *Perhaps this isn't so bad after all*, he thought, kneeling on all fours to scrub a bile stain off the floor. He had been wrong—the Satorians didn't need saving afterall. Hard work was a good prescription for squalor and destitution, and the euphoria of flowing alcohol and laughter was always the perfect cap to the day. It seemed to him that he'd wasted the last century of his life, alone in the wild, when he could have had this.

But in the back of his mind, he knew he was a void. The nagging anxiety of surrender ever reared its head as the buzz receded. It mostly came in the early mornings before he took his first sip, and it was a bitter thought, knowing that the bite of his hangover could only be remedied by the venom that stung him.

Last night had been a night to remember–or barely remember, in this case. Something about an anniversary, or a birthday, or a holiday–it didn't really matter. The drinks hadn't stopped flowing until the sun had started to rise, and Einar felt his head being lifted off the table by the back of his hair. He had apparently passed out, sitting at the table, along with a few other scattered men across the bar. He squinted his eyes, seeing a cheery-looking Valor's face uncomfortably close to his.

"At least you're alive!" he laughed. "Up and at 'em now–we've got cleaning to do before the 'day crew' comes in."

Einar stood, feeling a crack of pain running through his head as he steadied himself on the table. He hunched, retching all over it until his abdomen clenched, and the echoes of his empty gut resonated in his throat.

Valor grimaced.

"On second thought–perhaps you should have the day off. Go on, off with you to your room and I'll see you when you're feeling better. Hopefully sooner rather than later–we've got another day of feasting ahead of us."

Valor chortled as he turned away, and started shaking some of the other late-sleeping patrons from their tables. The laugh was not helpful to Einar's splitting headache. He wiped his mouth with his already-soiled sleeve and nodded a thanks to Valor before stumbling through tables and chairs towards the back of the tavern.

He pushed the door to his pantry open, steadying himself on the door jam before taking another step and falling onto his rumpled sacks. He was still drunk. He pulled the corner of one of his sacks over his eyes, for even the dull light that shone through the cracked door was too much to bear. He lay there, drifting in and out of sleep for some many hours, even hearing the sounds of the pub begin to pick up–laughter, the shuffling of chairs, and the clanking of mugs being slung to tables.

Hours passed again, and this time he woke to realize that he'd pissed himself. It was still warm, and leaked down his leg, soaking his already-unclean trousers until they dripped and the piss puddled onto the floor boards. He clenched his fist and beat the floor where his sacks were, his throat tight and tears blurring the sides of his vision. He was pitiful. His stomach churned, not only from the alcohol but from the knowledge of his lost capabilities, and how he'd regressed.

He stood up, steadying himself against the wall with one hand and looking into a small mirror that hung on the wall. He had only looked into it once since Valor gave it to him, for he hated the gaunt eyes that stared back at him. This time was no different. His once-shaven head, face, and neck now had the dark fuzz of growth on them–patchy at best. His beard was matted around his chapped lips, no doubt from the constant flows of liquids in and out, and his eyes were puffy and bloodshot. He stared into his own eyes for a moment, and barely recognized them for they flickered wild in one moment and to emptiness in the next.

He raised his hand, staring at it in the mirror as he did and wrote a rune, but there was no glow, no trace of gilded light hovering in the air in its path; nothing happened. The corners of his lips turned down, and he bit on his lip to keep it from trembling as leaned on the wall in front of him, staring longer into his empty eyes.

He inhaled again, focused, and wrote, but to the same result as before. He shook his head and sunk back to the ground, covering his face again with the sacks. The sounds of laughter wafted in from the room, and he gritted his teeth in anger at their mirth. He closed his eyes for a moment, but restless he could not sleep, so he sat, crossing his legs and closing his eyes. He breathed in through his nose, his wavering hand stretched out in front of him to write a rune.

187

There was no glow of finger, nor movement of air in the breeze that he commanded.

His throat tightened as he wrote again to the same result. He shook his head, exhaling and controlling his breath as his mind searched for his spirit. An hour passed, and he managed to keep his mind clear, despite the raucous of debauchery going on in the room next to him. He felt a shiver run down his spine as he wrote again, and finally the most gentle breeze brushed across his skin in the otherwise still closet.

He reached out again, focusing more intently this time, calling to his spirit. In his mind's eye he saw that it was weak, a mere wisp of steam where it was once vibrant. He had now written a hundred runes, and wisps of dull golden light hung where they were written, but they were not clear and crisp, only muddled and barely shimmer as he tried to commune with his spirit. He fell into a trance; he could finally feel it again—he was not alone.

Then, the door to the pantry burst open, and a large man's frame filled the door frame. He was in the midst of a laugh, holding a cock-eyed and mostly drained mug in one hand, and steadying himself on the jam with the other.

"Einar!" he yelled, "Get your ass out here, we miss you! Where have you—" but the rest of his sentence was cut short as he surveyed the shimmers of light hanging in the air around Einar and his trance. The ceramic mug dropped from his now unfurled hand, shattering on the ground and spilling its liquid along the ground. He stepped back, hands over his mouth as Einar's eyes opened to see him.

"Shit, no, no." the man mumbled, backing away further into the room. The laughter died down as the patrons' attention was caught towards the man. Valor stepped towards the pantry, seeing Einar and the runes and let out a groan,

He slammed the door and spun to stand between the crowd with his palms facing the man, as if to hold him back. "You're drunk—nothing to see here. Must've been your imagination."

"I know what I saw." spat the man, "he's an Erilaz." The laughter in the room quieted down at the words, and their attention was rapt on Valor and the closet behind him. The man pointed towards the closet,

"He's in there. Writing runes. I saw it with my own eyes! Einar is an Erilaz!"

Chairs scraped along the floor as men pressed closer to the closet.

"No, No." said Valor, "It was nothing more than your imagination–must have been an excellent batch! In fact, everyone's next round is on the house!"

But it was to no avail, for the patrons crowded closer to the door, pushing past Valor to get into the pantry. He tried to hold them back with his arms, but he was thrust aside and the door ripped open. Einar was then broken from his trance as he was grasped by his sleeves and dragged across the floor to the center of the room. Drinks were spilled, tables and chairs were thrust aside, and he was thrown to the center amidst the angry men.

Valor bellowed, raising his hand and writing a rune to lift a table and smash it across the backs of the aggressors. They were brushed aside by the table as it pinned them between other tables and chairs, making a mess of the tavern's furniture.

Before he could write another he was mobbed–crowded by men who grasped at his hands, tearing at his fingers until many of them were dislocated, and he too was thrown to the center of the room. Heavy boots smashed at both of their hands, and the fracturing of their bones was mixed with cracking floorboards. Their hands were now a pulp, splintered bones pushing through their skin and leaving them mangled and quivering.

The mob took to the streets and paraded them along, shouting "Erilaz!" as they went. Their cries echoed through the city, the mob's numbers growing with each block they passed. The two of them were pushed ahead of the crowd, often shoved so they stumbled, and each time they fell on their faces for they could not stop their fall with their ruined hands. Each time they were dragged up again with jeers and set again on their way, being spat upon and pelted by cobbles from the road.

They were brought to the center of the city, a large crowd having now amassed and chanting at them. As they came nigh to the city square, they saw the orb, glowing white at their presence, and the guards watching it warily. Already waiting for them there was the magistrate, guarded by a detachment of *Aetherblades*, having been alerted of the mob in the street. Their capes were crimson and gold, and their helmets had but small slits at their eyes. Their armor was of tempered ceramic, the innards being stuffed with thick padding, and even the joints were sealed shut. A thick cloth was hung over the inside of their helmets over their mouths, and the armor was polished in a flame-retardant, for they were prepared to battle with mages.

The crowd dumped the two Erilaz in front of the waiting magistrate, and he looked down at them over his nose as they were bound and hoisted to stand in front of him. He inspected them for a moment, asking the crowd,

"How then can you be sure they are Erilaz?"

A jumble of voices spouted out over one another, trying to relay the story of the inn, but he raised his hands to silence them, turning his head to inspect the orb. It was still glowing white, even more than before now that they were closer unto it, and whisps were reaching out from it towards the two Erilaz. The whisps' tendrils moved across them as if feeling them until it caressed both of their chests and entered into them.

There was no pain, no sudden jolt of agony, but melancholy and weariness coursed through their bodies, draining them, even as the orb pulsated and grew a little brighter. The orb elicited gasps from them, even as the crowd around grew more vicious in their cheers. Their heads hung as the magistrate motioned across the square, and it took everything in them to lift their eyes to see where he pointed. Cages were there, five of them in a row, set atop tall stone pillars that rose above the square and could be seen from almost anywhere in the city. They looked briefly upon them, but their heads hung again from exhaustion, and they collapsed to their knees in front of the magistrate.

"The laws of the land forbid magic, for it is aberrant, and leads to unnatural violence. I would ask how you plead, but it is irrelevant for the orb illuminates the truth."

Valor spoke, his eyes averted, and laboring with each word.

"Please," he said, "long have I lived here in Chromer–peacefully, and unknown to all here. I have never been violent, nor used it for my own gain. Mercy for my friend and me."

The magistrate shook his head, but Einar interjected,

"Use us." he said, "Against Satoria. I am from those lands but am now deserted from them, and I harbor ill will against your enemies. You do battle with them, but they do not view magic as you do, and will use Erilaz to waylay your armies.

The magistrate gestured,

"Do you not see this orb in front of you? We do not fear Satoria's Erilaz, for if they were to step foot in this city they would be weakened, as you are now. No, we do not need you, nor do we want you."

He stood behind them and grasped a handful of each of their hair, turning their heads up toward the pillars as he spoke,

"It is already decreed that all Erilaz will be sentenced to the cages until you have lost the will to live. Be it a year or a day, you will relinquish your spirit."

He let go of their heads, and they started to fall to their faces but were caught up by the guards and carried off towards the pillars. The crowd spread away from them as they went, and the tendrils followed them through the air, lapping at their essence.

As they were borne towards the pillars they saw that the pillars themselves were descending into the ground, each let down by a mechanism set in their base. When they were thrust into the cages they saw that there were metal gauntlets with unmoving metal fingers set into them. Their twisted fingers were jammed into the gauntlets where they could not even wriggle, and blood seeped from the gauntlets and dripped to the floor of the cage as the doors were slammed and locked.

They knelt in the cages, hands locked away and their wrists shackled as the pillars rose to their full heights, and the muffled sounds of the crowd carried up to them from far below.

Einar could not even look over towards Valor, but with his head hung his throat tightened and he said,

"I'm sorry my friend."

But Valor did not respond, and he leaned his head forward against the wall of the cage and stared at the crowd below.

Chapter 22

The days of their capture were long and tormenting. It was still the midst of summer, and the hot sun baked them in their metal cages, leaving burns on their skin whenever they fatigued and leaned onto a sun-seared bar. The tops of the cages themselves did not provide much protection from the sun either. As it passed over them from morning, to afternoon, to nightfall, it evenly reddened the skin on their faces and heads, leaving them blistered. Flies lapped at the excrement that dripped down their legs, and ate at their open wounds, and they could not fend them off with their latched hands. Though at first the shaking of their heads would startle the flies, the flies soon learned there was nothing to fear, and would not relinquish their grasps–still feasting.

The jubilation of the crowds in the square below had lasted a few days, but was now waning. At first, music, feasting, and vendors littered the square in celebration of their capture, for there had not been an Erilaz found in Chromer in a hundred years. But now it was passed, and the citizenry grew bored, and only the occasional Chromerian would shield their eyes as they looked up to see if Einar and Valor still lived. Even vultures circled overhead, often landing atop the cage with a clatter to peck at them through the bars before flapping off again. Everyone just waited for them to die.

The only civility of their circumstance was the child that was hoisted to them every morning on a cord looped through a ring atop of their cages. He bore with him stale bread and a flagon of bland liquid that was probably supposed to be soup. The first few days his hands shook even coming near them as he offered the food to their mouths, and it dripped down their chins. He also somehow managed to drop both of their crusts to the ground below where a flock of small birds gobbled it while they watched.

The boy's fear lessened as the days progressed, more and more of the little food making it past their chapped lips and into their mouths. The boy spoon-fed them, even gathering the courage to look into their eyes the last couple of days. They felt a bond with him as their only caretaker, even though they exchanged no words with him.

In fact, they hardly spoke to each other. There was not much to say, for they each saw the same things around them, felt the same pain in their forms, and each knew the fate that awaited them. They just waited to die.

But how long would it take? They were drained and weary, not only from the lack of sustenance and inability to sleep comfortably, but also from the orb. They still felt it draining them, even eyeing its whisps still exploring them as they sat, but it was not as intense of an exhaustion or melancholy as when they were next to it. Their distance from the orb seemed to force it to drain them through a thin straw instead of lapping them up from an open bowl, but it was little consolation, for they were still within its influence and their days were numbered.

Ten days had passed since their capture, and while they were not hopeful of survival they each had a grit to live, until their bodies would carry on no longer. The boy had already come and gone that day, and the heat of the afternoon was already rising.

From their vantage point atop the pillars, they could see the layout of the city. Set in its midst, where they were, was the city square, though inaptly named for it was circular in design. The orb was set in its center and surrounding it were shops and buildings and governmental infrastructure as seen in many cities. The pillars on which they sat were planted on the east side of the square, and to the north of the square a small way off was the citadel wherein the crown dwelt.

The city itself had expanded since its founding, and with each expansion over the centuries, there were now multiple layers of fortified walls, concentric around the city square. The city itself was not of a defined shape, however, for it spread out in this direction and that, new districts attaching themselves wherever they could, and new walls were erected as seen fit. This led to a maze-like appearance from above, where gates and walls-within-walls provided the ability to lock down certain districts of the city were they breached. Invading forces would certainly be caught between these divides, and waylaid in the city streets by missiles flung from defenders on the walls.

A vulture, growing increasingly bolder as the days progressed, landed on Valor's cage. Usually he gave a rattle to scare it off, but this time he could not muster more than a glance at it. Einar watched as the bird gripped the top bars of the cage, maneuvering itself around until it was able to sneak its head in through the bars. It snipped at Valor once, but could not reach him so it slid down along the side of the cage, trying to grip the vertical bars with its talons and get to him from a different angle.

Einar shouted and rattled his own cage, stirring Valor and causing the vulture to flap its wings and take perch again on the top of the cage, where it waited. Valor's breaths were labored and he pushed out raspy words as he turned to look towards Einar,

"Guess I, owe you one." It was the first time they'd exchanged words, let alone a glance, in two days. His eyes were bagged and bloodshot and he had to catch his breath to even finish the short sentence. Einar shook his head and returned his own labored response,

"I'm afraid you owe this whole situation to me."

Valor's head was leaned against the bar in front of him, eyes staring at the cage's floor.

"It was bound to happen eventually. I was careless myself at times. At least we had one last good run."

Einar's eyes reddened as he looked at his friend, but they could not even moisten. The vulture cocked its head and readjusted itself as it surveyed them. Again, it lowered its head through the cage to reach towards Valor, but even as Einar opened his mouth to shout at it again it withdrew its head from the cage, its gaze captured by something in the distance. It squawked and flapped its wings, rising to the air and joined a thin line of other airborne vultures moving across the city.

Einar squinted his eyes, seeing a lazy spindle of smoke drifting in the air near the outer west gate, and the bustle of movement in the streets. It was too far away to tell exactly what went on, but from his vantage point he could see the movement of groups of soldiers running towards the west gate, and the toll of bells clanging in the distance.

There was a deep rumble as if the earth itself moaned, and far away in an alley he saw a group of buildings collapsing upon themselves and sending a cloud of dirt into the air. The spindle of fire had now thickened, becoming darker and wider, and flames licked up from its source. It whirled, growing into a flaming cyclone that traversed along the length of a city street before dissipating, into a lingering cloud, and the sound of shouts on the wind now trimmed the tolling bells.

Einar watched as the carnage continued, moving from the outer gates through the city and nearer to them.

"Valor." His voice cracked in his throat once, then he said it again, louder. Valor stirred, looking once at Einar before his eye was caught by the hanging smoke and movement in the city streets.

He too peered down before Einar asked,

"A hallucination?"

Valor shook his head,

"No, I see it too, but I cannot tell what its cause is."

"An Erilaz." said Einar, "It must be."

Valor managed a wheeze,

"You tease me. There are no Erilaz here, nor if they came could their spirit persist in the presence of the orb. Look at us."

"Perhaps they are not yet within its influence. I see its gentle glow now, and its whisps hovering around us, but there is no other wisp moving towards the Erilaz."

"Why then do they come here to Chromer?" asked Valor.

"For us."

Valor shook his head.

"I cannot even hope it."

Einar looked again, seeing the commotion moving through the city streets like a flood pushing through a dry streambed. The Erilaz did not bother to walk through the streets, but instead carved his own straight path through the city and its walls toward them, and rubble and floating smoke were left in his wake.

From his vantage point above, Einar saw Chromerians scattering this way and that, lifeless bodies flung into the air and raining down on rooftops while the structures and fortifications of the city itself were undermined and crumbled. At the helm of their retreat was a man, his hood thrown back and hair tousling in the wind that gathered around him. He held in one hand in front of him a book, and he swept his other hand around, glowing in glory, tracing in the book the staves that bent the world to his will.

In front of him was the innermost wall that surrounded the city square, and it was tall and thick and many of the city's garrison were sentried atop it. The arrows they loosed were thick in the air, but brushed aside by a perpetual upward gust of wind that defended him as he walked.

And as he went, he still wrote, and the cobblestone pavers of the city's roads, thick and heavy, were plucked from the earth and loosed one by one towards the wall and its defenders. With each step, the stones behind him rose as if the whole road was unzipped, and each became a projectile that flew, arcless, toward the walls. The stones impacted the wall in a rhythmic cadence that soon turned into a dull drone that drowned out the rest of the sounds in the city. Wherever they struck, the merlons of the wall were shattered, pushing debris and bodies into the square where they now lay unmoving below Einar and Valor.

But it was not only archers and foot soldiers that attempted to waylay him, for cavalry had been summoned, and the clops of the horse's hooves on the cobblestones echoed through the city as they charged towards him. Pavers that had been readied to fling towards the walls now widely orbited him, and as the cavalry came nigh they were met with swiftly turning stones that punched through the horses and men. The men were flung from their mounts, even as the steeds themselves were torn asunder from their own bodies, and still the stones continued their orbit around the Erilaz. The armor of the men clanked on the cobblestones, and the bodies and limbs of men and horses alike thumped in the gutters. The line of cavalry was now but a heap, and the Erilaz picked his way through the carnage as he continued.

The man came into the square, peering up at the two of them, and Einar saw Naryan's face, jaw set, and a fury in his eye to discover him a captive. But even in that moment, the orb's tendril's sought him out, and as it grasped ahold of him his shoulders sank, the grimoire tumbling from his hand to the ground. The grimoire lay on its face, its pages crinkled in the dirt of the cobblestones, and Naryan looked down at the tendril that pierced into his form. It did not break his physical body, but reached through his robes and chest, and into his heart. The orb drank at his spirit, glowing brilliant while it did, and if taking it as an awaited sign, a century of guards flowed into the square from all angles towards Naryan.

They were not the regular soldiers of Chromer, but the Aetherblades, and their red and golden armor flickered in the brilliant light of the orb. They had formed a circle around Naryan, evenly spread, and they converged on him at the center while he fumbled on his knees to retrieve the grimoire. His hands shook as he picked it up, flipping to the desired page and tracing the rune. He then clawed at the wisp at his chest, seeing that the runes had no effect, and dropped the grimoire, attempting again to draw the few runes that he did know by heart.

A slight breeze rustled around him, but it was not the strength of the whirlwind that he had summoned. He saw then in the square in front of him the face of his spirit, and it was distressed and hazy while it struggled against the pull of the orb. Einar watched from his perch as the soldiers moved towards him, steady in their cadence and confident they would prevail against him in his weakness.

Valor, however, seeing now opportunity in the circumstance, took action, smashing his face against the bars set in front of him. Twice he did this, and a gash spread open on his brow, gushing blood to the floor of the cage where it pooled. He pulled himself to kneel and with his toe wrote a rune.

Einar heard the steel gloves in which he was confined strain, and though they did not shatter, their mouths peeled a little wider, and he was able to withdraw his mangled hands. Einar looked down at them even as Valor shook his head to clear the blood from his eyes while he scratched another rune with his toe. The blood flowing from his forehead formed a stream and bent through the air, coursing towards Einar's cage and finding his hands. His fingers straightened and his flesh ment before his eyes, and he heard the snaps of his bones as they fit again to each other and his hands relocated to his wrists. He examined his hands; before where puss and scabs had covered them, they were now pink and soft and he wriggled them to find they had their full mobility.

The erect stream of blood halted and dripped down again across valor's face to the cage, and he looked over at Einar,

"Call it even?" and he wrote another rune with his foot.

In the square, even as the soldiers came upon Naryan, the orb shifted on its pedestal, now grasped in the hands of Valor's spirit, and it burst into radiance even more than before. The orb moved, pushed through the air at first with great pace, but its speed waned as Valor's spirit lost its strength and influence to the thirst of the orb. Still, it was carried a little further, through a gate to the north east and down the road before there was a bright flash as Valor's spirit was fully devoured. The orb fell to the ground with a clank, its unnatural weight cracking the stones of the street, before rolling further down the road and coming to rest in a nook between two cobblestones. There it sat, throbbing in brilliance from Valor's consumed spirit.

Einar's throat tightened as he watched Valor's form slump forward against the cage, eyes empty, for he had given up his ghost.

Though it was impotent before, Naryan's spirit now grasped onto the earth firmly as it had been bade, for it was no longer within the influence of the orb's radius. The earth around him split open and cracks swallowed up a number of the soldiers, but the others still aggressed towards him from the other sides.

His hands now freed, Einar cast a rune and the cage's lock cracked, the door bursting open with the shatter of metal, and he leaped forward into the air, writing as he fell. His clothes flowed around him, and the wind caught him as he descended to the earth. Dark clouds above thickened, and crackles of static surrounded him, raising the hair on his neck.

The guards below looked up to see him descending upon them, even as cracks of thunder filled the square, the fury of consecutive lightning strikes smiting the ground where they stood. The earth was blackened from where it was struck, glassing the earth in those places, and his foes were cast to the ground.

Their armor, however, was strategically not crafted of metal, and only a few of them lay still, while others rose and again aggressed towards Naryan. Einar landed, set on the ground gently by the wind, and turned to the tall pillars where he had just been kept. He wrote, and the foundation stones at their bottoms cracked one after the other until each pillar was in free fall towards the center of the square. He came to Naryan who had written so that those soldiers nearest unto them had their ankles swallowed by the earth, and they each struggled to free themselves.

Einar grasped Naryan by the collar, writing another rune as he did so to raise the earth between them and the remaining soldiers, and they ran towards the square's west gate.

Behind them, they heard yells from the trapped soldiers as the pillars cascaded down onto the city square. The pillars, now falling, collided with each other in the air so that instead of only five falling pillars there were innumerable shattered rocks that impacted the ground, and they felt the thuds in the earth as they ran.

Through the city they went, not taking the maze of streets but leaving in the path of carnage Naryan had wrought upon his entry. Their retreat was void of conflict, for those who had lived as Naryan passed through had evacuated in the face of his might.

Chapter 23

"So, how'd you find me?"

Einar and Naryan now traversed the Chromerian wild, staying off the roads, and wary of pursuit.

Naryan studied Einar for a moment before responding,

"You were hard to find, I might say. Almost as though you didn't want to be found."

Einar shrugged,

"Perhaps not, but perhaps I didn't know what was best for me at the time. At any rate, I'm glad you arrived when you did."

"You did look like you were in quite the predicament. How'd you find yourself there? Losing your touch old man?"

Einar laughed,

"The young and brash certainly now rule the world. I will say, you would have found yourself in the cage next to me, had it not been for Valor." Einar winced as he said Valor's name.

"Ah yes, thank you for the compliment. Valor certainly is one of my strengths."

Einar swallowed, ignoring Naryan's confusion, and returned in quip,

"A new one, I might add."

"Perhaps, but now we've saved each other twice, so you can consider me your equal in all things."

"Indeed," said Einar. "I'm glad to see you've gotten some use out of my grimoire at the least." he nodded his head toward Naryan's pocket. "Skipped straight to the violence of it."

Naryan raised his eyebrows,

"A violence that saved you–let us not forget so soon."

"I shall not, nor do I believe you'll let me ever forget it either. But, let us pause for a moment in silence and consider the sacrifice of my good friend."

"Tell me more," said Naryan, "for I did see another up in the cages with you. Did he perish in the fall? Did you know him well?"

201

"Yes, we were close in the past, though separated by time and then rejoined–at least for a little while. I will mourn him when I have a solitary moment. And you should too–it is because of his sacrifice that we live. I saw you stumble."

Naryan looked at Einar,

"I felt weak. Consumed. Each breath was a labor, and I felt as though I would never recover from the exhaustion. What was it?"

Einar shrugged,

"The orb that was set in the center of Chromer–other than that I cannot say its origins or qualities. I only know what you know–and you should watch your hubris, for I was crippled by its influence for more than a week, whilst you could barely stand a few moments."

"I am reprimanded," nodded Naryan as Einar continued,

"It was Valor–my friend's name, who moved the orb away from us and it took his life as payment. We both owe him gratitude."

"I see. It is given then," nodded Naryan, and they walked in silence for a bit. After a while Naryan broke it,

"You still have not answered me as to how you came to be in Chromer, and why I could not find you after nearly two months of dedicated searching."

"I'm surprised that you found me at all," said Einar, "considering I aimed to not be found."

"Well," said Naryan, "it was only until recently that I could even perceive you, and then I came straight away."

"Ten days perhaps?" asked Einar, "For that is when I came to be captured and it took all my might to live, let alone shroud myself."

Naryan nodded,

"I suppose the count adds up."

They walked in silence again before Einar spoke,,

"What about you then? I have relayed my tale, but when I last left you in the woods you could barely wipe your own ass, and now you have mastered your spirit. What is your tale?"

Naryan smiled,

"A little silence, a little soul searching, a little longing, and staring my faults in the face all the while."

Einar raised in eyebrow,

"So, you are a changed man then? No more wine and fornication for you?"

Naryan laughed,

"Well, I would not have promised to be chaste forevermore, but after smelling piss and stale malt on you I may have no other choice but to keep away from vices. I dare not ask what took place to find you in this condition."

Einar looked down at his attire and realized that there was no way he was not putrid. The olfactory fatigue had certainly set in days ago.

"A bath, perhaps?" asked Naryan, though I hope you packed a bag of fresh clothes from Chromer–I forgot to grab a spare set for you on the way over to save your ass."

Einar chuckled,

"Well, your quip certainly hasn't changed in my absence. Yes, let us find an inn–though, it must be your shout for I've forgotten my purse."

"You never had a purse, old man–you forget that I've seen your house."

They found an inn in a small town quite a ways from the capital, and judging by the lackadaisical atmosphere, news of the incident in the capital earlier had not yet reached the people there. It was past midnight when they arrived, and nothing special set it apart from any other inn, so they decided to order a room, receiving more than a few stares and crinkled noses at Einar's presence. They paid extra for a bath and purchased a set of clothes for a few coins. The innkeeper swore that they were merely left behind and forgotten, but they were probably from a dead man. Hopefully they had at least been washed.

After they were dried and dressed, they headed to the tavern, finding the smell of the perpetual stew rather enticing. A barmaid slopped it into bowls on their table, and as she turned to leave Naryan tugged at her,

"We'll take two ales as well."

She nodded and headed to the bar, while Einar blinked and looked at Naryan,

"Not as chaste as I'd presumed."

"Well they're not both for me. You'll be having the other."

Einar shook his head,

"You know me, I don't drink."

Naryan broke into a raucous laughter that elicited a few stares.

"Oh please, old man, don't sit here and lie to me that you haven't been on a bender for the last two months. I smelled it on you the moment I came into Chromer. I'm surprised it took them that long to find you. I'd have been banging down every door in Satoria if I'd have smelled you from my castle. No, one beer won't hurt you. Moderation in all things my friend."

Einar shrugged,

"I suppose if you can manage it, so can I."

The pints arrived and he sniffed his, a flood of fuzzy memories from his time in Chromer rushing back to him. It had been at least ten days since his last drink though, and alcohol had a way of making people forget the suffering it caused.

Still, he took a sip, adamant that he would not let it control him, and set it down as he let the fizz play against his tongue.

"So then," Einar said, swallowing his drink, "I have divulged my ongoings to you, do tell of your adventures."

"Adventures? Yes–you could say they have been adventures." Naryan exhaled, sipping his own drink and getting lost in the candle that flickered on the table near them. "I have learned much, and then back-slidden, done things I'm not proud of, and become nearer unto myself. It is though I've lived an entire lifetime of lessons these past two months. I cannot tell you all that has passed, for I feel shame–believe it or not."

Einar tried to hold back a wry smile, but the corners of his lips turned up anyway,

"It's funny, Naryan, to hear you hold a mature conversation."

Naryan nodded,

"Matured, yes, I have matured, for the weight of responsibility now hangs on my shoulders." he gritted his teeth, "responsibility in what you have taught me, but also the responsibility of my kingdom, which I am currently failing.

"War runs rampant in my land, and I am torn between saving my people, and letting the usurpers fail at their own game." He took a sip and jammed the mug into the table, the foam sloshing over the edge. "I see people I know, and love, harmed by this war, and I feel as though I have the power to end it. Unfortunately, I am harassed by those just as strong who would see me exiled away from the throne. Solis and the other Erilaz do not seem eager to relinquish control of Satoria, and my allies tell me that he becomes stronger every day through devilish means.

"On the other side we have Chromerians, marauding through Satoria since Solis is an inept general and let fall the most defensible choke point in all of our borders. Solis does not have enough Erilaz to lay waste to the Chromerians who strike nimbly all over the soft innards of Satoria, nor do we have the numbers to spread thin and meet them in open battle.

"Einar," Naryan's eyes caught Einar's with a wild gaze, "If you had not restrained me today, I would have emptied all of Chromer. Looking back I thank you that you hindered me, for now it does not weigh on my conscience, but know that I would have killed every living thing, down to the dogs and rats, to end this war. I know that the citizens are not at fault, but I still would have done it. My hands would be bloody and I would have drowned myself in liquor tonight."

He laughed, holding his mug up to Einar,

"So, drink to mercy." Naryan said. Einar looked at him with a smile and clinked their mugs together, each taking a light sip.

"Don't be so hard on yourself." said Einar,

"I'm a failure." said Naryan, "I cannot rule nor save my own kingdom. I have no bearing on my own life."

"We just drank to mercy. Save some mercy for yourself."

Naryan shook his head,

"Come with me Einar. Back to Satoria. I must reclaim the throne–I can't do it without you."

"I like this new you," laughed Einar, "humility suits you well."

Naryan stared him down,

"I do not jest nor quip. Come with me, and we shall put an end to Solis and have peace again."

Einar gazed at Naryan, seeing resolve and pain juxtaposed in his eyes. Silence hung on the table for a moment before Einar shook his head,

"I cannot."

Naryan let out a guttural burst and scowled,

"Why not?"

"We cannot defeat Solis."

"If *we* together cannot defeat him, then I certainly cannot on my own. Come with me. It is our only choice."

"No, it is not our only choice. There is no need to return."

"What, and back to the woods?" Naryan scoffed, "shall we end our days two old men sharing a hut and foraging for berries?"

"I'm not sharing my hut with you."

Naryan slammed his mug on the table and spat,

"You always run–don't you? You ran from me in the woods, you ran from Solis in the throne room, in fact, you probably ran from Satoria all those years ago–didn't you? Where has it gotten you? You cry 'exile' as if your hand has been forced and you have no other option, but in truth you are afraid. Tell me then–why do you run?"

Einar narrowed his eyes and breathed in through his nose while he watched Naryan's chest rise and fall, awaiting a response. He thought for a moment, softening as he replied,

"Failure. I am afraid of failure."

"What then is the biggest failure?" asked Naryan, "to do nothing at all, or to fail while your conscience knows you gave your all?"

Einar shrugged,

"Do you know what I never told you, Naryan?" asked Einar, "I never told you why I came back to Satoria in the first place. I came," he paused and inhaled, "for hope. I hoped to bring life back to the people, but instead they turn and say that there is no magic, and that there is no hope, even in light of evidence. Now, there is violence; everything I have touched has turned to shit. Life was much better when I was alone in the woods–for myself and everyone else."

"Not for me." said Naryan. "You've enriched my life."

Einar bit his lip.

"One of a thousand, I suppose. And even now it is yet to be seen if this is for the greater good."

"You know what you need?" asked Naryan, "Grace–for yourself. You aid others, but now it's time for someone to aid you–and it's me."

Einar chuckled,

"It sounds to me like you're trying to enlist me on a violent campaign against Solis–I'm not sure how you're coming to my aid."

"I think you just need a good kick in the ass. Now is the time to face your fear. You've been putting it off for far too long."

Einar bit his cheek and looked at Naryan, and then slowly nodded. He picked up his mug, draining the remainder in one go and slammed it on the table.

He stood, turning his back to Naryan and strode out of the tavern and into the cool night air. There were a few men in chairs in the front, smoking pipes and laughing, and they took little notice as Naryan and Einar's feet crunched along the dirt path. Naryan stood behind Einar, watching him survey the stars, his arms crossed in front of him as he brooded. Finally, he turned on his heel and looked Naryan up and down,

"Fine. Let's go."

Naryan nodded,

"So be it. We leave at dawn."

Einar's eyes gleamed, his hands sparking as they swirled a rune in front of him. The wind kicked up around his feet, lifting him into the air and he floated, surveying Naryan.

"Dawn? My friend," he grinned, "We leave now."

Naryan raised an eyebrow, and copied the rune, his own feet lifting off the ground, and they whisked off into the night sky.

Nobody believed the drunks in front of the tavern.

Chapter 24

They had flown for more than four hours when they passed over the Shallows and back into Satoria. The sun was starting to glow in the morning sky as they passed the river border, and Naryan was thankful for the warmth that would soon come. The flight was cold, uncomfortably so, turning Naryan's hands blue while he felt his lips chap from the windchill. Still, it was much better than walking for more than a week, so he kept his mouth shut and eyes squinted as they were conveyed through the outer territories.

They flew not vertical, and not horizontal, but with a slight lean forward, and they controlled their trajectory by carving runes in each hand. Even after flying for hours the exhilaration of speed and height was to be unmatched. Not even a horse at a full gallop could run so fast. Tall trees and the topography of the land looked like a child's playset as they went, and the sprawl of flowering fields and meandering of rivers painted the landscape from their vantage point.

They were high enough in the sky to be out of reach of prying eyes not purposefully looking up, though when passing over the Shallows a vigilant Chromerian guard did point them out to another watcher with an outstretched arm. Not that there was anything he could do.

Naryan grimaced as he saw the ruin of the city for the first time, for it had been sacked, and he could see down into now-empty rooms, once covered by thatched roofs. Einar thought back on the night of the siege, and shook his head–perhaps he could have saved it, but perhaps he'd be dead.

Their altitude afforded them a wide field of view, and the day's walk of the hamlets' separation passed by in less than an hour. The wind rushed past their ears, making conversation inconvenient, but the view of forests, fields, mountains, rivers and gullies into a picturesque landscape, lending them brief serenity. It was easy to forget the hunger, filth, and war that was apparent when on the ground.

As they flew, their attention was drawn to hundreds of specs lining the ground in the distance, and slivers of smoke rising from a hamlet. War was still very real. Judging from their position they were in the center of the Satorian plains, nearing half way between the capital and The Narrows. The hamlets here were mostly small farming communities with little more than a town square surrounded by a few buildings, and homesteads sprawling out around them. Still, these hamlets comprised much of the outer Satorian territories, and the people that lived there would die.

Naryan banked in that direction and Einar followed, unsure of the former's goal. From their vantage they could see the Chromerian force encroaching on the hamlet's borders, and while there was a Satorian detachment there to defend it, their numbers were not enough. The townspeople were in the midst of evacuation, and a thin line of them departed into the fields on the far side of the hamlet from the skirmish.

The two Erilaz landed in the midst of the abandoned town square, their legs running and stumbling to catch themselves as they finally stood again after the long flight. Naryan looked to see the two opposing companies a few spear lengths apart from each other, shields raised, the sounds of chaotic yelling on the wind.

The Chromerians knew they outnumbered the defenders three-to-one on open ground, and they pushed forwards, encroaching on the land with every step. The defenders' backwards steps were proof that they were not confident in the fight, and they brandished their spears outward in deterrence. The Satorians were not in organized lines, but in tight ball, for they could not match the Chromerians' long ranks.

The Chromerians, sensing the timidity of their foes, pushed forwards, and battle cries came forth as they ran forwards, shields and spears raised. The two parties clashed into one another, the wooden clunks of shields impacting one another, trimmed by the clash of steel on steel and the grunts of wind knocked from men at the impact. The prods of spears wriggling their way between the shields to the men behind were accented by the screams of those who had been found as marks.

The walls of men pushed against each other, the front lines now trapped between their comrades behind while they were pierced again and again by desperate thrusts from their foes. But the Chromerians were too many, and the Satornian's footing faltered; they were pushed back as a group, many at the front slipping in the dirt to be trampled and slain by the Chromerian spears from above.

The Satorian front line was easily broken, and the rest turned to flee, those in back running first through the town square, and those that were towards the front now chased with the Chromerians at their heels. In the center of the square stood Naryan and Einar, and Naryan reached into his robe to withdraw the grimoire, flipping through it and resting his finger on the page. The fleeing Satorians shouted at them to run as they passed them, but Einar and Naryan were planted as stones in a flowing river while the Chromerians charged into the town, thrown torches immediately setting it ablaze, while those in front charged towards them with spears raised.

Einar wrote, and the nearest Chromerian had the spear ripped from his grasp and thrust into his own stomach. He tripped with a gurgle, landing with a clatter on the stones and ceasing to move as red pooled around him. Naryan too wrote, tracing the runes in the grimoire so that the small cobblestones of the hamlet's square lifted themselves up and shot forward as projectiles into the running Chromerians. Twenty had already fallen from the stones when Einar wrote again, this time commanding a tall flame be grasped from the fire licking the structures. It lashed through the air like the tail of a kite, passing over, around, and through the lines of the Chromerians that rushed towards them.The beards on their faces melted, leaving seared skin beneath, and they dropped their weapons, covering their heads with their hands and rolling along the ground as they screamed.

Still the tail of flame moved, and the Chromerians behind those that had fallen realized the detriment of their circumstance. A hundred more had already poured into the square but as they turned to run they were now trapped by their allies behind them, who could not see what befell the others in the square.

Naryan wrote, and the beams of a tall building burst, the whole side of its structure collapsing onto the entrance of the square. The Chromerians beneath it held their shields up as if to deflect the whole of the structure, but many were crushed at its fall, and those within the square ran towards the fallen structure, throwing themselves at it to hoist themselves over the debris away from the Erilaz.

The Chromerians no longer thought of aggression, only flight, and they scattered this way and that across the square while Einar's stream of fire weaved through them, and Naryan's stones revolved around the open square with thuds of impact on their bodies.

The Chromerians all now laid still, and silence settled over the square. The meandering stream of fire dissipated into a wisp of smoke, and the remaining paver stones fell and tumbled across the ground. The two Erilaz let their hands fall down to their sides, the cadence of their breath now slowing. Behind them, a rustling of movement and the patter of boot steps on the cobblestones caught their attention. They turned, to see there still remained ten or so Satorian soldiers in the street, eyes rapt on the two of them.

The soldiers solemn stares and grit teeth were mingled with uneasy shifts in their weight from between feet, and they shared glances with others. Einar watched as Naryan raised his hands, palms out in a gesture of empty-handedness towards the soldiers, but at this a few soldiers turned and sprinted from the scene without looking back. Naryan dropped his hands again, folding them at his front before taking a step towards the remaining group.

"Friends, I mean you no harm." he said, as he continued forward.

By the time he stood in front of them, there were only two men left. The one at the front stood with his arms crossed over his chest and his jaw set, eyes narrowed. The one behind had much

212

wider eyes, and he constantly turned to look behind them as Naryan approached.

"Where did the rest go?" Naryan asked,

"I do not know, but if you follow the trail of piddle I'm sure you'll find them." responded the first.

"Why do you also not run?" asked Naryan.

"If you meant to kill us you would have already–you're clearly capable."

Naryan raised his eyebrows and nodded in agreement.

"Do you know who I am?" asked Naryan,

"I can only assume you're one of those hooded men whom the queen has kept near unto her side."

"A good guess," said Naryan, looking at Einar who now stood next to him."

The soldier continued,

"Why you're just now deciding is the time to practice these magics is beyond me. Imagine how many fellow soldiers would not have perished on the battlefield if you had simply waved your pinky around like so. Why this town? I'm not even sure I know its name. In case you cannot tell, the soldiers were not keen on defending it with their lives."

Naryan cocked his head,

"Have we not been defending all of Satoria with magic since we arrived?"

"Have you?" questioned the man. "There are whispers among the people of magic being seen, but I have never heard of concrete witness, nor seen with my own eyes. Until now. Even if we go and make this known we will be silenced as lunatics or punished for drunkenness on duty."

"What about Sallow Hill? Have none spoken of that?"

"There was word at first of magic there, but it was quickly dispelled as myth. The word is that a home simply lost control of its hearth and burned the pitiful place to the ground."

Einar and Naryan shared a glance,

"And the soldiers that perished there?" Asked Naryan,

"Soldiers? Why would soldiers have been at Sallow Hill? Why do you ask so many questions–do you not know the answers?"

Naryan shook his head,

"It seems that both you and I are in search of answers we do not have."

Einar cut in,

"Someone still aims to keep this secret in the shadows."

The soldier looked them up and down,

"Will you now slay me for what I have witnessed?"

Naryan shook his head,

"No, goodman, I return to save the people, not to kill them. Come Einar, let us right the wrongs of the past, in blood if we must."

Einar nodded, and smiled,

"Your majesty."

The soldier cocked his head and shielded his eyes from the sun as he watched two Erilaz carve their runes, while the air lifted them into the sky in flight.

Chapter 25

The remainder of the way to the capital was quick, and the outskirts of the city were visible within minutes. A short ways out from it Einar and Naryan caught each other's gaze as they felt the presence of another's spirit probing them while they drew nearer.

"He knows we're coming." shouted Einar in the rushing wind. Naryan nodded and set his jaw as they came closer. They flew above the forest to the west of the city, crashing through the canopy and setting themselves on the forest floor. They then picked their way through the forest until they came to its edge, and wrote runes, bidding their spirits on errands away from them for a while so they could continue undetected.

They left the forest, walking the distance to the first buildings of the city's edge and mingling with those milling around the streets as they made their way towards the castle. It was not yet noon when they finally made it through the city and up to the castle's outer bailey and barbican.

As they approached they made to go through it, but the guards blocked their path.

"Halt goodmen," said the first guard, the others blocking their path, spears in hand. "What business do you have in the castle?"

"I come to see the queen," said Naryan, "I have business with her in court today."

"Do you have your summons then?" asked the guard,

"He does not need one," said a voice from the side, and an Erilaz stepped out from the shadow of the gatehouse. "He is expected."

Naryan and Einar eyed the Erilaz, but he removed his hood and beckoned them through. The guards parted without much more than a glance, and they passed through, following the Erilaz.

"Your coming has been seen from a ways off," continued the man, "certainly you know you are watched for."

Einar nodded,

"Yes, Argyle–I know this."

"Good Einar, for now I hope that we can speak of peace instead of violence. Solis awaits you."

"Perhaps his quarrel is with Solis," said Naryan, "but I am here for Rhondia. Take me to her."

The man stopped, gesturing forward with his hand towards the courtroom.

"Where one is, you will find the other. They await you."

Einar and Naryan looked at each other before continuing the rest of the way through the baileys and up to the courtroom. There were no guards to usher nor waylay them, and as they reached it, Naryan smiled at Einar,

"Back to where it started, I suppose."

Einar nodded but his lips were drawn tight, and he pushed open the heavy door to let light shine into the otherwise darkened interior.

Rhondia sat on the throne, and Solis stood behind her, arms crossed as they surveyed the two entering. The echo of their footsteps was all to be heard in the room, and they came until they stood in front of the usurpers.

"I miss the bustle of my reign," said Naryan. "It was once more cheery in here. Did you cancel court today, Rhondia?"

She did not smile, and her eyes narrowed as she watched him,

"Why do you come here, Naryan? Is it not enough that your life is spared? You were free to live as a sot, but now you are a thorn to be plucked."

"I come to take back what's mine."

"You have nothing, child." She stood, and they stiffened, but she did not aggress towards them, simply paced as she talked. Solis still did not move, but his eyes were locked to them.

"You think so small, for what little thinking you do, and everywhere you turn you cause ruin. You think you deserve the crown, but why should you deserve what you cannot even govern?"

"I could do better than this 'commander'" said Naryan, "for I've witnessed with my own eyes Chromerians roaming across our lands, pillaging the hamlets and defeating our soldiers. Even today we easily waylayed a Chromerian troop, yet you reserve the other Erilaz and sacrifice our men–for what?"

Rhondia laughed, a cold laugh that echoed through the courtroom.

"Again, you think so small. Yes, sacrifices–that is indeed what they are, but you could not see it if it were plain in front of you! Surely you know of the orb in Chromer–of course you do, for I know of your venture there. I will say that I'm quite impressed with the change set in you, Naryan. As impressed as I could be, I suppose.

"Nonetheless, for all that you have learned, you still do not see past your immediate goals, and you've thus used your newfound abilities for naught but your own selfish gain. Think bigger!

"The Chromerian military is superior in every way to Satoria's. But now, the Erilaz have come to aid us from the wilds at my behest, yet the they cannot aggress into Chromer for the orb thirsts for their spirits. Through a scheme we have drawn out the armies of Chromer and they will certainly congregate here, and the Erilaz will defeat them far away from the influence of the orb. Then, when their numbers are weakened, our armies will strike at the heart of their capital and we will have peace."

Naryan nodded,

"Peace through war. I see. Always aggressive, Rhondia."

"Better than passive. You have no drive or foresight."

"Perhaps these last months have changed me."

"Perhaps they have–but it's too late now. The plan is afoot and Chromer will fall."

"What about the people? Think of their people! Long has Chromer been in power over us, but they have not aggressed towards us until the fell murder of their king, no doubt orchestrated by you."

"The people." scoffed Rhondia, "The people! You lost your right to speak for the people when you murdered your own subjects in Grainridge."

Naryan growled and started to raise his hand, but Einar grasped it, halting his rune. Naryan pulled his hand away from Einar and pointed at Rhondia, but she interjected before he could speak,

"Ah, so we now see who is the dog and who is the master. I do trust Einar's judgment more than your own. He is smart to run when he sees his defeat."

"Yes, well I see two bitches in front of me," spat Naryan, "one a bitch for her demeanor, and the other a bitch for his submission."

Rhondia shook her head and let out a sigh,

"Oh, Naryan, when will you learn that a soft tongue will make you more allies than a sharp one. Nonetheless, the time for pleasantries has passed–clearly. If you have come to retake the throne, then take it. If not–depart and be banished forever from Satoria. Where you go–I do not care. I do not yearn for Solis to kill you, but he will if he must. Quick now, make your choice."

"Before I do," said Naryan, "I must know–why this secrecy? This magic is a tool that can change the lives of all who use it! I see now it has been suppressed from Satoria, and I am bitter for it."

Rhondia watched him through narrow eyes while he spoke. She thought for a moment before exhaling and answering,

"There are many things that have been long set in motion," she said, lowering herself back down to the throne. "Let me tell you a tale, one that starts well before your birth, and even long before the birth of Einar–but not before my birth."

The hairs on Einar's neck stood, and he watched Naryan stiffen.

"Long ago, when the states of Chromer and Satoria were both young, they were even more quarrelsome than of late, for this has been the first war with Chromer in even your lifetime. Two powers, vying each for control of the river, and the trade routes, and the forests, for at that time the borders were not as set as they are today, and the people in the wilderlands skirmished with each other for lands they laid claim to.

"At one time Chromer controlled nearer to us than the boundary of the river where the border now sits. In order to maintain and spread the foothold of the Satorian crown, lands were gifted to the bold who would pioneer and settle. Over time they crept into Chromer's outer borders, for in those days Chromer did not hold such power to keep control over that which they claimed. Satoria promised to defend the settlers, and their influence began to reach further and further into Chromer's territory.

"Each proprietor of their estate was gifted land a half-day's walk in every direction from its center, so that each manor was set a day's walk apart from those adjacent. In time these have become the hamlets that you know. Each lord of their land was entrusted with the defense of their own people and the conscription of well-equipped knights to the Satorian military. Thus they were able to field a force to contend with Chromer, and push their boundaries to the river.

"Yes yes, I know my history," interjected Naryan, gesturing with his hand, "For you made me sit through hours of it in my youth. Now bring us to your point."

Rhondia exhaled through her nose before continuing,

"At this time there was a great war in the far north, the makings, methods, and outcome of which is unknown to me. Many refugees came from the north, some coming to settle in Chromer, and looking for homes in the cities and countryside. They intermingled their lives and livelihoods within Chromer, and I even learned to love them as friends.

"Still, they were looked down upon as vagrants, and unnatural, for many of them brought from the north the knowledge to commune with their spirits through runes–as you have learned from Einar." she nodded towards Einar, "And you Einar, though perhaps you did not know your origins, your kin were at one time displaced by this war."

Einar made no sign of acknowledgment, but still listened to her as she continued.

"Now, their unnatural abilities made the Chromerians wary of them, and in time they were expelled from their homes, often with violence, and many of them did not defend themselves with their magic for they were not warriors. Those who did defend themselves laid waste to their offenders, but they all fell or exiled eventually, leaving an ill taste of magic in the mouths of Chromerians.

"They then dispersed for their safety, again heading south and coming then to the lands of Satoria. Here they set themselves amongst the hamlets, traveling throughout the lands and even settling in the capital.

"Now instead of eyeing them as troublemakers, the Satorians rather saw their power and knew that they could harness it to gain advantage over Chromer. While the northerners knew that it could be used for violence, they refrained from doing so, for they had no need. All of their warriors had stayed in the north to contend in the war, and the refugees were the remaining pacifists from those lands.

"Even in light of this, the Satorians still found them useful, and they learned their ways, at first expecting to take the knowledge and use it against Chromer. They soon found out that their needs were easily met, and they could provide for themselves and their own without needing to expand their lands and take further campaigns against Chromer.

"They offered peace to Chromer, and built this great city and others, laying roads, felling forests, and seeding fields in unprecedented time, so that they were prosperous. There was no longer a need for war.

"Chromer though, was wary of Satoria's new-found pacificity, for they were fearful that they would remember Chromer's violent transgressions, and raze their cities with their magic, unhindered. They plotted, knowing that they could no longer meet them in open battle, so they feigned joy at the peace accords that had been struck, offering up a royal marriage to bind the two states together.

"So I, the king's daughter, was sent, a young girl alone to marry yes, but also to infiltrate the court and learn what I could, and to erode them from the inside. And I learned their magic and saw their strengths, and their weaknesses and devised a plot to ruin them.

"Chromer bought and paid for the lives of poor Erilaz, so that their families would live in wealth after they perpetrated crimes against the public. Satorians then saw the danger of these men, calling them dissidents and saying that none should have these powers lest they go insane and turn to violence. Thus I wove the lie that these strengths were too much for the common man, and they should be outlawed, but my task was not yet done!

"This plan came to fruition after many years when finally they were weakened by their vices, and had forgotten their roots and the strength of their own spirits, and had all passed away. They could not trust those who still wielded magic, so they gave up the legal use of their power for promised securities.

"But any forbidden knowledge will not be lost, for there are those who keep its secrets and pass it along in rebellion–no, the only path forward was oblivion, so that all knowledge would fall out of memory completely."

"So then you are the perpetrator of this crime?" spat Einar, stepping forward with his finger pointed at her, "You have ruined Satoria and its people!"

Solis' hands, which had been clasped in front of him shook the sleeves off his hands, and he poised to write a rune, but Rhondia waved him back with her hand and responded,

"I see no crime, for the people should not have magic. It is too dangerous for the common folk."

"Dangerous to who, the tyrant?" replied Einar. "In that case, I would agree, but those with full bellies and happy lives have no need for aggression."

"And if those bellies are full of wine, they will still be happy and no threat."

"You do not trust the judgment of the people? Satoria lived in peace and prosperity for centuries! Who are you to claim that an individual is not worthy? You should remember as well as I, if you were here too."

"No, I do not trust them," she said. "See Naryan now who stands before us–a prime example. Within weeks of his communion, he has murdered hundreds."

"I did not teach him that." scoffed Einar

"Precisely–this violence is natural to those who lack temperance. Do you really think that Satoria is full of men of greater quality than he? No, they are all sots alike who steep themselves in visions of violence against their rivals. Satoria would tear itself apart."

Naryan's eyes narrowed and jaw set while he brooded on his actions at Grainridge while Einar continued,

"One thing Eludes me–why do you war with Chromer? Though I dispute your methods, you claim to have the best interest of Satoria at heart. This is curious for an agent of Chromer."

Rhondia chuckled,

"Well, let us not forget now that my handlers in Chromer have long perished, for they are not long-lived without the communion of body and soul as we have. At first, I felt it my duty to carry on their legacy and ensure the crumbling Satoria, and I completed my task, but I have long stewed on the role that I played and realized that I was nothing but a puppet."

She stared off into the distance, remembering,

"I will admit–I was bitter. I was thrown as a tribute to a land that despised my patronage, nothing but a sacrificial pawn put forth in strategy and then forsaken by my kin. I long bided, an entire lifetime passing me by while I rued this plan and those who set it in motion.

"I then meditated; What is Satoria? What is Chromer? Simply the constructions of weak men who squabble over dead fields and muddy rivers. No, I have loftier goals than those, for when Chromer and Satoria both conform, even the Dons in the far south, the Herzogs in the east, and the Dukes across the west sea will submit.

Naryan shook his head and laughed,

"And here I just thought you were simply an aimless bitch. Perhaps we understand each other a bit more now."

Rhondia shook her head,

"I think you feign understanding, for we are not aligned in any way. Let me ask you this–what would you do should you reclaim the throne?"

"I would save the subjects on both sides from certain death.You play this game with their lives."

"You claim mercy but slay the powerless." said Rhondia. "You are weak in your convictions. You also have no plan, nor would you do what needs to be done in the face of resistance. Your father too had the same impotence, for I showed him the power that could lay at our fingertips, but he would rather steep in wine and gluttony. It runs in your blood."

"Keep him off your tongue!" spat Naryan.

"It truly is a pity," Rhondia continued, "to see the lives of frail men pass them by while they solely live to eat and drink and indulge in their carnal desires. I have seen this again and again, for I am long-lived, and I have watched their often driven and vigorous youths decline into apathy and infirmary. Your father should be thankful that I delivered him early from an even more despicable end, for the advancement of age is not kind to those who resist it."

At her words Naryan snarled, carving a rune in the air to assault her, but Solis had already acted, and his own rune was already set in preparation. A bench near them spun through the room, but Einar too was ready, and a gust of wind pushed the bench to the ceiling, smashing it while he jumped onto Naryan to save him. The two of them fell to the floor and slid a short way, Naryan writing a rune as he fell, and a beam from the ceiling disjointed itself from the others to come crashing down to the throne. The beam itself was suspended as Rhondia wrote her own rune, and a rain of debris from the shattered plaster descended on her and Solis, basking them in a cloud of dust.

The beam emerged from the cloud of dust, spinning towards the two of them, and Einar cast a rune, snapping the beam in two and sending each half to the side of them, clattering along the floor and knocking into the other benches behind. The two of them untangled themselves and sprung up, hands poised and ready to write. There was movement from within the cloud of dust, and both Rhondia and Solis emerged from it, unscathed. Rhondia dusted her soiled attire with puffs, but Solis had bared his chest, opening the front of his robe and letting it slip off his arms behind him as he walked.

Hidden beneath the robe were inscriptions carved into his flesh; runes and staves covered his forearms and shoulders, traveling across his chest and down his abdomen. He shook his arms once to finally throw the robe to the ground and with glowing finger he traced the runes on his left forearm. As his finger glowed, so did the rune he traced, and the wind outside the building kicked up, soiling the blue sky until it was gray and tumultuous.

The two doors behind them had been left cracked but they were now thrown ajar as a burst of wind entered, rushing past them to then whirl around Solis. With the gale came sticks and stones, followed by debris and then the stones of which the courtroom itself was comprised. Einar too wrote, and up from the ground swirled his own wind, creating a protective funnel around them to brush away the missiles that Solis drew. The doors to the throne room were also torn from their hinges, but they were deflected by Einar's wind, and they wildly spun past the Erilaz to shatter onto the wall behind the throne.

While they were safe from the missiles blown in the air, they were still vulnerable from below, for Solis traced a rune on his other arm and the very floor stones on which they stood heated. They first felt warmth on their feet, then looked down to see flames licking up at the heels of their boots. Einar, occupied with maintaining the whirlwind shouted at Naryan through the noise of the wind,

"Write!"

"Write what?"

"Write!" Einar shouted again with furrowed brow. .

So Naryan wrote, and even as the stones were turning to turning to slag they fell away beneath them into a tunnel Naryan carved into the ground. They each spread their stance, catching their footings onto the adjacent stones untouched by the heat and tunnel while the shaft collapsed further down.

"Well don't stop now!" shouted Einar, so Naryan wrote again, and the earth below the foundation under Rhondia and Solis twisted, also dropping away to nothing below them. Rhondia was quick to write though, and even as the shaft appeared below them, some of the floor stones of the courtroom arranged themselves as a bridge beneath her and Solis, and it held them floating in the air. This brief reprieve allowed Naryan to reach into his cloak and grasp the grimoire. His fingers flicked immediately to the page he knew and spread it out in front of him in one hand, tracing the runes with the other.

The ceiling of the throne room unpeeled itself at its ridge, revealing the darkened sky above, and sections of the roof were flung away up into the air, disintegrating into smaller pieces as they flew.

Solis however, had his eye caught by the flame of brazier that had hung from the ceiling, and even though it was flung far away in the air now he drew the flame back towards them with the tracing of his fingers. By the time it arrived it had grown to a river that curved and flowed through the air like a coiling snake. It descended upon Einar and Naryan, but Naryan had written a rune again, and water welled up from the shaft beneath them, spouting around them and then whirled around by the whirlwind that Einar still maintained. The fire and water clashed in the air around them, billows of steam flowing from where they held their stance.

The fire dissipated, and the whirlwind still twirled, whisking the steam away from the two defenders and creating a clearing in the mist. Rhondia folded her arms, watching them, and Solis too dropped his hands, and the wind he'd summoned died down. Even far above the clouds cleared a little and the sun peeked a single ray through towards them.

The glow on Solis' hands softened a little, but the runes on his chest and arms still shown brilliant from where he'd traced them. Einar too released the rune, and his whirlwind died to a subtle breeze that brushed a few dead leaves along the stones around them. Both he and Naryan stepped backwards, away from the shaft beneath them, while Rhondia and Solis stepped down from the floating stones that held them.

The four Erilaz observed each other, the toll of the city bells in the distance the only sound in the air.

"Naryan, Naryan." said Rhondia, "You must have quit drinking."

"Mostly."

Einar kept one eye on the other two Erilaz, but shifted as he peered around.

"If you're looking for the others, they're not here." said Rhondia, "They're indisposed at the moment. I believe they found Sherry. "She nodded towards Naryan. "You may have taught her a little too much for her own good, and–she can't become a problem."

Naryan growled at Rhondia and clenched his fist but she clicked at him,

"Tsk Tsk, you've drawn a standoff from us here–I wouldn't push your luck. Be on your way." She shooed him off with her hand and Naryan caught Einar's gaze, shaking his head 'no'. Einar grabbed Naryan's arm.

"Let's go." he said, motioning with his head.

Naryan's throat tightened and he held back his lip's curl as he exhaled and tucked the grimoire back into his robe. He and Enair turned away from the other two and headed towards where the double-door used to be–but Naryan had feigned resignation. As his back was turned he flicked his hands to write a rune, and a fist-sized stone on the ground flew back towards Rhondia. He turned to watch its arc but her cool gaze had already written her own rune and the stone hovered in the air, halted in its path. It quivered, the two spirits striving against one another, each to move the stone, but Rhondia's was stronger and it slowly progressed back towards Naryan.

Solis too wrote a rune, and from the earth rose a massive pillar on which the corner walls of the throne room had been set. The entire corner of the structure crumbled as the pillar was lifted, and it shivered in the air to relieve itself of all the debris that clung onto it. Einar too wrote, but Solis had already sent the pillar on its way towards them. The pillar too hung in the air, Einar and Solis struggling to push it each against the other.

But Rhondia's and Solis' spirits were stronger than the spirits of Einar and Naryan, and both the small stone and the large pillar hung in the air quivering, the pent-up energy of death awaiting those at the receiving ends. As the moments progressed the missile edged closer and closer to Naryan and Einar, who could not hold back the strength of their two foes.

Part 3: The Speaker

Chapter 26

Even though he was left long behind, Sherry's mind could still hear the sounds of Naryan's slurred yells and the snaps of branches as he crashed through the woods behind her. She had managed to gain a little space during the chase, and had hidden behind a tree, watching him stumble off after her into the dark woods before she circled back around towards the caravan.

By the time she'd returned to the caravan, a few guards had started to venture into the woods, torches held high as they peered into the darkness, but she had no desire to be discovered, and instead lay dead still on the ground next to a log until they'd dispersed. She may as well have been dead—she felt nothing inside.

The guards now gone, she picked her way back to the road and followed it in the direction that she'd come: away from Sallow Hill, away from Naryan. She remembered that they'd passed through one of the hamlets earlier in the day and kept following the roads until she came to some of the homesteads far in the outskirts. A barn and silo were a ways off and after a while she came to it, passing through a small herd of cows and entering into the barn. There she found nothing more than a horse and some swine housed within.

She dipped her hands to the cold watering trough and lapped at the water until she no longer thirsted, before collapsing onto a half-eaten pile of hay. The moonlight shone in through a broken board in the ceiling and she felt at her tender groin through her clothes, for it caught her attention now that she had stopped to rest.

She lay on the hay, curled into a shivering ball with her throat clenched, and squeezed her eyes tight, but no more tears came. She was drained of them, and even her eyes hurt from the exertion. So did her heart.

Her sleep was restless, haunted by the gaze of Naryan's glazed eyes and the thrusting of his form as he held her down.

"You have to leave."

She must have fallen asleep, for the pinkened sky of dawn now peeked through the slat in the bar and a man wielding a wooden pitchfork stood over her, getting ready to prod her with it.

"You damn drunks always think they can just sleep wherever."

Sherry sat up and showed her hands,

"I'm sorry–I didn't have anywhere else to go."

"Well," the man feigned a prod with his pitchfork again, "go have nowhere else to go, somewhere else."

Sherry stood and the man backed up, at least resting the pitchfork's shaft on the ground instead of brandishing it.

"Your horse," said Sherry, "How much?"

"He's not for sale." he said, looking her up and down, "And you don't have enough anyway."

She reached to her side and pulled out her coin purse, which jingled as she did.

"This should cover about two horses," she said, throwing the pouch towards the man. "That's more than enough for your inconvenience."

The man caught it against his chest and started to protest, but looked inside the purse and thought better of it. Sherry had already mounted the horse, which stamped its hooves a bit as she grasped onto his mane, and she prodded it towards the road.

The horse trotted along, and it seemed happier to be bearing her than plowing a field first thing in the morning.

"What shall I name you?" she asked it, peering down at it, and seeing its head turn and eye peer at her. The glint of the rising sun in his black eye caused her to turn and see the sun rising over the mountains to the east; its light bringing the hope of a new day.

"Daybreak–that's your name," she said, leaning forward to pat his cheek. "You're the fresh start that I need." Daybreak blew through his nostrils as if he approved, and continued trotting on.

She didn't once push Daybreak to a gallop, and waited as often as there was a rest stop while he watered. He was not a courier, nor a war horse–not like Nightmare was bred to be, but he was still large enough to carry her with ease. She saw that his shoulders were strong from plowing fields, and that he was not skittish.

She rode on, coming to the capital before the day's end and riding through the city streets and straight towards the castle. Her manor was still a few hours ride, and she and Daybreak needed to rest. Through the outer barbican she came, nodding at the guards who nodded and recognized her, but kept their mouths shut at her haggled look. She came to the stables, guiding Daybreak to a trough filled with hay, where he gave no hesitation to diving in. She beckoned a stablehand over, directing him to tend to Daybreak, and headed towards the inner bailey, and the castle.

She sought Shawn, for he was somewhere to be found here in the castle. Their family's status lended him command of a company, and in light of the pending war he was certainly caught up in the development of Satorian defense strategy. Just over a week had passed since the declaration of hostilities by Chromer, and there was no time to waste.

She didn't often spend time in the council chamber, for the discussions there were usually in the realm of commerce and politics, and she did not care for those. Still, she knew where it was, and headed there in search of her brother. Through the inner bailey she went, her walk speeding into a hustle as she lifted her dirty dress so it did not catch her heels. She saw in front of her the steps up towards the corridor where the council chamber was, but as she neared them she heard her name called out across the inner bailey,

"Sherry." it was not a question, nor a request, for Rhondia's voice could even make a simple name a command.

She saw Rhondia coming towards her from across the bailey, and glanced up the steps again towards the council chamber before stopping and turning to address her,

"Dowager queen Rhondia–how do you do today?" She nodded her head forward in respect.

Rhondia's gaze kept Sherry in place until her walk brought her to stand in front of Sherry.

"I am well," said Rhondia, "though I see you look worse for wear–out of place for a courtier's daughter I might add." Sherry shrugged. Rhondia studied her for a moment, but then her brow furrowed,

"Did you not depart here with the king's convoy? You'ver returned already? Where is he?"

Sherry shook her head as her eyes reddened, but kept her lips pursed so they would not quiver.

"Speak now." Continued Rhondia, "Were you waylaid? Where is the king? We received a pigeon yesterday requesting aid."

Sherry continued shaking her head side to side before her brow finally furrowed and she quivered and grasped onto Rhondia's arm. Her breaths were short and shallow and her strength could not hold back the sobs. She collapsed to her knees before bending over at Rhondia's feet and grasping onto the hem of her dress as she cried.

Rhondia bent down, holding onto the crook of Sherry's arm to help her up. Sherry's knees shook as she tried to stand, and she leaned heavily onto Rhondia.

"Hush girl," said Rhondia, "catch your breath–come this way." and she led her up the stairs and through the corridor into a leisure chamber, dismissing a few courtiers with little more than a glance. She ushered Sherry to sit into an armchair, and drew her own chair next to it, her hand resting on Sherry's knee until she was able to catch her breaths, and her tears subsided.

"Firstly," said Rhondia, "I must know–are they safe?"

"I...I do not know." said Sherry, her words accented by the sobs of her catching her breath, "I departed from them well into last night."

"In the night?" asked Rhondia, then aside to herself, "that would have been before the pigeon was sent."

"Pigeon?" asked Sherry. Rhondia nodded,

"We received word that the king and his guard were defending one of the hamlets from a Chromerian brigade–they would have already done battle by now. I am hoping for another pigeon shortly with news."

"No," Sherry shook her head, "I know nothing of that."

"What happened then?" asked Rhondia. "How did you come to be here?"

Sherry's lip trembled again, but she bit it and looked into Rhondia's eyes,

"I was with the king." her head moved side to side again and she swallowed, before continuing. "I was with the king. We had a dispute, and I left."

Rhondia's eyes were intent on Sherry's, but her gaze softened and she shook her head,

"Naryan holds you high in his heart–I would not concern yourself with a little fleeting anger. It will pass."

"No," said Sherry, "you misunderstand. I am spurned."

"Naryan is fickle," smiled Rhondia, "I would not put weight into his words–only his deeds. Come now–I will have a maid attend to you and escort you to your manor. You may keep her there as long as you desire comfort."

Sherry interjected, her voice rising as she spoke,

"Well, I am spurned by his words, but claimed in deed–even against my will."

Rhondia's smile faded.

"I see." she said, as she shook her head, "I do pity you–but I am powerless in this regard for he is the king. Though, I do grieve at your abuse."

"What then should I do?" asked Sherry, "For I have desired him since our youth and the dream of my future is now turned to ash."

Rhondia shook her head,

"I loathe to bear this bad news to you, but you never were his future. The path before him is surely a marriage of convenience, for his will is tied to the wellbeing of the kingdom, even to his regret. You are no daughter of the Concordian courts, nor of the kingdoms across the sea where an alliance might be had. Even the blood of a Chromerian princess would be held in higher regard. There is no gain for Naryan to marry a courtier's daughter, for though you love him, the institution of marriage is not for love.

"No, no king for you, kind Sherry–and I see the pain in your eyes as I speak this hard truth to you. Find a nobel and chivalrous knight who holds you in high esteem and does not abuse you and cast you into the darkness. This would be better than to pine after a king who will sire you a bastard and consider you no more than a thorn in his side when you have aged–merely a mistress. Consider another–a good man, for Naryan clearly is no such thing–and you will learn to love them."

Sherry laid her head in her hands and wept again, so Rhondia wrapped her in her arms and consoled her until she slept.

Chapter 27

It was early in the morning of June 19th when Sherry awoke. It was very cold, and still dark. She'd bidden one of her maids to rouse her in the middle of the night, and though confusion took hold for a brief moment as the servant shook her shoulder, her mind quickly cleared and she rose, aided by the servant as she donned her clothes. They were not the fancy attire of the courtroom, but warm riding clothes, and the servant threw a heavy cloak across Sherry's shoulders as she left her room.

Another servant waited for her near the manor's stables, lantern held high in one hand, and Nightmare's reigns in the other. He was already saddled, and Sherry pulled herself up onto him by the horn, fitting her feet into the stirrups and grasping the reins in her gloved hands. Nightmare pranced and settled, glancing over at the other two horses near him who were hitched to the fence near the barn.

The other two horses belonged to Shawn, and his squire, and Sherry turned to see the two of them emerging from the main manor of the house. They trudged down the short path, the lantern held by the squire and swinging as they approached. As they came to the horses, Sherry could see the mist of their breath dissipating into the darkness around them, and Shawn looked up at her,

"I didn't think you'd actually make it, little sister. It is a bit chilly this morning."

"I'll brave the cold for you, brother." He nodded and smiled.

"How could I ever doubt you? You're the most reliable person I know."

He too hoisted himself up onto his horse, and the squire tightened straps holding saddle bags that bore Shawn's armor, before also mounting. He looked to Shawn, who nodded, and the squire spurred his horse forward to lead the way with a pole-mounted lantern. Shawn and Sherry followed on their horses down the path towards the capital.

They took the ride at a leisurely pace, not pushing their horses, for there was no need. It was a few hours to the capital, but they did not speak much for they rode single file and huddled deep in their cloaks to keep warm.

Light began to paint the edges of the sky in the east as they approached the outskirts of the city, and they rode through it, seeing the people stir and start the day. The clops of their horses' hooves on the cobblestone streets echoed, following them until they left the city's innards and started on the slight ascent to where the castle lay. Reaching the outer barbican they found that the night torches were still lit, and the guards nodded in acknowledgement as they came through the gate and entered into the outer bailey.

They continued through the outer bailey, arriving at the stables and dismounting while a stableboy gathered their reigns to tether the horses.

"Water and feed them." Shawn commanded the stable boy, "but keep them burdened and ready for we'll be departing again within hours."

The stable boy nodded, and the sound of splashes of water pouring into a trough could be heard as Sherry and the two others exited the doors and began their walk toward the inner bailey.

Silence was the mode for the morning, but Sherry looked over to catch Shawn's gaze as they walked. His face was clean-shaven, and his jaw cut a sharp line at the bottom of his profile. He smiled in return to her glance, and they continued up the steps towards the council chamber.

Warmth emanated from a well-fed fire in the council chamber, and as soon as they opened the door to the corridor, they were welcomed in from the chilly dawn. Shawn removed his cloak, handing it to his squire, and bidding Sherry to wait for a moment. He walked into the council chamber, emerging a few moments later and nodding to her,

"They're all here." he said, motioning towards the room, "We now must talk strategy. I'm sure you could sit yourself in the corner if you'd like to listen in…"

She shook her head,

"I didn't think so," he laughed, "are you saying that you came all this way for me? Take off your cloak–stay a while! I'm not leaving immediately."

She stepped forward, wrapping her arms around him and resting her head onto his shoulder. He too embraced her, and even though he released the embrace she still held on a bit longer.

"I'm going to miss you," she said. "You've become a good man."

Shawn laughed,

"You act like you're about to give my eulogy. There isn't a reason to worry–I'm not going to be on the front lines. Father invested quite a bit in my education–I think they'll be putting that to use, rather than the strength of my arm."

"Good," she said, "Father wouldn't be able to bear it if his only son perished."

"I'll be doing no perishing," Shawn replied, "though I don't doubt that you'd brandish your own sword if the time came, and make father proud."

"Ok, enough talk of perishing," she said, embracing him again. The echo of footsteps filled the hallway and she glanced around Shawn's arm to see a guard approaching.

He was close by, and through the apertures of his helm she saw Naryan's eyes piercing into hers. She gasped, nearly releasing Shawn, but Naryan's eyes widened in warning, and Sherry held Shawn in the embrace.

"It was nice of you to come see me off." Shawn said, finally releasing the embrace and putting her at arm's length to look at her.

"Be safe brother," she said, fighting the urge to turn and watch Naryan.

"I'll be fine–really. I'm there more for show than to do battle. I'll be mostly strategizing in the commander's tent sipping a goblet of wine."

She finally pulled away and smiled, but her mind was on the cadence of Naryan's footsteps retreating down the hallway.

"Farewell then," she said.

"I'll see you within a month," he winked, "Chromer will wish they'd stayed on their side of the White River."

With that, he turned, squire in tow, and walked into the council chambers. As soon as he disappeared, Sherry turned to see Naryan's shape turning the corner far down the corridor. She hurried after him, as fast as she dared.

Sherry mounted Nightmare, and left Naryan lying on the green patch of grass, not even giving him the satisfaction of a glance back. Her mind was still racing from the excitement of the escape from the castle, and the magic that he'd cast to save them. She didn't know what to think, she just needed to get away.

She was at least telling the truth when she'd told Naryan that she needed to go back home–lest her father worry. What she didn't say, however, was that she couldn't bear the sight of him a moment longer without either breaking into tears, or tearing his heart out. Such were the feelings of lingering love, and betrayal.

Still, she'd smiled at their farewell, giving him the best courtesy she could muster, but there was truth in her words when she'd said that she no longer trusted him. How he couldn't understand that–she just didn't comprehend. It was almost nice to see him beg though–and it was certainly nice to tell him 'no'.

It had been just over a month since he'd raped her, and less than two weeks since he'd disappeared from the castle. It was hard to believe he was already as different a man as he claimed. He seemed honest when he said that he'd changed, and she could see that he had changed some, and some were in ways she'd never have expected. His normally clean-shaven face had grown a few weeks of a beard, and though she'd never have admitted it at the moment–it was becoming on him. Very unlike him, still, for he was of pale skin and soft hands–a true noble.

His attire certainly took some getting used to as well. He usually adorned himself in the latest fashion, and he spared no expense. He probably had more clothes than she did. The guard's uniform was a different aura than she was used to.

Those were not all that she sensed though. She noticed that he was less jubilant, for his light demeanor was one of the things that she'd liked best about him. There was also a certain new regret in his eyes instead of the blank stare of inebriation she'd become accustomed to. Even if the stare was often accompanied by laughs, she'd never loved it. She missed his deep gaze, one that they'd shared in countless nights of their youth. Perhaps he now had self-awareness of iniquities, but it was hard for Sherry to feel empathy for him when he still could not acknowledge the one thing that hurt her most.

But the worst part–she hadn't been prepared to face him. Even after a month of sleepless nights where she'd composed well-thought-out scoldings, admissions of vulnerability, and earfuls of wrath, she didn't know what to say when they finally came face-to-face again.

From the gossip here and there in the castle, and the position that Rhondia had elevated herself to–she'd thought Naryan was dead. Perhaps it was just wishful thinking so that she didn't need to hold herself accountable for what she truly wanted to say to him. Even so, when she finally did see him again, it was as though a ghost from her distant past was haunting her. She was proud of herself for what she had told him, but there was still more that she'd held in. If she'd started to let it out, it may have never stopped, so she'd just kept the composure of a lady, even in sight of her offender.

She was sure to think of the things she wished she'd said while lying awake tonight. The day had already gone so quickly–first the farewell to Shawn, then seeing Naryan, then their escape and–the magic.

The magic. She shook her head as Nightmare's trot carried her further down the road. She looked down at her own gloved hand and wriggled her fingers as if expecting something to happen. She'd forgotten all talk of magic since Naryan had gone missing. That night had shocked all other worries from her mind, and ever consumed her thoughts going forward.

Two times now she'd seen magic, and it was certainly undeniable. To think that Naryan had these capabilities was world-shattering. Perhaps that was the weight of responsibility that sat on him now–a new power at his fingertips and the ability to move mountains. He now really saw that he could hurt people. Not that he couldn't hurt people before–but it was more apparent to him now. What a pity, that it took him hurting someone else to grow up a little, when all she needed was for him to grow up for her.

Sherry arrived back at the estate a bit later in the day than she'd expected, but with daylight still shining. The journey back was as uneventful as it could have been, but it had passed quickly while her mind raced through the events of the day and her encounter with Naryan.

The ownership of the estate itself went back a few generations, for Sherry's forebears were themselves the ones who had homesteaded the land at the behest of the Satorian crown. While the land that their family held was no smaller than the territory of any of the hamlets, their manor was much more secluded, and the land less populated. Over time the manors held by other families had been sold, often by the recipients of hefty fortunes. The fortunes, not garnered by those who inherited it, were squandered–the land sold or chartered, and hamlets began to populate with citizenry where once a single family lorded over their land. The hamlets now were mainly stewarded by ranchers and farmers, and ultimately governed from afar by the crown since they had incorporated over time.

Their estate, however, was still held in their family, for her family was fiscally well-educated, and each was prudent with their heritage. Shawn and Sherry were to be no exception. It was one of the nearest estates to the capital, in fact, the nearest to the north of it, and it sat back from the main roads amidst green rolling hills. Their land was four kilogross acres, more or less a large square plot of thirty miles per side, and the largest privately-held estate in Satoria.

There were parcels spread throughout it, cultivated by the serfs they lorded over, and near unto the cultivations were their homes. The plots of land grew crops of wheat, and corn, other vegetables, and held orchards and vineyards. It was a bountiful estate, and the land was well-tended by the local populace.

Still, the homes were few and far between when compared to the residences of the other hamlets, and even the serfs there were looked upon as having good stature and good lords over them. While Sherry's family owned the land and certainly held those who dwelt there accountable to their feudal obligations, there was a sense of communal stewardship, and the serfs and the lordship banded together to reduce abject poverty.

As Sherry's grandfather always said, "I'd rather their bellies be full with the labor of their spades, than my belly be filled with the point of their spades." It was unfortunate that not all of the remaining estates practiced the same clemency. Thus the serfs that dwelt there were as happy as they could have been, being serfs, and the fruits of their land were marketed between all the serfs that dwelt there so that they didn't need to often travel the long distance to the capital.

She rounded the bend in the road near one of the final green hills before looking out over the small valley where their estate was settled. The brown path ran up towards it, following a stream that trickled down from a small mountain range. The water itself came near unto the west side of the manor, collecting in a swirling pool before continuing on down the stream. The pool had been dug out and lined with stones generations ago so as to provide fresh water for the estate, and it was its life-blood.

She dismounted Nightmare, gathering a bucket of water for the trough, and calling out to the stablehand. He greeted her, grasping Nightmare's reins and leading him towards the stables as Sherry walked the remainder of the distance towards the manor.

Still in her riding attire, she approached the kitchen, garnering a small meal of bread and fruits for refreshment, and rested in the shade of a jetty on the west side of the house, watching the sun set in the distance. After a while her handmaiden approached her,

"M'lady–I saw you from afar returning and wondered where you'd gone."

Sherry smiled at her,

"Well, you always know where to find me, Sondra."

Sondra nodded,

"Perhaps you'd like to bathe and sup?"

Sherry shrugged,

"I've just eaten, but a bath would be nice. Will you draw it?"

Sondra nodded,

"Of course."

She left, and Sherry waited a while longer until the sun had fully set before walking up the stairs to her chambers where Sondra waited.

The fire in Sherry's hearth was well-kept, and Sondra heated water there, filling the tub while Sherry disrobed, and slid into the water. Sondra cleaned her, often switching buckets of water from the tub for newly heated ones from the cauldron. While she cleaned her hair, she casually mentioned,

"I noticed you were later than expected today. Was all well with your brother in the capital?"

Sherry nodded, but did not speak.

"Did you enjoy your ride back then, m'lady?"

Sherry did not respond, and Sondra pried no further. Still Sondra cleaned and after a while, Sherry spoke,

"I saw the king today."

Sondra let go of Sherry's hair, letting it fall back into the water. She knew of what had transpired the night in the forest, for she had greeted Sherry upon her return from the capital, cleaning and attending to her while the events were relayed in confidence.

"I see. You have not mentioned his name in a while–I did not want to press…"

"It's fine," Sherry said, "He's been gone for some time–I thought him dead in my mind. Or at least wished him so–I cannot tell."

"If you wish him dead, I will not so much as whisper it."

Sherry smiled as Sondra helped her out of the tub, and they stood in front of the fire while Sondra dried her.

Sherry stared into the fire as she spoke,

"It hurt to see him–I cannot lie, for my heart clings on to him even though he has forsaken me. I've waited so long for him to grow up–you know I've pined for him since our youth, even holding on to hope that he would one day admire me.

"I will admit, sometimes I look at the man he's become with chagrin, for he has not turned out to be who I foresaw he would be in our youth. We used to ride, and fence, and compete in archery–and I admired the vibrancy with which he tackled the challenges in front of him. There was nothing he couldn't do if he put his mind to it, and I fell in love with his tenacity, and it compelled me to also better myself.

"My father and mother have long expected me to play the courtier's wife, but truth be told, I long for more. I have often worked hard to intimidate my suitors, telling myself I did not want them. But now I am nearly an old maid and there are many good men that have passed by. I fear to admit that I was just waiting for Naryan to notice me.

"I was at first happy to be kept close by his side, but always longed for more, for we jested and nothing else. And also we fucked–the feverish lust of carnal desires in our youth often fueled by wine and the vulnerability of my love. And while I then told myself we made love, I know what it was, and can lie to myself no longer.

"The more that Naryan steeped himself in wine, the more he stepped away from his vibrance, and the more that I saw it change him. It has changed me too, for I allowed myself to be drawn into it, to pretend that I was closer to him. But the dichotomy of laughter and sorrow are the only company in the indulgence of wine, not those with whom you clink glasses. Now I hate myself for allowing this change, for it is not a choice of good conscience. There will be no more change for anyone else, nor will there be forgiveness from my part, for long enough I have waited and it's time I move on."

Sondra robed Sherry, and braided her hair while Sherry's eyes were locked onto the fire.

"He is the king," said Sonrda, "I'm afraid there is little retribution."

"I do not seek retribution, nor penance." said Sherry, "remorse is the most I could hope from him. Though, I may never see him again, and this fret is all for naught."

"If you do not wish it, you do not need to see him again," said Sondra,

"No," said Sherry, shaking her head, "I don't. Even if he orders it I will not acquiesce, nor will I forgive. He does not even merit the breath of my words."

Chapter 28

It was now the third of July; Sherry's father was in the capital attending court, Shawn was off defending the honor of Satoria, and she–well, she was still despondent. She hated herself for it too–there was no reason that Naryan should keep slipping into her mind, but little thoughts here and there often reminded her of him, and she could not shut him out.

It had been two weeks since she'd last seen Naryan, and neither food, nor drink, nor sleep, had given her relief from the weight that sunk deep in her stomach.

As she'd become accustomed to, she awoke this morning after a restless night's sleep to Sondra throwing the blinds open and letting the sun stream down onto her face. Sherry covered her head with the pillow and groaned, but after a few moments she discarded it to the side and sat up.

"What will it be today, m'lady?" she asked, "More water, gruel, and resting by the hearth?"

Sherry shot her a sideways glance, and Sondra bowed her head,

"Apologies for the sarcasm. I'll put a nice breakfast together for you."

"No no–you're right." grumbled Sherry. "I dwell too much on it. But I will say 'yes' to the breakfast. Call Harold to ready Daybreak–I'll be going for a ride afterward." Sondra nodded and left while Sherry dressed herself in her riding attire and headed downstairs.

Breakfast was, as Sondra had promised, uplifting. The fresh cream and strawberries paired with bread baked fresh this morning was enough reason to shake the gloom off for at least a little while, and she headed to the stables with a spring in her step.

The day was still cool when she collected Daybreak from the stables and spurred him out down the road for a run. The fresh air was nice and it chilled her cheeks as she stood in the stirrups and felt the rhythm of his hoofbeats. Their cadence pounded on the compacted dirt road, resonating through to her heart.

She often grew restless at the estate. She had ridden every inch of it many times over since her youth, and while she was fond of its beauty, she was never meant to be a caged bird. She'd set out this morning for a quick sprint through the fields, but Daybreak carried her towards the open road. On it, she passed a few travelers at a hard gallop, and they peered after her with concern before she disappeared away from them in a cloud of dirt down the road towards the capital.

Daybreak has slowed after the sprint, and she did not goad him harder, letting him catch his breath and trot further down the road as the city grew closer. She'd never really planned to come to the capital today, but she was this far so she might as well enjoy it.

For all the time she'd spent at the capital, the city itself was not a place of deep familiarity. From the estate she always went straight for the castle, for that's where court was held, and also where Naryan was usually found. Today felt like a day to turn a new page, and she found herself dismounting Daybreak and entering into the city through the east gate. While other ladies may have turned up their noses to hay, manure, and the smell of slop, she was familiar with it, and didn't shy away from leading him through a bustling street where vendors yelled, hooves clopped, and carts squeaked.

She hitched Daybreak next to some other horses and paid a stableboy for his keep before setting off into the streets herself. It was a world that was strangely foreign to her–it was more wild, and unkept compared to the trimmed lawns of the castle, and the demeanor of the people around her were less reserved than those of the court. She felt the energy around her, and she loved it.

She realized that she hadn't eaten in hours, and a meat pie, a strawberry pie, and a beer soon found their way into her hands by way of coin. She walked for a little while, enjoying the streets and settled down on a stone wall set at the bottom of a small green hill wall, across the street from some shops. Growing up far away from the capital, and spending most of her time outside of the estate in the confines of the castle, she found the common way of life fascinating and that she stared at those who milled through the streets. Some had a clear purpose of where they were headed, and others seemed lost or confused as if they had nothing to do. In Sherry's eye, each of them had a fascinating story to tell.

Sherry's sonder was broken by a young woman who carried a baby wrapped in a cloak. The woman's head was drooped and the baby lamented in her arms as she passed. The gray skirt she wore dragged across the cobblestone street to soil its hem. The woman's gaze was averted as she passed by her, but Sherry could still see the woman's eyes lock onto the pies in her hand. The woman continued, without saying anything, but a few steps later Sherry called out to her,

"Stop. Come back."

The woman's head swiveled and she rocked her baby as she turned to face Sherry.

"Do you know if there's a festival going on today? It seems like there are quite a few people in the streets."

The woman shook her head and swallowed.

"I, I don't think so." She glanced down at the hand pie that Sherry held.

"Are you from here?"

The woman nodded.

"You look hungry," Sherry said, and held out her remaining pie to the woman. "Sorry, I know it's half-eaten–but it's all I have right now. Do you want it?"

The woman, wide-eyed, took a step closer to Sherry and her hand protruded from her cloak, grasping onto the pie and keeping eye contact with Sherry. Sherry let go of the pie and the woman held it in front of her.

"Thank you," she said, bowing her head a little. "I didn't know what I was going to eat today." She looked at the pie again and swallowed,

"Thank you." she nodded her head again towards Sherry, and her lower lip trembled a little as she looked down at the hand pie.

"Well don't let me stop you."

The woman brought it to her mouth without hesitating, sinking her face into it and breathing a sigh of relief as she did.

Her eyes moistened as she looked at Sherry and nodded, swallowing,

"Thank you." She said between bites, taking another and breathing through her nose as she did. Sherry saw that the pie was already gone, but the woman licked her fingers with the food still in her mouth.

"Tell me," said Sherry, "Where do you live?"

"Around here," motioned the woman with her free hand.

"Do you have a home?"

The woman shook her head.

"Where is the father?"

The woman shook her head again, and turned to go.

"No, wait," said Sherry, hopping off the short wall. "Guide me around the city today and I'll pay you."

The woman looked Sherry up and down. The shine of the silver clasps on Sherry's polished riding leather, juxtaposed next to the woman's filthy skirt, showed their difference in class.

The woman shrugged,

"Sure. What do you want to see?"

"I'm not sure," said Sherry, "walk with me."

The woman walked near Sherry, but still stayed a little ahead and did not look back as they conversed.

"What is life like here for you?"

"I don't know why you should be curious."

"I've never lived in a city before. What is your way of life?"

"What way of life is that? The one where I am hungry, and my child cries, for I cannot even nourish him with my body?"

Sherry bit her cheek,

"Do you not have parents, or brothers, or a husband?"

247

"I have no husband, and my child is a bastard." she said, "And in light of this my father and brothers would not have me in their sight."

"I'm sorry to hear that."

"I do not seek pity," said the woman, "you asked what the city is like, and though I would very much like to tell you that our bellies are as full as yours, and our clothes do not require mending, you would see that I was a liar. I do not know from whence you come, but it is certainly better than here–and I would beg you to take me with you, but I'm sure you would not have it."

"Why then is the city such a terrible place?" asked Sherry,

"There is no hope for me here. Many people are like me–scraping a living only due to the kindness of others, which is certainly few and far between. I cannot find work for I have a child, nor would the work I do be worth my time. It is better to have nothing and receive gifts of little, than to have a little and give my entire life to sustain it."

"Is the crown cruel to you then?" posed Sherry,

"The crown is of no consequence, for they do not care what goes on in the streets so long as it stays in the streets. They take their dues for the coffers and the men for their war, and leave the rest up to us. No matter who sits on the throne the outcome would be the same, so I do not care either way."

The woman looked at Sherry expecting a response, but their attention was then caught by a scuffle a little ways down the street. Those walking nearby steered clear of two men, both drunk, who yelled at each other with equally slurred voices,

"They're fucking dead. All of them–dead!" yelled the first, pointing his finger at the other man's chest.

"You're nothing but a crazy drunk" retorted the second, roaring a laugh and taking a swig from a wineskin. "Get your talk of magic out of my face. I ain't seen nothing of it and I'm tired of hearing your shit."

"You weren't there! I barely escaped with my life!"

"You ran?" the second man jeered, "Quite pusillanimous are you?"

"Fuck you!" shouted the first again, "What was I to do? The earth trembled and swallowed the buildings. They were going to burn him at the stake, but they perished instead. All of Grainridge is ruined since eleven days passed!"

The second man let out a more riotous laugh than before,

"A village drunk probably tripped holding a torch and lit a part of it up. Show me the proof of this mage you speak of, or get out of my face." He took another swig of wine from a flagon in his hand, and wiped his face.

"I have seen it with my own eyes! Do you not trust my witness, or the witness of others as proof?"

"No, I do not. I do not know you. Your witness counts for nothing."

"Come to Grainridge then—see how it is destroyed!"

"I don't have time to go to Grainridge. It is not even within the city. What happens there does not pertain to us."

"But you call me a liar," spat the first man, "when it is the truth! Simply because it does not happen here, nor pertain to you, does not mean it is not truth!"

"When a mage comes and starts burning the city, then I'll believe. Until then I say you're nothing but a loon."

A pair of guards, seeing the commotion, approached the two men who were oblivious to the crowd that they'd drawn.

"You two, what's this?" said the first guard.

"This man," gestured the skeptic to the other with a hiccup, "won't shut up about gods and magic and necromancers."

"I never said anything about gods or necromancers!" protested the first.

"Aye, but magic you did, and it's all the same to me." the other spat.

"Enough enough," interjected the guard with his hand up, "Word from the crown is that there's to be no more talk of magic or mages, or anything of the sorts. We can't be having riots in the streets again, so keep the tripe off your tongues and go about your business."

The first man protested but the second stuck his tongue out at him and took another swig of his wine while he chortled and turned away. The guards stood between the two men, the first watching the other disappear into the crowd whilst he grit his teeth, before they all finally went their separate ways and people milled again in the street where they had stood.

Sherry looked at the woman,

"Is this a common occurrence?" she asked. The woman shrugged,

"More common than uncommon, but it seems that even months ago this was unheard of. Something strange is afoot, though I cannot say what."

"What think you of magic?" Sherry asked,

"The woman shrugged again,

"I think it is of little difference to me, for I do not have that gift."

"But do you believe it to be true?"

"I believe it in my heart that something has passed which makes talk of magic afoot. Perhaps it is magic, or perhaps it is some ruse of conspiracy, but to what end I cannot say."

"Do you think that magic in the world would be for good or for ill? posed Sherry. The woman thought for a moment,

"Part of me says that it would be good, for life is hard as it is, though I see two different scenarios unfolding in my head. The first is that if everyone were to have it, then it would be as if nobody had it, and the inequalities in the world would be the same, for the oppressors would hold the same control over us as they do now.

"I also see another scenario, one where only a few have magic, and I say to this one that the few that had the magic would certainly rule over those that did not. In that case, the world would be just the same as it is now, only perhaps with different people dwelling in the castle than those that do now.

"So, in answer to your question, it makes little difference to me as to whether or not magic exists, for the outcomes would be the same either way; some of us have set unto their destinies grandeur and some of us squalor.

"You are well-spoken and well-thought," said Sherry, "you are certainly learned in language and mathematics at the least."

The woman nodded,

"That I am, for my family is heir to one of the hamlets and my father is magister there. Still, those disciplines lend no aid to my circumstance, for as I said, I am cast to the street by my family, and my child's sire is off to war." She shook her head and grimaced, "I believe that even were he not at war he would not intend to wed me. I have resigned myself to my fate."

"I have witnessed magic." whispered Sherry. The woman paused and studied Sherry's face before finally saying,

"I believe you."

"It is awesome, and wonderful, and terrifying, all at once." Sherry continued, "I've seen it twice now, once even not a foot away from me, and the spell saved my life. I foresee good coming again into the world, for though we are in different circumstances now I pity you– I could easily be in your place instead. Trust to hope, for hope is on the horizon."

"I believe you," the woman repeated, " but, as I've said, it still makes no difference to my life."

And she turned her back to Sherry and walked away down the street, disappearing into the crowd.

Chapter 29

The knock on the wooden frame of the parlor interrupted Sherry's thoughts as she gazed into the flames of the hearth. Sondra stood in the doorway and cleared her throat.

"M'lady..." she paused, as Sherry lifted her head to greet her,

"Good evening," Sherry responded. After a longer pause Sondra said,

"You have a guest."

The hour was late, and guests seldom ever came to the estate. Sherry cocked her head and studied Sondra, noticing that her eyes were wide, and she gave her a concerned look.

Sherry stood and watched as Naryan strode through the doorway. Sherry's throat tightened, but she stood tall and nodded. Sondra peered from around Naryan and shook her head before excusing herself and shutting the door behind her.

The two stood watching each other for a moment before Naryan took a few steps across the room toward her and grabbed her in an embrace. She stiffened, but draped her arms around him briefly before pushing him away and holding him at arms length to examine him. He was not haggard, but he was not clean either. He wore clothes that were a little too big for him and his beard was coming in even more than the last time she'd seen him. He wore a satchel strapped across his chest and his boots were dusty, for he had no doubt been walking along the dirt roads between the Hamlets.

"You look like you haven't had a bath in a month. Smells like it too." Sherry noted. Naryan grinned.

"I suppose it's been about that long."

"I'm not so used to seeing you in ill-fitting clothes that are more than a few weeks old and ne're worn more than once."

"Aye, I don't believe I've ever worn a set of clothes more consecutive days in my life." said Naryan.

"Is this the new favored fashion in the capital then?" she asked.

"I wouldn't know," said Naryan. "I haven't been back in quite a while."

"How long has it been since I've seen you?" she asked. "Two weeks?"

Naryan Nodded,

"To the day. Not that I've been counting."

"What brings you to my doorstep then? This is certainly a surprise, and I can't say one long watched for. I wasn't sure that I'd ever see you again."

"Did you hope for it?" asked Naryan.

Sherry turned and looked out the window into the black night. She ignored his question for a moment before responding,

"So where has the road taken you, if not to the capital?"

It was Naryan's turn for silence. He finally sighed and said,

"There is much to tell, but I am weary. Do you have a place for me to sleep, and we can speak in the morning?"

"Is this why you came?" snapped Sherry, "Since you have nowhere else to go?"

Naryan held his hands up,

"No no–I came because it seems you may be my only friend left in the world."

Sherry shook her head,

"It seems you aim to use me. Again."

Naryan Grimaced,

"If you are to turn me away, then say as much and I will depart."

Sherry's fierce eyes did not break away from him and they stared each other down for a moment before she softened a little.

"I will not turn you away," she said, "but it is only for the boy that I grew up with–not for you."

"I am no longer that boy," Naryan said.

"No, you certainly are not."

253

"Neither am I the man who exiled from the throne merely a month ago."

"I find that hard to believe," said Sherry.

"As do I." continued Naryan, "but as I said, much has happened and there is much to tell."

"Fine then," Sherry said, sitting back down into her armchair and motioning towards the couch across from her. "Some of it I know–you and Einar, alone in the woods, learning of magic. Of this I am still curious, but what other great changes do you claim?"

Naryan sat on the couch and rested his elbows on his knees while he rubbed his face before clasping his hands in front of him and starting,

"When you and Nightmare left me after we'd escaped the capital, I was distraught. I cannot ever say that I was well-loved in my life, but perhaps tolerated as the king's son, and when I acceded there was a further respect that came with the post. All that was gone in an instant, for when I exiled, Rhondia usurped the throne and all of that tolerance dissipated. When you left, I felt fully abandoned,"

Sherry cut him off with a barked laugh,

"*You* felt abandoned?"

"Do you wish to hear?" Naryan said. Sherry's eyes looked towards the ceiling and she shook her head, before saying,

"Continue then."

"You left me there in the grass, and Einar was already gone, and I had nowhere to go, no-one to turn to, and my pitiful thoughts ate at me from within my own head. As time passed, my ego could not handle the blows of rejection from you, from my step-mother, nor from my own subjects who did not even know me, and did not believe who I said I was. I could have let them end me and be done with it, but my stubbornness would not allow me to be defeated. So in my rage I killed them–those who disparaged me, those who turned me away, and even those who did no offense to me specifically yet were merely present in the face of my wrath."

Sherry set her jaw and turned up her nose towards him,

"So you come to me, confessing, in search of forgiveness, for the dead cannot forgive you?"

"No," Naryan said, shaking his head, "there is no forgiveness for this deed, for this was no righteous slaying done by my hand. It was wrath, plain and simple. I am confident I will take the remorse with me to my grave." He looked into the fire and exhaled before continuing,

"And so the people were killed and much of Grainridge was razed. I disappeared into the wilds, wandering aimlessly in search of death, but it would not find me. Neither did I have the will to take my own life, even though I so easily grasped it away from others, for I feel I do not deserve mercy from myself. I searched for Einar, hoping he could bring me relief and wisdom, but he has disappeared and I cannot find him, even with magic. I have given up hope of finding him, and I fear that he may be dead and that I will never learn more of my spirit.

"Grainridge–is that what you said?" asked Sherry.

Naryan nodded,

"Yes, that is where I was."

"I have heard talk of it–in the capital. People in the streets argue over whether or not the events there are true."

"I can assure you," said Naryan, "they are no fabrications–though I am not proud of it.

"There is confusion though," continued Sherry, "as to what is real and what is not. I myself, even having witnessed spells with my own eyes, do not know what to believe, nor what to think of the comings and goings of the other mages."

"What have you seen, and what have you heard?" asked Naryan,

"I do not know much, but I know that Rhondia keeps these cloaked men close to her side at all times. They go here, and there, sometimes within the castle, and often to the city and countryside, though I cannot say to where for I do not spend much time in the

255

city or capital. I only have noticed these strange figures around of late, for they were not here before.

"What's more strange is that they do not cast spells, nor flaunt their powers–in fact I would think them no more than monks or vagrants covered in their hoods, save when we escaped on Nightmare and were assaulted by the one. I think that nobody in all of Satoria knows what they really are, and it is curious to me that they are so clandestine."

"Curious, yes," said Naryan, "for I know little of them either, save that they and Einar know each other and have a history–whether for ill or good I cannot tell. I also find it strange that Rhondia would hold their power concealed. She is crafty, but I cannot tell what her plan is.

"Ah, Rhondia." he grimaced and tightened his fists. "Whenever her name crosses my lips it leaves a foul taste behind. She and I have never been close, but this treason is more than I can handle from her. I will certainly slay her when the time comes, for she has shown her true colors and taken this as an opportune moment to seize the throne. This is not only an offense to me, but to the foundational laws of Satoria."

Sherry stiffened,

"I know you and her have your differences, but she is not evil as you would presume."

"Why do you defend her? Do you not see she has supplanted me from the throne?"

"She has the heart of a mother."

"The two of us have cut any familial bond there may have once been–she is no mother of mine. What good is the heart of a mother if she tries to kill me?" Naryan scoffed. "I cannot see how you honestly think she is of good intent."

"You cannot judge my thoughts for you have not been where I have been." Sherry stood and walked to the hearth, where she stared into the flames, brooding. "In fact, when I had given up hope of life, and love, and was distraught at the bruises of your betrayal, she found me and consoled me. I have seen her in a new light."

Naryan shook his head,

"So now my best friend has taken sides with my greatest enemy–I cannot say how deep this betrayal cuts."

Sherry turned to him,

"If anything it was forced by your own hand–or the thrusts of your loins rather. I was foolish to loft you to such a high place in my heart."

Naryan stood and moved towards her in a few slow steps. He reached his hand out and grasped hers, holding it in front of him softly, and caressed it with his thumb as he spoke,

"I will admit–I have taken you for granted these last years, for I felt that you were a staple in my life to always be there–but now I have pushed you away. These last few weeks, in the face of my errors and solitude, in my heart, my mind was drawn to you and your goodness, and your empathy, for you have always been the rock on which I leaned in my life. I hoped that your wisdom would lead me out of this pit of despair."

Sherry shook her head,

"If you would have said these words to me but two months ago I would have accepted them, for I even longed for them, but now they are folly. You've spoken many words tonight, in humility even, but none of them are the ones that I have longed to hear."

"What then do you long to hear, Sherry?"

"I hear remorse from you, and I would say that your remorse is good, but you sound more sorrowful for those you have killed that you do not know, than for what you've done to me. They did not love you, and I, the one who stood by your side even when you were despised, am refuse in your sight."

Naryan gripped tight onto Sherry's hand as he spoke,

"I have been afraid to even admit it to myself, and dreaded to even stand in front of you, the offended, and repent of my sins." he swallowed and paused, looking down at the floor between them. His jaw quivered and lower lips turned down even as the sheen of tears on his eyes showed in the firelight. He then looked into her eyes, eyes that glared at him with righteous anger from her set face and he collapsed to his knees in front of her, holding her hand above his head in both of his own.

"I am sorry." he said finally, gasping between sobs "for forsaking you as my friend. I'm sorry for abusing your love. I'm sorry for violating your trust, and your body in my own carnal desires. I have no excuses, only remorse and repentance."

He did not look up to her, but kept his head bowed and her hand atop his head as he wept. Sherry looked down at him and heard the sniffs from his nose and the thuds of teardrops onto her carpeted floor, until after a while they subsided, staccatoed only by his sobs.

"Do you forgive me then?" Naryan asked without looking up at her.

Sherry bit her cheek and exhaled before answering,

"Now that I finally hear these words, even as I have longed to hear them and dreamt of them–they are empty. Perhaps not from your meaning, for as far as I can tell they are said in sincerity, but these words cannot mend the rift you have wrought in my soul."

She withdrew her hand from his, and his arms dropped to his sides. He did not look up at her, but stared at her feet for a while, before finally sighing and pushing himself up to a stand. He ran both his hands over his face and squeezed both his eyes tight before opening them again to look at her. Sherry saw that his eyes were red and bagged, and though she saw sincerity in his gaze her stomach turned in disdain.

"Sondra." Sherry called out. Sondra immediately opened the door, as if she'd been waiting outside of it to be beckoned. She scuttled over to the two of them, brow furrowed as she surveyed them.

"Yes, m'lady?"

"The 'king' will be staying the night here," she paused, "though not much longer than that I should presume. Show him to the guests quarters and see that he is well-attended."

Sondra nodded, and nodded her head towards Naryan,

"This way, your majesty."

Naryan turned and followed Sondra, but stopped at the doorway and turned to look again at Sherry.

"Will you ever forgive me?" he asked. Sherry's eyes locked with his, but she shook her head,

"I cannot say."

Chapter 30

Sherry awoke the next morning, much as usual, to Sondra throwing open the curtains. The sun shone down on her face as it always did, but she sprung up willingly and had Sondra help garb her in her riding gear. The clasps were all set, and her boots pulled tall, and they shared no discussion whatsoever of the previous night. Sherry walked down to the ground level, bypassing the kitchen and heading straight for the stables where she intended to take Daybreak on an early ride.

Out the front she walked, past a gardener tending to the hedge, and toward the stables where she heard the commotion of mucking from inside. The horses were all standing outside, tethered to the railing, but her saddles were still inside so she called out to the stable hand,

"Harold–halt the mucking a moment–I'm coming inside for my saddle. Or better yet, bring it to me, would you?" The sound of slopping stopped, and the sound of footsteps patting along the ground could be heard within. A grunt of him lifting the saddle came from within, followed by the crunch of dirt beneath his feet as he trudged toward the stable door holding the saddle. Around the corner he came–but it was not Harold's face she saw, but Naryan's.

"Where would you like it, m'lady? On Nightmare?"

His face was flush from the work, and a bead of sweat dripped down the side of his face. His hands and forearms were filthy, but he exuded joy nonetheless. Sherry crossed her arms,

"I didn't know that the invitation I extended to you would outlast the night."

Naryan adjusted his stance to hold the saddle against his hip,

"I thought I'd earn my keep at least."

Sherry looked him up and down and wrinkled her nose at the stench of urea.

"Have you ever mucked a stable before in your life? You know we have rakes and shovels–you needn't use your hands."

Naryan shrugged.

"I'd like the full experience the first time. On to Nightmare then?"

Sherry shook her head,

"No, I'll have it on Daybreak–I hope you're not getting horse shit on my saddle."

"I'll polish it for you if I have to. Which one is Daybreak? I'm not sure I've met them before."

Sherry nodded to the white horse down the line,

"There he is–saddle him up for me if you would."

Naryan walked to Daybreak and started saddling him as he spoke,

"He looks like a fine horse–did you pick him up in the city? And when? It must have been fairly recently–unless you've been hiding him from me for a while."

Sherry chewed her cheek before responding,

"I picked him up on the way back from Sallow Hill. I didn't quite want to walk the whole way by myself–if you gather my meaning."

"Ah. I see." Naryan held his tongue and didn't turn to look at her as he continued to fasten the saddle. A few minutes later he had pulled the final straps and bridled Daybreak, giving him a pat on the rump and untying him from the post. He led Daybreak to Sherry and handed her the reins.

"I feel I owe you reimbursement for his cost. Unfortunately, my income is indisposed at the moment so you'll need to be a little patient. Charge me usery if you see fit."

"I'll add it to your debt." she said.

Naryan turned and walked back towards the stables. She watched him enter into it, and shook her head with a snort as the sound of mucking continued from within. *Let him sweat it out–he deserved it after all the shit he'd put her through.* As she left she called out,

"When you're done–you should go."

There was no response from within.

She rode the bounds of the estate for a few hours, finally returning in the heat of midday and coming again to the stables. Harold was there this time, tending to the steeds, and she dropped off Daybreak to him without so much of a word regarding her earlier interaction with Naryan. She did peek her head into the stable, however, to see that Naryan was gone, and it was as clean as it could have been for a first-time mucker.

She headed back to the manor, cleaning herself and putting on casual attire before going to her favorite place on the west side of the house to recreate with a drink and lunch. The porch was near to the kitchen, and a window from the kitchen gave a view from the inside to the porch, and it was open to let in what little draft could be captured. Between the heat of the ovens within, and the heat of the day without, it was often quite stifling inside.

She sat, eating a charcuterie brought to her by one of the chefs, and sipped on a cool light wine from one of the many vineyards within the bounds of their estate. Sliced salted pork sausages, goat cheese inlaid with dried plums, a dripping pear, and freshly sliced bread topped with a thick slab of salted butter that sat atop it melting was her course today. Even the simplest things were glorious when one was hungry. She tore off a piece of the bread, ensuring to wipe up a pat of butter that had slid across her plate, but her attention was caught by clattering from the open window of the kitchen, which was considerably lower than usual.

Voices carried from within and she stood to investigate, setting her plate down on her seat as she walked toward the window. She stuck her head into it, the voices becoming clearer as she moved closer, and finally heard the words much clearer,

"Your majesty, I–I must insist. Thank you, but we have two more chefs on the way–we'll be quite alright!"

Sherry watched Naryan use both of his arms to wrestle a huge pot across the kitchen, banging into pots and pans that hung from the sides of the counters as he went. They swung back and forth as he passed, clanging both into the pot he wrestled, and into each other as a set of horrible-sounding wind chimes.

Naryan finally set the pot next to the fire and stood up, looking at the chef with a grin and wiping his forehead with the back of his hand and saying,

"There you go–no difficulty at all! What's next?"

The chef sputtered,

"Your majesty, you really shouldn't trouble yourself. I'm not sure there's any way you can make yourself useful here–it's not as large a pantry as you have up at the castle, so not much room to move around. Too many cooks in the kitchen, and all that."

Sherry moved away from the window towards the side door to the kitchen, hearing Naryan continue to protest about something, before she finally entered the building, rounded the corner, and confronted them,

"Ok, that'll be enough." Her hands were on her hips, and both the king and the cook looked up, startled at her presence. "Naryan, you heard him–you're not needed here. C'mon let's go." she motioned toward the door with her hand.

Naryan pouted a little but did as she asked, and behind him the wide-eyed chef nodded his appreciation to her. She ushered Naryan outside, pointing him to sit on the chair next to where she'd placed her food and asked,

"What are you still doing here?"

Naryan eyed her plate, grabbing a piece of cheese from it and putting it in his mouth as he answered,

"Making myself useful."

"You're clearly just getting in the way. I'm not really sure you're needed anyway–we've got plenty of retinue here on the estate. In fact, it's been running just fine for over a century as I've been told."

"I'm really just trying to help. It's the least I can do after all I've put you through. I am a penitent man." he reached forward to help himself again from her plate and she reached out and slapped his hand,

"Keep away from my food."

Naryan's chin dropped and he feigned indignation with a gasp, holding his 'injured' hand up, but wagging a finger with the other.

"You should be put to death for that–striking the king. You ought to know better."

Sherry pursed her lips and glared at him for a moment, but quicker than ever he reached his hand back out and grabbed half of her pear, leaned back in his chair, and munched into it. It took everything in her to keep back a smile, so instead she huffed,

"I won't let you ruin my meal more than you already have." She grabbed her plate, and sat back down to finish eating with nothing but the sound of the two of them chewing, and a steer mooing in the distance.

Naryan looked at her as she ignored him, chewing, so he swallowed his own bit of pear and leaned forward.

"You know–joking aside–I really am sorry."

"I know." she said without looking at him, and continued eating.

Naryan raised both his eyebrows and took another bite of the pear.

"So...where's your father? I haven't seen him the whole time I've been here."

"He's at the capital–you know, with the war and all. Quite busy. I haven't seen him around here much of late."

"Aah, so you're the lady of the house now?" Sherry nodded.

"I have been for quite some time."

"I suppose I should listen to you then."

Sherry raised her own eyebrows and nodded again.

"That you should–which is why I'm surprised you're still here. I've already asked you to leave."

The smirk drained from Naryan's face.

"I owe you a debt. My conscience cannot handle it going unpaid. Also–I've nowhere else to go."

"There is no payment for this debt." she said.

Naryan tossed the remainder of the pear to the lawn where a goose gobbled it up.

"So be it then," he said, rising. "I shall not disparage your will again."

Sherry held the food in her mouth as she watched him walk away, now the only sound was the clack of his boots along the wooden deck. She swallowed, calling out to him after a few steps,

"Nowhere to go?"

Naryan turned to her and shook his head,

"Nowhere. I am a king–without a kingdom."

Sherry sighed, then enunciated,

"You may stay here–" she said "but you will obey my every word and you will leave the moment you're told. Do you understand?"

Naryan nodded.

"Do not take my kindness as weakness;" she continued, "for I will not be abused again."

Naryan nodded.

"Thank you." he said. It looked like he meant it.

She gave him a curt smile, then grabbed her plate, sat down again, taking a sip of her wine.

"Would you like a drink, as the honored guest?" she asked, gesturing towards her goblet. He shook his head.

"Actually," he said, reclining on a chair next to her, "I've quit drinking."

Sherry raised an eyebrow,

"You're joking."

"I'm not."

"What's your reason then? Make too many poor decisions while inebriated?"

He conceded her point with a nod, but said,

"Certainly a benefit of my abstinence, but ultimately I cannot commune with my spirit when intoxicated–I cannot cast spells."

"Oh yes," said Sherry, "the magic. I'd nearly forgotten. I'll have to hear more of that."

"Yes, you will," said Naryan, standing up. "But another time. I've got keep that needs earning."

Sherry cocked her head,

"Oh? Where are you headed off to then?"

"Now that the stables have been mucked, Harold needs help unbaling the hay. He said to meet him before supper."

"I'm not quite sure where this work ethic came from. I don't know whether to be impressed or worried."

Naryan shrugged,

"I told you I was a changed man." he said as he walked off towards the stables. Sherry muttered under her breath,

"I suppose we'll see."

Chapter 31

A little more than a week passed since Naryan had shown up that night, but the days gone by were much less eventful than the first. It was now nearing mid-July. Naryan certainly did keep himself busy, "earning his keep" as he'd promised, and Sherry often found herself keeping an eye out for him as she meandered the grounds. Curiosity? Perhaps. She could not honestly discern if she was proctoring him, or pining after him, though the latter frustrated her, and at any thought of him she scolded herself and then found something else to be busy with.

He made no passes at her, which was a relief since she truly did want to help him—but she had no intent of playing the victim again. His relationship was now that of a tenant, and if that's what he wanted, then so be it. She did find it entirely strange, however, that he had come all this way to make amends, then keep away from her and bury himself in his work. Confusing, to say the least. Had he only cared about clearing his conscience, or was he still keen on mending their relationship? She did not know, and telling herself that she did not care was a lie.

Even as he was lost in his work, today she was lost in hers, as she'd spent much of the morning tracking the stewardships of the estate's tenants, and tallying their banalities. Monetary taxes were not the only collection from their tenants, though that was certainly part of it. Their storehouses were kept brimmed, and the harvests were already good this year, with plenty more ahead. What overflow there was would be sent to the capital for sale, to further fill their coffers.

It was not her first time taking part in the tally, but it was her first time with full responsibility since her father was currently engaged at the capital. Even excluding the upcoming sale of the land's produce, their ledger was very profitable this year. They had forgone this year's scutage by way of conscription of a few men in lessee families, in addition to Shawn's service. Even if his education did lend him an officer's badge, it was still a pretty penny that they normally expended so as to save him from enlistment.

Sherry shook her head, realizing that she was in the midst of writing the final figure in her ledger, and looked up for a moment trying to think of what it was. She remembered, scrawling on a scroll of parchment, and tucking it under her arm as she headed from the storehouse back toward the manor.

It was mid-afternoon and she was tired from the day's work and ready to recreate in her favorite spot on the porch. Behind her, the estate hands continued to separate barrels and crates of goods that were to go to the storehouse from those to be sent to the capital, and ahead of her, a gardener was on his hands and knees trimming the verge from the pathway. She passed the gardner, but heard him call out to her,

"M'lady."

She recognized the voice and turned to see that it was Naryan, who stood up and grinned at her.

"Oh—hello." she said.

"Don't have time to say hello to old friends, eh?"

"I honestly didn't know it was you."

Naryan shrugged,

"I guess I do blend in quite well these days with the serfs. Anyway—what do you say about dinner tonight? Just the two of us? You and a common folk?"

Sherry clasped both her hands in front of her and looked him up and down. He was garbed in coveralls blackened with soil at the knees, and with filthy hands. She looked back towards the estate and thought of a cool glass of red wine mixed with plum cordial. She shook her head,

"I'm not sure that's a good idea."

His eyes looked deep into hers for a while, before he finally smirked,

"Do you not find my work fit for your house?"

"Oh, I've not checked in on the quality of your work whatsoever, but I assume it satisfactory if the manor isn't up in flames."

"I think you at least owe me dinner for all the hard work I've been doing."

"I don't owe you anything." she snapped.

He grimaced,

"So be it." and turned to walk away.

She grumbled to herself for a moment, but called back after him.

"See those men down there, separating the barrels?"

Naryan stopped and looked at them, and nodded to her.

"It's supposed to take five of them until dark to finish. If you give them the rest of the day off and finish it yourself, I'll sit you down to sup."

Naryan counted the barrels under his breath,

"That's too much work for one person in that time."

"No dinner then." Sherry shrugged. She turned away from him to head back up toward the manor. Partway up the hill she looked back to see that Naryan had abandoned the verge and was headed over towards the storehouse at what she knew was his pace of determination; she rolled her eyes and continued up toward the manor where her drink and shade awaited her.

The manor itself was on a small hill that gave good vantage over its surroundings, including the ancillary structures around it. Leading up to the front double-doors of the manor was a wide stone staircase, and as she reached it, she heard the sound of voices and commotion in the air. Turning and looking out towards the storehouses she saw the men that had previously been manipulating the barrels and crates backing away from another figure who was certainly Naryan.

Even from her vantage point far above she could see the glow of the runes as he wrote, and the barrels that had taken two men to wrestle were now arranging themselves in organized rows. Most of the men, at first backing away from Naryan, were now in full sprints away from him, flailing their arms and yelling to others to also retreat. It seemed that one of them had even fainted at the sight of the magic and was laying face-down in the grass nearby.

Sherry sighed, even as Naryan enthusiastically waved up to her from down below as the final crates were settling down into their places. Upon hearing the manor doors creaking open behind her she turned to find Sondra greeting her.

"Sondra, run over to the kitchen–will you? Tell them to prepare a table for two in the dining room. The king will surely be expecting to dine with me tonight."

And so he was. Sherry saw that Naryan had at least taken the time to scrub his arms and put on some clean, no doubt borrowed, clothes before he came to dinner. He strode through the door trying to hold back a smile that instead came across as too smug of a smirk for her to not be annoyed. She too had cleaned up a little–only for the occasion–not for him, she told herself.

The table was already set and Naryan held out her chair for her as she sat down and placed the napkin on her lap. He strode to his char and sat down, also placing a napkin on his lap before eyeing her.

"You shouldn't look so proud of yourself." Sherry said. Naryan feigned offense,

"Ah. Me? You should be happy that I was able to save you an afternoon's wages for five men!"

"Sure, a little wages were spared, but now I've got four mens who no longer want to set foot near the manor, and another who is still shaking in the infirmary. I'd bid you to give him a well-visit, but he might faint again."

Naryan shrugged,

"Apologies–I meant no harm."

Sherry smirked,

"I suppose you didn't. You mustn't forget that these people have no idea of your newfound knowledge. I must admit–I'd nearly forgotten it myself. What, with you ignoring me and all."

"Ignoring you? I haven't been ignoring you–I've been lost in the work of earning my keep! I didn't want to bother the lady of the house with petty smalltalk."

"Yet," she gestured, "you'd do *that* to get my attention?"

Naryan mustered an innocent shrug.

"Though," she continued, "It eludes me why you'd subject yourself to such laborious work when you can simply wave your little finger around. Mucking the stables? On your hands and knees tending to the lawn? I could have sworn I saw you milking a cow the other day too. Your hands were too soft for such tasks a mere month ago."

Two servants entered into the dining room bearing their dinner, and filled the plates in front of them with roasted beef, fresh bread, and an assortment of sliced fruits. One of them eyed Naryan with gritted teeth, and they both scurried out of the room as soon as they'd served the food. Naryan continued,

"I have been a little too, let's call it 'liberal', with this newfound knowledge, though others might opt to call it reckless. I dare say I'd like to learn a little temperance and moderation. Call it a desire to build my character and learn humility."

"Words that I never thought I'd hear you admit."

They paused and looked at each other for a moment, before he leaned in a bit towards her from across the table and whispered,

"That was pretty great though–wasn't it?"

She scowled for a moment before leaning in a little and grinning,

"I must admit–it was."

Sherry reclined back into her chair and started on her meal, while Naryan grabbed her goblet and poured the contents of his own into hers. She eyed him before asking,

"So–you weren't kidding about not drinking then?"

Naryan shook his head, and Sherry said,

"Tell me more."

Naryan wriggled his finger to write a rune, and her goblet glided through the air to rest in front of her.

"You know," she continued, "I'd think this was wholly unnatural and terrifying, if it wasn't you who was doing it. I still find it uncanny, but knowing you–it is more curious."

Naryan raised his eyebrows and nodded in agreement,

"It took me some getting used to, and sometimes I find it surreal myself."

"So," asked Sherry, "how does it work?"

"How it works, I can explain, but why it works–I can barely tell myself."

"Go on..." Sherry prompted,

"These runes–they're a language, the language of the spirit. In writing them I am merely directing my spirit, who dwells on a different plane, what action I require of it in this one. We are," he paused, "more than this physical frame, though I would not have believed it without seeing it myself."

"You saw it?"

Naryan nodded,

"I ate a strange mushroom, given to me by Einar of course, and witnessed my spirit doing my bidding."

Sherry put down her fork without touching her food and looked at him,

"So you're saying that all these runes are just speaking a language that we do not know?"

Naryan nodded and continued,

"And our spirits are powerful–having dominion over the physical world that our bodies inhabit, but are subject to; we must commune with our spirits to shape the world to our desires."

"You're right," said Sherry, "I would not believe it if I had not seen it for myself."

"Do you want to learn?"

Sherry bit her lip to fight back a grin before nodding,

"Certainly."

Naryan stood, pushing back his chair.

"Well then–onto it! Come, stand here."

Sherry pushed her chair back and walked to him. They stood next to each other, and he held his hand in front of him as she watched.

"Hold your hand like this."

She did, and watched as he gestured with his hand, a soft glow emanating from his fingers as he did. In front of them, a chair scraped itself along the floor to pull out from its place beneath the table.

"Just copy what you did?" she asked. Naryan nodded his head,

"Yup–just like that. Exactly as I did it."

"Does it–my spirit–just *know* how to speak this language?"

"Yea, as far as I can tell." said Naryan.

"Can you write it again? I don't recall what you did." Naryan wrote again, and the chair scratched its way along the floor again. Sherry ran her finger through the air, but nothing happened. She exhaled a breath she'd been holding and shook her head.

"Hey, don't get down on yourself," said Naryan, "It took me a while to get it too. I actually would have been cross if you got it the first time."

Sherry let out a short laugh, and then focused again, eyes narrowed as she drew. A few more times she motioned with her hand, but still there was nothing.

"It's ok," Naryan said, "it will take some practice." he put his hand on her shoulder but she shrugged it off and continued to write, intently focused on the spot in the air in front of her.

"Here, watch again," said Naryan, "it looks like you're not quite getting the curve right." She watched him as he wrote, this time the chair sliding towards them and turning around. He twirled around and sat in it, watching her as she worked.

A few more times she tried, but still to no avail. Naryan stood up again, and paced as he watched.

"No, no," he said, smirking, "you're holding your mouth wrong."

Sherry scowled at his poor joke, tried a few more times and then plopped down in the chair with a sigh.

"Here," he said, reaching his hand out to her, "stand–and we'll try again."

She let him guide her up, and this time he stood close behind her, holding just below her right wrist with his right hand, and guiding it as she focused.

She traced the rune, and the slightest glow of gold emanated from the tip of her finger, even as the chair jerked a few inches before settling down.

"I did it!" she squealed, rotating toward him, "Did you see that! Did you see it?"

"Yes!" he said, even as each of their eyes caught the other in their close proximity. His teeth held back his lip, as his eyes narrowed and hers widened; time dragged on for a few moments and she heard her heartbeat in her ears. Her head swam as he leaned forward and kissed her on the lips, lingering only for a moment. She turned her head away from him, pulling back, even though their arms were still caught in an embrace.

He reached out and caressed her hair, but she would not look at him, and she shook her head.

"No."

His brow furrowed and he released her, holding his palms out towards her as he took a step back.

"I'm sorry," he muttered.

"It's fine." she said, but she shook her head, and studied the grain of the wood floor.

"Well," said Naryan, breaking the silence, "You got it a bit faster than I did at least. I shouldn't expect anything less from you I suppose. You're always good at whatever you put your mind to."

She tucked a strand of hair behind her ear and flashed him a curt smile,

"I suppose so. Anyway, thank you for showing me that. I think I'm going to retire now."

She could feel his gaze following her as she walked away from the dining room, until she rounded the corner to the entryway. She sped up when she was out of his sight, her feet moving quicker and quicker to take her up the steps of the grand staircase. She ran her hand along the banister along the top of the walkway overlooking the entry until she came to the hall that led her to the wing of her bedroom.

She was nearly at a jog as she went down the hallway, and finally made it into her room where she pulled the door shut and leaned her head against it as she caught her breath.

Chapter 32

Sherry managed to get another glow out of her fingers, but not much else. She shook her hand and wrote again, but to mostly the same result: nothing.

"Ugh, I'm never gonna get this."

They were out in the sun on a grassy hill a short ride out into the estate from the manor. It was still visible in the distance, and they had a clear view of the road leading through the estate up to it. Naryan reclined on the ground as he watched her struggle to not move a small rock in front of her, twirling a small stick between his fingers.

"Just a little more practice, I'm sure you'll get it." he said.

Sherry grimaced,

"You've been saying that forever and I've had basically no results." she slumped down onto the grass next to him and lay back, looking up at the sky.

"I mean," said Naryan, nodding at her finger, "at least you won't run into things when you're walking around at night."

Sherry rolled her eyes. Naryan smirked,

"I'm just looking on the *bright* side of things."

The comment elicited a slap on his arm from her.

"Don't you have some chores to do? I'm sure I can find something useful for your time."

Naryan shrugged,

"I think I've done everything required by the bailiff for the upkeep of your estate for the next month. All the people have found themselves with leisure time and they barely know what to do with themselves. At least they're not scared of me anymore, now that I'm doing all their work."

Sherry sighed,

"All I'm saying is that you seem to have picked up magic within a few weeks, and you're already competent, while I've been at it for nearly a month and a half with no results. I can write every symbol in that grimoire forward and backward, but to no effect except now I've got a glow worm for a finger." She looked at her hand with a scowl and wriggled a finger. "It's a little disheartening."

Naryan shrugged and continued to study his stick.

"I don't really know. Everyone should be able to do it just the same, at least that's what Einar said..." his voice drifted off.

Sherry sat up,

"What's the matter?"

Naryan tossed his stick away,

"Oh, it's just Einar...I've been searching for him but to no avail." he furrowed his brow, "My spirit cannot find him even sent out every day and every night, in every cardinal direction from here to the sea, and to the mountains, and even to Chromer."

"I'm sure he's fine," said Sherry

"Oh, are you? I'm *sure* he's fine with a bunch of other Erilaz after him, trying to kill him for saving me."

Sherry drew her lips tight as he continued,

"To you and everyone else, I'm an incredible magician, but to me, I am still a learner. I know so little, and my only teacher and my only friend has disappeared. I'm lost without him."

"Sometimes we need to find our own way."

Naryan stood up,

"Thanks, but I'm in no mood for speeches of inspiration." he held his hand out to her and she grasped onto it to be helped to a stand. She brushed the grass off her pants and looked at him.

"Why do you want to find him so badly?"

Naryan stared off into the distance,

"Perhaps call it friendship, perhaps call it loyalty–all I know is that he aided me in the darkest of moments when nobody else would, and for that I owe him a debt of gratitude."

"You'll find him." she said.

Naryan flashed a smile.

"Yes, I will." he said, mounting Nightmare as she mounted Daybreak, "For I plan on seeking until he is found, or I am dead of old age."

She looked at him and nodded, but then looked past him to the road which led to the manor in the distance. On it there was a carriage, escorted by two soldiers on horseback as it rolled down the path. Sherry nodded towards it,

"Look," she said, "Father must be back! It's been weeks since he was home!" She goaded Daybreak towards the manor and took off at a gallop, Naryan close behind. She grinned, thinking of his arms wrapped around her, while she felt the wind rush through her hair and the rhythm of Daybreak's hoofbeats as the manor drew closer.

They first stopped at the stables to drop off the horses with Harold, before making their way up towards the manor again. The carriage had arrived a little before them, and Sherry could not help but scurry a little faster towards it when they were close. There was already a group of people gathered round it when she came, but the furrowed brows adorning their faces caused Sherry to slow her pace.

The door to the carriage was open, and from it, borne on a stretcher, was Shawn, covered in a thick blanket and pale as he slept. A wail escaped her lips as she saw, and her stomach turned, causing her to fall to her knees. Behind her, Naryan caught her under her arms from behind and held her up, his jaw set as he watched Shawn being carried by the soldiers.

"Come, stand up." Sherry heard Naryan say, and she stood, burying her head in the nook of his neck, and allowing his arms to envelop her. She sobbed for a while, even until the whispers of the others died down and they dispersed back to their posts on the estate. She pushed herself back from Naryan, and she wiped the tears from her eyes and looked around.

"Take me to him. I need to see him."

Naryan nodded, and he held her hand as they walked towards the manor together. As they came to the front door, it opened, and the two soldiers who had escorted the carriage emerged from it, grim looks flashing on their faces as they saw her.

"My lady," said the first, holding his helmet under the crook of his arm. "Let us speak."

She nodded, and he gestured with his hand towards a bench in the entry of the manor.

"Please, sit if you will." She sat, and Narayan next to her. There was a long pause, wanting to speak first, until the guard finally broke the silence,

"He is not well. While I cannot say if it is a mortal wound, he certainly lays now in the balance of life and death. He must be cared for during all hours of the day and night, for he is with fever and fighting infection."

Sherry nodded,

"What happened?" she asked.

"He was wounded in a skirmish, pierced in his side with a misericorde while he was caught alone and swarmed from his mount."

Sherry covered her mouth and whispered,

"He said he was to do no fighting."

The soldier shook his head,

"There is no safety on the battlefield. He is no coward, but even when armored, one cannot prevail against many."

"How goes the war?" cut in Naryan, "I have heard no news."

"There is no good news to tell," said the soldier, "for the border was not held at the White River, and Chromer now occupies the Shallows. It has been so now for over a month, and we cannot stop them from coming into our lands unhindered."

Naryan grimaced and the soldier continued, "Their numbers are too great so we cannot defeat them in one fell swoop, nor can we spread ourselves so thin to defend all the lands that they threaten." he shook his head, "Many even throw down their weapons and desert in the face of danger, for the king is nowhere to be found."

Naryan opened his mouth to protest, but Sherry stood,

"Take me to him," she said, "I want to see him."

"My lady." nodded the soldier, and they followed him towards the room where Shawn was laid.

The blinds were drawn shut to keep the room darkened, and a nurse tended to Shawn's side. He was lying on his back, a cloth across his forehead; his eyes were closed and he was unmoving. His shirt was cut off and lying on the floor near him, and it was black from days of blood that had seeped into it. His wound was not a gash but a puncture, for the thin misericord had been thrust between the plates of armor at his ribs to find his soft innards. Thus, it did not seem a terrible wound at a glance, but with every rise and fall of his chest blood leaked out of the small hole, for it was a deep prick.

The nurse took her leave, and Sherry came and knelt next to him at the bed, Naryan standing just behind her with his hand on her shoulder. Sherry put her hand out to Shawn's, and felt that it was clammy. She caressed it and he stirred, opening his lids the slightest bit so that he could see them. He blinked a few times, finally realizing where he was, and his company. He tried to speak, but instead was caught up in a fit of coughing that he held back until they became little more than shallow breaths.

Sherry grasped tighter to his hand until he was able to regain his composure, before he looked over at them and, with long pauses between each phrase, rasped,

"Sorry, you have to see, me like this, little sister."

Sherry gripped his hand tighter,

"You told me you wouldn't get hurt."

"Now, isn't the time, to point out that, I'm a liar."

"Well, I missed you." she said. "Does father know?"

Shawn shook her head,

"I don't know, but I doubt it. I'm just one of many who may not return."

"Hush," she said, "You have returned."

"Aye, but many others will not. And for what? For him?" He nodded towards Naryan the best he could. "Many ask, why they fight for a king, who will not even show his face. But it seems he, he has been here, the whole time–philandering."

A fit of coughing and wheezing interrupted him again, and Sherry shushed him, but Naryan could not hold his tongue.

"It is not right that you have been sent to war–and it is not by my hand that this has been ordered. I do not sit on the throne."

"So, the whispers, are true." said Shawn, "that you cannot even rule the throne which has been given to you, so you have run away. Many times I defended, your honor behind your back, but I am played the fool."

"These are lies!" spat Naryan, stepping closer to the bed, "spread by whom and to what end, I cannot say."

"They are simply murmured by the men, who die for the kingdom, and to no apparent end."

"I have been usurped," said Naryan, "and she who sits on the throne does not care for the people."

"It must run, in the family." said Shawn.

"I care for the people!" said Naryan.

"Prove it then," said Shawn, "for it seems to all that you are a drunk and a coward, and the end of the kingdom is at hand."

"You know nothing!" spat Naryan again, "Of what I've done, and what I've gone through."

"Yes," said Shawn, "so many jugs of wine–it must have been hard."

"If you were not in this condition, I should call for a duel and check your tongue–you know not what you speak."

"No, I do not know of what trials you claim, but I know that you have not been at the battle fronts, defending your kingdom, nor speaking at the burials of the dead. There is no respect, left in, the kingdom for you. The men, do not even know, your face."

"Hush," Sherry said, and nudged Naryan back with her arm. "Whatever quarrel you have must wait–this is not the time or the place. Shawn, you must rest."

Naryan and Shawn's eyes lingered on one another each with a glare. Shawn's eyes eventually closed to rest, and Sherry released his hand and rose, kissing him on the forehead and ushering Naryan from the chamber.

As soon as they were in the corridor and the door shut behind them, Sherry hurried off along the hallway, faster and faster leaving Naryan behind as she went. He had to run to catch up to her, calling her all the while,

"Sherry, wait." he called, but she did not stop. Finally, he managed to reach her, and he caught her up into her arms, finding that she had tears running down her cheeks. She turned and buried herself in his arms and he held her while she sobbed.

"He's going to die," She said, looking up at Naryan and wiping her eyes with the back of her hand. "Isn't he?"

Naryan grimaced.

"I cannot say."

Sherry moved away from Naryan and looked back down the hallway towards the room where Shawn lay.

"He has always been my strength," she said, "for in my youth I looked up to my older brother. He taught me to ride well, to not fear a little dirt, and to cross my fingers at those who give me sideways glances. It is hard to see him in such a place of weakness, and know that we may have already had our last laugh together."

"Aye," nodded Naryan, scowling, "I hope he did not pass on to you the inability to hold his tongue. He certainly could use a little less sharpness. If he was not on his deathbed I would box some humility into him."

Sherry turned and slapped Naryan across the cheek, leaving a red mark and causing him to take a step back with mouth agape.

"You disgust me." she snapped, her eyes red from the mixed tears and anger. "Pull your head out of your ass. He lies, dying from fighting for his land, and you insult him because of your spurned ego."

"He, and probably a thousand others, think that I'm a coward that has left them for dead. They do not know the struggles that I've endured and the pain that I feel with the throne usurped from me. I did not send them to this fight, yet I am blamed."

"You always turn everything about yourself. You have no shame, even in the presence of a dying man."

Naryan's eyes flashed and he opened his mouth to speak again, but then he softened and nodded.

"You're right. I'm sorry."

She inhaled and nodded, her eyes now a little less menacing.

"I need some fresh air." she said, and they headed back down the corridor and out the front door of the manor. The air and sunlight of the exterior were refreshing compared to the heavy gloom of Shawn's room, but Sherry still felt no joy.

They each secluded themselves in different places in the estate for the remainder of the day. Sherry had spent the time in her favorite spot near the kitchen, and Naryan busied himself in the garden, surrounded by flowers that buzzed with bees.

Still, Sherry grew restless, and searched for him across the estate as she slowly walked, until she saw his form in the garden. She went to him, and as she neared she saw that he was sitting cross-legged on the ground, eyes closed and hands on his legs as he relaxed. There were runes writing and hovering in the air around him as he meditated.

She stood, watching him for a moment until all of the runes whisked away as though a breeze blew over them, and he opened his eyes. He nodded to her in acknowledgement, but said nothing. She sat beside him on the grass.

"What are you doing?" she asked, nodding to where the runes had just been.

"Searching." he said, "for Einar. He is still nowhere to be found.

"How do you search for him if you are here?"

"I command my spirit to search for his," he said. "Each of the runes is a place or a direction and a command to search therein for him. My spirit then goes to each of those places, and will tell me if he is there."

"So your spirit is not here with you now then?"

Naryan shook his head,

283

"No. But it will return shortly. Even though I have bid it to search far and wide it is of fleet foot, and covers vast distances in little time."

"So then," Sherry smirked, "I could now overpower you in your defenseless state?"

Naryan laughed,

"Aye, I suppose you could."

"Good, I've been meaning to give you a few welts for your comments of ego earlier today."

Naryan picked at the grass.

"I already apologized for that."

Sherry nodded,

"So you did–but sometimes words alone are not fit to heal wounds that the same tongue has wrought."

"I guess I'm learning that," he said. The two sat in silence for a little before Sherry broke the silence,

"I know how you can make it right. Everything."

Naryan looked over at her.

"Oh?"

She nodded.

"You know," she continued, "I've read your grimoire front-to-back a hundred times by now. I know all the symbols and their meanings as well as I can."

"Maybe better than I do," Naryan muttered.

"Perhaps." she said, "Have you read all of them?"

Naryan nodded.

"Then you've seen the magic concerning lifeblood?" she asked. Naryan nodded,

"Yes, I've seen those pages."

She stopped, and turned to him, eyes locked.

"That could be our chance to save Shawn."

Naryan looked back down at her for a moment, then shook his head.

"I'm not so sure about that. I've never done it before."

Sherry scoffed,

"All you need to do is write the symbols. It's not like you need to *understand* anything. It's how everything else works. Why are you so squeamish about it all of a sudden?"

"I've seen what it can do." he swallowed and shook his head. "Sir Sylvian–he perished by it, at the hand of one of Rhondia's mages. Solis is his name." he grimaced and looked at the ground. "The rune sapped the blood from his skin, all over him, as though he was pressed by a vice. It beaded on his flesh before flowing in the air like a twisted river. It wrung the very life from him."

"You would not chance it, to save my brother?"

Naryan shook his head,

"No. I would not chance it. I do not know what it could do."

Sherry glared,

"Fine then, I will do it."

Naryan shook his head,

"I wouldn't do that."

Sherry stood,

"Stop me then."

She turned to walk away, hearing him call after her,

"You can't even move a blade of grass! Do not force something you do not understand."

She ignored him, and went to the manor, shutting herself in her room and thinking on the runes deep into the night.

Chapter 33

Sherry lay in her bed, asleep, though her form twisted itself amidst the blankets as she dreamt. She felt as though she was in a deep cavern in the earth, and though the ceilings may have been high they were black and she could not see them; all she knew is that she was not in the free air.

It was dark all around her, and there was but a light emanating far in the distance ahead of her, but it did not lend her much vision. She felt as though she was constricted by the very air she breathed, and it pushed in on her from all angles, suffocating her. She labored with each inhalation but still pushed on through the darkness, to what end she did not know, but still moving towards the light.

Finally coming to it, she found that the light was not far off, merely so dim that it had seemed to be the distance. Rising in front of her she saw a shapeless and flowing form–knowing it to be her spirit as Naryan had described his to her. While Naryan had told her that his spirit was consumed by another, hers was not consumed, but wrapped and tied into a never ending knot. It struggled against the knots, but the knots were constructed out of itself, and so it was its own restraint. It pulsated as she came nigh to it, seeing it was the dim light.

She reached her hand out and her spirit fought against its shackles, whisps from it reaching out towards her as well to try and commune with her. But it could not, and even though she reached her hand towards it, nothing happened. It writhed again for a moment before calming itself and slowing its pulsing to an even rhythm.

A voice wavered through the cavern of Sherry's mind, a melodic tune that echoed ever so slightly as it spoke, and though she did not know the words, they were beautiful. She cocked her head, stepping around to examine her spirit and again it pulsed, accompanied by the voice, but it struggled to no avail.

It strained again, pulling against the restraints of its own form before speaking, the urgency in its voice echoing louder as its exasperation increased. It now writhed, pushing and pulling against itself as the inflection of the words turned to desperation, and it sank to the ground in defeat.

Sherry approached it, and it quivered at her presence, and she watched it as the pulses became little more than throbs, and the light dimmed even further.

A wisp of her spirit reached out, tracing in the air as it did and leaving the faintest glowing trail in the air behind. The symbol was familiar, though it dissipated within moments as she studied it. Again, the spirit wrote the symbol, and again Sherry read it, but still could not comprehend it.

She traced the symbol in the air with her own hand, and her spirit reacted, glowing a little brighter in hope, but the hope faded into nothing in a moment. Then again, all around her, she heard the whispers of an unknown tongue, strange sounds, but eloquent, echoing in the cavern. The sounds were fluent, but the voice was weak, and even as she raised her hand to trace the rune again the cavern rushed away from her and her spirit's voice transformed into that of another whispering her name as a hand grasped onto her shoulder and shook her from her slumber.

She woke, her own bed and room materializing around her and she sat to find Sondra holding a candle high in one hand while shaking Sherry with the other. Her grim face was the only illuminated thing in her room, and she spoke in a shaky voice,

"My lady–you should wake. Shawn is not well." she paused, "He would see you one last time."

Sherry's throat clenched and she threw back the covers, running down the hallway, her gown flowing as she went. Sondra too came, scurrying behind to illuminate the corridor and stairway as best she could, but Sherry knew the way and wasted no time in coming to Shawn's infirmary, leaving Sondra far behind.

In the room with him was a guard, and a nurse who was dabbing at Shawn's shining forehead with a damp cloth that she often dipped into a bowl of water held in her other hand. His bared chest rose and fell in an uneven cadence at his shallow breaths, and she could see that the skin around his wound was red and inflamed.

She rushed to his side, the nurse rising and moving out of the way, and Sherry caressed Shawn's clammy face, her furrowed brow coming near unto his so that she could look into his eyes. His lids were heavy and he fought to keep them open as he looked upon her. His lips curled into a smile as best they could, but their weight was too heavy for his defeated frame.

He tried to raise his hand towards her but could not, so she lifted it to her face as he rasped to her,

"Sherry…sorrow, does not suit you."

She bit her lip, her brow furrowed and eyes searching into his, seeing if she could glimpse any hope of life left in him. She saw none.

She rose and let go of his hand, letting it fall onto the bed beside him, and turned to the guard.

"Your sword." she demanded. The guard hesitated, so she strode to him, reached out, and drew it from its scabbard before turning back to Shawn.

"My lady?" asked the guard, but she glared at him, gripping the pommel of the sword in one hand and resting the blade on her other wrist. She dragged the blade across her wrist, feeling the pain of the slice as she did so, and white flashing in front of her eyes. She dropped the blade to the ground with a clatter as her head grew light and she steadied herself against the side of the bed. She held her injured arm up in front of her face, seeing the blood seeping from the wound and running down her elbow to land in a puddle on the floor with a stream of drips.

She took in a few deep breaths, regained her balance, and stepped forward towards Shawn, writing a rune in the air with her free hand as she did so. She heard her heartbeat pounding in her ears, and felt it in her chest and wrist as she traced the runes she'd studied in the grimoire.

But there was no glow of her hand, no tingling sensation in her fingertips as she traced it the rune that she'd read a hundred times. She traced it again, and again, her throat tightening as she did so, and tears blurring the room around her. The symbols had no effect, and soon she was made more aware of the dripping running down her arm and the growing puddle at her feet. Her vision blurred further, no longer from the tears in her eyes but from her lightness of head, and she leaned forward onto the bed with her good arm to steady herself again.

The guard stepped forward, offering his hand to her in assistance but she wrenched it away from him with a scream and collapsed onto the floor, now lying in the puddle of her blood as she curled into a ball and sobbed. The nurse bent down beside her, grasping up her arm to pressure the wound, and Sherry did not fight her as the edges of her vision began to darken and her breaths became more shallow.

Though her vision was graying from the loss of blood, she could tell that there was a commotion, for the door to the room burst open and she heard Naryan's voice commanding the guard to stay back. Sondra was with him, having fetched him, and she now felt Sondra's presence by her side next to the nurse, attending to her.

She fought to open her eyes again, seeing the blurry faces of Sondra and the nurse bent over her, and behind them she saw Naryan grasping up the sword that she had cut herself with, and dragging the blade across his own arm. He did not wince, nor gaze on the cut, but wrote a rune, his hand dazzling the room as he did so. The blood that should have dripped from his wrist to the floor instead flowed towards her, and the nurse released her arm, collapsing backward away from it as they did.

Through her half-closed eyes she saw the skin of her wrist mend itself closed, leaving fresh pink skin where before there had been a gash. The flow did not stop though, for Naryan wrote again and his blood now streaked towards Shawn's form on the bed, coalescing into a pillar that entered into the hole where Shawn had been pierced.

The hole bubbled for a moment and the blackened, foul blood that had been poisoning Shawn was forced out of the wound, the skin around it already beginning to fade from its inflamed crimson.

Naryan again wrote, and his own wound closed so that no more blood flowed from him, but his face was white and he steadied himself on the wall behind him before sinking to a seat on the floor. Neither the guard, nor the nurse, nor Sondra uttered a word, and Naryan rubbed his pale face in his hands as Sherry's eyes closed from exhaustion.

Sherry heard the voices of the Sondra and the nurse as she slept, and she felt herself moved, and stripped, and cleaned, for her clothes were still soaked in her blood. Still, she did not stir for she was drained of blood and energy. When she woke in the morning she was in her bed, and the afternoon sun was shining through her window.

"M'lady." She heard Sondra's voice from beside her, and turned to find that Sondra had seated herself next to Sherry's bed, waiting for her to wake. Sherry rubbed her eyes and then remembered the night before, looking down to her wrist and turning it around while she felt it with her other hand.

She turned to Sondra, who was watching her, and asked, "Was…?"

Sondra nodded.

"A peculiar evening it was–and no dream." she said. "I could not believe it myself if I was not there."

"Shawn?" Sherry asked, throwing back the blankets and standing. Her head spun as she did, and Sondra rose so she could steady Sherry. Sherry started moving towards the door, grasping onto Sondra's arm as she went.

"M'lady, you should relax. You certainly lost lots of blood."

Sherry ignored Sondra, locked her eyes on the doorway, and put one foot in front of the other, leaning on Sondra who dared not let her go. They went along the corridor and made their way down the staircase, heading towards the infirmary, but before they could make it there Sherry saw that the front door was open, and Shawn was standing there with his hands clasped behind his back, surveying the estate.

He heard their footsteps and he turned as Sherry let go of Sondra and ran towards him, throwing her arms around him and sobbing into his chest. Long they embraced each other, until they finally pulled away to look at each other's faces. Sherry saw that he was thinner than usual, but he was no longer deathly pale, his face now vibrant and full of color. He did not even lean as they turned and walked, but his stride was as strong as it always was, in fact she leaned on him to steady herself as they went.

"I can't believe it." she said. "I thought you were dead. I had given up all hope."

Shawn nodded,

"As had I. I was so far gone that I did not even remember where I was, nor the events of last night–though I hear they are quite the tale."

Sherry shrugged,

"What have you heard?"

Shawn chuckled,

"That my little sister cut her wrists in an attempt to use magic of which she knows nothing at all."

Sherry shrugged and smiled a little as he continued,

"Though, I cannot in good conscience scold you, for it was in an attempt to save my life. For that at least I am grateful."

"What then did you hear of Naryan?"

Shawn looked her up and down,

"That, little sister, is the most curious of the tale, for I have spoken to four witnesses all claiming the same. I have little recourse against their testimonies for I was asleep for it, and am now standing before you well, when I was knocking on death's door last eve. I suppose I have no choice but to believe them."

"You've spoken to four witnesses?" she asked. "You have not yet spoken to me, and there was only the nurse, and a guard, and Sondra…"

"Let us not forget Naryan," said Shawn, "for he is also a witness, and we spoke this morning."

"And how went that conversation?" asked Sherry.

"It was brief," he said, "though clarifying, and I feel I have misjudged him. I found it hard at first to take the words of a drunk at face value, but all signs point to his betterment and I have no choice but to believe him."

"Where is he now?"

Shawn nodded out towards the road.

"Leaving."

"Leaving?" Sherry brought in a sharp breath. "But not yet gone?"

"Only minutes ago."

Sherry pushed past Shawn, out the front door of the manor, sprinting down the dirt path that led towards the stables. She arrived, quicker than she ever had, to find Naryan leading a saddled horse out of the stable's door. She stood in front of him for a few moments, catching her breath as he surveyed her, before she ran to him and threw her arms around him.

He hesitated for a moment before returning the long embrace. She finally stepped away from him, pushing a lone strand of hair behind her ear,

"Borrowing a horse without asking, and leaving without a farewell? What have I done to deserve this?"

"Apologies, M'lady. I know you like to sleep in and didn't want to bother you." She smiled.

"Thank you." she said. "For Shawn."

Naryan nodded.

"I am drained and weary from the blood I gave last night, but I desire no pity, nor thanks. In fact, I am the one indebted to you."

"How is that?" she asked.

"I have thought on my previous inaction to save Shawn, and see now that it may have caused a deeper rift between us. I was fearful of the pain of injury in piercing myself to give the blood for the runes, and fearful of the pain of my ego if I could not save him. I see now I have kept this gift for myself alone. I have had the power to do good, but instead I have been living in fear.

"But when I came into the room last night, and saw you stricken to the floor, the fear left me, and action took hold. The thought of losing you was greater than all else. You've helped me conquer my fear, and for that I am thankful."

"You do care for me then?"

Naryan looked off towards the road for a moment, then at the sun, then back to Sherry.

"Yes, I do care for you, though fear has held me from admitting it."

Sherry's eyes softened as she looked into his.

"But now, I must go," he said.

"Go?"

Naryan nodded,

"I have found Einar."

"How?"

"Long I traced the runes in the grimoire to find him, but to no avail. Now, his spirit has been shown to me, but why it has taken this long, I cannot say. I am pricked with apprehension for he seems to be in the direction of Chromer, and he is not well."

"Stay," said Sherry. "You still must teach me the runes."

Naryan chuckled,

"There is no more teaching to be done, for you know them even better than I do. They are etched in your memory while I still require the grimoire." he patted at the grimoire stored in his robe at his breast. "No, what's left is to be done by you, and you alone, and it must be done in quiet solitude and meditation."

"Don't go. Things can be well between us again." she offered.

Naryan grimaced, and grasped each of her hands in his own, holding them while he looked down into her eyes.

"To what doom I go, I cannot say, but I know in my heart I must face what I fear. You have shown me that I must."

"If you go, you may not return."

Anxiety lingered as a growl in the back of Naryan's throat.

"There is no other choice."

Sherry raised her chin at him,

"This is my only request of you."

"You only had the power to tell me to leave," said Naryan, "never to keep me here."

"So be it." She pulled her hands away from him, and let them fall to her sides. "I will not beg."

Naryan exhaled through his nose before stepping to the horse, grasping the pommel, and lifting himself to the saddle.

"I hope that you can find it deep within you to at least forgive me for my errs," he said from his loft, before kicking the horse to gallop down the path towards the edge of the estate.

She watched him for a while until the dust of the path settled again and he was little more than a spec on a hill in the distance. She scowled and looked down at her balled fists to see that they were still shaking. It was probably just the guilt that prompted him to say that. He needed to hear that she forgave him–and so he was using her again if only to clear his own conscience. She would have none of that.

Chapter 34

Naryan hadn't given her many pointers in the way of meditation before he scurried off, and it was quite an annoyance. Sherry sat cross-legged in the garden, bees buzzing in the flowers around her. The constant prick of the grass through her skirt, the insects landing and crawling on her and buzzing around her head, and the heat of the day all contributed to distraction that she didn't need. All of that, on top of her preoccupation with Naryan's departure, made it an unfruitful meditation.

She opened her eyes and scowled, casually moving her hand through the air to draw one of the many runes she'd memorized, but of course, nothing happened. She looked down, flicking a stick away from near her leg before squeezing her eyes shut again and puffing her cheeks to exhale. She sat there feeling the sun on her face and nodding off into a sitting sleep, the buzz of the bees lulling her.

She was in the cavern again, watching her bound spirit as though it paced back and forth, unable to rid itself of its shackles. She looked, seeing again that the shackles were its own tendrils wrapping knotted and tangled so that it was restricting itself. She moved towards it, trying to touch it to untangle its tendrils, but her hands moved through it. It stopped, as though observing her for a moment, before Sherry said,

"What's wrong? I want to help. How can I help?"

A voice responded to her, a beautiful and crisp echo that seemed to drive fear from the dark cavern, but even though she heard them, the words meant nothing to her. Again she spoke to it, and again it responded in its melodious rhythmic poetry, but there was no comprehension between Sherry and her spirit. She shook her head, but this time instead of speaking, the spirit extended a wisp and drew in the air. This was no rune scrawled by a shaking finger, but a perfectly carved symbol drawn crisp and clear by a steady hand.

.   As Sherry read the rune the voice spoke again, this time not smooth, but staccato, as though it enunciated its syllables. Though the first rune hung in the air it wrote another and again spoke in its peculiar cadence so that Sherry realized the count of the symbols was the same as the count of the syllables and that words that it spoke were akin to the runes that it wrote.

She listened carefully to it as it wrote again and spoke again and this time repeated with her own languid tongue the sounds that she heard, and as she did, it seemed almost that the spirit grew a little brighter. She reached out her hand to trace her own symbol, but from far away she heard her name being called, and a bright light shone in through the ceiling of the cavern so that it soon took up the entirety of her vision. Again she heard her name being called, and the world of the garden rushed back to her and she found Sondra hiking up the small gnoll on which the garden sat, hiking her skirt up as she came.

Sherry growled in the back of her throat and clamped shut her eyes, trying to bring back the cavern, but the sounds of the garden again filled her ears, and the light of the sun filled her eyes, and she saw that Sondra bore with her a basket filled with her lunch. She exhaled before straightening her lips into a smile and waving Sondra to come over to her.

"You seem preoccupied–perhaps now isn't the best time for a game of chess." Shawn looked at her from across the small table where they were seated, only a pawn having moved in the few minutes since they'd sat down.

"I'm just thinking."

Shawn laughed,

"You've memorized a hundred openings to beat me, and you feign thinking?" he shook his head.

"No, I can tell when you're preoccupied with other thoughts, sister. What ails you? Naryan?"

She scowled and reached out to move her own pawn.

"How long has it been since he left? Nine days?" Shawn pressed.

Sherry shrugged,

"I don't know. I haven't been counting."

They moved the pieces a few times, Sherry coming ahead a pawn, and Shawn biting his cheek as he watched.

"So it is Naryan then?" he asked.

Sherry glared at him and Shawn held his hands up,

"All I'm saying is that you're easy to read."

She took another pawn for free and he grimaced

"At least, I wish I could read your moves the way I could read your face." he stroked his chin as he looked at the chess board, and continued,

"I know about you two–not that it's any of my business, but it's not hard to see."

"You don't know everything."

"Perhaps not–but I know he's the king, so you have good reason to swoon over him."

"There's no more swooning."

Shawn raised his eyebrows.

"No *more*? Aha! So you admit it then!"

"I don't want to talk about it."

"Ok, fine. All I'm saying is that as much as he and I have had our differences in the past, perhaps we have put that behind us."

It was Sherry's turn to cock her head. Shawn continued,

"On the morning he left, he came to me, and I thought he would point out how indebted to him I was for the magic he's suddenly pulled out of his ass–say, you haven't happened to learn any of it, have you?"

Sherry shook her head.

"Another sore subject."

Shawn continued,

"Nonetheless, as pompous as I assumed he would be in the light of my living by his hand, he mentioned nothing of it. I wasn't quite used to his humility. Perhaps he's growing into his kinghood.

297

Ah yes, and he did tell me about the whole Rhondia ordeal, and how she's usurping him. I'm honestly not surprised, knowing her, but it does lend a little more credibility to his disappearing in the midst of a war…"

Sherry captured a knight for free this time, and looked up at him as he rolled his eyes.

"You really shouldn't let your knights get caught out alone." Sherry commented dryly. "They tend to die that way."

Shawn shook his head with a wry chuckle,

"Why you little brat–as soon as I'm off my deathbed you're right back at me with the quips. I should probably be offended at that."

"It was a piece of advice, really. Given with love."

Shawn nodded,

"Ah yes, tough love. We all need it sometimes. So long as you forgive me for nearly dying on you, I'm sure we can move past it."

"Sure, I forgive you." She promoted her passed pawn to a queen and watched him fumble about for a few moves before she snagged his hanging queen without penalty. He picked up his king and tossed it across the room in mock frustration. They both laughed, before Sherry looked him dead in the eye and remarked curtly,

"But don't do it again."

It was now evening, and Sherry sat alone in front of the fireplace. The fire itself was now little more than a low glow that cast its dim light just in front of the hearth. She was looking over a stack of parchment where she had copied runes from the grimoire so she could study them. Really, she really had no need to study them any longer, for they were memorized in and out, but she absent-mindedly looked them over and traced them with her finger as she flipped through the pages.

Naryan had refused to write the runes for her, spouting on about how his spirit would think he was commanding it and try to enact all of the commands. She'd managed to copy everything, and of course, her spirit had not so much as budged a chair. She scowled, now running her finger over one of the staves. It was a set of runes to command movement, and she held her breath and looked hard at the chair adjacent to her as she traced it. Still, nothing happened.

It was useless–she'd never been able to do it–why did she think it would change now? Each of these pages was just a reminder of her failure, and a reminder of Naryan.

She crumpled it and tossed it into the fire, watching the flames lick at it and grow a little higher before she then looked down at the next page. This was the first rune that Naryan had really tried to teach her–a rune to command the soil. Her face grew hot at the embarrassment she felt when she could not cast it, and she thought back on how he'd tilled an entire garden row in a minute, but would have taken two men all afternoon. She clenched the paper between her hands, thinking of his smug face as he turned to her with a flourish after he'd done it.

This too she tossed into the fire, and breathed a sigh of relief as she did. Again she held the next page up, and the next page, until each was but a bit of glowing ash now resting at the bottom of the hearth. She looked down, finding that she had but a final page left and she read it, seeing that it was a commandment to move wind.

She looked into the fire, seeing that the paper fuel was now dissipated, and intended to fuel it with fresh air. She set her jaw, tracing the rune with her finger pressed hard into the page, but nothing happened. She crumpled the final parchment and stood, stepping to the hearth to throw in the final memento. She watched it blaze for a moment before dying, and she moved backward to sit again in the chair.

As she went to sit, however, she misjudged the position of the chair and stumbled, falling backward onto it. She missed it as she fell and it put her off balance, throwing her sideways off the chair. Her head made contact with the wooden arm of her chair and darkness enveloped her consciousness.

Her mind woke while her body lay on the floor, and she felt herself pulled up to a stand. Her spirit hovered over her, the familiar environment of the cavern materializing as her surroundings. Her spirit surveyed her, as if confused, and she watched it patrol in a circle around her.

"Can you speak to me?" she asked as it approached her.

Though she had not exerted herself, her voice echoed through the cavern, filling its every corner with the sound of her speech. Her spirit swirled around her, and its glorious voice filled the cavern, the remnants of her own speech's echo drowned out by its harmony. The words, however, were foreign to her, and she shook her head.

"Do you understand me?" she asked. The curious tongue again echoed through the cavern and her spirit was suddenly in front of her, surveying her. A whisp emerged from its form, drawing a rune in front of her. She looked it over, squeezing her eyes shut to burn it in the black of her vision while she thought back to the grimoire. She'd memorized hundreds of symbols and their meanings, and the ways that each morpheme could form each word, and the words could be drawn together to form the clauses of each stave.

"To see? To hear? To read? Yes, to read!" Her spirit glowed a little in affirmation and another rune was drawn in front of her, while the first was blown away on the wind. She looked the rune over once before nodding,

"To speak."

That rune too dissipated, and another was drawn in its place–a combination of the two before.

"Read and speak." Sherry read aloud, even as her spirit's voice rang clear in the cavern. Again, it spoke, the sounds emanating from it the same as it had just done. Sherry opened her mouth and repeated the sounds, her languid tongue unfamiliar with itself as she copied the sounds. Her spirit repeated it again and again, and she parroted the sounds until her tongue loosened and the words flowed a little better.

It wrote again, then spoke the words that it wrote, and Sherry echoed her spirit as the symbols materialized and then were whisked away. The sounds became familiar as she continued, and she found that each sound was paired with a morpheme of the stave so that the sounds themselves formed the very words that she read. The minutes stretched to hours, and hours stretched to days and sleepless nights, and years became centuries of communion. For an eternity she was there, listening and speaking, and finally, understanding the runes that she wrote. They were no longer curious symbols to be blindly written, but commands to be understood and obeyed–the practical language of spirits.

And as she learned, she did not simply learn the commands of the grimoire, for patterns emerged from the words to be found and understood in words of common meaning. It was now if she'd spoken the language since birth for she fluently conversed with her spirit. Each word she repeated ten times, a hundred times, a thousand times, until it was as though they had always been a part of her being, and would always be with her.

Now, being learned in the language itself, she began to become aware of the secrets of the ether, and she became wise beyond her years, discerning the falsehoods she once thought truest in her world. She laughed at the folly of riches, and scorned the petty squabbles of superficial connection that she had lain awake fretting over deep into many nights. Most of all, she understood that it was all for naught, but a game of rags and pity in comparison to the purity and communion of spirit.

It was love, in its truest form, the love of oneself, but not the love of a conceited ego. It was unity and fellowship, as it was meant to be, not the blinded wanderings of a spirit severed from its form. The truest evil was severance from her own self, and now she felt the truest good. But the eternity was now coming to an end, for time is a fickle thing.

The cavern, once the most corporeal settings she'd known, now glowed a little thinner, its walls seeming to fade to translucence. The things she had learned began to slip away into the recesses of her mind, and the wisdom and histories that once were clear in her memory began to fade. She thought on them, finding the memories harder to recognize amongst the haze of her mind, and the more she gripped tighter to the thoughts, the more they slipped through the cracks of her thoughts.

The cavern now seemed far away, a place of distant memory, as her room began to materialize around her. She shouted out to her spirit, though it was already a great distance away, and the echo of its voice responded,

"At least remember the runes."

She thought then on the runes, for the speech associated with them too faded alongside the wisdom of a hundred lifetimes. A thousand more questions flooded into her mind, for an eternity was still not long enough to answer all she longed to know. She called out, her voice echoing along a black corridor the only question that now mattered,

"Why will you not read the runes?"

Her spirit responded, but the warbled words had already lost their meaning. It rushed further away from her, little more than a white wisp, sitting on a distant plane as her consciousness returned. Knowing it was no longer understood, it now wrote a rune, and though it was a thousand miles away it seared into the black of the vision behind her eyes, and she spoke aloud to herself as she thought on the symbols, grasping at their meaning.

"Grace." her own voice echoed, a little more melodious than she was used to.

She woke, her eyes red with tears and a feeling in her gut of the loss of communion with her truest friend as it disappeared into the ether.

Why have I been sleeping on the ground? This isn't very comfortable.

She sat, and pulled herself up again to the chair as she felt the back of her head. The memories faded a little more into the distance as a knock came at her door.

"Come in." she called out, and Sondra entered.

"M'lady–I heard a noise. Are you alright?"

Sherry looked up, She nodded, and swallowed back the tears, now rubbing the back of her neck.

"Yes–I was just at the fire–and then…I must have fallen. How long ago was the noise?"

"I was walking near to the door only moments ago, and I am here now."

Sherry nodded,

"I'm fine–I must not have been out long."

Sondra bowed a little and backed out of the room, closing the door behind her.

Sherry walked over to her bed, collapsed into it and pulled the covers over her head as she closed her eyes. She fell asleep quickly, though the dreams she had that night paled in comparison to the vision she'd had of her spirit, and she still felt the lack in depth of knowledge that was again out of her reach.

Chapter 35

"Happy birthday, little sister." Shawn stood at the bottom of the stairs, smiling as he waited for her.

Her feet pattered down the steps as she ran to him and hugged him.

"I thought you'd forgotten!"

"September the 10th? I don't think I'll ever forget this day. One of my earliest memories–meeting my little sister for the first time." he tapped the side of his head with his finger, "it's seared into my memory–the day mother and father's attention was no longer solely mine."

She rolled her eyes and scoffed, but gave him a big smile.

"I'm going on my birthday ride–are you coming?"

Shawn looked down at his own attire,

"I don't think I'd be dressed this way if I wasn't."

She smiled and nodded in agreement, practically skipping past him, out the door, and toward the stables. As she went, she saw that the groundskeepers had set a long table in front of the manor comprised of lengthy   boards laying on sturdy barrels, and large white cloths covering them. They now set chairs around its perimeter and were now placing pastries, meats and cheeses and wines along its length, and streamers set on tall stakes were driven to the ground. She turned to Shawn,

"Did you tell them to do this? Unless father sent a pigeon…"

Shawn grinned,

"Aye, it was me. Don't go getting all sappy now–perhaps I'm a bit more sentimental since I've knocked on death's door."

"Thank you." she said, "I've needed this."

He nodded and smiled, and they continued past the party setup toward where Harold had the horses already hitched and waiting for them. He tipped his hat to her for her birthday and they mounted, and headed off into the fields. She felt the sun's warm rays pushing through the cool morning air as Nightmare pinned his ears back, forcing her to grip him tighter with her legs. The sun's position in the sky had not quite yet matured and she felt dew from the tall grass collecting on her riding pants as they galloped through the fields.

She normally would have pressed for a longer outing, but after a few sprints to satisfy her annual birthday ride, she nodded back towards the manor to Shawn. Her mouth watered at the thought of the prepared foods she'd seen being placed on the table, and she raced back to the manor faster than they'd left.

The horses were panting when they finally cantered back up to the barn, and they dismounted–a little out of breath themselves from the exhilaration of the wind rushing past their faces. She took off her riding gloves and wiped a little moisture from her eye before patting Nightmare and hitching him back to the side of the barn.

Shawn too hitched Daybreak and looked over at Sherry,

"He's a good ride. Where'd you pick him up?"

"Over to the east." Sherry gestured, waiting for him to finish the knot. "I've nearly forgotten to ask you–where is Paladin? Is he kept at the castle stables?"

Shawn rested his hand on Daybreak's side and looked at the ground.

"No," he said, shaking his head, "he is a casualty of war."

Sherry brought in a sharp intake of breath and watched Shawn swallow and pet Daybreak's side. After a few moments he looked up, and her eyes blurred when she saw that his too were glazed over.

Sherry often busied herself in the keeping of the manor, or busied herself with her horses and the beautiful landscapes of the estate. She did not want for anything, and since Shawn's revitalization, she'd been overall ecstatic. It was a sobering reminder that things outside of the manor were not as well as they often felt in the moment.

Shawn shook his head,

"Let me not dreary your day with my sorrows. We have all year to be woeful, but only today is your birthday."

He moved to her and they hugged, a bit tighter than usual, before continuing up toward the party.

Surrounding the table were many of the manor's servants, and even some tenants of their estate had been invited to ride from their homes this morning to attend the party. Most of them she'd known well since birth, and some were mere acquaintances to her, known as an orchard keeper, or shepherd, or brewer, and only a few new faces. Still, they were staples in her life, and she was happy that they were there to celebrate her day.

They were all simple folks, happy to be invited to the manor for any joyous occasion and Sherry was quite happy to be in their company today instead of surrounded by stuffy courtiers gossiping about one another and dressed in stiff corsets. She and Shawn walked arm-in-arm together towards the lot, smiles adorning each of their faces, and her mouth watered a bit just seeing fresh pitchers of grape juice.

"The lady of the hour first." Shawn motioned with his hand for her to proceed, and she skipped forward, grabbing the top plate from a tall stack and proceeding down the table.

At the end of the table fresh pastries were stacked into tall towers, the glaze still dripping off of them, hot from the ovens only minutes ago. Ahead of those were platters of fresh fruits gathered from the orchards and picked fresh from the vines, perhaps even this morning. Bowls of cream sat alongside them, ready to be plopped onto mixtures of the fruits, and even as she surveyed the table, a baker walked with bags of warm bread to be placed along the other foods, while the butcher sliced honied ham from a thick chop.

She moved along the table, filling her plate to the brim as she went, and the others fell in line behind her, chattering. She wasn't sure if there was to be enough room on her plate for the fruit-filled pastries at the end of the table, but finally decided that it wouldn't hurt to just toss it on the top of the rest of the food. A cherry tart caught her eye, the center a dark crimson and the edges

306

perfectly browned in the oven and she reached her hand out to grab it.

A man stepped in front of her and reached his own hand out, grasping it first. She took a step back and cocked her head to look at him as he surveyed the tart for a moment. He then turned to look in her eyes as he bit into it, a little of the cherry filling pushed out the sides. Bits of it clung to the side of his beard as he chewed. He did not look away.

Sherry stepped to the side, as the people around her sensed a disturbance and looked up, quieting.

"Please," the man motioned, "have one. They're delicious." His tongue licked the corners of his mouth and he took another bite.

"Do I know you?" Sherry asked.

The man shook his head as he finished the cherry tart and licked the tip of his fingers.

"No, I don't suppose so. You never quite know what's going on outside your little slice of heaven, do you? Did you forget there's a war going on?"

Shawn stepped up next to Sherry,

"Mind your manners or I'll have you expelled. Who are you?"

The man stood casually in front of the crowd and shrugged,

"Nothing but a courier. I come to bring you to the capital," he nodded towards Sherry, "m'lady."

"Under whose order? Father's?"

"Yes." the man nodded.

Sherry scowled,

"Show me his seal."

The man grinned and held his hands up,

"Ok, you've caught me. No, not your father–this order comes from higher up."

"Higher?"

The man nodded.

"The crown."

"I should say I do not think that the king would have requested me, for he is indisposed and not at the capital." said Sherry. The man's eyes narrowed,

"I know this as well as you do," said the man, "but no, not the king. Her majesty has requested your presence."

"Let us see her seal then," said Shawn, holding his hand out.

The man looked at Shawn's outstretched hand, expectant of a letter, but he shook his head and crossed his arms,

"I do not bring a seal, just my word."

Shawn's eyes narrowed,

"What good is the word of a man whose name I do not even know?"

"I am Vasta. Are you ready to go M'lady?"

Shawn Shook his head,

"I forbid it. I will not send my sister off on an unknown errand with a strange man."

"This is no request."

Sherry watched Shawn's brow furrow and jaw set as he locked eyes with the man.

"Why then," said Shawn, "is she so urgently requested?"

"Enough." said a voice as another man approached them from the side, writing runes as he walked. The people behind Sherry and Shawn ducked away as two nearby chairs flipped through the air and caught them behind their knees, knocking them to the seats and hovering in the air overlooking the scene.

Yells emanated from the bystanding serfs as they scattered away, the table's boards turning on their ends and spilling the contents all over the lawn.

Vasta clicked his tongue,

"Tsk Tsk, Torve, the queen said not to make a scene–first to see if the girl would come willingly. Now you've wasted all this food."

"Well she clearly wasn't intending to come." gestured Torve at them, "her brother babbling on about the crown's seal. I thought he was dead anyway–or deathly ill at least." he said as he looked Shawn up and down. "Doesn't seem to be doing too poorly to me."

"The queen said she felt that her spirit was kindling–perhaps she healed him."

Torve scoffed,

"You give her too much credit. Kindling, perhaps, but that healing would take some skill. Nonetheless, you were quibbling too much and we're short on time. We must return before the boy-king does. Rhondia's got some use for the girl."

Sherry and Shawn, though hovering, were within earshot of the two Erilaz below. She looked over at her brother, who caught her glance. His knuckles were white, gripping the sides of the chair's seat, and his eyes glared at them as he whispered to her through his teeth,

"It's only eight feet. We should jump. I'll distract them."

Sherry looked down and shook her head. *Only* eight feet looked like it would hurt from where she was sitting.

Though the serfs had initially scattered, they were now standing what they considered a safe way off, watching the scenario. Torve motioned toward them and looked at his friend,

"What are we to do about them?"

Vasta looked down at a rock and kicked it with his foot, before squinting and surveying the serfs.

"Eh," he said, "let them be. We just need her."

"What do you intend to do with me?" Sherry asked.

Vasta looked up at her, then back at the ground and drew a rune. Beneath him a pillar of earth rose, growing from the earth itself with him atop it until the grinding of earth halted and he was level with her in the floating chair. He looked into her eyes and smiled,

"Oh, it's not what I want with you. It's the queen. All this meddling you've certainly been doing," he motioned at her with his hand, "I can feel you growing. It's like a signal for those who know how to look. We were looking for the boy-king to put an end to him, but found you instead. Perhaps unfortunate timing for you–you would probably have gone unnoticed any other time."

"Don't you touch her." spat Shawn, hovering on his own chair a few feet away. The man smiled at Shawn whilst reaching his hand out to caress Sherry's face,

"And what will you do about it?"

At that, Shawn yelled and leaped from his chair at the man, grabbing him around the waist and knocking him off his pillar. Vasta's flailing arm tried to write a rune as they fell, but Shawn gripped tight onto his elbow, pinning it to his side. The two of them fell together, each locked in the other's grasp as they came to the ground, knocking the wind from them both. They each lay there for a moment, their sides where they had landed in thick, dull pain, but Shawn saw that the Erilaz started to write again and sprung atop him, pinning his arms to the ground.

Vasta tried to twist his wrists out of Shawn's grasp and writhed his body beneath Shawn's, eventually arching his back and twisting Shawn off of him. The two of them grappled with each other along the ground, fists flailing as they went, a ball of turmoil that rolled in the grass.

Sherry grabbed onto the side of the chair, hung down from it, and dropped the remainder of the way to the ground to find Torve standing over Shawn and his adversary, a rune partially written in the air. He had paused though, seeing that he could not affect Shawn without affecting the other. Hearing the thud of Sherry's landing he turned, and moved toward her as she recovered from the drop.

She rolled away, striking him as he grabbed at her, but he had a hold of her arm, and threw her to the ground. She backed away from him on her hands and feet as he encroached upon her.

"Stop, or I'll kill her." he snapped, his voice barely raised.

Behind him, Shawn had mounted the Erliaz and was waylaying his face with his fists, though Vasta protected himself as best he could with forearms outstretched. Shawn heard the threat, however, and turned to see that Sherry was caught. Torve looked back at Shawn, who ceased the blows, and Vasta pushed Shawn off.

Shawn kneeled in submission but Vasta stood and hit him across the side of the head, laying him to the ground.

In all desperation, as Torve's attention was caught by the other two, Sherry raised her hand up, writing a rune. Torve's gaze spun to her, brow furrowed at the sight of her finger's movement, but there was no effect, and the tip of her finger did not even emanate a glow. Torve chuckled and shook his head,

"Had me nervous there for a second, but perhaps you're not as capable as Rhondia thought."

Vasta now repeatedly kicked Shawn, who lay curled in a ball on the ground, motionless. The Erilaz stopped to catch his breath and grabbed Shawn by the leg, dragging him beside Sherry and surveying the two of them.

"You are quite the handful." he said, spitting blood on the ground. He sneered and looked down on her. "She'll probably just kill you anyway. Perhaps I should save myself the trouble of dragging you back." Torve nodded in approval.

The first stepped closer, his shadow looming over the two of them and raised his hand to write the rune. Time slowed as she saw his golden finger tracing the symbol in the air, and the scene blurred and she watched. The blur continued, until colorful streaks were drawn across her vision, and the streaks continued until they were white. The white then grayed, and darkened to black, and she found that all that existed on this new plane were here and her thoughts. *It's so lonely*, her thought echoed through the blackened cavern of her mind, but there was a response, for her spirit spoke to her,

"This is unto death." she heard it say, "though you are not yet perished–you are seeing but a glimpse of eternity. There is emptiness and endlessness, though you should not fear it; it is not pain, nor evil, but solitude and unity."

"If I am not dead," Sherry asked, "then why do I see this?"

"I show you this, to show you what might be, and you have the choice in this moment to acquiesce to the darkness, or to fight again, and live in the light. If you wish, all can end here, and you will feel no pain in death."

Sherry let a long, weary sigh,

"Death isn't so bad."

"No, it is not, for death is only the end of this physical form. It is terrifying in this moment, perhaps, for life is all you know now, but after life we will commune again, and be as one, as we were before."

"It sounds as unto utter bliss."

"Still," her spirit continued, "death is not the greatest good, for in life there are many good things."

"Yes," Sherry nodded, "there are many good things."

"Tell me then," said her spirit, "what good things do you still wish to live for?"

Sherry closed her eyes and smiled,

"There are many joys in life. The taste of thick cream topping tart berries on a hot day. The wind pushing through my hair as I ride through the fields. The splash of a cold pool of water to clean the dust from my face."

"Go on."

"The tickle of wine flowing through my mind, the glow of a fire nearby as I watch the stars. The warmth of my blankets as I wake, and feel the coolness of the air in my room.

Her spirit sighed, and Sherry continued,

"A laughter so deep that my stomach aches. The lingering hug of an old friend who sojourns. The aegis of a brother. The deep kiss of a lover, the morning after."

"You falter as you recall the last one, for though I sense joy, it brings you sadness as well."

Sherry nodded,

"Yes, there is grief intermixed with the love, for though it is deep for my part, it is unrequited."

Her spirit responded,

"The purest love exists in a state of giving, not receipt. What does a mother gain from her child? To love truly is to not care what is gained from the other.

"But this love," her spirit continued, "while imperfect perhaps, *is* reciprocated."

Sherry snapped back,

"Either way there is pain, and it lingers in my heart. This pain is worse than death."

"Yes, yes–I feel this pain–It is real, but it is not insurmountable. True love transcends pain, for pain is for a moment, but love is enduring.

"But now, we come to the end here and I must ask, what gives you pause, and makes you desire to go on?"

Sherry thought for a moment and responded, almost in resignation,

"To give myself freely, to love and be loved, forgetting all past transgressions."

Her spirit sighed, a great burden lifted from it–as a tingle running down the spine and a breath of fresh air on a stifling day. The cavern then rushed with a mighty wind, even as her spirit grew steadily brighter until it was so brilliant that the cavern was awash with its glory. Sherry covered her eyes with her hands, but so brilliant it was, and pure white, that her entire vision was enveloped by the flash. Even then, as she felt herself rushing away from it, her spirit's now powerful voice echoed,

"In this moment of forgiveness, you have found your grace."

Then, it was quiet, save for the heavy breaths of Torve standing in front of her. The rushing wind had now retreated to the gentle breeze that blew across the estate, and the sun that warmed her face was but a pale fog in comparison to the light that her spirit had emitted.

She looked up, and a long moment dragged out as the Erilaz's finger traced the rune that spelled her doom.

But then, she glanced down to her side where her hand was propping her up on the ground and saw that in her trance she had scratched a rune in the dirt; it was nearly complete. She now moved her finger to finish the character even as the Erilaz saw, and his eyes grew wide at its glow. He could not even finish his own rune for in that moment both he and Vasta were drawn near unto one another, side-to-side, skewered by a stake that had torn itself from the ground and pinned them together.

Torve dropped his hand to his chest where he was gored, seeing a yellow streamer on its end painted red with his blood and flickering in the wind. The wheeze of their final breaths escaped as they tumbled to the ground, and Sherry scrambled over to Shawn, helping him to a stand. His face was bruised and bloody, and eyes were swollen to a squint, but he stood well enough, leaning on her before they collapsed into an embrace, each of them sobbing into the other's hair.

"I have to go." Sherry said, but Shawn grasped tighter onto her and would not release her. She felt him shaking his head against her shoulder.

"Don't leave." he said, "we have both nearly been torn from each other too many times now."

He reluctantly released her as she pushed away from him and wiped a tear from his cheek.

"I must go to the capital."

"Why? You're safer here."

"You heard them–they're going to kill Naryan."

"Fine, I'm coming with you." he let go of her and swayed, holding back onto her for support. She shook her head,

"No, there's no time."

"But you're not safe there."

"I'm not safe here either."

Shawn grunted and released her.

"Don't worry," she said, "it looks like I didn't memorize all those runes for nothing."

Shawn eyed the pool of mingled blood from the Erilaz laying on the ground and nodded.

"Go then go with my blessing–as long as you're home by supper."

She smiled and with her jaw set, she took off sprinting toward the stables. She reached it, pulling open the door and grabbing a blanket and saddle to throw onto Nightmare. All the horses in the stable sensed her urgency and hoofed the ground, blowing air through their nostrils in violent whinnies as she tightened the cinch round his belly and pulled on his bridle. Daybreak was in the stall next to Nightmare, and he banged against the walls as he watched her readying to depart. Her trembling fingers finally finished the clasps and she pulled herself up by the pommel, grasping then onto the reins and spurring Nightmare forward. He cantered into the daylight and wheeled from the excitement before galloping down the hill toward the main road.

Far behind her she heard the splintering of wood, and she turned to see that Daybreak had burst through the gate to his stall and tore down the hill after them. She leaned forward and whispered encouragements into Nightmare's ear, and the drum of his hoofbeats quickened, and the wind brushed faster against her face.

Chapter 36

The rhythm of Nightmare's hoofs pounding on the dirt paths of the estate had long gone, and his hoofs now clopped on the paved roads that signified she neared the capital. A few hours of riding had now passed her by, but they had gone quickly, for her mind was on the events of the day, not on the road ahead of her.

Her pace had slowed from when she'd first left the manor, on account of Nightmare's stamina, and she was cognizant of it. She'd galloped him as far as he could go before he slowed of his own will, but now managed to keep him at a healthy trot. Still, she had a strange calm to her anxiety, now feeling the full presence of her spirit, persistent in its existence. Not once did she feel alone.

She hesitated to push Nightmare harder, knowing that he had to make it the entire way, even if it was slow, and allowed him pauses to canter and catch his breath. She was glad when, during one of the canters, Daybreak finally caught up to them, breathing heavy, but not as tired as Nightmare who had borne her this whole way. At a stream crossing she dismounted and allowed the horses to water while she switched the saddle to Daybreak. A brief rest was all she allowed them before she ponied Nightmare to Daybreak and continued on down the road. The horses sensed her urgency and seemed to keep good spirits, in spite of the heavy riding.

It was late afternoon when she finally rounded the last bend that gave view to the tall spires of the castle in the distance, and she pushed the horses on even faster with the end in sight. When her stomach grumbled, she realized that she'd never eaten earlier in the day, but she pushed aside the thought as she passed through the villages that lay on the outskirts of the capital.

The roads were far from empty, for the citizenry went about their daily business, unaware of the stakes that were being bet for the kingdom. Perhaps, she thought, they wouldn't care even if they did know. Their lives were wholly unchanged by who ruled from the throne; taxes were still levied and conscriptions were still drafted.

She wasn't there for the stake of the throne though–she was there for Naryan.

Last time when she passed through the city streets she went slowly, meandering to watch the people and see the buildings, but this time she passed through without a glance, her eyes set solely on the castle. The day had been clear and sunny as she traveled the roads to the capital, but now as she galloped up toward the castle she saw that dark clouds had gathered from across the sky and now hovered over it.

There were no guards stationed at the outer barbican as there usually were, and she rode unhindered through the gate and through the inner grounds towards the inner barbican. There a single guard was, though he jogged toward her, hands held up. She wheeled Nightmare and looked at him.

"M'lady," he said, looking behind him toward the castle, "I would leave here if I were you. Something foul is afoot."

He did not stay to see if she heeded his advice but abandoned his post and took off toward the outer barbican. It seemed the entirety of both baileys were emptied giving an eerie aura to the castle that she'd never felt before. She kicked Daybreak forward but even as they passed through the barbican to the inner bailey he wheeled, stamping the ground and whinnying. Nightmare too hoofed the earth and shook his head, and she dismounted even as there was a rumble of thunder from overhead. Not too far away fingers of lightning spread themselves across the sky and a crack of thunder emanated from above her without pause.

The horses spooked and bucked, and the lead rope tore from her hand as they galloped off together, back the way that they'd come through the barbican. She shook her hand, feeling the burn of the rope and looked down to see that it was reddened, before her attention was again caught by a roll of thunder.

She approached the throne room, and as she did she felt the rush of wind and looked up to see the entire roof burst upward, large swaths of it carried and twirling away into the sky. Even from her distance the wind waylaid her steps and she fought against it to move forward, covering her face as she put one foot in front of the other.

She then saw a pillar of flame writhing down toward the open throne room, spinning around in a thin cyclone until it touched down out of sight. Though the fire was a ways off she felt the wind grow warm on her skin, and her lips and mouth dried as it blew across her. As she pressed on she felt the rumble of the earth beneath her, and she stepped to catch her footing, for the ground moved as the foundation of the building itself was torn up. She could hardly walk, for even the cobblestones of the paved road began to turn up from the soil. Though her footsteps faltered, her heart did not, and her fingers went to work, writing rune after rune so that the cobblestones held themselves low above the ground, and she stepped on them one at a time as they made a path forward for her up toward the throne room.

There, through the gaping entrance where the doors had been torn from their hinges she finally finally stood, taking in the scene set in front of her. Rhondia and Solis, descending upon their prey, a pillar parallel to the ground, hovering in the air and gaining ground with their every step. Naryan and Einar stood together, their backs to her and struggling to keep the missile at bay. The wind had died down, and the rumble of the earth had ceased, and all the birds had vacated the vicinity. Now, the only sound now in the still air was the heavy breathing of the two men striving for their lives, and the quiet taps of her footsteps on the cobblestones.

Rhondia noticed Sherry's frame coming in behind the two men and cocked her head.

"Hm," she said, "curious." and flicked out a rune with her hand. The pillar ceased its forward inching and went spinning wildly up into the air with a whir on a trajectory far away from the throne room. Naryan and Einar each collapsed to the ground at the release of their stress, and gasped for air as though they had been holding their breaths.

"I like what you've done with the place," said Sherry. "It's a much more airy feeling."

Rhondia's eyes narrowed, but she smiled,

"Now here is a face that I did not yet expect to see here until this evening. Where are your escorts?"

"I came of my own accord."

Rhondia let out the slightest bark of a laugh.

"Ha. I see. I feel you play coy, and there is more to the story, sweet Sherry."

"I killed them, if you must know. Both of them."

Naryan pushed himself up to one knee and turned to look at Sherry as she came to stand next to them. Droplets of rain began to patter around them in the open courtroom and leave darkened spots on the stone floor.

"Curious indeed. I should say that violence was not my intent–I hope that they two did not misunderstand it was an invitation, not coercion."

"It was clearly misunderstood."

"My deepest apologies. I suppose it's better that they'll no longer muss up my errands." Solis stiffened, but said nothing.

"Nonetheless, I'm glad you've come. You've arrived just in time to witness vengeance exacted upon your perpetrator. I think it's something you might enjoy."

Sherry shook her head,

"I do not come seeking violence."

"No," said Rhondia, "Yet it seems that all who gain this arcanic knowledge turn to it nonetheless. Three prime examples sit in front of me. All the more reason that knowledge of it should be quelled."

"And two in front of us." snapped Naryan

"Hush Naryan, the women speak." Snapped Rhondia. She stared him down to ensure his tongue was held before she continued, "Though you, Sherry, I do have hope for you. I feel the strength of your spirit, and you are of good character–this I am sure. You are someone who I could bring into the fold anew. I would teach you–hone you into a sharp tool that could be wielded with precision instead of wagged aimlessly about. You are calculated and cool, unlike these hot-headed men. You could do great things under my guidance. This is the invitation I meant to extend to you."

The rain thickened, and the five of them felt their clothes begin to soak up the water, leaving it heavier with the weight.

"I'm flattered to be considered–but why do you keep this for yourself? Think of the good if all men and women had this knowledge! There would be no sickness, no hunger, no poverty."

Rhondia shook her head,

"It is tried and true that violence reigns when people are given power."

Sherry replied,

"Why not use your own power in plain sight to help them, even if they are not taught? You wield this as a tool of control when you could do great good."

"If these practices were common knowledge," said Rhondia, "even if they were not taught, there would always be some who sought to learn it in secret, and they would certainly become violent. No, to keep it clandestine is the only way, for if it is not even known then there is no threat; accusations of conspiracy keep the populace blind and unaware."

"Fine," said Sherry, "I care not. We shall be on our way."

Naryan and Einar stood, and though their breathing had slowed their eyes were gaunt.

"Oh," said Rhondia, "Will you? If you will not stand by my side I cannot let you three prance away as though nothing has happened. You would certainly not keep shut your mouths in light of the knowledge you have gained–all would be for naught. Einar here is proof of that–even after hiding in the woods for a century he eventually came crawling out and pretending he had strength. No, there must be an end to this now."

"I did not come to hear your politics."

"Why then did you come my dear? To take the throne?"

"I came for Naryan."

Naryan stiffened, and Rhondia scowled and shook her head.

"This I cannot understand. I consoled you in the bereavement of your dignity, done by the actions of the man who stands now next to you. Do you not recall that day, Sherry, when you came to me?"

"I do."

"Do you not recall the night prior, one that you relayed to me in great detail, the comings and goings of this boy who I once dared to call my son?"

Sherry inhaled, now feeling her clothes sticking to her skin as the water had wicked through them, and the constant drum of raindrops on her head and shoulders.

"I do."

Rhondia shook her head,

"Even setting aside 'politics' as you so delicately put it, I stand before you as another woman and question your sanity. What weakness is this?"

"Love is my strength."

Rhondia scoffed,

"Perhaps I was wrong about you. What respect I had for you has dwindled, if you would toss away the offer of my support and crawl back to him." she spat. "This is a betrayal that cuts deep. I should not have thought that you hold your own self-worth so low."

"My worth is not low–I have found my worth and found that which I value."

"If you value him, then you are of no value to me!" Rhondia snarled. She looked towards the sky, writing a rune as she did, and the gust of wind that blew upon them chilled their skin. The raindrops that were falling around them soon turned to small bits of hail, and only a moment later the first icicle shattered on the ground near where they stood. Naryan looked up and saw a volley of the glistening shards descending upon them. He yelled, grabbing Sherry around the waist and diving aside with her, even as another smashed right where they stood.

Einar wrote, and a large panel of wood tore itself from the wall to hover above them, the icicles shattering along its top and sending bits scattering throughout the room.

Solis then traced a rune on his arm, and it glowed as a marble window frame behind him tore itself from the wall and went hurtling towards Einar's vulnerable frame. From his position on the ground Naryan wrote, and the marble cast itself into the ground, shattering and sending bits ricocheting along the walls.

Rhondia then wrote and the panel that had been protecting them tore itself from Einar's grasp, flinging itself away from the courtroom and leaving them exposed again to the falling shards. Sherry wrote this time, and wind blew horizontally along the courtroom, pushing the falling icicles off their path. But, the collision of the two streams of air of different temperatures mixed together, and a vortex spun down from the sky to the courtroom. Rock and ice and dust swirled around and around them as the vortex swelled, and it grew so large that the company was safely within its eye, even though the courtroom was continuously dismantled by the winds around them.

Solis then drew, and the marble throne dragged itself across the ground, skipping along at first before flying toward the other three. Einar drew and the throne halted in the air, quivering with the energy from each spirit striving against the other. But even as it quivered it continuously moved closer to Einar. Solis' eyes were wild and his jaw was stretched into a grin while his chest and arms glowed bright. Naryan saw their peril and he too wrote to push against the throne, but even he and Einar together could not match the strength of Solis' spirit.

Rhondia then, seeing the two of them were indisposed in their conflict with Solis, smirked, and started to carve her own rune to take advantage of their distraction. Sherry watched her write and saw into her intentions for she read the rune even as Rhondia's hands carved it, and its strokes had meaning to her. A cobblestone had plucked itself up from the floor of the throneroom to be thrown, but even as it was about to be sent its trajectory was changed, and it was instead flung backwards into the wall of the whirlwind around them.

Rhondia stared at the stone, then wrote again to pluck up another, but Sherry had already written and that too was tossed away from Rhondia's will. She looked up at Sherry, brow furrowed even as she started to write again, but with each brush of her hand Sherry had already read the rune and countered Rhondia's will.

Solis then, seeing what was happening, traced a rune on his arm and another stone plucked itself from the ground to fling toward them. Sherry saw it, and brushed away the stone but Rhondia, seeing that Sherry's attention was caught by Solis' movements, wrote again. The crumbled wall near them trembled and dismantled itself, a hundred stones falling toward them to crush them. There they were, caught between the tumbling wall with too many stones to write away, and the potential of the throne, waiting to pin the three of them against the wall.

Sherry then heard the echo of her spirit's voice in her ear and understood its speech. She opened her mouth, speaking in kind, and from it flowed the language of spirits which she had spent a lifetime between lifetimes mastering. Rhondia then heard the words coming from her mouth and cocked her head at the strange sounds, eyes widening at the realization. The command that emanated from Sherry was precise and swifter than a written rune. The century of stones that fell from the wall were each then caught by her spirit as they neared the three, and then were flung in succession toward Rhondia.

Rhondia wrote a rune and a single stone was deflected, but myriad others flew to her to pummel her frame, laying her to the ground. Sherry spoke again, her mouth and eyes aglow as she did and the stones were now directed toward Solis. He wrote, and the throne was swung in front of him as a barrier between he and the projectiles, and they shattered on the marble of the throne as they contacted it.

He again traced a rune on his arm and the throne was flung toward the three of them. But Sherry again spoke and the throne was then thrust into the ground where it broke into the cobblestones and cracked in two before resting, now sunken into the floor.

Solis was now in the air, flying up along the eye of the dissipating whirlwind towards its peak, and he disappeared into the clouds above. The wind died down and the clouds dispersed, and the dot of Solis in his retreat could be seen far away in the blue sky.

It was now peaceful, and a light breeze now brushed across their skin, but the sound of a wheeze and a cough caught their attention and they turned to Rhondia who lay broken on the ground. The three of them moved across the barren throne room to where she lay, limbs bent and face mangled, and buried amidst a pile of the stones she had meant for them.

Naryan looked down on her and said nothing, but Sherry bent down and looked into her fading eyes as Rhondia opened her lips for her final words.

"I did care for the kingdom." she wheezed. "And I did care for you. I can only hope he now cares for both in my stead."

Sherry held her hand as she perished, and let it go to stand up. Naryan exhaled and surveyed the decimated throne room and looked out toward the city through the gaping hole in the wall.

"Looks like there's a lot to do," he said.

Sherry looked over at him and nodded.

"Your majesty."

 M. J. Struven (or, Matt will do just fine!) is just a sarcastic, Rugby-Playing, beach-laying, beer-drinking, writer, who likes sushi too much. You'll often find him gaming into the dark hours of the morning--oh, and he scratches out projects now and then, too! Growing up reading names such as Tolkien, and Lewis, Asimov, and Card, has lent him his creativity, and style. He aims to entertain with fantasy and sci-fi focusing on resonating characterization and fluid dialogue, punctuated by scenes of conflict that leave you hanging on every word.

Connect with me for media opportunities, or just to see what projects are on the way! I love to talk to people.

Cover Art by Jono Vengoechea